THE RIPTIDE

Also by Gareth Rubin

Murder at Christmas (writing as G. B. Rubin)
The Waterfall
Holmes and Moriarty
The Turnglass
The Winter Agent
Liberation Square

THE RIPTIDE

GARETH RUBIN

SIMON & SCHUSTER

London · New York · Amsterdam/Antwerp · Sydney/Melbourne · Toronto · New Delhi

First published in Great Britain by Simon & Schuster UK Ltd, 2026

1 3 5 7 9 10 8 6 4 2

Simon & Schuster UK Ltd, 7th Floor,
199 Bishopsgate, London EC2M 3TY

Simon & Schuster Australia, Sydney

Simon & Schuster India, New Delhi

www.simonandschuster.co.uk
www.simonandschuster.com.au
www.simonandschuster.co.in

The authorised representative in the EEA is Simon & Schuster Netherlands BV, Herculesplein 96, 3584 AA Utrecht, Netherlands. info@simonandschuster.nl

A CIP catalogue record for this book is available from the British Library

Hardback ISBN: 978-1-3985-3543-5
Trade Paperback ISBN: 978-1-3985-3544-2
eBook ISBN: 978-1-3985-3545-9
Audio ISBN: 978-1-3985-3547-3

Typeset in the UK by Palimpsest Book Production Ltd, Falkirk, Stirlingshire
Printed and Bound in the UK using 100% Renewable Electricity at CPI Group (UK) Ltd

FSC
www.fsc.org
MIX
Paper | Supporting responsible forestry
FSC® C013604

For Phoebe

Chapter One

I never had my parents to thank or berate for my name. I owe it to the man who took me in and raised me. It was, he assured me, a strong name. A regal name. A name to inspire awe in others – all things that I would require in life, given my bleak start.

In my formative years, it became a child's game to me: I could hop, as if playing grandmother's footsteps, to its sound. *Ly-san-der. One-two-three. Ly-san-der. One-two-three.* It would take me three paces, then stop.

No, I never paused to consider how the name had been thrown over my original one like a cloak. From the earliest times that I remember, it was the only one that I knew. And it was a game to play.

So it was not until I was thirteen years old that I began to wonder about my first given name. The one that my parents must have chosen for me. Could it have been Frederick, like Fred Gilly? Or Bernard like Bernard Mason? Was it Miles like Miles Albrough-Scott or Edwin like Teddy Het? The boys at school knew their true monikers, assured in their veracity by the presence of the parents who had selected them.

Ly-san-der. One-two-three. I whispered the tripping rhythm as I walked along the Strood, our sandy path to England. We – that is, myself, Fred, Bernard, Miles and Teddy – lived at Mr Tolson's house on the islet of Ray, which was part of the Essex coastline. I had, earlier in the year, measured the extent of Ray myself, pacing one-two-three along the longest of three edges, and then one-two-three along the shortest. After carefully measuring my stride, intense calculations had told me that it was one thousand, two hundred and three yards long but just one hundred and nine yards wide. All in all, it was a small islet. Big enough for Mr Tolson's home – named Turnglass House due to an unusual weather vane shaped like an hourglass – and little more. Ray would be cut off entirely from England when, twice each day and twice each night, the tides would rise and cover the Strood, the causeway to the mainland. (Then, though, we could still reach Mersea, a larger island with a village, to which Ray was an adjunct, if we traversed the Strood in the other direction, away from the mainland.)

From the big window in our schoolroom, where we ate and slept, as well as learned our times tables, I would often stare at night into the dark, to the mainland, where, one day out of the year, a group of people assembled at the Peldon Rose inn to show me friendship and sympathy.

This night, Mr Tolson referred to smilingly as 'the Gala'. And it was thence that I was headed, in the year eighteen hundred and four, when it came upon me stronger than ever before to wonder what my true name was.

I stopped and blinked into the black water that was lapping at the side of the Strood, hoping in my childish way that my name would magically appear to me, written in sparkles on the surface or the twisting seaweed below it. It was not. The glittering spots of the reflected moon danced here and there, and I fancied for a second that they circled around to trace out a grand letter 'O', but it was gone in the blink of an eye, replaced by more darting sparks. I turned and strode on, towards the Peldon Rose, where my friends awaited me with charitable hearts; for, unique among my schoolfellows, I had to earn my keep.

I was a tall, slim lad, with thick curling black hair that I could not tame. My eyes, green, I always thought quite large for my face, which might sound odd, but if you were to see me, you might think so too. I wondered about my nose. It was what they called 'Roman', which excited a thirteen-year-old whose tutor loved to teach of the classical world. Did that make me a little bit Roman? I hoped it did.

As I walked, I bore in mind that the Strood could be treacherous and you had to time your crossing because the tide rose quickly to swallow the causeway; and if you were caught then by the water's cold fingers, you would be drawn out into the boundless ocean. The riptide, as the local people called it, swept you away without warning or mercy. I grew up with the riptide, although I little knew then that another one, harsher yet more subtle, had been always all around me from my earliest age.

Still, here was the Peldon Rose, a long and low rustic country inn. White smoke was pouring from its chimneys, a raucous rabble was cheering inside and the landlord, Walter, bubbled up in emotion as I entered.

'Lysander!' he cried, actual tears welling in his eyes. 'My boy, *our* boy! Come, come!' And he threw a flabby arm (for he was very fond of his own wares) around my shoulders and pulled me into the ensemble.

My entry was greeted with a cheer as great as if the King himself had called in for a jar of ale. These were my people, and I never have and never will forget the love that they showed me.

'Friends!' yelped Walter, who had a piping voice that he always strained to make himself heard. 'He is here. Our own Lysander Rose. Come, Lysander, what will you sing for us this time?'

I flushed with pride. It was not an emotion that I had much call for at that time – my schoolwork was well, but I took care not to make it too well, lest my classmates find another cause for mockery; my family was unknown; and my place at the school precarious.

Mr Tolson, grinning like a cat, pushed through the throng, holding his violin aloft like the holy grail. At this sight, the crowd erupted again, some yelling for their favourite ditty, others simply for 'Song! Song!'

'Patience, Tom. Calm yourself, Peggy!' he laughed gaily. He was a joyful fresh-faced man, often finding entertainment in the smallest things, and his pockets were always spilling intriguing and unexpected items for later examination. His dress could also be a little disordered, but never unattractively so. 'You will have your song; will they not, Lysander?'

'Yes, sir.'

'Then let us give them "The Lincolnshire Poacher".' And he struck up the first chords of that joyful tune. He was a good player, his long and slender fingers were graceful as a sylph's. His face, one that I always see before me as the picture of charity and good faith, contorted here and there with concentration, even though it was a simple melody.

I jumped in on my cue.

When I was bound apprentice in famous Lincolnshire,
I served my master truly, for nearly seven odd year,

I had the first few verses to myself before the others all joined in, unable to hold themselves back from the lyrics of defying the law and running rings around the slow gamekeeper. After that 'Down Among the Dead Men' got them all clinking their tankards together.

Here's a health to the King and a lasting peace
To faction an end, to wealth increase.

For an hour I sang, until my throat could take no more, no matter how my audience importuned me. 'No, no, friends, that is all for this year,' Walter proclaimed at the top of his voice. 'Now the minstrel has sung, he must be paid.'

Mr Tolson plonked onto a stool, stretching out his worn fingers, and Walter scurried throughout the company, proffering a small linen bag, cajoling the company to drop crowns, shillings and pence into it. 'Now, Morty, I am sure you can add another half crown. Look, Rick's put a whole one in himself. Thank ye. Come on, Alec, time to cough up, the boy must have vittles, you know. Aye. Thank ye.' Five minutes later Walter disappeared behind the bar whence he served his wares. I knew he was totting up what was in the bag, and calculating how much he had to add himself to bring it to the level needed to pay for my board with Mr Tolson.

'I do declare,' he yelped, 'We have a full eleven pounds here.' And another shout of joy erupted, with my schoolmaster looking worn out and best pleased.

They fell to slapping each other on the back, and pinching my cheek or shaking my hand. I felt the mother's milk of belonging in that damp air. And there is no feeling that can hold a candle to it.

There was more jollity for another hour before I went home, after being treated to a tankard of small beer, as Walter insisted befitted a wandering minstrel, with my hand in Mr Tolson's. I betook myself to the schoolroom, where the sound of gentle snoring – not so gentle in the case of Teddy Het, who always sounded like a mill grinding barley – greeted me and my stomach unknotted itself. I had not even noticed the tension within my innards, for while the Gala was a high point of the year for me as a night when my pride found a rare place to flourish, it was also a high point for my schoolmates to rib me for my lack of family and means. I would have to deal with it on the morrow, of course, but for the remains of that night, at least, I could have a heart full of joy.

In that long room, with bare boards on the floor and tall windows that looked out on one side to the land of England, I kicked off my shoes, pulled off my homespun stockings, my patched breeches and shirt, donned my nightshirt and crawled onto my horsehair mattress.

'Charity boy.'

It was whispered in the dark. I knew the voice. Bernard Mason. His lungs were powerful, like his frame. And then it was answered by a sniggering from the opposite side of the room. That was Fred, who always followed his master, Bernard's, lead. The soft laughter emboldened Bernard. 'Sing to us, charity boy,' he said.

The barb struck home, yes it did, and yet the pleasure of the evening lent me fortitude. Regardless of Bernard Mason, I fell asleep under a blanket of joy.

Chapter Two

I woke the next morning as the first gilded light flooded through the windows. I was usually the first to stir, and I lay there watching the sun's beams creep around to the schoolbooks on the shelf, the box of chalk that was destined for slates to tell sums and the little wooden boxes on the top shelf that contained our personal possessions – while the others had keepsakes of their families, perhaps a book or Bible and a few wooden toys, mine contained but one item: a silver watch, made, according to its face, by 'Scholl', which I had come to conclude was a German name.

The timepiece was scratched and bruised in places and the glass over its face was chipped. I knew every imperfection in that watch, and even though it was kept on the top shelf, I would look at it each night and very gently wind it, to keep it softly ticking. It was my only true possession and somehow the veneration I had for it kept it safe even from Bernard, who, I think, knew that if he touched or interfered with it, I would have torn him to pieces. Sometimes I would hold it and try to divine my name, as if the sounds were set into the very metal. But all I would hear would be the soft *tick tick tick*.

Teddy's snores were lighter now – they reached a

crescendo in the darkest hours of the night before falling away into gentle wheezing around dawn. Bernard slept with his usual grimace. It was a pity because I could tell he was, by nature's hand, a pretty boy, with black curls framing a face that went cobnut-brown in the sun. He was a year my senior and his limbs, too, were excellently made so that he could have been a fine player of sports if he had not expended most of his energy on teasing and mischief. He had been handed a plate of natural gifts and turned his nose up at them, choosing instead to scrabble in the mud of fury towards those he could not subsume to his will.

I loved those minutes on my own with only the sounds of human sleep around me and cawing gulls overhead. I was alone to dream of a future when I would be free to follow my open path, when I might have a slice of bread and cheese in my hand and a few pennies in my pocket, and I could seek my fortune in London like Dick Whittington or on the seas like the boy in one of our Sunday stories. No time holds promise like the first few minutes of a summer's day. I knew it then and I know it now even more.

And so I was in perfect happiness when I saw Fred's eyelids flick open and he stared at me, as if wondering why I was free and not being ribbed by his captain. '*Psssst!*' he hissed at Bernard. 'He's awake.' There was an urgency there, as if any moment when I was not being taunted by one or other of them was an abomination. Bernard moaned a little, but remained asleep. 'He's awake!' Fred reiterated. He knew his role in this little pandemonium and he was not going to miss out on it.

'Shut up,' muttered a new voice. It was Miles, the

oldest of all of us and the sleepiest. If he could have slept eighteen hours out of the twenty-four that God provided he would have been happy as the lark. He was a full sixteen years and it was rumoured between us that he and Mr Tolson's daughter, Iphigenia, who was a twelvemonth younger than Miles, were in love and would soon be married. I cannot recall how the rumour began, but I suspect Miles was its origin. I knew not why, but that intelligence was bane to my innards. Every time it was mentioned, I felt sick and sullen. It was only as I aged a few years that I came to realize why.

Neither Fred nor Bernard would refuse Miles's command. For Miles to the rest of us was like a kraken to a sailor – dangerous, capricious and likely to rear its head when least expected. Solidly built and unallied, he followed his own whims, which mostly rotated around food in the way that our world rotated around the sun. So long as none of us poked the kraken, and so long as it was fed regularly, it left us alone and we were all the better off for that.

And so, as ordered, Fred shut up.

This left me a further glorious ten minutes of daydreaming, when I pictured myself on the road to London with thruppence jangling in my pocket; perhaps joining a company of soldiers called upon to rescue the King from robbers, or to save a wealthy baker of sweetmeats from an undetermined danger that nevertheless left his stock wholly intact and available as a reward to his saviours.

In time, Teddy's snuffling became regulated breath, and Bernard's soft moans became awoken yawns. Our morning symphony drew to its end.

We crawled out of our beds and took turns at the stone basin to wash our faces. I was the last in the line, for although I was not the youngest, I was the poorest, and that trumped rank by age. I did not mind so. It gave me a chance to pull faces at Bernard's back while he tried to wipe away the night's grease. 'Out of my way, charity boy!' he cast in my direction but it was mostly for form's sake, and I paid little heed. I pulled on my stockings and patched breeches and tugged at my hair to make it one-quarter respectable before Iphigenia brought us in our slice of bread and cup of sheep's milk to break our fast.

Her mother had died during Iphigenia's infancy and the daughter had grown up taking on the tasks of adults and she always took the first lesson of the day, which was arithmetic (her father preferred losing himself in the histories of the Caesars of Rome and the battles of the Greeks).

So we sat with our slates and abacuses and fretted over the numbers that Iphigenia cast at us.

I wish I could say Bernard was the dunce of the class, but in fact he had some talent for mathematics and was able to perform the calculations well. He could have solved most in his head alone, had he wanted to.

Arithmetic for two hours in the hot summery room drowsed us until, our stomachs rumbling and complaining, we were brought a second small breakfast consisting of toasted bread with a smear of fat. Then, as we were licking our fingers and touching them to the crumbs on our plates to lift those mouse-like morsels, our schoolmaster himself entered, with a genial expression on his face.

'Today, gentlemen, we reach the time of tragedy! The downfall of the greatest statesman our world has seen outside these isles. Do you know of whom I speak?'

It was Julius Caesar. It was always Julius Caesar when his face shone like polished brass and used those tones of adulation. Something that I have come to understand about Mr Tolson, now that I am a man, is that he loved us, his wards, but no less than that he loved humanity and the noble instinct in mankind. He admired all that men and women could be; and the chiefest form of that was the instinct towards righteousness – not in the religious form, for he had respect for those not born into our mother church, but in the sense of doing what is *right*, without a thought for any other consideration.

'No, sir,' four of us said as one. But not Bernard, who, I believe, gently snorted in some derision.

'Julius Caesar!' our teacher announced happily. We feigned astonishment. 'As the Bard wrote: *I am constant as the Northern Star, Of whose true-fix'd and resting quality, There is no fellow in the firmament.*' He sighed in contentment and we spent the rest of the morning hearing our master talk of the great qualities and greater triumphs of this scion of Rome.

Mr Tolson's small innovation to common pedagogy was to introduce athletic aptitude into the day, so that at three by the clock on the shelf, we would each day run twelve times around Turnglass House without stopping. He informed us that the great houses of learning – Winchester, Rugby, Eton and the like – swore by such measures, although I had an inkling that their exercise would have been grander than a dozen rings of a house, and avoiding the neighbouring mud flats. Fred would occasionally lie in wait, exhorting Bernard to thump me as I ran past, but I soon developed a sense of their presence and waited until they grew bored with lurking and resumed their own runs.

And so our regular day's education came to a close. But on that particular day, it did not mean the end of my day's duties, because it had become custom for me, the night after my Gala, to attend the Rose so as to offer more thanks to those who had contributed to my benefit. This partly took the form of my helping Walter in any small way I could, such as collecting empty tankards and sweeping some of the muck from the floor of the taproom.

The construction of the Rose is such that it holds two bars. The main bar, which is the first you come to when entering the pub, and a little snug, which is where those who order Walter's fowl stews sit to sup. There are large fireplaces in both, with wide chimneys. I was collecting the wooden bowl that had contained Peggy's food while she and Walter nattered about the price of bread when Walter happened to glance back towards the main bar. I saw his face turn ashen and his jaw drop almost to his chest. Confused, I stopped still, with the bowl in my hand and a cloth in the other.

In an instant, he grabbed me by both shoulders. 'Lysander!' he hissed, like a snake.

'Yes?' I said, staring at him, almost dropping the bowl in my astonishment. Was he having a turn of apoplexy?

'Lysander. Do what I say. And no argument!' His voice was strained and low, as if whispering through the night to a band of brigands.

'I shall,' I answered.

'Walter? Whatever is—' began Peggy.

'Hush!' he commanded her, lifting a finger but without turning to see her. 'Lysander. The chimney. Get inside it. Climb!' I blinked. All I could guess was that he had seen something utterly incredible and dangerous in the outer room. I shifted my head so I could see around his to glance out. He slapped my cheek. Not so hard as to really hurt me, but hard enough to make his intention clear. 'Climb.' And this time it was a growl, like a maddened dog. I could see nothing past him. But I did hear something out of the ordinary. The usual hubbub had dissolved, and there was now but one voice. I could not make out its words, but it was a gruff man's accent. And then I caught sight of Mr Tolson, backing into the snug doorway. He too looked concerned. He glanced to Walter and Walter nodded, full of meaning. At that, my tutor's face became as desperate as Walter's. 'Inside,' Walter said for the third and final time. And this time I did as I was told.

I scampered to the fireplace. It was a large but simple one surrounded by an inglenook wherein two wooden wing-sided chairs had been placed. As I found myself utterly confused and staring up into the flue, I heard the gruff voice come a little closer. Although the words themselves still escaped my hearing, some animal instinct told me they were a danger to me. Another voice rose up in annoyance. And then the shoving around of tables or benches.

'Quick!' hissed Walter, pushing me hard.

'Yes, go!' muttered my schoolmaster.

'But—' I began, until Walter positively threw me onto the hearth, and turned so that his back was to me. And at last I pulled my thoughts together. These men loved me and if they were telling me that I must climb for my life, then I must climb.

I put my head up inside the flue and instantly a shower of soot fell into my eyes, grating them with pain. My yelp of distress brought only a warning to 'hush' and 'climb!'

At that, my hands found little fingerholds in the crumbling and burned masonry. Then, with great effort, I pushed off with my feet and braced my back against the bricks behind me, so that I could grind and shuffle my way up. It was fortunate that I was a slim boy and the chimney was a spacious one.

A yard up and an urgent rapping on the outside of the flue, like a tapping of knuckles, suddenly sounded. I halted, my heart in my mouth, realizing that the constant falls of soot and scraping of my feet must have seemed like an alarm bell to anyone searching the inn.

I froze solid against the invisible bricks, hardly daring to breathe – though the smut in the air made that unpleasant enough – and waited.

The boards of the snug creaked as a new figure entered the room, and my two benefactors shuffled slightly. I would swear that I heard them breathe.

'Good day to you,' Mr Tolson said. There was a pause. No shifting about. 'You are not from here, I know.' A slight creaking. Even in my eyrie I could tell there was movement as the newcomer slowly paced around the room.

'Am I not?'

It was a gravelly voice. The accent was not local, but then I had little idea whence it came.

'I think not, sir.'

'Think what you like.'

And then the sound of one of the benches scraping a little as it was moved. 'You are weary.'

'I am. But it will not hinder me.'

'In what, sir?' Walter burst out, his voice tremulous. There was a long silence. I had the feeling that the man was sizing up my two protectors and they were not enjoying the sensation.

Mr Tolson rejoined the conversation. 'Maybe we can aid you?'

A dull tapping on a table. Five or six little strokes. One of the tankards, I was sure, as if the stranger were tapping out musical time in boredom. The sound somehow seemed to run through my feet and calf muscles, which were beginning to feel the strain of my position.

'Do you know me?'

'Not at all,' Mr Tolson answered immediately.

'Seen me before?'

'No. Never.'

'You are certain.'

'Quite certain.'

'The man out there . . .' I began to wonder how long I could stay there stock still. 'He did not welcome me.'

Walter spoke up. 'I am sorry for that, sir. I am the landlord. I welcome you.'

'And my friends?'

'They are most welcome.' So there were others. I did not think they were in the room, so they were perhaps on the threshold, enabling him to swan around like an invading general.

'You the schoolmaster?'

'The schoolmaster?' Mr Tolson asked, sounding flustered by the words.

'You heard what I asked.'

My feet were beginning to give way. I braced my palms against the sides too, trying for any grip. I did not know what danger this man was to me or to those around me, but I knew that I had to stay hidden if I could.

'Yes, sir. I am the schoolmaster.'

'Schoolmaster.' He hissed it to himself, as if wrangling with the idea. 'Who are your lads?'

If I had been breathing at all, I stopped then.

'My pupils? I have four.'

'Their names.'

'I . . . err, I am not sure that—'

There was a crashing sound as a table was overturned and its tankards went rolling across the floor.

'Their names!' yelled the gruff man.

'Mason, Albrough-Scott, Gilly, Het!' Mr Tolson burst out.

'No more?'

'No more.'

'And who are they? Who are their people?' the man roared, kicking, by the sound of it, the overturned table.

'Mason, his . . . his father is a milliner on Mersea. Gilly, now, his parents are farmers near Colchester. Albrough-Scott, he . . . he—'

'He what?'

'He . . . yes, I remember. Devonshire. Somewhere in Devonshire. I . . . I only correspond by letter. With the mother.'

'By letter?'

'Yes, by letter.'

'That must have cost a pretty penny.'

'I . . .' my benefactor flustered.

'How much?'

'A . . . a shilling each one.'

The man seemed to accept this. 'Did you ever meet her?'

'The mother?'

'Who else?'

'I . . . I did. A most respectable lady. Her husband is a printer of books.' I could hear the desperation and self-doubt in his voice.

This reply left a pregnant pause in the air. 'A printer, schoolmaster?' the man asked after a while.

'Y-Yes, I believe so.'

'You see this?'

I wondered what the stranger was holding or displaying.

'Yes.'

'Did he print it?'

So it must have been some sort of book, I thought.

'I . . . could not say.'

Then there was an extraordinary sound, as if the strange man had slammed something down on one of the tables. 'Look closer,' he growled.

'I am looking, sir. I could not say who printed it.'

'You would not lie to me, would you, schoolmaster?' He sounded like a jackal before a deer.

My muscles were burning and I knew that I could not stay put much longer. I tried as silently as I could to press myself up, finding another foothold to my right.

'Of course not, sir. I do not . . . I do not know who you are, but I would not lie to you.'

'Take me to your boys. I want to look at them.'

'Sir, please,' Walter's voice intervened. Maybe he heard me twitching about and was doing his best to mask the sound. 'If you—'

'Take me to them,' the man reiterated. And his voice brooked no argument.

'I will,' Mr Tolson said wearily.

There was no more speech, but a further shifting about as the newcomer stood and then a pattering of steps. I waited. As soon as I could hear nothing, I started to gingerly lower myself down. But then I stopped: what if it were a ruse to get me out of my hiding place? What if the stranger had an inkling that his quarry – if that was what I was – had gone to ground thereabouts, and the best stratagem was to sit tight until I showed myself? I was paralyzed by the confusion.

'Lysander.' I knew Walter's voice. It was low and urgent. 'Lysander, come out. Be quick.' But was he speaking freely or under duress? If I dropped down, would I immediately feel hands on my neck? 'I said be quick about it! You are safe.' I calculated that even if I were not safe, I could only have remained there another half minute before I fell out. And so I whispered a prayer for sanctuary and preservation, and dropped hard to the stone grate. To my relief, there was Walter and no one else in the room. But on the threshold were the staring faces of my friends at the inn. None of them spoke but all had the same look of concern. 'Who can take him?' Walter asked no one and all.

In the corner of the room, I saw one of the familiar inn tables overturned onto its side. Yet there was something most queer about it: in its centre one of Walter's meat knives had been stabbed into the wood. And that was not all: the blade held in placc what seemed to be some sort of pamphlet. As it was, it looked like a playbill posted on a wall, but with a threat of violence pervading it.

There was a mumbling in response to Walter's question, my utter confusion being ignored. A few offered to take me in and it befell to Walter to decide my destination. While they spoke low and urgent, I went to the table and managed to free the knife. I took up the pages it pierced, seeing them to be a sort of chapbook of the type they called a 'penny blood': a violent and salacious account of ill doings. This one blazed the title *The Murderous Deeds in the Village of Lorne in France and How They Brought About the Bloody Revolution. The First Part.*

By a Gentleman of the Law

Most strange.

I turned over the first page but was pulled up by Walter. 'Morty, you take him,' he was saying. 'I will send for you when it is safe. Go now, go quick!'

There was no more discussion and Morty, a young buck around twenty years old, took me by my arm. I surreptitiously slipped the chapbook into my jacket.

Still without the faintest idea of what was in occurrence, we ran out the back of the Rose, flitting between trees and low walls to hide our escape.

Half an hour's run later, my feet rubbed raw in my leather boots, we came to Morty's little cottage, which he shared with five or more family members – I was not clear how many. For his mother he came up with some excuse for my presence, apparently enjoying the subterfuge.

After a while, the simple domesticity calmed me, and I was gradually able to slow my tumbling mind and turn it to the one clue that I had as to what in God's name was happening: the chapbook that sat within my pocket. I betook myself to a corner and, by the light of a tallow candle that reeked fatty fumes through the house, opened the penny blood and began to read.

PROLOGUE

17 June 1789

The glass in the Hall of Mirrors reflected a thousand sun-bright candles, a flickering firmament of miniature stars that God himself had set to surround noble King Louis of France. The very room in which they shone had been built so that the silk-clad visiting dignitaries would henceforth know that here, in Versailles, lay all the wealth of the world, atomized into a royal house chosen by the Almighty as his very own. Above them, the vaulted ceiling, emblazoned with a rich panorama of hard war and luxuriating peace, said that within this nation all the elements of the earth had combined to form a land higher in His love than any other. It was truly a kingdom divine.

I watched all bow low as Louis and Marie Antoinette passed by. His pace was stately, as needs be when weighed down with the heavy diamond-and-sapphire regalia of his sublime rank. Her heaped and moulded hair pouf, dressed tonight with miniature trees replete with grapes and tiny orange-fruit, ensured that her stride was equally sedate. And yet she was keen as ever on joining the gaming tables, to lose half her husband's, and our starve-stomached nation's, wealth. Someone muttered that her dress tonight was trimmed with marten tails.

As they walked, we followed.

Had it been the King's afternoon passage to his cabinet, the route would have been lined with petitioners on bended knee, hopeful of a few seconds' words into his ear - petty disputes about neighbours encroaching on grazing land, or murderous accusations of political disloyalty against enemies. But this was the time for pleasure and as Louis paraded on towards the Salon d'Hercule, the Queen skipped to the gaming room. She was doing well not to wrinkle her nose at the all-pervading summer smell of urine that reeked from the two hundred and fifty privies stationed throughout the palace.

Yes, while Versailles was still renowned the world across for opulence, those of us who lived and worked there knew the truth: that the headstrong days of the Sun King, Louis XIV, were past. Now numerous rooms were shut up, corridors in ruins. Many an old aristocrat claimed the corruption stemmed from the edict that all subjects of France, from the lowliest peasant to the highest duke, had the right to wander the palace and view the King at meals, or at play or even a-bed in the morning. I gave this explanation little credence, and considered instead the well-meaning dimness of the monarch and the fact that supporting America in its war of independence against Britain had bankrupted us.

In the gaming room I noted the Duc de Coigny, Comte Esterhazy, and in the corner: the Duc de Lauzun. Lauzun was keen to show off his *redingote*, our French interpretation of the long English riding coat that the young rakes were sporting. The Queen bade them all sit and return to their cards and roulette wheels and I was relieved to see a marble perfume burner at the edge of the room, sweetening the air with jasmine.

For an hour I watched the cards dealt and the wheels spin. I observed the powdered faces and luscious wigs. Even one dashing young man who had ventured to show off his real hair.

'Are you looking for a game, sir? Join us. We play faro!'

The voice was attached to Gaston de Rotanne, the pudding-headed son of the Comte de Rotanne. I had a fractious history with the comte, and only knew Gaston by sight and preferred it that way. But I sat at the table and took a hand.

We played, he won and my small store of livres diminished.

'Lady luck is not with you,' he chuckled, his fat lips stretching out.

'She seems to have had a better invitation.'

'She sits beside me tonight.'

'No doubt.'

'She is not with the Queen either,' he added, watching Marie Antoinette lose another pile at the vingt-et-un. 'The King wants for money,' he whispered. 'His debts are so great, my footmen are richer than him. But do not think that means he will give in to the traitors like Robespierre. Damn lawyer.'

'I am a lawyer.'

He stared at me. 'You do not look like one.'

Perhaps, perhaps not. For the record, my hair is dark, like the men of Piedmont, and I did not pomade it like most of the nobles of court. I was fortunate that the military battles I had fought had left me with nothing worse than a slight white scar along the bottom of my left jaw. The one bullet that I had taken had passed through my right calf muscle, hurting like hell, but resulting in no lasting damage. My subsequent life as a lawyer rarely required feats of strength, but still I was above average in height and tried to stay in good form by playing *jeu de paume* and lifting the heavy tack in the stables. I was thirty-four years old and did not wish to end my life as a fat lawyer dying at my desk with my hand clutching my chest.

It was then that something caught my eye. It was that as Gaston expertly flicked the cards to the players his wrist action always seemed to stutter, catching breath just before releasing the card. It seemed a curious tic. And after watching it for a minute, I realized why it did so: as his hand moved, it passed above a golden goblet of rich yellow Madeira wine, thus allowing him a glimpse of the card's face reflected in the surface of the liquid. I had seen card-men with hands better than surgeons. Gaston de Rotanne was a cheap street poacher by their standard.

'Another round?' he enquired.

I hesitated before replying. I did not relish a petty contretemps. 'Something tells me I will not win tonight,' I said, glancing at the cup.

His eyes narrowed. 'You have something to say, sir?'

I stood wearily. 'I have many things to say, and yet custom and courtesy . . .' I waved away the final words.

'And what is that meant to mean?' he demanded.

'Only that a game of chance clearly means one thing in the servants' quarters and something else entirely in your lordship's presence.' It was foolish to do this in public but I was tired of the pretence. I folded my cards and left the table.

'Sir!' he bellowed across the room, silencing all talk. All eyes were on us. 'I demand your name and your title.'

I did not turn around. 'My name is David Sévine,' I said. 'I have no title to speak of.'

'Then I . . . then I . . . My father shall hear of this!' he blustered.

But I kept my back to him and left the salon. I already

knew the evening was doomed before it had begun, and it was far better to get out now before the bitter end. I gazed along the corridor, where a mouse looked back at me, blinked in agreement, then insouciantly slipped back through a hole at the bottom of the wall. Even it could tell there were better places to be. Mentally complimenting the creature on its sagacity and good taste, I headed back to my chamber.

18 June 1789

I was shaken awake the next morning. The hands that gripped my shirt were attached to a tough-skinned servant in cream livery. Two others stood behind him. My head ached and my mouth was dry. The one room I had to my name - where I ate, slept, and performed my duties recording and deciding upon humble petitions to the King from nobles of his realm - was coming into focus.

'All right,' I muttered. 'Deliver your message.' Outside the window I could hear the gentle sound of the King's woodwind quartet playing to rouse him more gently from his sleep. My own quarter in the rear of the palace was generally serenaded by water dripping from the fracturing pipes.

The message, it turned out, was in the form of action, rather than verbal. Indeed, they set about destroying my quarters in a fashion that spoke of practice: breaking the furniture and sweeping all my books and papers from the surfaces where I had discarded them, in a perfect semblance of anarchy. There went the Marquis de Lambert's suit for a new waterwheel on his estate, there the dowager marchioness of Rouen's pleas for her daughter to be presented at court in the hope of marrying before she reached fifteen.

From my bed I watched them go about their work and reached for a cup of water. There seemed no point in attempting to dissuade them. My chamber door, which I noted was now hanging from one hinge, shuddered as another figure hove into view.

The Comte de Rotanne strode in and peered around, as if seeing a hovel for the first time. 'So, this is where you live, Sévine,' he said. 'Little better than a pig.'

'Good morning, Comte.' I had half expected his visit sooner or later.

'It is not a good morning,' he replied. 'Neither for you nor for me. Last night, in the presence of Her Royal Majesty, you accused my son of dishonourable conduct.'

'Actually, I accused him of–'

The closest of his three lackeys threw a punch directed at my head. I can't say he did it well because I was just able to shift out of his reach so that he overbalanced and his knuckles cracked the wall plaster.

'Stop,' the comte ordered him in irritation. 'I have seven or eight witnesses from last night that will swear before the *lit de justice* that it was you cheating at faro, not my son.'

I knew that he would indeed. Some men in our court used whips to pursue their aims, one or two used whispers. What set the comte apart was his skill at manipulating both weapons. In the service of France - the France he and the bewigged clans saw - he maintained a veritable army of intelligencers from fine ladies passing on poisonous rumours to taproom snitches dripping dirt into his lieutenants' ears. Then his other employees would be called in. But it was an army to marvel at from afar, not close enough to be struck. Had my head not been pounding due to the previous night's bad wine, my stomach might have twisted in greater fear.

Instead, I lay back on the bed and rested my forearm across my eyes, as they stung still in the sunlight. 'No doubt you have, Comte.'

'You are no gentleman, Sévine. A lawyer never is, of course. You were never much of a soldier either.' He had seen me attempt the army life when we fought in the American war for independence. He had been my commander, indeed, and an efficient one given grudging credit by the British whom he routed on more than one occasion. He had a talent for noting and taking advantage of the smallest battlefield factors so often overlooked by lesser officers: the food his men had eaten, the manufacturer of the muskets, the length of time since the opposing troops had been paid.

But it was during the Battle of Yorktown that he gave me orders to attack a well-defended and strategically important outpost with a small squad. I considered it an ill-planned mission that would end in our death or capture and insisted on a different plan. He ordered me on penalty of a brutal punishment to do what he specified but I promptly ignored his threat and followed my own stratagem. To his chagrin, I met with grand success and was toasted by his brother officers, who guffawed at how absurd his plan had been.

The result, predictably, was fury on his part, and my expulsion from the army by his command. It was only the noted success of the mission that saved me from the rope, I suspect. I was sent back to France.

In time he returned, lauded for the victories he had gained; but every time I had been within his line of sight I had felt the chill of a man who wished my life to end before his eyes.

'You are quite right, Comte. No point wasting energy on

my person. Best if you just leave and forget all about me.' It was more blind hope than expectation but my pockets were empty and we both knew his were full of silver and schemes.

To answer my low expectation, one of de Rotanne's men set a stool upright for him. He tested it and, finding it acceptably stable, rested his rear upon it. 'I will not do that, Sévine,' he told me.

'Pity.' God, how I meant it.

'Because I also know what you are, I know whom you associate with.'

It was fresh information to me that I 'associated' with anyone to speak of - certainly, few that would have moved in de Rotanne's orbit.

'In all honesty, Comte, right now I wish to associate with no one and nothing but the nearest privy.'

'Society, Sévine, rests on honesty,' he continued, seemingly unhearing. 'And I am minded to go straight to His Majesty's person and present such evidence about your cheating.'

'No doubt, no doubt,' I said. I knew this was not the end of the conversation. It was the preamble and no more. I had been through many preambles in the courts. They were to be endured before the true fighting began.

'But what would that accomplish?' he mused.

'What indeed?'

'No, I have a better purpose for you, Sévine.' I could feel him coming to the point, which was a relief. 'The Three Estates are about to present their suits to His Majesty regarding the direction - indeed, the very constitution - of France. Utter impertinence. Louis was set upon his throne by God himself. They question the King, they question God.' I was of a mind to suggest that if our Heavenly Father had truly favoured Louis and France, He would have made him a town locksmith, for the King's curious hobby was designing and installing door locks and such a quiet life would have left him happier and the national purse distinctly less empty. 'I know you have sympathy with some of the more radical elements in the Third Estate. Lawyers. You are all the same.'

'I will not dispute that.' I hardly got on with other lawyers any more than he seemed to - hence my banishment to the backwaters of the law, dealing with tiresome petitions Louis XVI would never read.

'It will be your duty now to get talking to them. To join their little salon discussions. Discover their plans.'

'Influence them?'

His eyebrows rose. 'Indeed, when the time comes. You guess well.'

'It is astonishing that I need to cheat at cards.'

I did, indeed, know a few members of the Third Estate. When the King had been forced, due to the emptiness of his coffers, to recall the Estates-General, the elected body that had last met in 1614, many had feverishly speculated who would be chosen for the Third Estate, the one made up of commoners. Along with a spattering of minor landowners, doctors and journalists, there was certainly a preponderance of lawyers, some of whom I had come into professional contact with. They were, for the most part, young and radical in their ideals regarding the transformation of France - thus setting them on a course of dangerous collision with the aristocratic Second Estate, and the First assembled from the clergy.

'Robespierre.' His voice darkened. 'A seditious dog. Get to know him in particular. He is about as welcome here as a two-sous whore in the Convent of Saint Alice.'

'All right.'

'And send me frequent reports of what you find. If you fail to, I will importune His Majesty and you will be lingering at his - and my - pleasure in the Conciergerie.' That prospect did send a little shiver of doubt through my gut. Even in the Bastille, life was not too bad if you had the money to pay for your own room and decent food, but the Conciergerie was more egalitarian in its approach: duke or beggar, life within its walls was as foul as a wound washed in ditchwater. 'So, reports. Frequent and accurate - I no more want embellished intelligence than I want a dearth of it. You understand your orders?'

'I do, Comte.' But I was trying to cudgel my pounding head into finding the best route to scupper ever taking up my enforced role as political weasel. I do not like tattletales and had no intention of becoming one. And, in addition, I suspected that if the mood took him, the comte might well inform upon me to the very men he had set me to infiltrate, and that would be the end of me.

'Then we are finished here.' De Rotanne looked about the room. 'Something tells me this was no better before my men arrived.'

'You are probably right there.'

He gave me a final glance and departed, his men in his wake.

'You can come in now, Francois!' I called out through the doorway a few moments later. 'Just stop lurking. It is very disconcerting.'

I heard laughter and then saw a face I welcomed more than I would any other at that time: a fine-looking man, though his blond hair was beginning to recede from his forehead.

And here was Francois Merrin, the Baron d'Agnes, perhaps the last friend I had left in France or her colonies.

He was not the poorest aristocrat in France - there were some no better than peasants, farming dry patches of soil for scrawny vegetables - but he was well on his way.

Allow me to tell you.

Francois and I had been close during our childhood. The Barons d'Agnes were feudal *seigneurs* of the village of Lorne. His father's poor head for estate management and a penchant for being defrauded by fast-talking Parisians offering stakes in non-existent sugar plantations had conspired to reduce his already small fortune to the level of a Rouen tailor.

I was born in Lorne. My father, a man prone to bouts of anger, had been offered ownership of a nearby coal mine, giving him high hopes of social advancement. When I was ten, my mother died from the bad water. As a result, Francois and I were taught as one by the local priest. Then we had grown up. Somewhat.

'Oh David,' laughed Francois as he surveyed the chaos left by de Rotanne's men. 'What have you been up to?' I was about to explain when he lifted a palm to me. 'Actually, no need to answer, half the court is talking of it.' I lay back, grateful that I was not required to recount the episode blow-by-blow. 'You did the right thing, though. No one will be playing faro with Gaston de Rotanne any time soon.'

'No doubt I shall receive my reward in Heaven.'

'Well, it will not be this side of the pearl-decked gates, old man. What did the comte have to say?'

'He has invited me to wed his daughter.'

He burst once more into laughter. 'Even if de Rotanne had a daughter, something tells me he would rather she die of the pox than join you in marriage. Oh well, if you will not tell me, you will not tell me. But it would be best if you absent yourself from Versailles for a while. Come and stay with me. Come home. You cannot avoid it for ever.'

'I could come,' I said, more to myself than him. The comte would be outraged at my discarding his orders for a second time, but the alternative would be the low life of an informant, and an informant who could not even trust his own spymaster.

Francois seemed delighted. 'Wonderful. We can hunt, play billiards, even read if you like.' I would not have objected to a chance to open a book or two that had nothing to do with long-forgotten legal cases. And it would give me a chance to see Father Dollet once more. According to Francois, our old tutor had become something of a radical priest, influenced by the political reformist writings of the Abbé Sièyes. 'You know how it is really as dull as ditchwater there. But I must go soon.' A troubled look passed across his face. 'To be straight with you, old man, I have something of an ulterior motive in getting you down there. There is something I want to ask your opinion on.'

'Go on,' I said, intrigued.

'Well, you have been to some strange places and seen odd things, have you not?' Well, I had, but this was a curious turn for the conversation and I wanted him to get to the meat of it. 'You see, some of the local girls - mostly aged eleven or twelve - have been telling of strange sights on the road and in the fields.'

'What sort of things?'

A pink hint of embarrassment rose in his cheeks. 'Look, it seems madness to state it, and yet they are talking of . . . having seen witches.'

'Witches?' The superstitions of countryfolk were rarely far from the surface, but it was odd that Francois was joining them.

'Witches in flight. Or the water in their cups boiling and steaming as they bring it to their mouths. Things as . . .' He trailed off. 'Now, the Bible tells us witches do walk among us - and yet I baulk at the thought that they would choose Lorne as their bolthole. No doubt there is some more earthly explanation.'

'No doubt.' We were in an age where science was rapidly supplanting such mediaeval absurdities, but the knowledge would take generations to permeate the fields and lanes of our country villages, even those within a day's walk of Paris.

'Yes. All folly, and the girls will surely calm as they are married off. But still, I feel a great responsibility to these people.' He looked distraught at the thought of his villagers' worry. I was proud, then, of my friend. It was touching that some seigneurs truly cared for their tenants - and something to be encouraged, in order to bring succour to those whom life too often trod underfoot. I may have had the comte breathing wine fumes down my neck, but I knew I was more fortunate than many to have a full belly and warm clothes when I needed them.

'So I see.' I hauled myself to my feet for the first time. 'All right,' I said. 'I will come.'

Would that I had not. There would have been less blood soaking the dry soil of Lorne.

19 June 1789

I left the palace by coach the following afternoon. The King and all his entourage were in the chapel and it was easy for me to slip away unnoticed by de Rotanne's lackeys. There was a constant traffic to and from Versailles those days as the deputies to the Three Estates came and went. Usually they would arrive with faces full of determination and optimism, and leave with aspects of frustration and misery. But the struggle for power between the three orders seemed to be sifting down. The priests of the First wanted to keep their heads down, lest their cushy clerical sinecures be taken from them. The aristocratic Second had absolutely presumed their wishes - primarily for lower taxes and some oversight of Royal spending - would be the sole focus of the assembly. And yet the upstart commoners of the Third had come armed with lists of grievances and - far worse - solutions.

I had never thought to have seen it, but the position of Louis XVI of France was beginning to look precarious. One shock to the system and it might all fall to the earth like a rotten barn.

I pondered as we drove towards Lorne.

A settlement of no more than a hundred souls eking out a living from the poor arable farms around, it is about a league from the road that runs from Versailles to Paris. It is not remote, and yet it is somewhat isolated for the reason that there is little reason to go to or from it: a church and Francois's tumbledown baronial pile. There is an ageing monastery nearby but even the white-clad Order of the Brothers of Mount Carmel was then shrinking and folding in on itself.

Two hours bouncing through ruts had left me stiff when we turned off the main road. The path from thereon was actually better than the main highway, due to its lesser use, and we managed to pick up speed.

The first houses appeared. Poor farm cottages with scraggy cows chewing cud, sad-looking dogs sniffing at the earth. A few workers standing in the field, leaning on their tools, too few crops to keep them busy.

In the village proper, the main street boasted the church and the better-made houses. Some had two storeys and all had plots growing fruits and vegetables. They were thatched with the barley stubble gleaned from the fields after harvest-time. From this street little tracks and alleyways branched off to dark one- or two-roomed homes where twelve children had been born and three survived past their first birthday. In the doorways, small, filthy faces peeped out. Their residents worked as labourers for the larger farmers during the grape and corn harvests and scratched what they could from their own little yards.

No, my friend, the rural idylls you read of exist only in the minds of men who do not live in them.

The coach stopped outside the church and I entered, walking the length of the nave, my footsteps ringing despite the building being nearly full of muttering and whispering sinners waiting for evening Mass to begin. Above them, the church windows showed eleven scenes telling the stories of the apostles; but the window behind the altar, instead of the normal imagery of God upon his throne, showed the martyrdom of Saint Pierre, to whom the church was dedicated. Pierre had been crucified upside down, believing himself unworthy to die in the same way as our Lord and Saviour. Below that window, bracketed to the wall, there was a wooden crucifix, with a life-sized painted and gilded figure of our Lord upon it, his hands stabbed through with iron staves and a look of such bottomless sadness on his face that one feels as his mother must have done to see him so used.

I looked for my old tutor, Father Dollet, as I entered the church - I had been greatly looking forward to seeing him, as the main compensation for my enforced return to Lorne. But he was not yet present. I had taken only a few paces when Francois sprang up from the front pew. 'David!' he cried happily.

'Hello.' I clapped him on his shoulder. It was a relief to see him, even though it had only been a day since we had been together.

'You are late. But better late than never. And now you are back where you belong,' - I was not hugely pleased by that description, quite unconvinced it was true - 'we can start feeding you up. You are so thin these days, your cheeks are positively sunken, you know.'

He pulled me down to sit beside him. It was an unusual pew, seating just two people in the dead centre of the front row, no doubt constructed to display the wealth and importance of those for whom it was reserved. But Francois, a good man, had none of the airs of his ancestors; the powder-blue frock coat that he wore was not much fancier than my own. (The lace of his cravat was brilliant white, though, while mine was the grey of a hundred washes.) Of course, the rest of the simple countryside congregation was dressed in similarly greyish shirts, dark loose trousers and rough brown waistcoats so I was in good company.

'How does the old place look?' Francois asked me.

I gazed about. 'Not a stick of change.'

'De Rotanne did not nab you on your way out, then.'

'I would guess he is noticing my absence right about now.'

'Ha. That would be quite a scene to behold. He does not like you very much.'

'No.'

At that point, a short and delicately boned curate entered from the vestry with a billowing white alb over his black cassock and ribbon collar, an altar boy padding in his wake. I was delighted to see Father Dollet looking a lot greyer but no more fragile than I had last seen him so many years earlier.

The congregation stood as he climbed into the dark-stained wooden pulpit, opened his book and began to read a lesson. It was the description of the Last Supper. But after a few moments he lifted his eyes and I saw in them a sudden glint that I had forgotten sometimes resided there. He paused and turned a number of pages in the gilt-edged book before him. The lesson abruptly changed to the story of the return of the Prodigal Son. I noted a wry glance in my direction. He had a sly old wit, Pierre Dollet.

As he read, a murmur arose like low wind through a forest. We turned to see four people entering the church, the apparent cause of the minor commotion. One was a dark young woman aged in her twenties, with curls of thick hair brushing the top of a simple dress. Beside her was a man in his forties, a good-looking fellow with a handsome round face, budding mouth and fair hair. He had a big, powerful frame. But there was something muddying the fine face - a haunted expression and a flitting about of the eyes as if he had something to be wary of. Behind them walked a boy aged around fifteen years, with hair the colour of the man's. He was making a point of the interruption they had made to the service, enjoying the attention. That attention was in no small part a reaction to the figure leading the others.

She was a woman, tall and graceful, clad in fashion that drew attention for its fine taste without a hint of gaudiness. The neckline on her dress rose high and the skirts blew out gaily from her waist. As she came properly into view, I saw her handsome profile, a white powdered cheek with black, straight hair falling to her neck but no lower, in contrast to the fashions I had seen in Versailles. Other than that, I could make out little because a veil fell from the brow of her hat to her lips. As she walked to the front of the church, a ripple of attention followed her. She sat, seemingly unaware of the sensation, in the second row.

'Do not worry, my friend, you will meet her later,' whispered the baron with a grin. If I had told him I was not interested in doing so, it would have been a lie.

Father Dollet, who had looked up from the ink on his page and watched the woman's entrance along with the others, shook off the interruption and returned to the words of the lesson: 'When he came to his senses, he said, "How many of my father's hired servants have food to spare, and here I am starving to death! I will set–"'

'Repent!' It was a voice crying out from the back of the room. We all turned again at the interruption.

'Sweet Jesus,' Francois muttered, blasphemously, to himself.

I saw a man whose skin was stretched across his bones like paper. Despite that, he did not, in fact, look old, at least not in the number of summers he had seen and winters he had faced. This man who wore no shoes could almost have been born on the same day, thirty-four years earlier, that I first mewed, amazed and saddened, in this world. Indeed, but for the yellow of his skin, which was seeping into his eyes, and the lack of muscle, our appearances were not dissimilar, I noted. And he was dressed in clothes that had once been good but had faded and torn.

He continued his cries, now reciting the Denial of Christ by his apostle to whom the church was dedicated. '"I will tell you the truth," Jesus said, "Tonight, before the cock crows, you will disown me three times." But Pierre said, "Even if I must die with you, I will never disown you."' He stared at Father Dollet. 'Is that right, Pierre? *Ad poenitentiam te adducit*? Do you repent your deeds?' The priest looked too shocked to reply.

'Cotillard,' Francois muttered in answer to my unspoken question. 'He is, whether or not you will believe it, my former lawyer.'

The fact did not even surprise me.

'Are you ready for a judgement?' Cotillard called out. And then he crossed one foot delicately in front of the other, stretched his arms out straight from his shoulders and dropped his head to his chest, in a mirror of the painted and gilded wooden holy image below the stained-glass window of Saint Pierre.

An hour later, in an atmosphere where a sense of interruption, of imbalance hung in the air like thick incense, despite Cotillard's subsequent enforced departure, I watched the penitents queuing for the confessional. As a child, I had kneeled so many times in that box, wondering where my words would end up. Although I came early to the conclusion that those words ended up precisely nowhere, I still believed there is something very beautiful about the sacrament of penance: people asking forgiveness for the wrongs they have done to other men as well as God. That said, it was almost two decades since I had done it myself.

The confession box was of the ornate Spanish style - perhaps modelled by someone who had trained in sparkling Barcelona or dusty Madrid. Entering, I pulled the curtain to, leaving myself in a comforting semi-darkness, and kneeled, waiting for Father Dollet to speak to me through the wicker grille. Then the pink, white-grizzled cheek of the priest appeared. 'My child?' he said simply.

I cleared my throat. I would not have been going through this if Francois had not pushed me into it, saying that in Lorne anyone failing to confess would be viewed with deep suspicion. At this moment I was uncertain if relating all the black marks on my conscience would affect me any more than it had done sixteen years previously when I had last gone through the ritual. 'Forgive me, Father, for I have sinned.'

'How long has it been since your last confession?'

'Two weeks.'

'And what sins do you have on your conscience?'

'Most of them.'

'My son, most men have most sins. List yours,' he told me.

'Wrath. Lust. Envy. Sloth. Some pride. Not gluttony or avarice.'

He thought this over for a second. 'Well, then let us be thankful for only five of the seven.'

I suspected he had guessed my identity. 'Any instructions, Father?'

'Say about a thousand Hail Marys and as many Lord's Prayers as you can squeeze into a day. I have a feeling I will be hearing you again.'

'Yes, Father.' There was something I had been wondering for a very long time and now seemed the perfect moment to sate my curiosity. 'Father, can I ask a question?'

'Please do. It will make a pleasant change.'

'Do you ever get bored with the same confessions over and over?'

He paused. 'My son, allow me to let you into a little secret - so long as you vow not to reveal the secrets of the confessional.'

'Pone, Domine, custodiam ori meo.'

'I see you have had a good teacher.' So he had indeed guessed. If Father Dollet had any sin, it was for occasional self-regard. I peered through the grille, and could just make out his left hand resting on his lap. On the little finger was his signet ring, which had always fascinated me as a boy. On its face were Father Dollet's initials set within a scroll to indicate his scholarly nature. 'Well, the truth is, after all these years, it would have to be quite spectacular to surprise me.'

'Thank you, Father.'

I hoped he could see my smile through the dark. I also hoped the next whispering penitent would at least have an interesting story to tell.

'You look like you enjoyed yourself in there,' Francois told me, with a bemused expression on his face as I blinked a little in the light from the candelabras set around the nave.

'Best confession I've had in years.' Which was true.

Behind me, the tall dark-haired woman whom everyone had stared at entered the box. She turned so she was facing me and lifted her veil. For a moment I saw a delicate face with hints of the Orient, before she pulled the curtain across and hid herself once more. Perhaps Father Dollet experienced ennui even when hearing the illicit thoughts of attractive young women. More likely he looked forward to it all week.

'I would pay dearly to know what sins she has on her conscience,' said Francois. He grinned.

A few minutes later, the priest emerged from his box and I positively bounded over to see him.

'My son,' he said, wrapping his arms around me. 'It has been too long.'

'Father. You look well. For your age.'

'Ah, the one fate a man cannot escape,' he said, passing his hand over the greying hair. 'David, I am so glad to see you. I want to talk to you about the nation, about its people. Look around you. They need someone to take up their cause.'

I was a little taken aback by this immediate bent of the conversation. 'I am not the one they need. But we will talk.' There was still a queue of penitents expecting his absolution. 'Will you come to dinner at Francois's?' I asked.

'I cannot tonight. But tomorrow for certain.'

'I look forward to it more than I can say.'

I left it at that and we bade goodbye. I pictured us sitting up chewing the bones of a partridge and pouring the wine - I had a fond memory of him introducing me to the mead produced by the nearby Carmelite brothers, an order to which he had belonged before he left to join the priesthood.

Outside, the early-evening sunlight felt warm on my skin, which had been cooled by the dark church. 'Ah, the Gypsies,' remarked Francois.

'What?'

'The Gypsies. Our village Gypsies.' He pointed along the street to a family of three. 'They came here about, oh, twelve years ago.' A small couple aged in their fifties were dressed as drably as all the other peasants. The father had a bald crown among his dark locks and a worn-out expression as he gazed down at a rough table that sported a few wooden items for sale. His wife looked jollier. She was plump with rosy cheeks and was knitting a shapeless grey object that could have been the beginnings of a hat or baby coat or man's jacket. They stood, having no chairs. Their son, tall and proud with shaking curls, wore a red bonnet and watched as the congregation filed out of the church gates and past their stall. A pair of bustling old women paused in front of the table and the older man looked up expectantly as one picked up a delicately hewn and beeswax-polished wooden horse. I could see that he felt too deep a connexion to the toys he had carved to ever want to see them go, but it was a matter of necessity. No man can eat his own talent. Still, the women soon put the animal down and moved on. There was something of relief in the man's posture as his prized work remained unsold.

Francois and I strolled away and were about to climb into

his dilapidated carriage when we were distracted by a rising noise. It was mocking laughter and we craned our necks to see what was going on.

Four young farm labourers had left the church and were at the Gypsies' stall. One, who was more sturdily built than the others, had the toy horse and was waving it in the face of its inventor, who looked downcast. 'Three sous?' he demanded. 'It's not worth shit!' To make the point, he rubbed it through the channel between his buttocks. His friends sniggered and nudged each other. The toymaker's son made to snatch it back, but his mother gently placed her hands on his arm. The heavy-set labourer took the rear legs of the horse in one fist, and the front in the other and slowly prised them apart. The rear pair came away in his hand, to the howls of his friends. 'Well, now you can charge six sous!' he declared, dropping the contents of both hands on the table.

'David,' Francois called after me as I walked briskly towards the gathering, which had attracted a couple more onlookers. I heard but ignored him and pushed one of the smaller labourers out the way. I think he might have resisted if I had not been dressed as a man from the city, albeit a shabby one. I was now in front of the group.

'I will pay six sous for it,' I said.

'Six, sir?' asked the old man, uncertain about what was happening.

'Ah, so you drive a hard bargain, monsieur? Eight it is.' I reached into my frock coat and pulled out a purse.

'It is broken,' stated the dumbfounded heavy-set labourer.

'You need not state the obvious.'

The group of young men looked to each other for guidance while I counted out the coins on the table. The toymaker looked bemused, his son looked curious and it was left to the mother to be grateful. 'Thank you, monsieur. A present for a boy?'

'Yes.' I stood with my back to the four behind me.

'Thank you, sir,' said the woman again.

'It is my pleasure.'

I saw Francois at my shoulder. 'Good evening, your lordship,' the woman said. I heard in her tone that she had rarely uttered these words.

'Good evening. How much is the pig?' he asked lifting a fat wooden creature from the stall.

'Two sous.'

'Surely eight, like the other.' I was grateful for Francois taking up my cause. 'Stand aside, Philippe.' The heavy-set labourer, who had edged close to the table, retired a step. 'Good afternoon, Jacob,' he said, addressing the Gypsy boy. For his part, that boy inclined his head a little, without overt commitment.

'Eight then, monsieur.'

'Then I shall take it. I think we should take home one of your wares that is still intact, should we not David?'

Lorne sits on top of a low hill, with the chateau d'Agnes sleeping in the valley below it. A tree-lined tributary to the Seine, carpeted at its edges with water lilies, runs through the valley, splitting the house from the hillside. In the middle of the river, where it bulges out like a man in his middle age, there is a small thickly wooded island where a collection of little buildings peeps out through trees. Since we were in Francois's carriage we would have to go via the long roundabout path to the house, instead of straight down the hillside and across a thin wooden bridge. The carriage, with its livery painted on the side in fading green, passed fields of cereal shattered in the setting sun, the stalks withered and brown. The farmhands stood idle, staring at their meagre crop and Francois looked out sadly as the wheels blundered through dry potholes. It was, indeed, a saddening sight to witness hard-working men know that their families would be hungry again that night.

We rounded the valley, drove across a wide stone bridge, and down a track until a break in the trees allowed a brief glimpse of his three-storey grey stone chateau with two wings and twin turrets that were topped by unmoving, collapsed flags. It had been built in the early days of the Sun King and over the following century and a half it had been allowed to fall into genteel decay, such that the top storey was disused, with the windows boarded up.

Above the doorway the shield of the barons d'Agnes was embossed in lichen-covered stone. Crossing under the lintel we entered a neat lobby with passages leading off to the two wings and one backwards towards the kitchen.

A couple of rusting, ill-assembled and toppling suits of armour stood with mace and battle axe, ready to defend the house, although they looked as if at any moment they would more likely fall apart and pour onto the black-and-white chequered floor. As happy ten-year-olds we had done imaginary battle with these knights to defeat invaders and terrible monsters.

'Peugere will show you to your room,' Francois told me, indicating his ageing butler with bushy eyebrows, who silently turned and walked towards an oak staircase lit by glowing candelabras.

Pictures lined the wall as we climbed: portraits of men in a series of changing fashions from military to civilian-noble. But at the very top step a smaller painting seemed out of place. It was new and showed a woman lit from a different source than all the others. Where the men had been in daylight, this woman had been painted by the pale light of the moon. She was in a room where oak panels could be made out, and a table from which sheets of music fell to the floor. A harpsichord stood in a corner as if it had been abandoned just a moment before, and the woman was by the window, leaving a shadow behind her. Her straight black hair was lost in the shade as it fell to her shoulder. But what drew the eye was that her visage was turned away from the viewer, looking out the window as if there was nothing on the viewer's side of the frame that she needed, all her life was there in that room or outside. All that could be seen of her face was a single white-powdered cheek. And yet it was enough to recognize her.

'Who is she?' I asked.

Peugere raised his thick eyebrows sadly but made no reply. After more silence, he began to wend his way once more. I decided not to press him. If he did not want to answer, it was not my place to pull it from him with thumbscrew and Spanish boot.

At the top of the stairs a corridor stretched east and west. The floorboards complained as we walked but somewhere behind us I thought I could make out the sound of plucked strings. Yet when I stopped to listen they had passed - if they had been there in the first place - and there was only the rasping breath of my impatient guide taking me to the final room on the wing. 'It is not the best in the house,' he mumbled.

'No, I do not suppose it is. But it will do fine.' It was faded but clean enough.

'Would you like me to unpack your trunk, maître?' he asked, pointing to the case, which had been brought up earlier.

'No, thank you.'

Dinner that night was a joy. No talk of court, no talk of

the Estates-General. Just Francois and me denting the wine cellar that his grandfather had established. Oh, the pleasure of careless hours!

In the dark of the night I was woken by a light shining in my face, piercing my sleep and sending a white sweat rushing across my skin. I jerked straight up, my heart pounding. It felt like the continuation of the dream that had me in its grip, something unnatural and inverted. Francois's face loomed into the candlelight. 'We have to go. To the church. Now,' he warned me. His voice was low and the urgency was all the more for it. I could see that this was no prank.

No more than three minutes later, our horses were leaping over ditches in the dark, the only light coming from the lamps fastened to our saddles. The animals seemed as surprised and worried to be woken as I had been. Francois's caught his flank on a nail and leaked dark fluid as he jumped over a hedgerow, galloping at full fury. We did not use the bridge but forded the river on horseback to save seconds. Then we climbed the hillside, leaning into the horses' sweating necks to keep from falling.

At the top of the hill, I followed my friend along the lane to the main street, and then we were outside the church. The baron jumped from his horse without bothering to tether him, and I followed.

A single step inside the doorway was enough to understand the urgency. Those dark pews, the Spanish confession box that had heard my words and the stone pillars that held up the roof were untouched. But there on the altar, lit by a faint white moonlight filtering through the windows high in the walls, was a strange and evil sight. A sight to sicken even an old soldier such as myself.

The bloody crucifixion of Father Dollet, the man who

had taught me to read and write and had been more father to me than any other, had been performed with ritual care. The cross that had stood over the altar had been taken from its place and Father Dollet's arms tied to it under his shoulders to hold him; then his palms had been nailed through to the crossbeam. His right foot had been crossed over his left and a single long iron nail hammered through them both, breaking the warm skin and the delicate bones and the strings of flesh that make us move, into the wood below, where his blood had congealed into black gobs.

But there was an aspect to this crucifixion that was something quite unlike, and even worse than, that of our Saviour. This crucifixion, which seemed to fill the whole room, grotesquely mirrored the great portrait above the altar, which depicted the death of the church's patron saint: Pierre, who had deemed himself unworthy to die like the Son of God and had therefore been inverted, his head to the ground and his feet in the air.

The foot of the cross before us lay on the altar table, while the top rested on the floor, so that the priest's head hung down, and his jaws rolled open. And beside the pain, there was obscenity. His black cassock had been lifted up at the waist and anything he had worn underneath was gone, showing his private parts to the world.

And finally, the blood that had poured to the ground had come from a precise wound on his neck, betraying his life. The sight sickened me, as if my body had been wracked by the miasma of a thousand dead. It was worse than anything I had seen on the battlefield, worse than anything I had heard from the criminal pits of the cities. Those all seemed somehow part of the natural order, no matter how harsh. Yet this sight was something from beyond nature.

On his face was not the sadness of Jesus of Nazareth, but

with closed eyes and a lolling mouth, Father Dollet, that charitable, world-loving man, had a look that spoke of a pain piercing into the lowest depths of humanity, into all that sets us apart from the insensible things of this earth. The man had been debased, turned into something animal, robbed of all that he was.

Something changed in me then, as if it were my own blood that was ebbing away into the unseen ground.

'For God's sake, get him down,' whispered Francois as he stood, as amazed as I was.

I looked around to see whom he had spoken to. There was a man standing in the quire in a grubby nightshirt, his legs bare. Rolls of fat showed through the spattered material around his waist.

'Wait, no, let me see him first,' I ordered, motioning the man back. I kneeled to closely examine the cross and what it bore. Dollet's mouth was open, his tongue grey. The bags under his eyes bulged. He could have been weeping. A thin twine wrapped many times from his shoulders to his armpits and around the wood, cut into his flesh, leaving it an angry red, which became the colour of milk whey where the blood had failed to flow, dammed by the ligature. And finally, there were the hands with the offending metallic stakes through them, with that faint blue glow that all metal has in cold light. The nails looked like they could have come from any home or farm where furniture is mended or fences constructed. Slowly and delicately, because it felt as though I were touching the wound on a living man, I felt the gaping hole on his neck. The blood had run out and pooled on the ground - enough for me to smell it. But the blood on my fingers was warm. And as I examined the wound again there was a howl from the villager behind me.

'Jesus, our Lord! Look!' He pointed to the head of the

murdered man. Inches from my own, the priest's eyes suddenly flicked open and a low groan hissed from his parted lips.

'Christ!' I yelled. 'He's alive! Help me get him down!'

Our hearts pumping, we lifted the foot of the cross from the altar. I wanted nothing in life so much as I wanted to be able to preserve him. All the while the moaning of Father Pierre Dollet filled our ears and echoed through the nave, bouncing off the bare walls and returning from a hundred directions like the sound of the hopeless crowds in hell.

'Who are you?' I asked of the rotund man in the nightshirt.

'Jean-Michel Hubert, monsieur. I am the baker.' He sounded as if he were on the verge of tears. No one would have blamed him.

'Be careful, do not shake him about,' I said in a tone I hoped was firm but unlikely to trigger the baker's final collapse into dumb shock. The cross and its mutilated cargo touched the stone floor.

'What should we do?' I was not even sure who had asked the question. I was staring into the priest's eyes - eyes that reflected in them a journey to places he had described a thousand times in church but never expected to see. The lids had only opened a fraction, and the head had turned away from the light still shining in a single dust-floating beam through the high window. In a heartbeat they flicked open so wide that I started back, as if the man on the cross were trying to see all the way back to the lands he had just departed. In those eyes there was fire and anarchy. His body began to shake, vibrations that set the wood chattering on the stone.

'Hold him down!' I ordered the other two. Even then I felt uneasy, as if I were the one doing violence to my old tutor. The others grabbed the priest's chest and legs but it was Father Dollet's hands that moved. And, incredibly, before

I could act to prevent it, his left, then his right palm ripped away from the wood. The iron nails tore through ligament, muscle and bone to remain in the cross while the bloody flesh flew away towards me. Those gored hands gripped my wrists and our two fleshes became one. His eyes seemed to recognize me, returning to the days he, I and Francois had spent turning the dry pages in his books. Somewhere deep, I had a glimmer of hope that the memories would bring him back to us.

But from inside the brittle shell of his body, a sound rose that his mouth attempted to turn into meaning. 'The . . . I . . .' It was more breath than words, something from the time before language. 'The butterfly!' I put my ear beside the old man's lips, hoping to hear more, but all there was was a shallow sigh from the lungs. Then his head slowly fell back to the wood to rest and his eyes closed. I pressed my head to his chest, listening for the drum-beat of life. But all was empty.

There would be more acts to perform, but none was life-urgent now. I sat back on the floor and slumped against the pew, my head spinning.

'What did he say?' Francois asked after a while.

'He said, "The butterfly!"'

Francois's brow furrowed in confusion. 'What does that mean?'

'I cannot tell.' Was it to do with his death? Maybe he believed himself an insect? And yet at the moment of death, a man may simply speak words without real meaning. 'Let us untie him,' I said eventually, giving in to the confusion, letting it win for now.

We drew the nail from his feet and loosened his bonds. I saw on his left hand the signet ring with a device of his initials set upon a scroll. I remembered what he had once told me: it was to remind him too that you had to study words to truly understand them.

All I could do for him now was to lift his feet, then legs, then buttocks to put his thin undergarment, which we found beside the altar, back on him and offer him whatever famished dignity we can have in death. As I did so, I noticed another sign of humiliation. A single long nail, rough iron and the length of a finger, had been inserted into the man's rear passage. The three of us gazed at each other before I gently removed it.

But then the light from the lamp beside the body showed me something else. Squinting, I brushed the cooling flesh of the curate's left buttock with my fingers, touched them together and held them up to the light to see them better.

'What is it?' asked Francois.

It took me a long time to answer. 'A man's seed,' I replied. I watched Francois sit, lost for words, unable to comprehend what had happened. As a lawyer I had once or twice known cases where men had forced themselves on another in such a fashion. I watched Francois struggle with the thought. 'Who will take charge of the body?' I asked eventually.

'I will send a messenger to Dom Mathieu, the abbot at the monastery,' he answered, distractedly. 'David, this is . . .' He could find no words.

I saved him the trouble. 'Have you any idea?' I, for sure, had none. And my bewilderment at what I had seen and touched had not yet turned to anger, though I knew it would soon come.

'No. Nothing like this. Not ever.'

'Never, sir,' added the baker, Hubert.

My vision fell on the carving on a tomb. It showed an angel grabbing a dragon by its throat and hauling it out of a tower. I did not know what the tower represented - this corrupt world, maybe. 'Well now it has. We will have to deal with it. Somehow,' I said, my weight against the pew where Francois and I had sat together a few hours before.

'Can we discover who did this?'

'Yes. And then, as seigneur, you will punish him accordingly.' I had an inkling to enact my own law, but suppressed it. France's law would do better. Indeed, it could inflict a greater amount of punishment than I could alone. I would watch it avidly. Francois looked down at the outline of the corpse; the blood had stopped flowing and was turning solid. 'He was a good man.' There was silence. 'Francois, what do . . .' I broke off. I had been distracted by flickering brightness and distant sound heard through the open door. At this hour it had to be connected with our current situation, but I could not guess how. Then I understood. I spun around to the baker. 'Who did you tell?' I demanded. 'Who?'

'Monsieur, I . . .' he stuttered. Francois had jumped up, as if shocked by lightning, and had run to the door, staring out. 'I told Philippe.'

'David!' Francois cried. I could see the fear in him and he had good reason for it.

I sprinted to join him at the door. The light had been a glow from distant torches. 'Where do they live?'

'The edge of the village.' We had no time. All time had been twisted out of itself. We burst out into the night.

The air should have been still but it was moving. Far-off shouts were cutting into it that had no place between those silent onlooking houses. 'Down here!' Francois called as he pushed through a path between hedges that allowed a man but would have defied the horses. It widened into a lane that seemed to lead nowhere but empty fields. Then, at the end of it, a show of light that had no promise of dawn in it beckoned us urgently on.

As my chest heaved I could not tell whether the blue glow that was taking over my vision was from the short breaths ramming into my lungs or from the colour of the cold pre-dawn bushes that were rushing past me. The glow we had seen widened out into true light and the noise sharpened into two human voices, one yelling in anger and one crying in fear. It was a tiny cottage with a meagre plot of vegetables and fruit in front of it. God alone knows how anyone could grow something in that sterile soil. And now, kicking down the few stalks and ripping up the plants, the garden held five men, lit by an enclosed lamp and two open blazing torches. Four of them I recognized as the labourers from outside the church after Mass. The fifth man appeared to be a friend recruited from his bed for the night's work. In the cracking wooden doorway, barely large enough to fit him under the lintel, stood the son of the Gypsy family. He was wearing a grey nightshirt that must once have been white and had probably been his father's in a lost time. By his side hung a sickle, gripped in his hand. From his stance, from the tension in his bent knees and the angle of his elbow, I could tell that the weapon was not an idle threat.

I could now put sounds to their sources. The boy's mother was behind him, crying. Tears were rolling down cheeks that had been rosy when the light had been from the sun not from oil burning behind glass, and flames flying as the men holding torches waved them through the stagnant air.

'Get back!' I snarled at the men.

'Philippe! Do as he says!' shouted Francois, confirming my order. The group's leader, the heavy-set labourer who was clad in the same clothes that he had worn during the day, was within an arm's length of the son guarding his family home. It seemed to me that had we not appeared at that very moment there would have been more blood that night. At the sound of his name Philippe jerked around, each of his hands grasping a wooden stake.

For my part I have fought alongside - and against - Christians and Jews, Mohammedans and heathens. Assyrians, Nubians, Croats and Gypsies. I have been swindled by all and tricked all in return. The only species of man I have come across that I thought utterly foul is the one I saw right then with stakes in his two hands.

'He was seen, sir,' Philippe growled to Francois. And by the glow from the lamps, I saw him properly for the first time. His face could have been handsome - it was strong - but flab around the jowls had stretched it out. Marks of the pox showed on his cheeks, darkened as they had been by many hours in the sun.

I stopped charging only when my face was inches from Philippe's, my fingers twisting into the cloth of his shirt.

'I told you to get back,' I said quietly. I could smell drunken fights on his breath. 'Now move.'

Philippe's mouth broke into a grin. There were the fumes of decaying food and ale. 'You will make me? But we found a murderer. If you stop me from taking him, then it will be your head too on the block. That is the law, no?' He puffed up his chest like a pigeon. It would have been comical but for his smell and the flickering light that gave us all an aspect of madness.

Francois arrived, puffing, to stand shoulder to shoulder with me. I was glad of his comradeship. Perhaps I would have challenged these men alone but I could have been far from certain of victory. Francois's title alone was worth an army. 'What are you talking about?' he demanded.

'He was seen. The young one.' He raised a pointed finger

towards the boy in the doorway. 'Running away from the church. Do you not see?' He looked triumphant and his words carried a powerful message that indeed struck me and gave me pause. He widened his voice to all his followers. 'Do you not see?'

Out of the corner of my eye, I saw movement; the one labourer without a torch or lamp had skulked to the shadows beside the door. Now he showed himself at speed, rushing headlong into the young man in the doorway. He was bigger than the dark-locked boy and managed to knock him to his knees, prompting a scream from the mother, who threw her hands around her son's neck. She was pulled away by her husband, who showed himself in the black interior for the first time. But the boy had fallen to one knee, a position that gave him more strength than his opponent had expected and he lifted his sickle with a straight arm, into the other man's jaw. The farmhand reeled back, clutching his hand to the cut, blood running over his wrist.

It was Philippe's yell that alerted me to his own sudden movement towards the door. But he also had a powerful frame and it was thudding past me. I hooked my arm under his and curled my leg around him so that for an instant we were one creature. A second later my weight had upset him so that we spiralled down and his heavy torso lurched over, his hands shooting out to cushion his fall.

The roar that threw me off seemed to rise from deep with the animal that was Philippe. I saw two of his friends stoop to help, with the sickle-cut man above us looking dumbfounded at the scene he had begun.

'All of you get back,' cried Francois, pushing one of the two aside. 'Or I will throw you out of your houses.' At this threat, Philippe stopped his attempts to extract himself from my grasp, and I pushed myself to my feet. By the lamplight, which cast shadows so long that they merged with the night, I saw the boy standing grimly in his doorway, the sickle by his side, now with a red stain down the hilt and dripping to the soil. It recalled the body we had left only a few minutes before. It was just a pity that it was the curate dead and the farmhand alive.

The three remaining labourers had retreated to the edge of the small yard, preferring to watch for a victor to emerge than help him on his way. The two holding torches dropped them, leaving only the oil lamp casting shadows over the scene. The shades warped and spread on the dirt and rough grass. Philippe twisted his body over so that he could see Francois. I thought about breaking Philippe's nose on the heel of my boot, but there was probably no need now. He spat on the ground.

'Get up,' Francois ordered.

'Take this dog away,' Philippe said.

The one who had attacked the boy moved closer, into the circle of light that was binding us together in this night of sweat. I could see a rift in the flesh - it was deep enough to see the bone and that probably meant the skin and muscle going black and perhaps spreading. Let him fall where he was, for all I cared. The foxes could have him. I glanced over at the boy. He was standing again as he had before - filling the narrow, low doorway, his weapon in his hand. His parents were nowhere to be seen.

'I will deal with you properly tomorrow,' Francois told Philippe as the big man stood up. I noted with satisfaction that a twinge of pain crossed his face as he unfurled his back. 'For now, you will tell me what you were talking about.'

'What was I talking about?'

'Do not be facetious.'

'Do not be what, sir?' The baron said nothing. 'Well, this one was seen outside the church.'

'By whom?' I demanded.

One of the three holding back at the edge of the garden spoke. 'By me, monsieur.'

'When?'

'I would say an hour and a half ago, monsieur.' That made it a little before midnight. 'I had got up to . . . to do my bladder, monsieur.' One of his fellows suppressed a snigger. 'And when I emptied my pot out the window I saw him come out of the church. Then he ran away.' All turned to stare at the Gypsy. Francois swallowed. I guessed my friend was beginning to doubt he had done the right thing after all in preventing the lynching of this young man. If it turned out that he was indeed guilty, the aftermath would do no one any credit, least of all us. And I, more than anyone, wanted to lay hands on my tutor's killer. I could not help the suspicion rising. But suspicion makes more fools than judges. I have lost count of the times I have seen an innocent man look guilty as the devil, and the guilty appear as white lambs.

'You are sure it was him?' I asked.

'Aye, monsieur.'

'All of you, stand at the edge of this garden. Do not set foot on it unless I tell you to,' I said. Then I addressed the one who had said and done the least. 'You, go around the back. Do not let anyone leave.' The man, clearly one of life's followers and too stupid to have an original thought in his head, carried out the instruction. I turned to the doorway. 'Young man?' He met my gaze but said nothing. 'You have nothing to fear from me. Will you give me what you are holding?'

'No.' His voice was low and husky. It carried determination. He had already shown that determination and while my bulk was his and half again, I did not want to force any crisis.

Francois spoke: 'What would you say to this. If we come in, you stand on one side of the room, and we stand on the other, and we leave that in the middle. You are younger than we are - if we rush you, you will get to it first.'

The young man did not move a muscle, his gaze searing into me in a way I had seldom experienced. Then he stepped backwards into the dark interior, his face and eyes being the last to disappear into the black. Francois and I glanced at each other, then edged into the gloom, the door closing behind us.

There was no light inside so we felt our way with our hands and feet. It was about four paces until I encountered something smooth, curved and wooden. I explored it with my hand and felt it move, spinning around, and a thread slide across the back of my hand. The family were weavers. Their people, by tradition, moved from place to place, buying and selling whatever they could. But this little family had clearly decided to put down roots in one place. I circled around it and felt a bare, rough table press into my hip. Francois knocked into something else that scraped and rocked on the floor, a chair.

'You are at the wall,' we heard. The young man had stayed by the front wall and silently listened to us blunder about before choosing his moment to speak. The entire cottage was a single room and we were indeed at the rearmost limit. I felt some sort of curtain to my right, dividing off the sleeping area from the living area. Maybe the parents slept behind it and the son slept in the main area. The father was good with wood, so they likely had some sort of bed in there, perhaps the boy had a straw mattress or even a bed to himself if he was lucky. The parents were not to be seen.

They were probably behind the curtain, holding their breaths and listening.

The room was even darker than I had expected, the windows being shuttered, and an unwelcome tide of doubt washed over me. If it came to a struggle, I was not sure that the two of us would have an advantage over the one who knew where he was and where we were. And that one had seemed competent with his improvised weapon. Francois had offered this deal and the boy had seen better than we had that the exchange was all in his favour.

'Have you put down the sickle?' I asked. There was the sound of something being deposited on the floor. 'Thank you.'

'It is Jacob, is it not?' Francois's voice sounded dull in the dark, the walls were too ill made, too soft from the lime plaster to reflect sound.

'Jacob.' His voice was soft too.

'How old are you?' I asked.

'Nineteen winters.' I judged the sound. It seemed like he had moved to one of the adjoining walls and I stared all I could to make his shape out against the blank darkness but it was in vain.

'My name is Sévine,' I said. There was no answer. 'I am a lawyer.'

'Good for you.'

'And I was a soldier.' I thought this might carry more respect - the law had not been kind to Gypsies. Not of late, nor had it ever been.

'A hero of the American Revolution,' said Francois.

'Did that man outside see you coming out of the church as he claims?' I asked. There was no answer but breath. The parents, if they were there and had not escaped through some rear window, were as silent as the grave. 'He says he saw you. Why would he say that?'

'He saw me.'

A rush of movement at my arm told me Francois was going for the sickle. 'Wait!' I hissed, grabbing him. His attempt was an idiotic move. But he shook me off and I could hear him rooting about on the floor for upwards of five seconds.

'Do not bother. I still have it,' came the voice through the dark. I allowed myself to grin in the black where I could not be seen - unless, after so many nights in the dark, the boy had grown eyes like a bat.

'We made a deal!' insisted Francois, outraged.

'You are on your knees trying to break it.'

'Francois,' I said, dragging him up. 'If he had wanted to cut our throats, he could have done so twenty times by now. Is that not true, my young friend?'

'Yes.'

'Then we are at your mercy. So, will you grant us the boon of answering our questions?'

'Yes.'

'You were seen coming out the church.'

'I was.' He did not hesitate. It could have been either the directness of an honest man, or the practised lie of an easy sinner.

There was no point in exercising lawyer's sophistry. 'Did you kill Father Dollet?'

'No.' Again there was no hesitation.

'Did you see him?'

'I did.'

'Was he on the cross?' I sensed Francois stiffen his limbs, as if the very words brought back that terrible moment when we had been presented with a crucifixion no congregation would ever venerate. I pushed the image from my mind.

'Yes.'

I thought this through. 'Did you see anyone there?'

'Not exactly.'

'What do you mean by that?'

'Before I went in, I saw someone in the graveyard. But I did not really see. I could not see a face, just darkness there.'

'He had no face?' I asked.

'That is how it seemed.'

I took the information in. 'Just one man?'

'Just one.'

'Then what?'

'I went in. I saw the priest.'

'And you left him there?!' Francois burst out, incredulous. 'In God's name, why?'

'Because of this.'

There was silence for a long time. 'I understand,' replied the baron eventually. 'Yes, I understand.'

I placed my hand on Francois's arm, then spoke again. 'What were you doing abroad at that time?'

'Hunting.'

'What for?'

'Deer.'

'Poaching,' stated the baron. 'Those are the King's deer.'

'I think he has enough of them.'

It was a fair point to make.

'Did you see anyone else abroad?' I asked.

'No.'

'Father Dollet was a friend to me. An old friend.'

'I am sorry that he is no longer.'

'What did you think of him?'

He paused. 'He seemed . . . fair.'

It was true. Yes, Father Dollet had seemed fair but a niggling doubt crept into my lawyer's brain: could that seeming have hidden many a sin? Well for now, I wanted to believe in him. 'We will leave you,' I said.

'Very kind of you.'

I allowed myself to smile once more. 'You and your family will go about your business as usual but I suggest you stay out of the village. Come, Francois.'

We groped our way outside. Emerging from total darkness to lamplight was like the dawn of creation, although this one was uglier than that described in the scriptures. The unshaven, sweat-laden men we had prevented from meting out what they considered justice were, as they had been instructed, at the perimeter of the little garden, pacing like the Indian cats in the King's collection.

'Shall we grab them, monsieur?' one asked, stepping forward. He shone his lamp in the direction of the door.

'Did I tell you to walk on the garden?' I barked in return.

'M . . . monsieur?'

'Did I tell you to walk on the garden?'

'No, monsieur.'

'These people are not to be touched. You will go home now and you will not return here, do you understand?'

'But–'

The Baron d'Agnes stepped forward. His villager stepped back the same distance. 'Go home.'

The three farmhands whom I could not name glanced at each other then slowly began to shuffle away. Through the dark I heard the fourth, who had been stationed behind the low building, tread in the same direction. Last to leave was Philippe, who cast a long look into the doorway then departed.

We watched them disappear up the lane, after which we too walked up the stony path. When we had reached a distance where I was sure we could not be heard even through the still night, I spoke. 'He is lying,' I said.

'The boy?'

'Yes.'

'About what?'

'Well, for one thing if he had been hunting deer, he would have had a crossbow to hand, yet he decided to defend himself with a farm tool. Why?'

Francois stopped to think this over. 'Yes. I see. But if you think he killed Father Dollet, what are we doing leaving?'

'I do not think that. Why on earth would he? And in the middle of the night then go quietly home where the trouble would follow him and reflect on his parents? No, I think he had another reason for his travels that night. And I think you have a few days to find out what it is, before your loyal villagers return here. And this time they will make sure no one sees them coming.'

Some sort of illness had erupted in Lorne and a feeling in the pit of my stomach told me that there was more to come. I had spent my childhood desperate to leave the place that held my father, but I would always feel protective of the village. We are all tribesmen, really. And the desire to avenge my old tutor's death was strong. As we walked, I felt another pang of revulsion at the sight of him and what had been done to him.

'What do you need from me?' Francois asked.

'I shall go where I want and speak to whomsoever I want. You must make it known that I act on your authority.'

'Consider it done.'

'And Francois, one more thing.'

'Yes?'

'Never enter a dark room with an angry man holding a sickle.'

He nodded. 'Yes. That does seem good advice.'

After the tumult, it was strange that the lane was quiet again. In the bushes, animals rustled, disturbed by our footsteps that were so unexpected at this time of night. 'The boy's family are weavers,' I said.

'Yes. When they are not working on farms. Fourteen hours each day at that wheel. All three of them.' I could see them on low stools, sometimes talking, sometimes silent. Used to nothing more than each other's company as the wheel spun and spun all day long. And when it spun no longer, the father would whittle and carve cheap toys for his table outside the church on Sundays. 'There is a local organizer. He supplies the yarn and they turn it into cloth. Most of it is cheap, for the local markets, but some I have seen is of fine quality - I would wear it myself.'

'How much do they earn for that?' I asked.

'Thirty sous per day.'

'Well, that is enough for one of them to live on.'

'Quite.'

We walked on to the church, where a group of villagers had gathered outside the door - apparently word had spread. The fool Hubert, the baker who had found the body, hung his head and shuffled away. I fought back the desire to give him a taste of what he had nearly brought down upon the cottage we had just left, but I ignored him and entered.

The nave was more silent now, now that we knew what was there. We did not approach the body; we merely gazed, barely able to comprehend. I had seen the effects of hatred before - bodies battered or stabbed many times - but this, this came from madness.

Back outside, one of Francois's servants arrived puffing and panting on foot and his master dispatched him to the abbey so as to inform Dom Mathieu what had happened and beg that holy man to take into his care the *corpus sanctus* of his former brother.

'Did anybody see a man on the street tonight? A stranger or one whom you know well? He might be one of your neighbours,' I called out to the small crowd. They looked at me without a word. None said aye and none said no. Francois glanced at me. 'If he is your friend, do not fear for him,' I added. 'If he has no guilt on his conscience then he is in no danger. But we must speak to him to see if he has information about what has taken place in your village, among your homes, this night.' They remained as dumb as corn stalks. 'You try with them,' I muttered, frustrated, to Francois.

'Maître Sévine carries my authority,' Francois called out. 'You must answer his questions. Did you see anyone - young or old? Man or woman?'

There were a few mumbled responses that indicated no one had been awake until we had chased after Philippe and Hubert had raised the alarm.

'What about Cotillard?' Francois said to me. 'You saw what he did in church today.'

Certainly the lunatic lawyer's ravings rained suspicion upon him. 'Have him brought here.'

'Does anyone know where the madman Cotillard is?' Francois asked.

'He sleeps in the fields,' a crone replied. 'He roams.'

'She is right. He really could be anywhere,' Francois intimated to me. 'By night we will have no chance of finding him.' He instructed the villagers to lay hands on the man if they saw him and march him straight to the house.

The only thing left to do was to thoroughly search the village for any interlopers. I organized the mob into threes to look for anything or anyone strange. These were people who had rarely strayed beyond the next village and would know if a stone was out of place. They flitted away through their lanes, eyes narrowed in suspicion, clogs rattling on the stones.

'Can you think of anyone who might have wanted to do this?' I asked.

'Not one,' Francois replied. 'Who kills such a man as Father Dollet? And in such a fashion?'

I could not begin to answer that question. 'How has he been these past years?'

'He seemed fine. He would come to lunch at the chateau sometimes. Happy enough. You know he is progressive in his political thought and his theology but not aggressively so.'

One by one the villagers trod back, dejected and fearful. 'No one, monsieur.' 'We saw nothing.' 'It is quiet. We saw a fox. Nothing else.' I dismissed them all to their homes. There was no point in all of us missing a night of sleep.

We talked, Francois and I, for the next two hours, sitting in front of the church while we waited for the abbot to arrive. We did not say a great deal. I think neither of us wanted to think any more than we had to about what lay in the building behind us, cast adrift on the floor. We ranged over the poverty of the crops, the game he had bagged. At one point he started telling me about a wench he had known when visiting a friend in Chartres, but he thought better of it.

After a while I could make out his features without the lamp. It was not yet dawn, but that strange time before the sun has truly risen. I calculated that it must have been around four o'clock and a number of cockerels began to make their presence known.

Then between their calls came a rattling sound. The sound of wheels banging through the creases of the dry road. A cart, drawn by a donkey, hove into sight, carrying two men wearing white habits with dark monastic scapulars - long cloak-like strips of cloth hung front and back from their shoulders. The Carmelite brothers had always fascinated me as a child when they came into the village or passed through it.

The donkey clipped closer as one of the men flicked its rear with a crop. Then it stopped in front of us so that I could see the driver's bald head emblazoned everywhere with blue veins, red threads and brown spots like a hellish *Mappa Mundi*. The monk's head creaked around to me. 'Where is he?' he asked. But he asked with only half his face, the other half remaining static. I could not help but stare. That unmoving side sagged, fleshy like an overripe pear, and the words that echoed from the half-closed mouth had a moaning, animal resonance to them.

'Peace unto you, holy brother,' I replied.

'And to you. Who are you?' he groaned. His grey tongue hung over the lower lip, the tip tasting the air as do sunbathing snakes.

'My name is David Sévine. I am a lawyer.'

'Lawyers. Man's law. Not God's.'

The other man, aged perhaps sixty and scarcely any younger than the first, although he at least had some strands of fine white hair to show for his pate, intervened. 'Brother Henri, now is not the time. Now is not the time.' He climbed down from the cart. Francois knelt to him and I did the same. So this was the abbot, Dom Mathieu. '*Benedicte*, my sons,' he said, nervously making the sign of the cross above us. 'And rare have been the times when more was meant by that word, by that appeal to our almighty Father for protection and benediction.'

'Dom Mathieu,' said Francois, kissing his ring. I followed suit.

'Stand up, my son.'

'Thank you for coming, Dom.'

The abbot nodded his head sadly. 'He is in the church still?'

'He is.' Francois glanced at me. I could read in his expression a foreboding of having to show the abbot the body of his former religious brother. He paused. 'What were you told about Father Dollet? About how we found him?'

'Found him? Nothing. I . . .' He broke off and looked worriedly at Francois, then the church. 'Tell me.'

Francois told him how we had found the curate martyred like his namesake, Pierre the apostle, with his body inverted to the sky. He did not say what foul violation of his dignity I had found when I turned the priest over. That would stay between me, him and Hubert - so long as the baker had learned to keep his tongue in his head; and if he had not I would teach him the lesson tomorrow. As Francois told the story, Brother Henri began to mumble a prayer. From what I could tell, it was an invocation against the Evil One. *Too late*, I thought.

20 June 1789

I woke a few hours later, I guessed by the height of the sun. As I lay, the night's events seemed like a foul visitation of visions, but I knew they had been all too solid. I washed in the cracked pewter basin, donned fresh clothes and left my room. At the head of the stairs, a door presented itself ajar. Through the gap I spotted the edge of a harpsichord. As I drew nearer, the door opened, exposing the young dark girl I had seen at Mass. Her eyes looked on me with surprise and she seemed to catch her breath for a second before looking quickly behind her.

As I followed her line of sight it seemed as if the sole female portrait by the stairs had come to life, for there was the white-cheeked subject, looking out the same window, with music falling from the table, the abandoned harpsichord in the corner of the room, bereft of its player. The light that made her glow was the sun, not the moon, but when she turned, her black hair and pale skin seemed to have been coloured with the same paint as the canvas. As the corners of her mouth began to pull up and out into her cheeks, the girl between us gently closed the door. In the pit of my stomach, I felt a sense of unease.

When I entered the breakfast room a minute later, Francois, Baron d'Agnes, was looking at some papers. He did not notice my presence until I was standing over him.

'Oh, hello, David,' he said.

I dropped into a chair to look at the food on offer. I did not want any of it. There was no need for a preamble.

'Do you truly think you can find whoever killed him?'

'I will try,' I said. 'God knows if I will succeed.' The thought of action perked me up a little and distracted me from the heat in my blood. 'First, I will visit his home. And once I have dealt with the present, it will be time for me to delve into the past.'

'While you are out, I will search for Cotillard. Though it will be only slightly easier by day than by night.'

'Take a couple of men with you. We know not what he is capable of.' I went to the cabinet by the side of the room, poured out two glasses of cognac, and handed one to Francois. 'Now, let us not remember how Father Dollet left us, let us remember what he did for us.'

'Agreed.'

'To Pierre Dollet.' We clinked the glasses together and drank.

Then he picked up a letter he had been reading. 'I could happily be without letters like this today,' he said, shaking it. 'Do you suppose my creditors would like to take my estate in payment for my debts?'

'I am afraid not.'

'I have even quietly put it about that I will sell my *seigneurie* and estate. I will keep the house itself, though.'

Even if he kept the house, selling all his estate and rights as feudal lord would leave him without any income - the rents and barter quit-rents from his tenants and villagers. He would be left with a title, a shabby house and little more.

'Any takers?'

'Absolutely none,' he grumbled. He played thoughtfully with the bread and jam in front of him.

I changed the subject. 'Who is she, Francois?'

The baron smiled for the first time. 'Aha, I knew you would ask sooner or later. That, my friend, is the great Juliana Archer.'

I wracked my brains. There was a faint glimmer there but no glow of recognition.

'Surely . . . No? Well, that is a shock, what with you living in the palace. She was once a sensation. The soprano setting all the stages alight with her strength of voice. The purity like crystal. I spent night after night watching her. And not just me - the King too.'

And then I did remember. She had been a favourite of Louis's. Not a feted Chief Mistress, as Madame de Pompadour had been for the last monarch - indeed, the current Louis was often roundly, publicly mocked for his lack of a mistress, which marked him as a void of virility - but a regular dalliance of his. 'She looks exotic, does she not?'

I had to agree that she did.

'They say her mother was Chinese. It was Archer - her husband, Gregory Archer, you saw him yesterday in Mass - who discovered her singing for coins in some Italian tavern when she was young. He took her to England, trained her, and turned her into an English beauty. And the lucky so-and-so married her, to boot.'

Good old Francois, a dimpled nose could always lift his spirits. I could not honestly say I enjoyed the opera. I had gone a few times with eager acquaintances over the years and had feigned pleasure but inside I had been counting down the minutes. 'Well, the King had enough of her eventually - perhaps Marie was getting jealous, I do not know, so they have come to stay here for a while. Them and their son, Charles.' He was the boy I had seen behind them in the church. I suspected there was a little more to Francois Jacques Claude Eric Merrin, Baron d'Agnes's motives in allowing Juliana Archer to live within his walls than simple and unadulterated charity.

'And the girl with them?'

'Juliana's maid. Catherine.'

The girl, demure as any maid had to be while at the same moment possessing within her bosom every secret of her lady's, had intrigued me, for I have always been drawn to keepers of secrets. I was right to be so.

Out in the chateau's stable, the horses raised their heads as they recognized Francois. The mare I had ridden the previous night was out, taken by a groom for some exercise in the fields. 'You can have this one for your stay here,' Francois told me, leading me into one stall where a beast stamped his foot.

I swept my hand along my mount's neck and breathed in

his musk as it mixed with the less pure aroma rising from a dung heap behind him. He was black but for a streak of white on his nose and his ankles.

'He looks strong. What is he called?'

'Jackdaw.'

'Do you breed from him?' I could see him having a fine brood.

'Oh no, this boy is a gelding, not a stallion. We castrated him when he was a year old. Now he has all the fun in the world. He mates with all the pretty mares and fathers no foals at the end of it. Would that we humans could be so safe in our tupping.'

'Still, no one asked his permission.' I tried to imagine how gelding would be and it sent a shiver up my spine.

Francois chuckled and scratched the horse's nose. 'Should we say, "Dear horse, how d'ye fancy castration? We will leave you the pole, just not the two round things that hang down. No?" No. Anyway, the important bit is still there and in full working order, still pumping out the juice, but it contains no baby Jackdaws - those are made in the bits we took away.'

'They are?'

'You never knew?' He chuckled.

'I never asked.'

'Man or beast, it is the same. If you ever fancy rutting until your heart's content but without the danger of some child one day turning up at your door and calling you papa, all you have to do is have your stones removed. In the case of Jackdaw, I oversaw the removal of his myself.'

'A strange entertainment.'

'Not much else to do around here, old man. And look.' We lowered our heads under Jackdaw's belly. 'Which of us can boast one that big?'

Father Dollet's home was a two-storey well-thatched cottage. It had probably been built by an ancestor of Francois's hoping for eternal reward after a lifetime of whoring. I pushed open the door and stepped into a scene I well remembered from my childhood. Father Dollet was a worldly divine, with many works of literature, history and even a few musical scores lined up on shelves that ran around the main reception room. The books covered history and natural history, but also geography, with works on the Indes and China, such as Marco Polo's *Book of the Marvels of the World*. On its own table rested a flute that I vaguely recalled him playing from time to time.

I sat at his well-polished writing desk and turned to the sheets upon which he had been making notes. They were on fine writing paper, heavy and strong, a cream colour, covered with notes for what looked like a sermon on the deadly sins. But what was stranger was a note at the bottom, set at a different angle to the rest of the writing, apparently written at a different time. 'A man dreamed he was a butterfly. When he awoke he could not tell if he was a man who had dreamed he was a butterfly, or a butterfly dreaming that he was a man. But what did HE dream before he changed?' The script was slightly different to the rest too. It was by the same hand, yet it was prettier, slower, more ponderous with long loops.

A man dreamed he was a butterfly. But what did HE dream before he changed? It had to be the same thought that had fallen from his lips with his last breath. But the meaning was hidden. I tapped the pages, hoping for inspiration, but none came. Instead I tried the drawers of the desk. All men have secrets and need somewhere to hide them. The drawer to Father Dollet's desk was locked, which made me suspect his were kept there.

Usually, men are so lackadaisical they will lock away their most prized possessions and leave the key on top of the safe; and yet, try as I might, I could not find the key anywhere. It was a solid piece of oak too, that desk, so I could have smashed my way in, but it would have taken tools, time and sweat.

Instead I trod another path.

One unexpected repercussion of the King's hobby for making locks was that I had, out of curiosity, at one point read a few pamphlets on just how they were made. Of course, when a man knows how to design a lock, he also knows how to pick it.

This was a simple type, I saw, a warded lock - the modern lever lock had made peeping into a man's private affairs a good deal harder. But with this design I only had to fashion an L-shaped pick and it was as good as open. In the kitchen, I found a fork that would do well, once one of its prongs was efficaciously bent close to the tip. And then the drawer was open without a whimper. Fond as I was of the curate, he was dead and gone, so I had no moral conundrum about rifling the contents.

What a curious trove was within.

The first objects that came to hand were a pair of calf-bound books. One was a *Petit Albert*, the *grimoire* of household magic that so many countryfolk had hidden under their pillows. I opened it to find a spell to produce a Hand of Glory.

> Take the right or left hand of a felon who is hanging from a gibbet beside a highway; wrap it in part of a funeral pall and, so wrapped, squeeze it well. Then put it into an earthenware vessel with zimat, nitre, salt and long peppers, the whole well powdered. Leave it in this vessel for a fortnight, then take it out and expose it to full sunlight during the dog-days until it becomes quite

> dry. If the sun is not strong enough put it in an oven with fern and vervain. Next make a kind of candle from the fat of a gibbeted felon, virgin wax, sesame, and ponie, and use the Hand of Glory as a candlestick to hold this candle when lighted, and then those in every place into which you go with this baneful instrument shall remain motionless.

Yes, many countrymen fully believed that, like the gaze of a basilisk, Hands of Glory could paralyze anyone in their vicinity. They would also open any lock and shine a light that only the bearer would see. But acquiring the hand of a dead criminal was no simple task - even cutpurses had family who would protect the corpses of their kin. It is strange: the mother of a wayward son may refuse to speak to him for her entire adult life, but when he is dead she will walk ten leagues through a storm to protect his lifeless body.

The other book was an English tome entitled *The Discoverie of Witchcraft wherein the Lewde dealing of Witches and Witchmongers is notablie detected, in sixteen books, whereunto is added a Treatise upon the Nature and Substance of Spirits and Devils*. The Protestant English never did go in for brief or poetic titles.

I flicked through it, expecting it to be in the same vein as the other book and yet it seemed almost diametrically opposed in outlook: the author, one Reginald Scot, seemed of the mind that witches were no more real than fairies and dragons - the commonality of the idea that they existed could be best traced to market-day conjurors. Burn a witch, he was saying, and you burn only a deluded or slandered soul.

> I pray you believe my writings, wherein I will prove all popish charms, conjurations, exorcisms, benedictions

> and curses, not only to be ridiculous, and of none effect, but also to be impious and contrary to God's word: I should as hardly therein win favour at their hands, as herein obtain credit at yours. Nevertheless, I doubt not, but to use the matter so, that as well the mass-monger for his part, as the witchmonger for his, shall both be ashamed of their professions.

A tract for which the author or bearer could have been gaoled - or worse - in Catholic lands! I was astonished. I had long known my old tutor to be of the reformist wing of the Holy Mother Church, but this level of scepticism seemed to me to be far beyond his taste.

It all set me thinking. Francois had initially asked me to come to Lorne to look into strange whispers about witchcraft among the villagers. Had Father Dollet too been approached by a parishioner worried about sorcery? Was it even possible that the priest himself had come to suspect unnatural happenings? I could not credit the idea that he was himself directly involved in such goings-on. It would have been impossible for the man I had known.

And yet, my thoughts ran, why should I know my old tutor's mind? Could it not be the case that he had either hidden a part of himself from me when I was a youth unable to comprehend the nuances of the world, or he had simply changed as the years turned, as we all inevitably do? We presume to know the people we like, but we are no more likely to hear the inner thoughts of our friends than our enemies. I resolved, therefore, to keep a more open aspect, for now to see him as a stranger, no more my mentor.

There were a few political tracts too in the desk. Recent works, including a copy of the radical priest the Abbé Sieyes's seminal *What Is The Third Estate?*, a similar one entitled *The Constitution* by a journalist named Marat of whom I had heard, and a few other similar pamphlets.

'Why, you sly old dog,' I said to myself with a chuckle as I picked up a more-thumbed work. I was rather surprised to see it there. It was the notorious *The Sunrise*, the scandal-sheet that had described the libidinous orgy Marie-Antoinette had supposedly conducted to greet the dawn at Versailles some five years earlier.

Its courtly author had never been identified, but his (or her) witness of Marie 'serving' the servants one after another had turned the public favour distinctly away from the Queen. The publication had spread through the inns and market-places of France like the Plague, and thenceforth she was always a Viennese strumpet laughing behind the back of the dimwitted Louis. Was this sort of thing Father Dollet's reading matter these days? He certainly had depths of which I was not aware.

I replaced it to examine a large pile of letters. These were intriguing - as well as from France, some were sent from England, one from America, and a brief scan of the contents confirmed his interest in the new beliefs regarding a man's place in the world and the state. My curiosity was heightened when I found, at the bottom of the pile, a letter unlike any of the others. It contained a very brief message and no addressee name nor a signature. 'I thank you for your letter. I am intrigued to discover what you have for me. I shall wait for you on July the 19th at three o'clock. The Queen's theatre in the palace grounds will be remote from prying eyes.'

So my old tutor and confessor had requested a meeting to be held away from 'prying eyes' at the palace, and with a man who had not signed his name. I was elated. Such a secret was surely a part of the hidden truth of his death. I examined the page in detail. The writing was an educated, florid hand but the paper not of the finest quality. There were—

The sound of the back door opening made me halt and slip the letter inside my jacket and stand to receive whoever was about to appear. By and by, a woman like a ball of scalding red flesh seemed to roll into the room and yelped when she saw me waiting for her. She steadied herself on the door jamb and looked about to dart away when I reassured her that I was no Mephistopheles come to collect her soul, but a friend of the baron, examining the terrible death of the man whom I guessed was her employer. After leading her to one of the seats, which she stayed in for just enough time to stabilize her breath, before jumping back out at the impropriety of her familiarity with the furniture, I gleaned that she was, indeed, the poor, poor curate's live-in housekeeper, named Josette, and she knew absolutely nothing about anything. Possibly even less than that.

'Can you tell me who Father Dollet's friends were?'

'No, monsieur.'

'But he had friends?'

'I do not know, monsieur.'

'No, of course. Do you know of anyone who would wish to harm Father Dollet?'

'No, monsieur.'

'Do you know who has written to him?'

'No, monsieur.'

She did not know where he had been, what he was doing in the church, whom he had seen or what appointments he might have had that day - she did not know what appointments he might have had on any day between the Fall of Man and Doomsday. That she knew her own name was something of a miracle. She showed me around the house and said that she could see nothing out of place.

'What sort of a man was Father Dollet?'

'What sort of man, monsieur?'

'Yes.'

She thought hard for a long time. 'A priest, monsieur.'

'Thank you,' I said as I went to the doorway and threw my coat around me. Looking down, I noticed something. Just inside the doorway was a thin line of what looked like seeds. 'What is this?'

'Nettle seeds sir. Boiled.'

'Why?'

'To protect against the Evil Eye, sir. It is in the *Petit Albert*.'

'I see.' Yes, even in the house of a priest, the household magic was at play.

'There are witches about, sir. This keeps us safe.'

I gazed at the thin line of seeds. Unless the supposed witches skidded on them and dashed their heads out on the floor, I doubted they would be of great help. 'Is there anything else you use for protection against magic?' I enquired.

'Yes, sir.'

'And what would it be?'

She looked shifty, and then reached down the front of her smock. For a brief, terrible, moment I thought she was going to expose her bosom to me, but instead she drew up a leather string, with something attached to the end. It was a grubby piece of paper, stained with much sweat and grime. It was divided into segments, each with a number inside. This numerology was common in the countryside where the innumerate attached great power to little scratches of ink they could barely begin to understand but knew held great influence over their days. After all, numbers, those magical things, decided whether they would eat enough bread that day, or present sufficient chickens to their seigneur such that they would not be thrown out of their hovels. 'The talisman in the Seal of the Sun, sir. It will keep me safe from sorcery.'

'More from the *Petit Albert*?'

'Yes, sir. My cousin suffered badly from a witch in her village. She lost three babies to that harridan. But now she wears the talisman and she has had two healthy, bonny girls.' Her eyes narrowed. 'You believe, do you not, sir?' and a realization began to dawn on her that perhaps I did not. She was welcome to her Dark Ages beliefs but I was put out by her assumption that my scepticism made me the fool in this house. 'But sir, there are witches about Lorne.'

This had been, indeed, the reason for my very presence in the village.

'Have you seen them?'

'Not I. But others. And the death of Father Dollet was the work of the Devil, their master. All the village knows one who has seen them. It is their work, sir.'

I could not rule it impossible. That they were truly in league with Satan and able to perform sorcery, that was impossible. That they *believed* themselves to be in league with him, that was perfectly possible. The knowledge of witches was all around them, instructed by priests and peasants.

This woman, too, was immersed in such country beliefs, which was why there was little point in telling her that the talisman in her breast was no more use than any other scrap of paper carrying the faint odour of sweat. And, I supposed, if it gave her comfort in a world that sometimes seems implacably opposed to human safety, then there was no harm in it.

Yet as I left, I too had something hidden on my person.

Within my jacket I had the unsigned letter arranging a *sub rosa* meeting with Father Dollet. He would not be able to keep that appointment. I would. And I suspected that I would have to assume his person to do it. But first, I had another visit to make.

Here ends the first part of The Murderous Deeds in the Village of Lorne in France and How They Brought About the Bloody Revolution.

Chapter Three

And that was it. Nothing more. The rest was to be read in a forthcoming part. I found it a strange tale, but then I was myself caught up in another strange tale. And so I put the chapbook aside and went to take the barley soup that was proffered to me by Morty's mother, before curling up on the floor to sleep.

I spent a week at their cottage and had to endure sneering visits from Fred and Bernard, tasked as they were with discreetly bringing me food and fresh clothing. But behind their contempt, I could detect a degree of curiosity – even envy – for the odd events that seemed to be enveloping me. It must have looked more mysterious and exciting to those who were not, as I was, wholly bewildered and fearful. The worry was exacerbated by the fact that my schoolmaster stayed away, so I was unable to ask him for an explanation of what had occurred.

I was glad to leave at the end of the week. Most of the village seemed to consider themselves protectors of me, a foundling. They were charity overseers assigned the task by Providence. Yes, I was, in many ways, more a child of the whole village than the school. But Morty's mother had always stood distant from me, perhaps divining something of ill-fortune about me. I could not blame her for that, I suppose. The way of my coming into the lives of these good people must also, to those of a more watchful nature, have evoked alarm and apprehension. I saw her, one or twice while I lodged with her, watching me sidelong with unease before she edged away, back to her cooking and darning.

When the time came, Mr Tolson made a point of not making a grand occasion of my return, acting as if I had been away for but a day – to suggest, I surmise, that the danger, too, was of an ephemeral sort. But as soon as I found a moment when the other boys were out of earshot, I burst out with a hundred questions about who the stranger was, what he wanted, if I was in peril and the like.

'Lysander,' my tutor said, stroking the pate of his head uncomfortably. 'I know that you want to know so much – and, indeed, you have a right to know. But there is a time and a place, and this is not it. I will tell you when you are older.'

'How old?' I demanded, for the first time outraged. For I reasoned with myself that this was not his knowledge to hold, it was mine to know. 'How old? I am thirteen.'

'Yes, thirteen,' he said to himself, his face contorting a little in pain, and I could see that he was wrangling his heart against his head. But his head won out the battle. 'And thirteen must seem to you like adulthood. But when you are twenty, you will look back and think you are a child who—'

'A child!' I yelled. 'I am not a child!' Of course, only a child yells so. 'I want to know.' His eyelids dropped and he shook his head a little. 'Did the man come here?'

'He did. He spoke to your schoolmates. Then he went away.'

'Is he still out there?'

'No, no, he is gone. I set Walter to watch him leave. He rode away with his men.'

I had not realized he was one of a gang. 'How many men?'

'Three. He had three with him.'

'Is that why you could not fight him?' Every adventure story I had read, every history of Rome or Greece, had told me that fighting the invader was the simple answer to everything.

Even in his concern for me and the situation, Mr Tolson could not help but twitch a half-smile at my question. 'Yes. That is why I could not fight him.'

I took this information and thought it over. 'Will they hurt me?'

'No. You have friends, Lysander.'

At that, my eyes blurred a little with water. For you, who have always had friends, will not credit how strongly this could affect one who had always wanted them.

'Will he come back?' I asked.

'I doubt it. He found nothing here and there was nothing to make him think he ever would find anything here.'

I hesitated before speaking. 'Bernard did not say anything?'

Another little smirk. 'Bernard Mason said nothing. For once.'

It was all so much, and I needed time to think. I hugged my knees in a corner of the schoolroom and pondered, and Mr Tolson went to instruct my schoolmates on French grammar.

Whence the schoolboy's sense of Fair and Unfair comes is a mystery. But it is surely the strongest categorization of all to a youth. And as I surveyed my situation, I decided it was utterly Unfair. Not only was this man – a man that I had not so much as seen! – an apparent danger to me, but I was not to be permitted knowledge of how and why. Unfair in every degree.

That sense never left me, but did dull, over the course of the month and the one that followed. In time, I resumed my studies, and did my best to avoid Bernard's barbs and occasional fists. In fact, all fell back soon enough into its former routine.

As such, one morning I awoke at six. Normally I would have rolled over and slipped back into sleep. But because the day heralded my annual visit to Cambridge, I had barely risen before Mr Tolson himself appeared in the doorway, beckoning me.

'Now, Lysander,' he said. 'Today is to be a special day. Do you know why?' I feigned ignorance. I cannot say for certain why I did so, but I always did. Perhaps it was because the occasion carried such promise that I felt if I placed too much store by it, God would be angered by my presumption and dash my hopes. 'Today we will go to Cambridge. It is your birthday outing.'

My birthday had been arbitrarily set as midsummer day, and when I was a few years younger, this had enabled Mr Tolson to portray our trip to the Cambridge Summer Fayre as a treat to mark the ascent of another twelvemonth. He had not known that even then I had realized there was an underlying reason for the two-day visit – after all, why I should be so favoured, when the other boys were not, would have taxed even the sharpest mind. And for all my faults, I was no halfwit. I knew why we went each year. And when I had learned my letters, there had been no chance at all of the subterfuge remaining.

'Thank you, sir,' I said. 'I am most grateful.' Behind me, I heard Bernard repeating my words in a reedy, mocking voice, and Fred's answering laughter. I ignored them. A pebble in a stream will not feel the chill water.

Mr Tolson ruffled my hair – another annual ritual – and bade me make myself ready to travel, for we had a good walk before us and then a journey by staging coach. All this was familiar to me and after washing and dressing, I followed my pedagogue down the stairs, into the hallway where Iphigenia handed him his travelling jerkin and we both pulled on our boots and set out into the fresh air.

Fresh it was, with the smell of the sea salt and the beached sargasso weed upon it. The sun felt warm on my cheeks and they flushed as we skirted the mudflats and hopped over the mounds and pits in the earth between our stone home and the Strood.

Leaving Ray meant leaving the greater part of my world. The other part included Cambridge and Everywhere Else. Everywhere Else encompassed London, where the King resided; France, where no king resided because the last one had had his head chopped off; Africa, where there were lions and giraffes, and the Moon.

After an hour's tramp, we came upon the Cambridge coach. A further five hours' travel and there they were: the final landmarks on the path to the great daffodil-yellow city. This horse trough, that little church. The last landmark was a water conduit, one they called

Hobson's Head, that brought fresh water to the local populace. A little line of women with wooden pails stood chatting before it as they waited to fill their vessels.

'What a wonder!' Mr Tolson said to himself as he gazed out at the noontime scene and the city. 'I tell you, Lysander, there's no other city in Christendom to match it. Not even London!'

I loved to hear him pronounce the name of our nation's capital, because it seemed to me to be an incantation, a charm to engorge our muscles and our spirit.

I too was excited to see the city spreading out, as the light fell on the towers of the great colleges, casting shadows here and there. They moved like fingers when we moved, writing out the letters of my name, if only I could see their course. My name, my origins, I had realized, were hidden somewhere in the city. That was why we came back year after year. Mr Tolson had never told me that in so many words, but as I had grown older and listened harder and with more comprehension, I had worked it out.

'Will we be successful today, sir?' I asked.

Mr Tolson looked a little shifty and uncomfortable at the question. I could tell he was wrestling with the question of when he should acknowledge the true reason for our yearly trip, for he knew I had long since stopped accepting it as a mere birthday treat.

'I . . . I hope so, Lysander.' I waited for more, hoping there might be a few words of explanation. For all my speculation – some of which had fairly hit its mark – I wanted an honest description of what we were shooting for. 'We must . . . have faith. That is all.'

'Is that all, sir?' I was a little crestfallen.

'It is . . . all. Yes.'

He looked a little ashamed, which was not my intention one bit. So I did my best to brush it off and seem innocently excited about the day, as if I were still ten years old and under the illusion that we were there only for me to taste the treats of a city of ten thousand or more souls.

The coach halted at an inn named The Ram, and we descended, ready to walk to our final destination. Finally, we took a little wooden sign from my teacher's bag. It had already been my companion for three of these visits to Cambridge and I had a sinking feeling that it would be with me for three more. And then thrown in the sea as a failure.

I placed its string around my neck and let it hang against my linen shirt that was the colour of buttercream and traced out the words with my fingers.

Do you know me? Do you know whom my parents are?

I knew those words so well.

'Well, Lysander, are you ready?' Mr Tolson was beaming at me, as if he was certain that we would have the happiest of outcomes from the day.

'Yes, sir. I am.'

'Then onwards! We march to our future, Lysander, and nothing holds more promise than that.'

I turned the wooden sign around, so as to hide its motto until we arrived at the event itself.

We took no provisions, for the food on sale at the Fayre was part of the mythology of the birthday treat.

There was never cause to ask the way to Midsummer Common, for half the folk of the county were afoot then, hoofing towards the great festival. Single men and maids or whole families of ten were skipping past grand King's College, whose magisterial golden chapel reared up from the river Cam like a lion; then before huge Trinity College; and through the near-deserted market square until we came upon the Common itself.

I can describe it as nothing less than a fireworks party! There were flashes of gold and red tents between faces of the crowd; tumblers bursting and spinning in the air before being caught by their fellows. Other men and women on stilts stepped through like giants and bent down to play tricks on the dwarfed patrons. Music – a blasting and militaristic sort of music that I had never before beheld – started up somewhere and I peeped over the heads of the crowd to see whence it was wafting. I snatched glimpses of a six-piece band of trumpets and other twisted brass instruments that I couldn't identify, hooting a merry march as they stomped through the people.

The music made me want to fall in like a foot soldier – I knew that our country was at war with France and there was glory to be had fighting their general who was called Boney. To take our King's shilling and join the army was the height of bravery! There would be songs sung about you and weeping maidens would hug and kiss you goodbye. All that was promised in the foot-stomping rhythm of the snorting trumpeters before me. And there! There was the recruiting sergeant behind the band, in his dashing scarlet uniform. He was talking to a couple of keen young men. You could see the pride in his face and the awe in theirs. Oh, those two youths would be bidding farewell to their families soon, I knew. Goodbye to the grey horizons of East Anglia. Now bound for sunlit foreign adventure and escapades!

'I think you are a bit young for the regiments, Lysander,' chuckled Mr Tolson as he fanned himself in the sultry air that was abuzz with insects. 'Now, hurry up. That barrel of eels will knock you down if you are not sharp about it.'

'Yes, sir.' I jumped aside to let the fish pass.

'And take no food from anyone unless I have seen it first. They say half of these pies are stuffed with cat meat.'

For half an hour we swanned around, watching the showmen. One corner of the Common was given over to the Gypsies who came to read palms and tell fortunes in shabby tents; or to buy and sell horses. They travelled in painted caravans and sat in rings, smoking their arm-long pipes. Not far off, a preacher shouted from atop an upturned crate, warning of lust, gin, and the Devil's work.

Each year I saw more of the Midsummer Fayre and fell to love it more. For a boy whose life was restricted for three hundred and sixty-three days of the year to the walls of his schoolhouse, who had come to understand that there was a danger to him where the island ended and the world outside began – and yet he was not permitted to know the nature of this lurking danger, whence or why it followed him – the Fayre was all the light and possibilities of the wide globe. Oh, I loved it dearly.

'Now, Lysander, I think it is time for you to display the sign.'

I winced. 'Sir? Five more minutes?'

'No, I think we should get started on our purpose.'

It was a slip of his tongue, but I noted it. Our true purpose. No more subterfuge that this was my birthday gift.

I sighed and the tips of my fingers touched the sign around my neck, which was, for now, turned inwards so that its legend was invisible. I hesitated, hoping for the intervention of fate or man to stay my hand.

'Go on, Lysander.' I glanced at him and then, without looking at it, turned the sign outwards.

Do you know me? Do you know who my parents are?

Four words. Then seven more. Eleven that told my life's story.

Few in the crowd paid great attention to the sign – for only a handful of those on the field, in truth, knew their letters. A few passers-by paused their journeys and peered – one young woman audibly mouthing the words to herself – and followed with befuddled countenances; but little came of it. I did not mind this for it allowed me to enjoy the sights and noise that surrounded us for just a little while longer.

But time, that old reaper of wheat, waits for no one. And, as the nearby church struck one, my tutor nodded knowingly to me, quite cognisant that I would understand his meaning. Without speaking, we walked to where a small and rickety stage had been nailed together for the purpose of allowing musicians or tumblers to perform willy-nilly. At that moment, a strong man was finishing his turn, having lifted a tree trunk above his head, while a sad-looking woman went through the crowd, soliciting coins as pay for the entertainment. He lifted his palms in gratitude and climbed down.

'Time for your second gala, Lysander.' Mr Tolson put his hand on my shoulder and squeezed, before turning the sign inwards once more.

'Yes, sir.' I swallowed hard. This was always a nerve-wracking moment. The promise of all that you wish for is always the hardest thing to see before you, lest by rushing towards it, you break it to pieces. My feet were unsteady on the ladder up to the stage.

'Remember how much you enjoy singing before others,' my benefactor whispered in my ear as I hauled myself up. 'Think of your friends in the Rose.' And it settled me a bit. I pushed upwards with renewed determination and expectation.

The stage was only a yard or so above the ground, and yet it felt to me as I stepped onto it that I was higher than a church steeple and the focus for every pair of eyes in a league or more. I steadied myself, and opened my mouth. I found Mr Tolson was right: transmogrifying the faces before me into those of my friends at the Peldon Rose gave me the self-belief to lift my voice in song.

When I was bound apprentice in famous Lincolnshire,
I served my master truly, for nearly seven odd year,

I sang as strong and sweet as ever I had done. As a result, the half-dozen ranged around me grew to a full dozen, and then twice that, including one of the jackanapes men on stilts who were striding about and playing japes on all and sundry. He wore a cloak of blue stripes and a tall hat festooned with waving peacock feathers of all colours. By the time of 'Down Among the Dead Men', there were more still, and they were chanting along with my words, knowing them well from their own inns and alehouses. I was enjoying myself so much that I barely recalled my true purpose in the performance, and it was only my benefactor's gesturing that reminded me. As I let the last note fall, I turned the sign so that the people before me could see it.

The first to read my announcement was the stilts-man. He stared at it, his lips moving as he slowly read the words, working them out to himself. Then he blinked a few times and his face cracked into a chuckle and a long laugh that sounded like nothing so much as a cawing seagull. He was guffawing at me and my cruel situation. I had experienced many reactions to my place in the world but not, to my memory, this mocking one. Instantly, on that hot day, I felt an icicle thrusting into my chest.

His avian screech attracted the attention of others around us. Most of them were none the wiser, for they could not read, and so for their benefit he yelled out the meaning of the legend upon my sign. 'The boy's lost his ma and pa! Do YOU know them?' he cawed at all and sundry. The icicle in me exploded as I saw he was only becoming started with me – and those around were taking up his mood, encouraged by his volume. Some chuckled and grinned, as if I were one of the booth spectacles, not a warm, living human child in need of kindness. I looked to Mr Tolson, whose countenance was troubled, but he rallied and gestured me from the platform, then pulled me away through the throng.

'Ignore them, my boy. We shall go this way.'

He gently but firmly propelled me between bodies, and it was only a few paces before we were swallowed by people who had not seen my performance or the man on stilts and his mockery. But I realized that I had covered the sign with my arm. My teacher did not mention it.

'Why did they do that?' I asked, for I had endured harsh words from one or two of my schoolmates but nothing like this from strangers.

'They probably thought it was some sort of comedic performance.'

Although my schoolmaster often saw the best in people, I am not convinced that he believed that the people around me were so innocent of ill-feeling.

To distract my mind from what had occurred, he bought me an apple dipped in honey, and the sweet taste on my lips took the edge from the pain that those people had inflicted on my soul. Still my cheeks were hot, though.

'I think we should go to our lodgings,' my teacher told me. His voice was a little weak and forced, for he too had been upset by the turn of the crowd from friends to bullies.

I nodded and we set off along the riverbank in the direction of the colleges. But we had gone a few hundred yards when I stopped and stared at the rippling water and then my master. My mind had revolted and I knew that I would, no, *could* not take another step until I knew the honest truth.

'Mr Tolson, sir,' I said. 'Where do I come from?'

He froze in the middle of his stride. He did not look at me but I saw his breath escape him.

'Oh, Lysander,' he said, more to himself than to me. 'Oh, Lysander my boy.'

And he dropped onto the bank and let his feet, shod as they were, trail in the water. I did the same. The flow was cold. 'I will tell you all I know. It is not much but it is all that I can offer. You will be, I think, fourteen years old tomorrow.'

'You do not know?' I was taken aback. I had celebrated my birthday each year, at his instance, so how could he be uncertain even of that?

'I do not. My boy, I am sorry for all that I have presented to you over your years as fact, when the truth is it is little more than speculation.' I was silent for a while. He was too, allowing this to sink in, as preparation for what was to follow. Then he continued. 'It was, as you know, seventeen ninety-two and I had only had my school for three years. There were few pupils, but I would like to think that I was respected within the community.

'It was midsummer and the late evening of a Friday. I was in the Rose, eating a supper – the pupils and my daughter were being overseen by a woman from Mersea I sometimes used for the purpose. There had been a summer storm and the fishing boats had stayed in port. It was quiet, just two or three of us in the inn. When the door opened, we were expecting a familiar face to enter and ask for a cup of ale. Instead, it was a handsome young woman, white of face and utterly soaked to her skin. And in her arms, there was a pretty child with hair like a crow's feathers.

'This young woman came in nervous. I will not forget that she looked all about the room before her foot crossed the threshold. It left such an impression on me, no doubt, because we of Mersea are so much at home in our small world that when it is interrupted, it sets us unbalanced for a while. But politeness soon reasserted itself in our breasts and Walter asked her for her fancy from the bar. "I must get to Cambridge!" she blurted out, taking no heed of what he had said. "Can I get there tonight?" "Cambridge?" he replied. "Not tonight, not with all the will in the world." And he pointed out to the foul weather. "It's five hours' ride on the best of days. In this, you'd die of a chill on the way." And at that she looked quite wild. "Die, I . . ." she blurted out more to God than to the rest of us. And she looked down at the child in her arms, who was a year or two of age, and stroked its cheek. "No, I shall not!" The baby gurgled and laughed at that.'

Here he stopped and took a swig from his flask of water and wine. 'Walter looked at me as if I should know what to do, or what the meaning of all this was. But I was as flummoxed as he. So on he went. "There will be a coach at noon tomorrow that you may take. Horace drives it. It's old but moves well enough." At that, she closed her eyes and swayed a little, as if to faint. Then she shook her head. "May I sit here?" she said. "Why yes," Walter told her. "Always a warm welcome at the Rose for any that needs it." And she took herself to one of the tables. Without asking, Walter gave her a cup of small beer and she drank, then poured a few drops onto the baby's lips. It seemed to revive them both a little. "I have no money for a coach," she said. "It is all gone. All that I brought." I knew that Walter would not ask her a penny for her drink, but no funds at all would not go in her favour regarding her journey. It occurred to me that I did not even know where she had come from: out of the storm, and no more than that.

'"You are trying for Cambridge?" I said, attempting to commence conversation. "Are your people there?" "Safety is there," was her only reply, though, listening to her accent, I should say that she was a native of that county. I was about to ask her whence she came – the Peldon Rose was on no route but to or from Mersea, and I could not fathom a reason for her to visit the island without baggage or money – when she spoke again. "May I wait for the coach here?" and she turned her face to Walter, for she had discerned that he was the landlord. Her expression was – how must I say? – a concoction of powerlessness and defiance; desperation and yet resolve. For one moment it was one, and the next moment it was another. Walter was about to speak when she forestalled him with her raised palm. "I said I have no money. But if you can lend me the cost of a coach in the morning, I have this as surety that I will return with twice what I owe you." She reached into the pink cloak around the child and pulled out a pocket watch and offered it to us.

'"There is no need for that," Walter said, folding her fingers over the watch. "We believe you. Always a warm welcome at the Rose to those that need it. Why, you look half-dead on your feet. Let me take you up to the room above and you can both have a sleep. I shall wake you in the morning."'

That room was a rickety structure of wood that had been built onto the top of the inn. It was directly above the taproom, but accessed by a staircase on the outside of the building, used for occasional travellers or when Walter had had a drop too much of his own wares and his wife insisted he snore like a pig on his own for the night.

'I must own that I would, for my part, have given in to my shameful curiosity and have exacted some more information from her before showing her up. But Walter did not. And now I regret most dearly that I did not stay his hand and ask but a few questions of her before she wearily trod the stairs up to the hire chamber. I listened to her feet – slow and thudding, as she carried the weight of the child and the hard and mysterious journey that had brought her to our doorstep. Then Walter's voice, muffled through the floorboards and her final words that I could just make out: "Thank you, sir. You are a kind man in a harsh world."'

And Mr Tolson whispered again those words to himself, too quiet for me to hear, but I could see them form on his lips and then fly away with the summer breeze. He took a moment to think to himself, before speaking again. For some reason, his voice became a little darker and more melancholic then.

'And so Walter came back down and we looked at each other not quite sure of what was in occurrence. "A bit rum this, is it not, Leo?" he asked of me. I had to answer in the affirmative for it was "a bit rum", as he and the local people had it.

'We sat there for another two hours or perhaps more. Him smoking his pipe and me smoking mine. From time to time we would speculate on who the young woman was: a traveller who had badly lost her way, perhaps. Or a relative of someone on Mersea who had thrown her out after a disagreement. "A young criminal on the run?" Walter suggested at one time. But none of these propositions satisfied us, and we fell back to our quiet ruminations. That is, after all, the life of our little society: much time for thinking over occurrences out of the daily ordinary. At one time – around nine o'clock, I believe, Walter took out his backgammon board and we had a little game. We were in the midst of it when the door blew open once more, slamming back with the wind. There stood a man. A hefty man with a countenance that I would not cross.'

I knew where the tale would stop next. 'The man who came looking for me,' I said.

'Yes, lad. That is him.'

I took a moment to absorb this. 'What did he do?'

'He did nothing, just stared into the inn. He seemed about to speak when there was a whistle outside and he looked back over his shoulder. Someone was hailing his attention and he drew back from the doorway and shut it again. Well, Walter and I just looked at each other at this strange turn of events. "I should get up and see what is the matter," he said. "Yes, I believe you should," I replied. But neither of us wanted to. There was something diabolical outside, it seemed.

'It took us some seconds for our curiosity to overcome our trepidation and then we stood and started to go outside. But we were forestalled by the noise of a most furious explosion of violence erupting from the room above us. There was shouting, screaming – though we could not make out a word of it. After stopping agog at the sound, we rushed for the door. Try as we might, though, we could not force it open – something had wedged it shut hard. Walter looked panicked, as if we had been caught in a trap; and we both put our shoulders to the portal and shoved. It moved no more than half an inch. And then there was the smashing sound of furniture overturned and splintering. "Out the back!" he yelled. There was a small exit at the back that he only used for taking deliveries down to the cellar. All the while, the commotion was getting more furious – and then, suddenly, there was utter silence. We charged to the rear but found it locked and the key nowhere to be seen.

'Back we went to the front door, determined to open it if it killed us. We threw ourselves against it with all our weight and managed to bust the bottom planks of it and kick the rest open. We found it had been wedged shut with sticks and large stones planted into the wet soil. We dashed around to the staircase that gave way up to the hire room. In the dark – it now being fully night with little moon – I thought I saw something metal flash some way off and I was about to investigate when Walter grabbed my arm and pulled me, harrying me upwards with him. "Come on!" he was yelling. My God, how I regret now that I did not follow that glitter of light.'

He rubbed his brow and thought for a moment.

'But then, I tell myself, had I done so, all might have turned out worse and bloodier than it did.' And he glanced at me. 'Forgive me if I made the wrong choice in the moment. I cannot tell if I did.'

'Sir, whatever you think is right, I know is right,' I replied. And he placed his hand on my shoulder.

'We entered the chamber. There was little furnishing in the room: a bed, a table and stool and a garderobe. But what there was, was in utter disarray. The table had keeled over, one leg snapped off and dangling from splinters. The sole blanket was on the floor and the garderobe was tipped over, its doors face down to the floor. There was no one there, that was clear, so we dashed back outside and scanned the night. We rushed around – staying close to each other for protection, that went unsaid – and looked where we could, but we are not bats and cannot see in the dark. All we found was the abandoned inn and the lights from Turnglass House shimmering on the water.

'"Can you hear horses?" Walter demanded. We both strained our ears, but first there was nothing more than the sound of the waves. And then something else. It wasn't horses' hooves, it was something a lot more human than that. It was the sound of a child crying. We ran back to the room and lifted the garderobe. And as the doors opened, there you were. Frightened, bruised, but alive. A healthy boy, terrified but alive. And clutched in your hand was that silver watch that has been your only possession since.'

Chapter Four

I did not want to hear any more. I got to my feet, without looking at my school master, and I began to walk, then run, and then sprint along the river's edge. I had no thought in my mind of where I was heading. My head was full only with images of a woman, wet through her clothes, appearing in an inn, seeking sanctuary, finding it, then having it taken from her. Of a man in the night who stole her and left her child. Of that poor child on the floor of a room he had never seen before, bereft of his mother. I felt sorry for her and for me. The cruelty of it all was something I had never before felt, because I had never before known the story. Then I did and I swear to you now, I wished myself back in the woollen comfort of ignorance.

I tore through knots of happy folk on their way to the Fayre, past landing jetties and boathouses, with no idea of direction or destination.

As I ran I heard my name shouted from behind me. Mr Tolson sounded panicked by my flight. He was chasing after me. The sound brought me back to earth and I let my feet slow and then stumble to a stop. I slumped against a tree trunk into which two names had been carved by young lovers and I looked up to the sun, as if its beams would shoot knowledge into my brain. The light burned into my eyes. It ended when Mr Tolson stepped between me and the star.

'Why would you never tell me?'

'A dozen reasons,' he said. 'But chiefly that it was always easier not to. Forgive me.'

He had never before asked forgiveness of any of us, of course. Least of all me, the boy who had always relied on him.

'What happened next?'

He sat and took off his shoes. Perhaps the action was to give him time to decide how open and transparent to be with his intelligence.

'Next? Next, I took you up. You were howling for your mother, as babies will do, of course, but you became quiet as soon as I wrapped you in my arms.' Here, he smiled a sad smile. 'You always were a thoughtful child.'

That was true, I think, although how much of that was nature, and how much was foisted upon me by constant unresolved wondering as to my own past, my own true name, is uncertain.

'Maybe you already had a thought that I would ensure your safety.'

For want of something to do, though my muscles ached for some sort of action, I tore some dry yellow grass from the baked soil and chucked it towards the running water. It tumbled to the ground well before it reached the river's edge.

'We were in a quandary then. We could have run back out to search for your mother – presuming that she was your mother, for I have never been certain on that point, of course – and the man who took her. But we now had a precious cargo. "Shall we go after them?" Walter asked. "We cannot take that risk," I said, lifting you. "Whoever that man is, he is a danger. This boy is safe now, not so outside wandering about in the dark."

'And I have relived those words a thousand times, Lysander, trying to decide if it was the right decision. Should we have gone out? Maybe we would have overpowered the abductor. Maybe he would have overpowered us – do not forget that he had a mate with him: whoever had whistled a signal to him when he was at our door.'

And I felt, I think, the same mental turmoil that he had felt for a decade. What if? *What if? What if* he had gone out and rescued my mother? But otherwise, *what if* he had gone out and we had all been murdered? My heart wished he had taken the chance, but my head knew he had chosen rightly.

'So what did you do?'

'I kept a hold on you. I can't quite comprehend why, but I felt as protective of you as I did when I first held Iphigenia. Blood is not always thicker than water, you see. Then Walter and I went to the stairs and kept watch for a minute. I confess that we felt our nerves hard for that minute, for we had no idea how many of them there were or how much evil they would wish upon us. But nothing was stirring as far as we could tell, so we took a chance and ran as fast as our old legs' – he cracked another pained smile – 'could take us, back to Turnglass House. We didn't even stop to lock up the Rose. The tide was rising – I should have returned an hour or two earlier but all had been so strange that I had forgotten the time – so our feet and breeches were drenched by the time we achieved the island. And I was so discombobulated that I nearly stumbled into the mud flats.

'Walter and I said nothing as we came into the house and locked and barred the door, and snuffed all the oil lamps so the whole house was black, which amazed the woman who was there keeping watch on the children. The man who had taken your mother was a stranger, so there was little chance that even if he walked across the Strood he would ever know the house was there. He would walk on to Mersea, and possibly drown on the way as the tide overtook the path. With the lights gone, we peered out the windows, until we calculated that the tide was high and Ray completely cut off from the mainland. It was only then that we felt safe. We made up a little bed for you on one of the settles and stayed there, waiting to see that nothing untoward happened. After an hour, just watching you sleep in the candlelight, I sent Walter off in our boat to raise Mr Jasper, the Justice of the Peace, and to bring the beadle too.

'Another hour later and we were in a ring around you, scratching our heads for what to do. We resolved that you were safest there, and Jasper would make enquiries wherever he could about a missing young woman with a child – we did not want to make a noise about it, in case it brought that man back. So over the following week, we did all we could, asking of porters and coachmen and ferrymen. No one had the slightest knowledge. All we had was you.'

And those words resonated in my head, because all I had ever had was me too. I had always felt alone. The scanty description of the mother I had never known changed that only for the worse, as I now felt something torn from me. She was only a pencil drawing – thin, monochrome and barely fleshed, but still she had been real, and she had loved me. And then she was taken away from me. It is strange and difficult to describe the feeling and its intensity. I can only portray it as a physical harm, as if a part of you has been taken and pain will numb but never dissolve away.

'I resolved to become your guardian until the time when we could trace your family. We knew it was no certainty that we could do so, yet I was confident that we would. I am sorry to say that that confidence was misplaced. And my idea that your mother was a native of Cambridge, and that if we attended the Midsummer Fayre we would doubtless meet one who could identify you, proved equally optimistic. We failed.'

'You did not fail me,' I said, in all my infantile attempt at good grace.

At that, he perked up a little. 'Thank you, my boy. I appreciate the sentiment.'

'What after that, sir?'

'Without a loving home to go to, there was never talk of sending you anywhere, and so you stayed. I kept hope alive of a reunion with your people, but . . .' He hesitated, before continuing in a sadder tone. 'But it lessened with the years. And perhaps we must now admit to ourselves that it will likely never come. But! That means Iphigenia and I have the joy of your presence until the day comes for you to leave and pursue your own fortune.'

I was not wholly comforted by this attempt to turn my disappointment into a boon. 'What will my fortune be?' I really had no idea.

'Whatever you want it to be, Lysander.' He put his hand on my crown and ruffled my hair. I lifted my eyes to the bright sky. Slipped between the rocks of humiliation and loneliness that had seemed all about me that day, I did spy a pink future that my teacher was holding out. Every child dreams, and the child without a true home dreams the most.

I picked a brown pebble from the soil and pitched it into the river with a plop. It felt like pitching my fate – I knew not where it would end up. 'Shall we return to our lodging?' Mr Tolson asked, after I had reflected for a while on what he had told me.

I silently assented and we began trudging back through the hot, busy streets. The smell of the horse dung was high and it produced a sour miasma for our journey.

Our lodging was with a local woman in a narrow lane. Our landlady fed us and, afterwards, Mr Tolson asked if I wished to accompany him as he sought out some interesting tracts on King Solomon's rule of Israel in Trinity's College's famed library, but I declined, feeling restless and not attuned to ancient history, no matter how fascinating and instructive.

Out he went and he must have lost track of time for there was no sign of him by eight o'clock. Idle with my thoughts, I betook myself out into the street to kick my heels and wait for him. But as I leaned on a wall, a gang of scholars emerged from evensong and headed north, talking loudly of their desire to return to the Fayre. And without a conscious thought to do so, I fell in behind them.

It seemed to take longer to reach the Midsummer Common than before, and that was not the only difference. The dimming light had unleashed a spirit of bacchanalia that pervaded the air. There were no sacrificial animals or livid dancers spinning madly around the site, but there were many men and women retching from a surfeit of strong drink. All was lit by bonfires and torches.

I found the students amusing to follow for a while as they ran riot among the stalls and tents. One insisted on throwing aside his academic cap and walking on his hands, much to the amusement of his friends. I was laughing at him, the humiliation of the day forgotten, when someone to my side called out, 'Boy!' Thinking – rightly – that this was aimed at me, I saw, standing between two tents and shaking his head at the student antics, a man in the latter part of his life, with a bushy beard dyed green as an oak leaf, that made him look like the Old Man of the Woods. He was dressed in strange garb – a flowing gown with stars sewn upon it. He would have looked Mad Tom had he not been at the Midsummer Fayre and clearly a conjuror. But a conjuror of the second rate, it seemed, and down on his luck. He presented to me a ha'penny in his hand, and flipped it in the air. But as I watched it tumble back down, it entirely disappeared! And I own that I gasped. He opened his hands to show they were empty. It was a simple trick but one that I could not fathom then and still cannot. 'Good magic, no?' the old gent asked.

'Yes, good.'

But then a look of curiosity seemed to creep into his looks. 'You are sad,' he said quietly, his brow furrowing. 'You are laughing, but you are sad inside, I can tell.' His speech was rough-hewn, as one who has had no schooling but that of the folk of the fields and bracken.

'How can you tell?' I blurted out, for he was undeniably accurate in his assertion.

'It is my gift. Among others.'

At this, a healthy scepticism entered my thoughts. I feared not black magic, but even at that age I was able to discern nonsense. My attitude must have shown on my face.

'Oho, you do not believe me?'

'I . . . I am not . . .' I stammered, unsure how to remain truthful yet polite on that score.

'No matter. I have seen young men like you often enough. I care not.' And he shrugged and turned to walk away.

'No, wait!' I called, not wanting him to leave, for I thought there might be more tricks to see. And I went around him. 'I am sorry. I did not mean to be—'

'Rude?' he suggested.

'Yes, I think so.' I was a little confused by exactly what offence I had given. But he softened.

'Well, I am used to it. It is far from the worst I will suffer this night.'

'What do you mean?' I was again a little lost.

'I mean that those students or the people from the town will be happy to pay me tuppence to tell their fortune now, but by midnight they will be banging on the side of my caravan and telling me to leave or be burned to the ground as a follower of the Devil.'

I looked at my shoes, somehow ashamed, as if I were one of that crowd. He saw the look on my face, and clapped a warm hand, with dirt under his nails, on my shoulder.

'Oh, worry not. I will be well gone by midnight.' And he chortled at a private joke. Then he stood back and pulled my hand to him, opening out my palm. He studied it and furrowed his brow again, as if he had seen something that demanded deeper examination. Then he lowered my hand and looked deeply and penetratingly into my eyes. 'Come to my caravan,' he ordered me. It was an instruction, one that brooked no refusal and expected none either. Palm readings were by custom the work of Gypsies, but perhaps this man had the gifts he claimed.

He led me through the stalls to the far corner of the field. It was an isolated spot, part-shielded from the revels by a few willow trees weeping to the ground. There was a small arched wagon painted red and green on the side, with two dozing nags harnessed in. A door behind the driver's box gave entry to an interior with a round table covered in red cloth and simple stools on either side. There were a few racks on the wall holding the normal necessities of life: a smattering of wooden and pewter dishes, a loaf of bread, a flagon. On the table there was another pewter dish, inlaid with a scrolling design, that held a pile of dry leaves and herbs. An emerald green woollen scarf lay beside them, and a red candle floated in a bowl of water, sending waves of reflected light around the darkened room. The room smelled thickly of the herbs.

'What is your name?' he asked.

'Lysander Rose,' I said quietly, uncertain of myself.

'Say louder.'

'Lysander Rose,' I repeated, finding my voice.

'I am Roberto.' He stroked his green beard and sat before me. 'You have been searching for something. For someone.'

How he knew, I could not tell. But sure I had been searching for someone that day, and every day I had attended the Midsummer Fayre. I had never found her. And a spark of hope leapt inside me. Was this now how I would find that woman who gave life to me? I scoffed still at the thought of divination – and yet, he knew something of me. What else did he know? What could he tell me?

'Do . . . do you know?' I asked hesitantly. I did not want to mouth the words, as if doing so would break any spell that was hovering over us.

'I know many things, Lysander. And you know more than you realize. You must simply remember them.' At that, he lifted the floating candle from the water, and doused the woollen scarf in the water, soaking it. Then he sat back a little and put the flame to the dry leaves. They crackled and sent a burst of green-tinged smoke into the room. He put his hand to the back of my head, gently pushing it towards the clouds rising. 'Breathe it in, and soon you will see before you what you seek.' I did as he asked, sucking in the smoke, which was cooler and smoother than the tobacco that I had sometimes taken in the Rose. Like the tobacco, it made me light-headed.

'More,' he demanded, as I took it down into my lungs. 'See before you what you desire.' Again, I followed his order, my vision swimming. My thoughts tumbled, and I could tell it was too much; it was bad smoke and I opened my throat to tell him, but that just sucked down the thickest cloud of the green fog and I half twisted, half fell, to see him with the soaked scarf over his mouth and nose, shielding him from the poison that he was forcing into me. And then my cheek hit the table and a man entered the wagon and snorted in derision and I saw nothing more but the stars of the night.

I believe I woke a few times. I recall sensations more than thoughts: the feeling of iron nails in the floorboards pricking my back as the vehicle shuddered over the baked roads. Sharp pain as the base of my skull thumped up and down when we ran over craters on the highway. I seem to remember trying to lift my head but finding it had the weight of an elephant and falling back into black sleep.

And then I woke with a jolt as freezing water hit my face. How long I had wavered between sleep and wake I cannot say, but it must have been a number of hours because my shirt was wet through with salty sweat and the only light came from a spirit lamp shining in my face. I put my hands up to blot it out and they were smacked away.

'You look at me,' said a voice. And even before my mind had sucked in its sound, I knew who was speaking. A man I had never seen although he had been walking behind me for most of my life.

'Who am I?'

I surprised even myself with this question, which I croaked more than spoke. I had thought it to be *where am I?* when it formed on my lips, but then it blew into the air as the question that saturated my mind. *Who am I?*

His answer was to smirk, and then open his mouth to reveal a row of short teeth, stained black. 'You want to know, do you, lad?' And he gurgled a little laugh.

He was of medium stature. Well fed, it seemed, and

well formed as the farm hands I had seen when Mr Tolson had taken me to the market in Colchester. His features were somehow too small for his face. His hair was mostly gone, but some remained, clipped short around the lower half of his skull. I would have put him around the middle years of life. But what was most notable was that he must have suffered some terrible accident or assault, for where his left eye should have been there was a brass eyepatch, tarnished green, around which the flesh had knitted itself, and held in place with a leather thong.

He was wearing rough, working man's leather jerkin and trousers spun of grey wool. He stared at me before smiling contentedly to himself and retreating to the edge of the lamplight to sit in what had once been a leather easy chair, but was now a skeleton of leather and stuffing.

I took the chance to glance about. I was in a musty little room, alive with mould, stinking of damp, where the floorboards were badly warped or missing in their entirety. The wracked easy chair was the only furniture save for one other item: a large bed made for a married pair. It too had been eaten by the damp, so that the mattress was a heap of hemp. Wherever we were, it had long since been evacuated, and the bed must have been too heavy to extricate.

'May I stand?'

No answer, so, gingerly, I lifted my head from one of the rotten boards. My cheek stung where it had rested on the head of a nail, and dizziness made me falter – the after-effects of whatever burning drug I had breathed. I tried to stand, and then realized that it was not only my injured state that was preventing my movement. My ankles had been shackled and chained one to another like a convict.

'How do they feel?'

I had no answer to that.

'I've had their company one or twice myself. You will get used to it.'

'But . . . why?' I asked. 'Why me?'

'You shall know in time.' And he gently tapped his metal eyepatch with a dirty fingernail. I could not fathom his meaning.

I winced, not through the dull pain that still swamped my head, but as the enormity of the situation fell upon me like a typhoon. I was hobbled like an animal, leagues – as far as I knew – from any friend or help, and at the mercy of the man who had stalked me from my youngest time. I bent over and retched. What came out of me fell through holes and splits in the boards to whatever lay beneath the house.

After emptying myself, I managed to pull myself upright. But even then, something felt very wrong with the scene around me. Everything looked skew-whiff and I could not understand, until I realized that I was standing straight up, but the walls were leaning, as if the house were staked to the ground but trying to pull itself free.

Glancing at my captor for permission and finding no refusal, I moved stutter-fashion to the window, which leaned with the rest of the house. There was no glass in it, and probably never had been. It had only wooden shutters that were hanging down on broken brackets. I put my head outside and was met with a sight that was such a strange one that I briefly forgot even my terrifying predicament. For my head was hovering twenty yards or so above the surging sea. We were on the very edge of a cliff – indeed, from what I could tell, the part of the building's floor on which I stood was resting on nothing but empty air. I yelped and jumped back, retreating quick to the rear wall, which I hoped was planted on solid earth.

My gaoler laughed and pointed a dirty finger to another, smaller, window in the side wall of the room. Hesitantly, I made my way to it. It showed me the view along the cliff edge and a dozen or so cottages within a few yards of the precipice. All were dark and rickety and must have been as abandoned as ours. There were other houses further back but I saw no more sign of life in them than in the ocean itself. I stared down at the pulsing water and as my sight adjusted to the moonlight, I was certain I could see something in the sea – it was tall, solid and square, thrusting up from the waves. It . . . yes, it had to be. There was nothing else it could be. It was a church bell tower, being sprayed all around by white foam as the waves broke on its stones.

'Do you like Dunwich?' I was so astonished by what I could see that I did not even turn around. 'Big port once, then the sea took it.' He seemed to amuse himself.

'Are we alone?' I asked. Somehow there was still a spark of hope that there would be others around to whom I could appeal for salvation.

'Aye.' And his satisfied voice told me that he knew exactly what had been in my mind.

'What do you want with me?' I had no idea in my head as to what my destiny would hold – and it was that void that terrified me more than if I had known I was marked for death.

He took out a little knife and began paring his nails. I felt a twist in my stomach, as if I were going to retch again, but there was nothing there to purge now and the muscles twisted on emptiness. Why would he keep it from me? I could not resist, whatever it was, so why keep those secrets? Something in my mind reached back to our scripture lessons with Mr Tolson, when he described a fallen angel, Astaroth, the keeper of secrets. This man before me, with three days of beard, an eye made of brass and dirty fingers became entwined with that demon, and thenceforth each time he spoke, I mentally prefaced his words with 'Astaroth says . . .'

The other one, the one who had called himself Roberto, entered the room, sipping from a flagon. Astaroth stopped him as he passed and roughly took the flask, drinking deep before handing it back. I was thirsty but was too afraid to ask for anything. Roberto took himself to the edge of the room and sat, leaning his back against the mouldy wall, staring at me.

'I think that will be the last time you speak to a conjuror,' Astaroth said to himself. Roberto caught my eye and shrugged nonchalantly, as if his offence had been of the mildest sort and he felt not a whiff of guilt or remorse. It was just 'how it was' and no more. These two men who had abducted me and were propelling me to something evil: one who felt his action amusing, and another who felt nothing at all. I knew not which of them was the more wicked. 'And your schoolmaster will learn to keep his lips buttoned too. You never know who is listening.' I thought that was perhaps intended to convey the meaning that Mr Tolson had mentioned to someone his intention to bring me to the Fayre, and that is how they had come to grab me there.

'What time will the boat come?' Roberto asked his commander.

'One hour before dawn. Get the dice.'

They played for an hour for small coins that I did not recognize, ignoring me. I tried to think of ways to escape, but they knew there were none. A mouse could have run faster than I. I listened for the sound of any other voices or footsteps but the world was silent as a grave. In a fit of bravado I told myself that I would leap from the window to the sea below and swim for my life, but I could no more have done so than I could have flapped my arms like wings and flown away like a bird. So I sat and watched them play. The game only ended when Roberto, who had won almost all of Astaroth's money, said he wanted to play no more.

'We play until I say we have finished!' snarled his commander.

'I will play no more.' And he stood.

Astaroth grabbed him and pulled him back down. 'You do not hear me. We play until I say we have finished.' And he opened his jerkin, tore a knife from a leather belt and stabbed it into the rotten floorboard no more than an inch from Roberto's hand. I shuddered, for I had not yet seen a weapon, and I felt that I was destined to be acquainted with it sooner or later. Roberto knew what his companion was made of and he relented. In an hour, the fortunes had been reversed and Astaroth had all the coins in a pile. He laughed in triumph over his underling, who, for his part, seemed to take it well enough, without complaint.

The next few hours passed coldly. We three sat in a candlelit triangle of frozen hell, no words exchanged, barely a movement made, until Astaroth dozed off, his head on a pillow made from his folded coat. And then it was only me and Roberto. I could not sleep because my nerves were taut. He remained awake through will, I believe; for after half an hour of snoring from his companion, he rubbed his jaw thoughtfully and spoke to me.

'Boy, the last time we saw you, we left something. Did you read it?'

Read it? What was he— and then I remembered. There was the strange penny blood chapbook that Astaroth had pinned to a table with a knife through it, as if he were murdering the pamphlet.

'I . . . yes.' I stammered, confused.

'Did you take it as a warning?'

I blinked and shook my head. He chuckled to himself. 'You should have.' And he stretched his fingers to the pocket of Astaroth's coat and gently plucked something out. He held it out for me to see, twisting it – as he had the coin when in his conjuror guise – dextrously between his fingers. Then he flicked it to me. It skidded on the rotten floorboards.

I saw instantly what it was: another chapbook cheaply printed on quarto pages. With trepidation – for there seemed great danger in touching something stolen from Astaroth – I lifted it to my eyes. *The Murderous Deeds in the Village of Lorne in France and How They Brought About the Bloody Revolution. The Second Part.*

By a Gentleman of the Law

'Read it,' hissed Roberto. 'Learn your history.' And something made me do as he said.

The heyday of the Carmelite order of monks was centuries in the past and the smallness of the abbey before me - not much larger than the house of a Paris bourgeois - seemed designed to broadcast a poverty of public interest as much as a poverty of strongbox. I had always been suspicious of a church that both drowned in silver and pleaded beggary. But still.

A brother of the order in its distinctive white habit with black scapular shuffled out when he saw me approach. He looked along the dusty road I had walked, about a league from the village. 'Who are you?' he asked, as if he was uncertain why anyone would approach except to beg alms or deposit a sick parent with relief.

I told him my name and asked for the abbot. He seemed glad it was not something worse. A couple of minutes later Dom Mathieu appeared. He was a welcoming man, far more than many an abbot of the more austere orders, putting an arm around me to guide me through the door. I could see a small courtyard in a southern Iberian style.

'Dom, I would beg to talk to you of Father Dollet.'

'If you wish,' he allowed. For certain, he did not seem too keen.

'And I would like one last time to examine his mortal remains.'

'Come this way, I will show you.' He led me into a dark

room lined with shelves like some sort of library of medicine or the cupboard of an especially inventive poisoner. Father Pierre Dollet had been laid out in a fresh winding sheet and washed clean of blood. I hoped that the monks had not noticed what other fluid had lain on his skin. The old priest deserved dignity.

'You have been very respectful,' I said.

'He was once a novice in our order.'

I looked closer at the body. There were the ligature burns from the twine around his upper arms, the stigmata from the nails. I could now better see the gaping wound on his neck. It was more substantial than I had realized the previous night when half of it had been covered by the clotted blood. Battlefield necessity had taught me the preliminaries of the major veins of the human body. The wound appeared to have been made by a single thrust from a thin blade. 'Why did he leave your order?' I asked.

The abbot lowered his voice.

'It is a painful subject, my son. Why do you need to know?'

'In order to do God's will.'

'My son, you will not get around me that way.'

'Dom, I apologize. In order to catch the man who did this, put him on trial and have him punished.'

'Punishment means death?'

'In this case, I am certain that it will.'

The abbot sat on a three-legged stool in the corner. Through the window I glimpsed the abbey's small farm at the rear. A few ragged cows and near-feral goats dragged grass out of the earth. There was a yard full of chickens, with a huge black cockerel presiding over them magisterially. 'Our order is dedicated to the preservation of life. Not plucking it away. You understand me?'

'I do, Dom. But life has been plucked away already. We are not introducing death into this world.' I respected the feelings of such men as thought life to be sacrosanct. But my years had taught me to be circumspect. Take a life to protect a life: that was the way of this world. It was far from perfect. And I hoped the abbot would put his scruples aside for a few minutes.

He remained silent while he thought. 'Pierre Dollet left after an incident of which none of us is proud.'

That was a strange thing. 'May I ask what nature of incident?'

'I would not have put it to my lips if I had been unwilling to fill in the details. He was accused of a sin. Theft. Something trivial, I recall - a few pots worth sous, no more.'

I pondered for three or four seconds whether to believe him. I did not.

I asked a few more questions and learned something of Pierre Dollet's character as a young man - welcoming and pleasant - but nothing of note to my enquiries, and therefore bade the Dom a good day.

On my way back to the village, I passed within sight of Father Dollet's cottage. His slow-witted housekeeper, Josette, was walking towards it, carrying a basket. Something caught my eye: on the lower storey - the priest's study - a figure passed by the window. I stopped and stared. Who would be allowed in the house when the housekeeper was abroad? No one with permission to be there. I ran towards the house. Josette seemed to notice me and stopped on the threshold to watch my approach. I shouted to her. Whether she understood or not I couldn't tell, but that figure reappeared briefly at the edge of the window - too distant to make out who it was - and was gone. I charged past her, into the curate's study. There was no one there. I ran out the rear door, which stood open and looked all around. The tiny kitchen garden blended into the woodland that bordered the village and I hurried through, into the trees, watching for signs of movement. But there was nothing. Whoever it was had managed to steal away from me. I cursed my luck that I had not walked just a touch faster, to arrive at the house half a minute earlier.

Back inside, I examined the study. It took me seconds to see what the thief had been after. The locked drawer, which had contained the curate's secret correspondence and the strange books on witchcraft, had been wrenched from the desk, busting the lock, and was now empty.

'The books. The books that were here. Have you moved them?' I demanded.

'No, sir,' replied Josette. Tears began to roll down her cheeks.

I placed my hands on hers. 'Be not distressed. It was not your fault.' I blamed myself for leaving those items in place, rather than taking them with me when I had first seen them. *Idiot!* I thought.

'Will I be blamed, sir?'

'No, not at all. I will see to it that you are not.'

'Thank you.'

At least I had disturbed the thief, perhaps before he had completed his task, I told myself as I walked out, kicking up dust.

I wanted to speak to the baker, Hubert, who had found Father Dollet in the church. While I walked to his shop, I set to thinking about what was walking the alleys of Lorne. Nature, the church and sorcery - these were the three forces that French villagers knew shaped their lives: whether the sun shone in summer decided whether you would eat that winter; when the church bell rang you had to leave what you were doing and assemble to hear the priest's instruction; if a witch cursed you, the bloody flux would wrack your body until your last breath escaped and you were destined for the boneyard. All three forces unseen, yet utterly tangible.

Hubert's bakery was a long, low building that was sweating hot inside. The plum-coloured cushions of flab rolled from the baker's smock and peeped over the top of his trousers, glistening with moisture. Behind him the ovens were tended by two girls aged ten or twelve years, one blonde, one with dark hair. As I entered, Hubert was kneading dough, his hands grimy with unknown soil. I made a mental note never to eat a loaf that he had made. Upon seeing me he stopped dead and the two girls behind him halted to watch.

'You two go and bring in more wood or I will pull up your skirts and make you sorry,' he said over his shoulder. They obeyed and left through a rear door I could not quite make out. The baker's knuckles restarted their chore, driving harder into the dough, punching then folding, as the heat from the open oven seemed to grow ever more oppressive. I felt myself drenched under my shirt as if I had been transported to the gates of the underworld guarded by this Cerberus. I decided to make it a short visit.

'Hello, Hubert,' I said. The baker nodded his acceptance of the address. 'Last night, why were you the first in the church?'

'Because I found him, monsieur. I found Father Dollet.'

I would have to make things simpler for my new friend. 'Yes. I did not make myself clear. How did you come to find him?'

'I light my fires two hours before dawn, sir, so the bread

is ready at dawn. I passed by and saw the door open. I thought it strange and came in to see. Then . . .' His hands stopped kneading.

'Yes. I understand.'

'I didn't see anyone, sir. Nothing. If I did, I would say.'

'I believe you. Tell me, can you think of anyone who would have any reason to kill,' the baker flinched at the word, 'Father Dollet?'

'Only the Gypsies, sir.'

'How so?'

'It is in their nature. They steal babies too.'

'Forget about the Gypsies,' I said, simply too tired to educate the dolt. He seemed bemused by the instruction. I suspected he thought about them a lot. 'Had Father Dollet made anyone angry? Had anyone ever accused him of doing something wrong? Such as stealing from them?' The abbot had told me Pierre Dollet had been expelled from the order for such a misdemeanour so I had to keep an open mind, no matter how unlikely - indeed, offensive - it sounded to me.

'The priest?' His mouth fell dumbly open again. 'The priest steal?' He looked around his shop as if Father Dollet might be hiding in a recess ready to thieve some of the moulding produce.

'Never mind,' I sighed.

At that, there was a shuffling behind me and I looked around to see the man I now knew to be Gregory Archer, husband of the famous opera singer who was Francois's guest in the chateau. He had a leather satchel over his shoulder and was wearing clothes for tramping through the forest.

'Good morning, Monsieur Archer,' said the baker.

Archer offered his hand to me. 'Gregory Archer. I

understand we are inmates of the same asylum.' He spoke precise French with a strong English accent. Up close, his face was lit by humour, a warm glow in the cheeks and deep blue eyes with laughter wrinkles in their corners.

'David Sévine.'

'We should talk. Let me buy one of Hubert's loaves and we can walk together.' I left it to Archer to decide how wise he was to eat some of the bread I had seen the baker kneading. He could have rinsed it in a ditch and it would have come out cleaner. 'I have stolen a little cheese from the kitchen of our host and intend to go to the river to do a little composing. Shall we go there?'

'Gladly.' It would do well to try to gain what intelligence I could in a more relaxed place. He handed over a sous and we strode along the road in silence before turning onto a path that took us up the hillside to look into the valley where the tumbledown chateau of the Barons d'Agnes rested, and then along to the golden fields that were being tilled. I breathed in the air - it was like sugar compared to the town rot that normally filled my lungs. I felt - just a grain - at home.

Archer took from his satchel some paper, a small inkwell with the lid screwed on, and a quill, which he cut. He dipped the pen in the ink and began drawing lines on the paper. I found it somehow comic to think of this big, powerful man, who was two inches taller than me and built like a warrior, quietly creating chamber music.

'What are you composing?' I asked after a while.

'It is a church piece about the life of Saint Anthony.'

I thought back to the matter at hand. 'Did you know Father Dollet well?'

'Not very well. He was friendly enough and Francois had him to dinner at the chateau once or twice.'

'Which? Once or twice.'

'Twice, I think.'

'Did you see him at other times?'

'Only for church services.'

'He was in the church very late that night. Can you think of any reason for that? Had he ever mentioned to you working that late?'

'No, and never.'

'The night he died,' I said. 'You were at the chateau?'

'Yes. We were all together in the music room - us, Catherine, Charles. Practising my son's singing. We went to bed, oh, close to midnight, I would say.'

'And you saw nothing of note?'

'Nothing of note.'

I let the breeze play on us for a while before resuming. 'Tell me something: You have a village moonchild, have you not? A man who was Francois's former lawyer, is that right?'

'Ah, Cotillard.'

'That is him.'

'Mad as Orlando.' He waited. 'Handel? No?' I had disappointed him. People with a passion believe all others share it - still, at least Archer's obsession with music was more palatable than Francois's interest in how castrated horses could still produce seed. 'Well, anyway. Cotillard. Yes, strange case. You see him about the place and I have spoken to him once or twice. Quite clever, I think. But absolutely a lunatic. What do you want with him?'

'You were in church yesterday.'

'Oh. Oh, yes.' He put down the quill and sheet of paper on which he had been completing a stave. 'Yes, I had actually forgotten about his performance then. It does put rather a . . . look on things. Well, if you want to speak to him then good luck finding him. From what I can tell he sleeps under bushes.' He chuckled. 'I did spot him last week in one of the hay barns but he is just as likely to be in Toulon or Seville or in your bed right now, for that matter. I would try thinking of the one place you would never think of, and then look there. That is where he will undoubtedly be.'

'I thank you for your advice.'

'Do not mention it. Just pay me your usual rate.'

'I am afraid it would not even buy your breakfast. What of the other people of the village? Do any of them act strangely?'

He dipped his quill thoughtfully in the ink. 'I will tell you one thing: I work at night when it is quiet. Sometimes, if I want to be inspired to compose a dark and stormy piece, I go to the roof to look up at the black sky. And more than once I have been up there and seen that Gypsy boy, Jacob, creeping about outside the chateau. No reason to be there that I know of. It always seems to be around eleven o'clock.'

'Is that right?'

'It is. And now,' he said with perfect lightness, 'I will throw in one last piece of advice.'

'Please do.'

'It is to stay away from my wife.' My expression did not change. 'Now, that sounds like a threat and I do not mean it to be. After all, you are the hero of the battlefield, I am just a poor music scholar. What could I do to you?' He opened his arms. 'No, it really is advice. She will not do you any good at all.'

'I am curious,' I said, 'as to whether you ever gave the King the same advice.' He made no answer, but went back to his composition.

Advice. It comes in many forms. I wish I were better at taking it. Most commonly, it is after the door has closed behind me that I realize I should have stayed outside. For the time being, I concentrated on Archer's information rather than his suggestion.

I found the hay barn where he had spotted Cotillard and entered warily - for sure it was highly possible that he was the one who had attacked Father Dollet so brutally. If it turned out that Cotillard were the guilty party, I would make him pour blood and tears of regret before I handed him to Francois for the law's own reproach.

A strong smell of damp wafted around me as I entered the barn. Bales of straw were stacked in one corner but there was no sign of human habitation. I stepped outside and blinked in the low afternoon sun, to refresh my lungs if nothing else. Then my brow furrowed and I returned to the stack of bales in the corner of the room. There was something about the arrangement. The main deposit was stacked to form a neat plateau at the top and if you looked at the pile the right way, what looked at first sight like a cascade of bales beside it could otherwise be seen as a series of steps to the top. I climbed up, the grass proving itself quite sturdy under my foot.

At the summit I found a series of human possessions: a few mismatched clothes including some breeches, a hair shirt and something grey that resembled a nun's wimple - none of which I believed Cotillard had bought - and personal items such as a pocket book and quill pens. Here he was, living in an eyrie like an eagle, and stealing like a magpie. What was possessing him to take these items? They were surely of no practical use. I suspected it was something deeper: perhaps a need to connect with people, taking something that contained their essence. It was not malicious, but it was strange. What bearing it had on the death of Father Dollet, however, was yet to be discovered.

Descending from the height, I made out a sound: soft

reedy notes from an instrument coming and going indolently with the drifting breeze. I would hear a pair, then nothing. Then a full phrase with a gentle and undemanding rhythm, followed by silence. I stopped to listen properly but it seemed that whenever I was still and straining to hear, I could detect nothing. I drifted out the door in pursuit of it. It was coming from the direction of the river.

Walking down to the copse-lined flowing water, I heard it more clearly - it was a pretty melody.

The source, I soon found, was on the other bank. From where I was, I saw again the dark girl. She was playing a clarinet on the other side of the water and had placed sheets of what I presumed were music on a rock in front of her. I waited, listened, could make neither head nor tail of the music - it could have been modern or old - but found it quite pleasant leaning against a tree trunk and forgetting for a few minutes about my quest and the ugliness at the top of the hill behind me. After a while the deep vertical scores on the bark began to ache into my muscles so I shifted to find a new spot. As I did so the music ended abruptly and I saw the girl shade her eyes from the sun to peer in my direction.

'Hello?' she called over uncertainly.

I was a little sheepish for having been discovered in my surreptitious audience. 'Hello,' I replied. She froze for a moment, then hurriedly began to dismantle her instrument and gather the sheets. 'No need, mademoiselle, I assure you.' She stopped for a moment, and seemed to recognize me as I came closer, but said nothing. There was no bridge but someone had piled stepping stones in the river, which was so low in volume now that they were only just below the surface. I stepped on the first, then the second, which wobbled under my weight but I regained my balance. The third was fine and it was only when I came to the fourth that I slipped and sat down in the water up to my midriff. The girl chuckled. 'Thank you, mademoiselle,' I said, crawling out, my breeches sagging.

'Watch you do not fall, maître. The water is deeper than it looks.' Like her employer, she had an English accent, though hers was softer - as if she too was of the countryside.

'Is that a fact?'

'You tell me.'

'It is a nice place to practise,' I said, shaking my legs.

'You look like a dog after it has gone swimming.'

I quietly abandoned all plans at retaining my dignity. 'You see,' I said. 'I just tried to change the subject, and there you go changing it back again.'

I think she had had her fun. 'You are right, maître. Yes. It is a nice place to practise.'

I took off my shoes and poured out a stream of water. That was the end of those shoes. They were not for country wear, it seemed. 'Although inside would be safer,' I muttered.

'In some ways.'

My ears pricked up. 'Is there some way it is more dangerous?' Perhaps it is a failing of my legal brotherhood that we always look for the thorn on the rose.

She looked down. 'No.' But she smiled and relented. 'I am not supposed to play this.' She held up her clarinet.

'Is it not yours?'

'Oh, yes, it is mine. But Monsieur Archer says it is a vulgar instrument fit only for peasant weddings. He thinks that I am practising this.' She pointed to what I thought was a viola at her feet.

It was my turn to laugh. 'Well, I do not know anything

about music so I will take his word for it. But if you want to play at peasant weddings, then I say go ahead and practise.' I saw her reaction. 'Oh, I am sorry, I did not mean it like that. I think you should play whatever you want to play.' I sat on the rock, angling my legs towards the sun so they would benefit from the heat. They would still be sopping, but they would be warmer. I had enjoyed a while's distraction from my cause, and wanted to eke out a few more seconds of it. 'You know who I am?' I asked.

'Yes.'

'You know what I am doing?'

She spoke quietly. 'Yes.' She sat on the grass and drew her knees into her chest.

'Do you know anything that can help me?'

'No.' She did not meet my gaze. That is always the simplest sign of something to hide.

'You were in the house last night?' I asked.

'Yes. Just as every night. With Madame Juliana. After dinner she sang while I accompanied her on the harpsichord, and her son, Charles, practised until we went to our bed chambers. It was like any other night.'

'What can you tell me about your employer?'

'Monsieur Archer?'

'That is him.'

'He is . . . good to me.'

I waited for a moment, but there was no more coming. 'How did you come into his employ?' I asked.

'When I was a girl, I lived on a farm near Cambridge. But our animals did not do well and there was not enough food for us all so I left for the city. I sold drinks and oranges at our opera house and I saw his wife sing. There was no one like her.' A light shone in her eyes. 'No, not Charlotte Brent, not even the great castratos Farinelli and Marchesi who were courted by kings - they could not hold a note to her. There will never be another like Juliana. Then, when I went to London, I presented myself to them at their door. I had this in my hand.' She lifted her clarinet. 'I said I would be her maid for no more than my lodging. Monsieur Archer laughed at me and said that if I broke my clarinet in two, he would take me. That was twelve years ago. I have hardly been away from them for more than a day since.'

'And are they good to you?'

'I can't think of anywhere else in the world I would rather be.'

'Your French is very good.'

'They made me learn it. Every day, two hours. Then we came to live here eight years ago.'

'So, you were all together last night?'

'Yes, maître. Madame Juliana and I share a room and Monsieur Archer is in a room further down the corridor. Charles has a room below ours.'

'I have failed to ask your name.'

'Catherine.'

'And you may call me David.'

'Maître Sévine, I am sure.'

I did not want to embarrass the girl. 'If you prefer. What was it you were playing?'

'Mozart.'

'Mozart?'

'You have not heard of him?' She seemed incredulous.

'His name rings a bell.' It was a distant one but I didn't want to look a philistine in front of the girl, especially since she had just laughed at me falling into the river. So I just smiled.

Silly vanity.

*

A vole rustled into the undergrowth. At least I thought it was a vole, a black creature is hard to identify when the sun has long since gone down. The remainder of the day had passed and Francois and I were wearing dark capes on either side of a thin, pale tree trunk looking up at the stars. I checked my watch: a silver German timepiece that was the only thing of value my father had ever given me. It said it was a few minutes before eleven.

'Women?' asked Francois.

'None for a long time.' I shut the watch tight and placed it back in my pocket.

'Then I should take you to Madame Celine's in Versailles some time. Nice girls. Clean. They serve most of the court. They say the Prince of Conde likes to dress in girl's clothing for it.'

'It does not surprise me.'

I could hear a pause as Francois worked up to a question. 'Do you think you will ever marry?'

I watched a night bird flap its wings through the leaves. It appeared a ghostly white that seemed to glow in contrast to the dark, and then flitted away. 'No. I do not think so,' I said.

'Would you be open to it?'

'Francois, if you are proposing to me, then you have not thought this through.'

He chuckled and gently thumped me in the back. I was saved from having to more fully address Francois's point by a movement in the house of the Gypsies. The dark door shimmered with a shape that became a figure in the very dim light afforded by a half-moon and the stars. Francois and I presumed - hoped - it was Jacob, but we could not be certain. We saw him walk twenty paces along the path before an oil lamp sparked up and the silhouette told us it was indeed the son of the house who was going for a stroll in the fields surrounding Lorne at eleven o'clock at night, as Archer had suggested was his strange - perhaps guilty - habit, which the Englishman had witnessed on previous nights.

The fact that he was holding the only source of light for leagues meant it was easy to watch him from a distance. As he took the path to the village we wondered if he was heading for the church or perhaps the hovel of another peasant. But then he turned off the path and went through the gap in the hedge that led down the hillside towards the chateau.

We kept a long way behind him. Indeed, we could not in truth tell which direction he was facing at any moment. He tramped and stumbled down past the disturbed sheep, one of which sprang up and trotted to the far corner of the grazing ground, causing the others to follow. Their grubby white coats looked like a strange sea wave breaking on a beach.

Soon he was at the river's edge and stealthily crossing the bridge, after closing the lamp's shutters so that only the thinnest beam showed him where to walk. 'Why did he do that?' whispered Francois.

'Too close to the house. Might be seen - especially on the bridge.' We were now about a hundred yards behind him.

'Should we cross too?'

'No, let us see where he goes first,' I said.

We stayed low on our side of the river and watched him go around to the western wing and sit down on the grass. 'What is he doing?' Francois asked.

'I would bet you a hundred livres he is looking up at that room.' I pointed to the last window still lit from the inside. 'Whose is it?'

The baron burst into a supressed sniggering. 'My scullery maid, Alice. Oh dear. Oh, my Lord! We nearly lost a night's sleep to watch a love-struck adolescent moon over a kitchen girl. Oh, for the love of all that is holy, let us go to bed before he starts writing bad poetry.' He stood up from his crouching position. 'Come on, I have had enough of watching Romeo. And I agree that Juliet is a peach worth the plucking but I intend to observe from the comfort of my bed from now on.'

I remained where I was. 'You go, I am not tired. I think I will stay here and take the night air.' It was a warm night and I had no objection to seeing some more of it.

'Oh, as you wish. Well, now I will have to go the long way around across the stone bridge. All right, old man, I will see you tomorrow.'

'Sleep well.'

As my friend groped his way across the turf, dirtying his shoes with pellets of sheep dung, I laughed at myself. Not everything in Lorne carried sinister meaning, it seemed.

I had soon had enough of this romantic vigil, though, and thought it time to head for my own mattress. I stood, shook some blood into my thighs and worked out the path to return. As I made my first step, however, I saw Jacob also get up. The thin beam from his lamp turned towards me and I had but a moment to throw myself down onto the ground and pull my cape over me. I stayed still, lifting only the corner of the material so that I could watch the progress of the spark drifting through the landscape. It moved back over the bridge, up the slope, following the tracks it had made in the other direction. It came within fifty yards of me, then thirty yards, then ten. I was hardly scared of the young man but it would be easier for me if the villagers were not on their guard about being secretly observed. He came within five yards, and then passed, making no sign of having seen me. I waited until the glimmer from the lamp was almost at the crest of the hill before I stood up. The glow reached the path at the top and began to move along it, but it did not turn right as it would need to in order to reach the boy's rough home. It turned left and continued into the village.

His brassy lamplight illuminated doorways and glinted on windows, all shuttered. One or two had candlelight peeping through cracks in the shutters, but it was now near midnight and no one looked out. The shadows thrown by the lamp looked, if anything, like the ghosts of three hundred years of past residents being born, marrying, multiplying and dying. I hung back; the hard ground of the street could betray me more easily than the turf and cow dung of before.

We reached the church, which was locked and the key in Francois's strongbox. My brow darkened even in the night as the boy turned up to the door. He placed the palm of his hand upon it as if trying to divine what lay within, then he took a step back and looked up at the tower, the great iron bell swaying gently despite the lack of breeze at ground level. I saw him flinch and the glow from his lamp sped towards the gravestones at the side of the church. Dimly I was aware that my hands had become fists. There was a movement. A shadow thrown by the lamp hit a gravestone and warped onto the ground where it blended into the darkness behind a more elaborate tomb. I tensed my calves and put my weight on the balls of my feet. I waited, as did Jacob, but there was nothing more. A stray dog, perhaps. The lamp was shone around the churchyard but all was empty.

The boy hung his head before he set off again on his previous path, away from his home.

Once beyond the last house of the village, the way wound down the other side of the hill into open countryside. Farm animals lay sleeping in enclosures and grazing pastures. It was nearly an hour of walking through the night before we reached the road from Versailles to Paris. The beams from Jacob's lamp turned in a full circle and I had to fall flat behind a ridge in the ground and pull my cloak around me in order not to be found out. Then I heard a soft shoe step.

I watched as three men - I presumed they were men - arrived from the direction of Versailles. Unlike Jacob they carried no lamp, but just like him they made no sound. They met without words and, without ceremony, returned to the road. Once they had melted into the gloom, I followed quickly lest any others come. The darkness allowed me to remain undetected behind the men I was following, but Jacob's lantern meant I could see them still, I just had to keep my footsteps quiet. And as we moved off, our destination was clear. We were for Paris.

We walked for another hour or two. First, we saw sleeping inns. Then a few large but decrepit houses, summer residences for dandies who had been bankrupted by our wars of the last century. After that, dirt roads became cobbled streets with open gutters swishing along the rats and their feed. Great piles of manure sent a miasma into our noses, whipped up by a sudden sharp wind that belied the season. By day these streets were crowded with hawkers of food and clothes worn by five or six before you. They were streets where you kept one hand on your purse and the other on your breeches lest you be relieved of one or the other. But by this hour even the unluckier thieves had gone home, and bare-teethed dogs fought over scraps. A warped and cracked blacksmith's sign swung in the wind, slowly screeching out its presence. The sound of cartwheels on nearby cobbles conjured for me - I do not know why - the image of a body being taken from a house. It was by now close to three in the morning and I was foot-sore and beginning to wonder if this moonlit excursion was worth the trouble. How far into this belly of the French empire would we travel?

Soon houses of six storeys high were abutting each other. Even the bridges across the brown Seine were crowded with them, so that the occupants could look out onto that flow of muddy water speckled with waste and corpses. We passed the new Ecole Militaire, an impressive building with its clean, strong lines, edging the green Champ de Mars that had already hosted many a ragged crowd shouting for change.

And finally, here was our destination: tucked into a lane, an inn with a single candle alight in a dirty lower window. I stayed back and watched my quarry enter the stable to the side. I was tense, desperate to discover the purpose of this footpad union.

Creeping forward, I put my eye to a knot in the wood. Acrid smoke, from a pipe rather than a fire, filtered out, making me blink painfully when I tried to look through it.

'He is right!' I heard snapped through the wood. It was a man's voice - young, but I did not think it was Jacob.

'He is wrong. It will do more harm than good.'

'It is worth the chance.' This one, I believed, could well be the young man I had been following.

'Have you calculated the risk?'

'Yes.'

'Do not be absurd. What do you know? Child!'

'I would rather be a child than an old man to whom no one should give a second thought until his funeral.' The wood of the wall shuddered harshly as something slammed into it. 'Is that it?'

'Jacob!' said another voice, smoothing the ruffled feathers.

'I was not the one who tried to throttle my brother.' I turned this over in my head. Did Jacob have a brother? It could not be the old man, so which of the other denizens of this rude hut had tried to strangle him in the past ten seconds? Then a different connotation of brotherhood formed in my mind.

'Let us move to another matter,' said the emollient voice.

'Gladly.'

'"Gladly" says the child,' muttered the old voice.

'Albert, please.'

'All right, all right.'

'The demands.'

'Yes, yes. The demands. All the good they will do.' That was definitely Jacob.

'Are they all finished?'

'All bundled up nicely in a little scroll tied with dainty red lace with pictures painted on it.' Jacob, once more.

'Is he serious?' asked the old man.

'Of course I am not serious. It is a piece of paper. Folded once, if you want to know.'

I had counted four voices but had seen none of the speakers. I searched along the wood until I found a break between the planks. Smoke hissing out scratched at my irises but I saw that there were more men in there - perhaps ten in total. Most speech was from the four in the centre of the room: Jacob; a grizzled-looking white-head who needed someone to shave him; and two others who looked like smallholders - hefty arms but underfed. The room itself was a cypher - the short tallow candle barely illuminated their faces, outside their circle there was only gloom.

Jacob turned away from the others to face the wall behind which I was hiding. I drew back quickly. My heart beat harder against my chest; if these men were desperate, they were dangerous. 'Is this it, then?' muttered the young man. 'With history and right on our side, with all that is happening throughout this nation, we are to write words on a paper and no more?'

I wondered what, if anything, this had to do with the death of Father Dollet. I was beginning to suspect that the answer was 'nothing at all' and I had wasted a night's sleep.

A new voice spoke nervously. 'Step by step. Why rush into this? We do not need to throw ourselves into the river. Anything could happen.'

'We sound more like the aristocrats and less like ourselves by the day,' said Jacob.

So, my suspicion had hit the mark. Not murder, but political fervour.

'Revolutionary' was a word that was starting to appear on some lips. Could it find a place here? Perhaps it could.

These men were the sleeping members of the Third Estate. They were the countless poor of the towns and villages; few able to afford meat, far fewer able to read. But they were whispering to each other, encouraging one another to make demands. They wanted their bellies full, their children no longer subject to the whims of their feudal masters. They had never before thought of change, but now that their wealthier cousins - the doctors, the lawyers, the grain-sellers - were talking of grabbing some power for themselves in the land, the country mice were beginning to have ideas of their own. Could they rise up in their teeming masses? I had seen the self-same men and women in Virginia don uniforms and wield guns to face down a royal master and a class of nobles who saw them as no more than fodder. The first stage of rebellion was always this: men at night in a smoky room, talking, combining and planning.

And this was exactly what de Rotanne and his ilk feared most: the spread of ideals from the lawyers to the weavers. Lawyers could be paid off with a few livres. The roadmakers and ostlers before me tonight were harder to buy because they were a sea of starving anger.

Jacob was clearly for direct action - a description that covered a multitude of sins - but those who opposed him wanted to write peaceful petitions to the King. I knew Jacob's method was likely to fail and the other approach was utterly guaranteed to do so. But no one was asking me.

No, instead the brothers talked for an hour. Always Jacob was in favour of action, always Albert was in favour of their group sitting on their hands. Always the third man, who did not swear as much as the fourth man, was in favour of writing things down and 'seeing what comes'.

The group finally broke up - without any strong resolution that I could identify. If France's myriad of other political groups and clubs were the same, nothing would ever change in this nation. That would be a tragedy that only history could judge. A part of me wanted to get into this room and wring some sense into those who wanted to 'wait and see' if things changed without anyone pushing it. That would hardly have been politic at this juncture. After bidding each other farewell, the men left at one-minute intervals, clearly nervous for their security. Jacob was the last to depart, placing on his head the red bonnet that I had first seen him wear outside the church. I followed a short while later, stalking out along an alleyway, and thinking of my bed at the chateau.

I saw the ripple in the shadow beside me just in time to avoid the fist cracking into my temple. It passed by close enough to feel the air on my skin. I was lucky my assailant was unpractised in close combat and he had gone for my head when a blow to the body would have been more reliable in the dark. Hardly seeing him, I brought my elbow into the mass that I could sense to my side. It connected hard and he fell on his rump, splayed across a cart - he must have been hiding behind it to launch his attack. Surprising me, however, he did not stay down but leaped up again like a farm cat and it was all I could do to pin him to the ground. It was Jacob, I could just make out in the starlight. This would teach me not to consider youths defenceless creatures.

'Who are you?' he growled as he struggled hard against my grip.

'Sévine.' He went limp and muttered a strong oath. I could tell there was no more danger to be had from him and relaxed my arm. I offered a hand up. He took it. Without a lamp it was near pitch-black, so I tried to discern from his breathing how he stood, and how we stood together. 'I am not working for the King, the Duc d'Orléans or any of them, so you need not worry,' I told him.

'I know you are not. They would hardly employ a man unable to keep his voice down when watching a man's house,' he muttered. 'Yes, yes, I heard you both outside my house, discussing the baron's favourite brothel.'

Well, that was somewhat shaming. 'So, if you knew we were there, why come here?'

'I thought you left me at the chateau. I saw you leave.'

'You saw one of us leave.'

'Next time I will count the footsteps.' He found his cap on the ground, brushed the black city grime from it and lifted it to his head.

'That would be better for you,' I told him. Now that we were clear, I found his annoyance rather amusing.

'What did you hear?' he asked.

'Enough.'

'Will you inform the baron?'

His air of unconcern was clearly a bluff. The law and the caprices of his seigneur could do him much harm for the night's activities.

'As far as I can tell, you have not - yet - done anything illegal. Your group of friends likes to meet in stables in the middle of the night. It is not my preference, but I do not think prison is the answer.'

He paused. I knew he was appraising me, my words, my intentions. The night seemed pregnant with ideas and danger. Throughout the city, there were other meetings like his. 'You could join us,' he said carefully, cautiously.

And for a moment, I was tempted. The rot in our land had to be excised, I was sure. But I had had enough of the fights to bring such a catharsis. In America, I had too often seen the sour side of great victories. 'I am a man who cannot be quiet when spying, remember?'

He huffed and looked along the lane. 'You will be more use than Jean or Christophe with their endless petitions. And a devil of a lot more use than Albert. As if the King has ever even considered granting the Third Estate any of our needs. He will agree to changes and then when all is settled, quietly forget them. All that these papers will do is fuel the fires underneath his bath.'

'Let us imagine you are correct.' He was, of course. 'What is your plan instead?'

'We must unite. Organize. Seize the day. Find others who understand their own plight and don't just say that it is God's will that their children's stomachs bloat with air through lack of bread and meat.'

In the still air Jacob and I looked out through the veins of France. There were no lights to be seen. I knew that the boy to my left wanted to change that. He could not know on what level we shared beliefs. All creatures attract those like them, perhaps.

'Son, do not judge those people too harshly. Two decades from now, when your nose has been rubbed in the self-same dirt year by year, you might well think the same as them.'

'I fear I will. But I hope I will not. My God, there are some devils in this land!'

That word made me stop. 'What do you mean?'

'Gluttonous lords who eat in a day what we have to eat in a month, and have us turned out of our homes if we ask for a crust more. They are devils, for sure.'

'I thought you meant something else,' I said. I was, in fact, somehow relieved to understand his more innocent meaning.

'What do you mean?'

It was my turn to hesitate. 'Josette, Father Dollet's housekeeper, believes there are witches about. She points her finger to them for the murder of Father Dollet.'

'Witchcraft?' He sounded surprised. 'I give it little credence myself.'

'But there are many who believe fervently.'

'Well, yes.' He hesitated. 'There was a woman who lives out in the woods. In Lorne. She claims she can cast spells if you pay her enough. Probably mad. I have no idea if she is still there. Mother Bassot, or Bassette I think.'

'Thank you.' I would have to speak to this Mother Bassot or Bassette. Was she wrapped up in the mystery? Perhaps. Or perhaps she could shine a lamplight upon it.

I filled my lungs with the city's foul air. I had learned something tonight, something about France and where the country was heading. I had learned that even in the most modest village in a backwater of France, there were men who were plotting rebellion. Their numbers were small, they were surrounded by those who feared a direct assault on all that they knew, but they were there. And they were spreading from town to village, village to town.

Still, it was a way off the strange and bloody affair I was probing - at least, it appeared so in those dark hours - and I needed sleep to refresh my brains. I would have a full day on the morrow. 'It is a long way home and I am already ready for my bed,' I said wearily. He too was in need of sleep. We set off on the long walk back to a village at the heart of broken and blooded France.

21 June 1789

Upon rising the next morning, my mind was still muddy as a farmyard from interrupted sleep. But as I left my chamber, I became aware that the mud was being pierced. Delicate notes, almost metallic, were blowing through the air, growing as I neared their source. The door of the music room was ajar again. I was about to knock on it when it swung slowly away from me. Juliana Archer was at the harpsichord, playing and humming words in Italian to herself.

I entered to see that there were many instruments all around - flutes, a viola, and a pianoforte. She paid no attention to me, continuing her humming. I stepped forward to the very centre of the room and still she made no acknowledgement of anyone but her and the ghostly composer of the words she was singing. Behind me I heard a rustling and turned to see the skirts of Catherine flow out the room. Then she stopped, glanced back at me and smiled. I could not help but return that smile. It was a reflex that came from a part of me that did not think, only felt. Then she was gone. 'Good morning, maître,' I heard called from halfway down the stairs.

'Good morning,' I replied, not knowing if I was speaking loudly enough for it to reach her.

I must have been, because a further 'I trust you will have a pleasant day' drifted up from somewhere more distant.

For a moment, I could not recall why I had come to the room. My mind was fixed on the swishing skirt and the smile that had flashed.

I took a moment to return to my thinking being. 'Madame Archer . . .'

She held up the index finger of her right hand without looking at me. Then it dropped to the keyboard to execute what I realized must have been a complex piece of work even for an expert performer. As it ended in a waterfall of notes her face burst up and threw itself back in laughter. I studied her eyes; they were a pale blue in the powdered white. 'Is it not divine, Maître Sévine? Is not Gluck to be worshipped like a god?' She rose and held out her hand. 'It is Madame Juliana, not Archer.' I kissed her fingers and waited for her to sit again, but she did not. Instead, she went to the window where I had seen her twice before - once in a painting and once in person. I saw the powdered cheek in just the same place as before, then she turned her smile to me. 'I have heard a little of you. Do you enjoy music?'

'I know very little of it.'

She stopped dead. 'Then we will have to teach you.' She began to play again. 'What would a man like you enjoy?'

'I have heard of Mozart.'

Her smile erupted. 'That is a good start. A once-in-a-lifetime talent, Herr Mozart. And he is coming into his finest work now, I feel. A good place to start . . . Ah!' Her fingers froze, then started moving again on a different work. It had a strangely thudding rhythm, handfuls of chords followed by lightly skipping notes. 'His *Sonata No.* 14 *in C minor*. An easy one to start with. So, this will be your first lesson. What do you think when you hear it?'

I was at a loss.

'Close your eyes and see it as a play.'

I did so.

'What is happening on stage?'

'I see a villain pursuing his quarry.'

'Ha!' she cried. 'Excellent. That is perfect. Not what I see, but an excellent interpretation. We will make a maestro of you yet. You came across him in Versailles?'

'Yes,' I said. I had no trouble lying. I suspected she was no stranger to it in her time.

'It would be an honour for me to sing before him. Well, perhaps one day. When we are no longer ignored by the King.' She burst into laughter. 'For now, we must act as rustics and dance among the fields.'

'The girl,' I said.

'Catherine?'

'That is her. Do you treat her well?'

Juliana laughed again. 'Why, you are quite the knight in shining armour. We treat her very well. I am fond of her. I can see you are getting that way too.' She stopped playing. 'She came to us as a child, you know. She is a woman now. Oh, we give her her freedom - my husband even pretends he does not know she plays that terrible folk horn. And she has mentioned you too.' She looked up demurely.

'Oh dear.'

'Now, Maître Sévine, is that the attitude to take when a charming young woman displays her interest in you?'

'Sometimes. You understand that I am attempting to ascertain what happened to Father Dollet?'

'A sad affair,' she said. 'He seemed a gentle man.'

'Did you know him well?'

'Hardly at all. He came to dinner a couple of times during which he spoke about the King's profligacy, which he denounced. I am not fervent in my religious devotions, so had little call on him as a spiritual or moral guide. My husband is more particular about attendance and confession and the like.'

It was not useful information. 'Do you know of anything that could help my enquiry? Have you seen anything out of the ordinary?'

'Absolutely nothing, Maître Sévine. We have not been here long enough to notice anything that would be out of the ordinary. I am sorry to disappoint you.' She lowered the lid on the pianoforte. 'Will you join our stag hunt tomorrow?'

I nodded.

'Good. I will look forward to it.' And at that, she swept out past her portrait above the stairs.

My encounter with Juliana had been curiously unsettling. A magnetic beauty, for certain, and even I could tell that she was a musical talent, but there was something askew about her too. As if we were all just seeing her portrait, and not the true woman behind it.

As I reached the hall, I saw the butler, Peugere, and caught up with him. 'Peugere, I heard something yesterday.'

'Maître?'

'There is a village witch-woman, Mother Bassette or Bassot.' His expression fell into anxiety.

'Mother Bassot?'

'I want you to tell me about her. You look worried.'

'I . . . I am not, maître. It is just . . . what she did.'

'And what *did* she do? That is what I want to know.'

He licked his lips before carefully relating the tale. 'She fell out with Antonin, a farmer close to here. He is a poor man, he has only two fields. He came home one day and found her in his house. She had drawn a circle on the floor, out of chalk, and had set a crucifix in the middle. She had spat on it, maître. He drove her out but she cursed his cows.'

'And?'

'They died vomiting, that night after he fed them. I saw them myself. She admitted it was her work. She called Antonin all manner of hellish names and laughed at him.'

I suspected that there was a more earthly explanation for animals that die vomiting. We need no Lucifer when we can sprinkle lupin or water hemlock into a bale of hay.

But it did occur to me: some people - men, women, children - believed themselves in league with the Devil, just as many more believed themselves in communion with God. If Mother Bassot had happily slaughtered her neighbour's livestock, perhaps to ingratiate herself with Lucifer, it was not out of the question that in time she had enlarged her purview to killing men with the same aim. And the ritualistic and utterly wicked aspect of Father Dollet's death was clear as a spring morning.

'What of her now?'

He avoided my gaze but said nothing. He was hiding something, that much was obvious. I needed to speak to her, to look into her face as I asked her whether my old tutor had died by her hand. 'Peugere, I want to know,' I said more forcefully. He stared at the floor. He was afraid, I could see. 'Take me where she is.'

*

My nerves strained as we walked out across the sun-blanched turf towards the river. I did not fear that a sorceress might enchant me, and hardly more that an old woman might attack me with mortal blows. But I wanted to lay hands on whoever had butchered a good man. If she were evasive or held her tongue, I would force the truth from her using all the methods I knew.

The water was teeming faster than three days before. I could see fish below the surface, spurting with the current. Wordlessly, Peugere led me on, tramping through bracken and between rabbit holes. Despite his age, he set a good pace, surefooted from a lifetime of walking that ground.

For close to an hour we walked, and with every step I wondered more where we were heading. We left the village and Francois's home well behind, out of sight entirely, behind a bend in the river valley. The plants grew wilder and trees sprouted around us, moistening the air. Eventually, well into the forest, our path only denoted by the course of the river itself, we crossed through a small clearing and found ourselves staring into a deep silty pool fed by the river, but languid and still, as if waiting. The place had an oppressive air, secluded from most of the light. Beside us was a small rocky outcrop over the water. For the first time since we had left the house, Peugere looked at me and I knew he was troubled to be here.

I waited for him to explain. Then I grew impatient. 'Peugere, I want to see Mother Bassot.'

He looked confused. 'But I have brought you, maître.'

I scanned for a hovel or even a shack in the trees. Nothing. 'Where is she now?'

'Now?'

'Yes.'

'Why, in there.' He pointed to the silty pool. My heart froze. 'They bound her hands and feet. A year or two ago.'

They had drowned her. By fire or water, a witch's life had to be forfeit. So, screaming and spitting, no doubt, she had been lowered into the pool to fill her lungs with silt. My God.

By the sound of it, her guilt for the death of her neighbour's livestock was certain. But she had had no part in the death of Father Dollet, that was even more certain.

And yet the manner by which justice for her true crimes had been exacted was vile. Are we not better than that? Have we not moved since the mediaeval times? For two years this woman's flesh had rotted in that water, torn by fish and all the creeping creatures that span the land and water. Denied a burial as well as a trial.

Peugere beckoned me to the outcrop of rock and bent down. He plucked at something and I saw there was a rope, tied to a metal pin that had been hammered into the stone. The rope trailed under the water. I did not need to ask what horrific remembrance of a crime was on the other end of it. What a foul charnel house that place seemed to me.

'What should we do?' Peugere asked me simply. He trusted that I, an educated man, would have the answer to such a question. I was not so sure - how many people had been in such a place and known the right course of action? He lifted the rope and put it in my hand. I tested it. It was slack for now. Unsure, but unable to avoid trying, I pulled it towards myself. Slowly, it became taut, straightening into the air, dripping cold liquid back into the water below. I reasoned that I should have confirmation that this was true, not some false rumour or misdirection.

I tightened my grip. I could feel tension in the line - something heavy on the end beginning to move. As Peugere watched, a look of worry creeping across his features, I pulled the rope's load towards us. Whatever it was, was long dead and I had no fear of it. But it was sickening to think that on this line was a rack of bones that had once caged a life.

The water above it moved as it came closer to the bank. Spurts and waves erupted. And before I knew it, the pool was spewing up the dead, as a horrifying mass of grey hair gripping a yellow skull broke through the surface. The rope had been tied around her neck and a head devoid of flesh or humanity was now in the air for the first time since the witch had been thrown into the cold water. We were staring into the empty orbits that had once held her eyes.

She had once believed she could summon the Devil's spirit. Now she could not even summon her own.

Peugere groaned deeply at the sight. He, like I, carried the guilt of knowing. We stood, my hands numbing on the wet rope.

'What now, maître?'

'Now?' Now that I had seen for certain what the local superstition could provoke, the animal within us all that the law attempts to bind into courts and warrants, there was little to do but leave her to her grave. Little but that. 'Now we cut the rope and let her sink.' I let the line slip through my palms. And her bones slipped back into her grave. But the greatest, most dangerous question had not yet been asked. 'Who did it?'

'Who did it?' He looked at me with confusion, unable to comprehend that I could not see. 'Why the village, maître. Antonin's family starved without their cows. He has eight children - now they beg on the road. And she was a witch. So the village did it.'

My vision fixed on the ripples in the water. The village did it - whether it was one of them or all, they did it as one. The village of my childhood that I had once thought of as a peaceful and simple place. It had come together to tie and drown an old woman. And that was the moment that I realized I truly knew nothing of the country.

I began to dread what else I would find if I stared into dank copses and lifted rotting trunks.

'Did the baron know?' I asked.

'No.' He looked sheepish. 'He was not told. I knew nothing myself until months later.'

'Do not tell him now,' I said. I was uncertain if I would take that task on myself or simply leave the bones to sink in peace.

I was in no mood to talk as we started away from that desolate, oppressive place. There were primaeval forces at work there: fear and hatred rooted in a cutthroat nature that I could not understand or grasp. I felt as if I had waded out into the sea, only to find the waves higher and the tide faster than I had thought. Men drowned that way.

And my mind went back to what Peugere had said: 'The village did it.'

A collective act. Sometimes, when men bind together, they will perform acts that, alone, they would find mad or abhorrent. *The village did it.*

I looked sideways at Peugere. I was about to ask him a hard question. What else had 'the village' done? What was it capable of?

But I kept those words caged.

Walking back through the small clearing, I noticed something I had not seen there before: at its edge was a curious pile of stones. They had been placed by human hand - a small regular three-sided pyramid, each side three stones long. And poking between the stones, animal bones boiled or picked quite clean. At once a look of anger darkened Peugere's face and he kicked the stones apart.

'What is it?'

'A familiar's cairn,' he muttered in reply.

'A what?' I could not take my eyes from the pile of rock and bones.

'Witches are attended by familiars. Bird or cat spirits. They live in such cairns and follow you to your home.' He stared all around, distressed. 'They are strong. They can throw a man to his death.'

I wondered if I had not previously seen that shrine, or if it had not been there prior to our presence. No, I was certain it had not been there before. Someone had followed in our wake and set it there for us to find.

'Are there others like Mother Bassot?'

He glanced at me, then into the trees. He knew who I meant by 'others'. He nodded. So she might be rotting in the foul water but that did not mean that the witches were gone from Lorne. What had they to do with Father Dollet? I would have to drag that truth from its own mire.

Francois had first asked me to come back to Lorne because some of the local girls had talked of seeing or meeting witches. With all the arrogance of a Versailles courtier, I had scoffed at the idea. But now the laughter had drained away and I needed to ask him what he had been told. I strode back to the house as quickly as I could. But I was to be disappointed.

Chapter Five

I froze hard, as an icy hand grabbed the back of my neck. Astaroth snatched the papers from my grip and glared first at me, then at his comrade. I feared that this would be the end of me. But Astaroth's fury did not fall on my head. He extended a dirty finger at Roberto. 'I shall put a knife in your belly for this,' he growled. And I believed him. I think we both did. Then, glaring still like a demon, he slid the chapbook into his jerkin, looked outside the window to see light rain coming down, and declared: 'It is time.'

At that, I was led hobbling outside onto the windy cliff. A spray from the ocean bathed our faces, coating us in salt and stinging my eyes. 'This way,' ordered Astaroth, gripping my shirt and dragging me along a path between the hilltop houses. But the fetters on my legs made the going so slow that Astaroth became frustrated. 'I shall release you, but if you run, I shall shove you over to break on the rocks,' he warned. I believed him entirely, and put any such thought from my mind. Between an uncertain fate and certain death, I chose the slight possibility of survival. 'When we are in the boat, stay still and quiet. It is three days' sail and I want to hear no crying upon the journey. And none when you get there, either. The Circle will be less forgiving than me, I warn you.' At another time, the strangeness of his last sentence would have given me cause to question it, but then and there I had more present dangers on my mind.

He unlocked the chains and they fell away, revealing welts forming in my flesh, which smarted with the salt spray. The path led through what had been the churchyard, half of which had fallen into the waves along with the church itself, leaving long-forgotten gravestones prickling up from the earth like hedgehog spines. Roberto, in front, had a heavy stick that he used to whack grabbing weeds out of the way.

As we walked, those two stared out to sea, where the rain seemed darker and heavier than inland, on the guard at all times. We were between two headstones no more than a foot from the edge of the cliff when Roberto suddenly halted hard and pressed his finger to his lips. Astaroth, like a cat, tensed, glaring into the wet shadows, ready for anything. After a moment, Roberto spoke in a low voice. 'That game of dice,' he said.

'What?' the fallen angel retorted.

'You thieved all my money.'

And at that, by the light of the stars, Astaroth and I caught sight of Roberto's furious face and then his heavy stick whirling around to strike his commander on the cheek with all his might. The fallen angel roared in pain and staggered backwards to the limit of the land. His rearmost foot floundered in the air, trying for solid ground but finding only a void. He wheeled his arms, grabbing at nothing but the rain, and a thrust of Roberto's staff sealed his fate, driving him over the edge. It all happened so quick, and yet seemed so slow, that I recall every change in Astaroth's expression, from shock to rage to a sort of resolve as he fell.

And yet. Yet! I was wrong. He was not done! For as he slipped down towards the surging sea, his strong hands clapped onto a soaked headstone that projected from the last inch of England. With an oath of fury, he held there, shouting death to Roberto and demanding that I aid him. Even if I had not been rooted to the spot by fear, I doubt I would have gone to help the man who just seconds earlier had been leading me to an unknown but surely foul fate.

'No man thieves from me!' crowed Roberto, dropping to the ground to tear his comrade's hands from the wet stone. But still the fallen angel was not beaten, and instead of fighting to retain his grip, unlatched his fingers and wound them into Roberto's damp jerkin, drawing him to the terrible edge. As he did so, by the light of the moon I caught sight on the inside of his right wrist of something stained into the flesh: what sailors and soldiers called a 'tattoo'. It was a circle picked out in blue-green ink, bulging with the effort in his muscle.

'What say you now?' he cried, above the rising roar of the rain, into Roberto's wan, drenched face.

I scrambled a pace or two away, watching his body swing in the air, held by the gravestone and his new captive's footing. Roberto fought as best he could, but could not disentangle himself. Instead, Astaroth's weight dragged him closer and closer to his own death.

'Let me go!' he screamed, the triumph in his voice having tumbled into the cold depths below.

At that Astaroth's face cracked into laughter; he knew

the fight had turned. 'If I go, you go!' he yelled. And I saw the headstone that was holding them both to the cliff shift in its base, lifting up from the soil. *John Goode. Taken to the Lord December 3rd 1702.* And then it was right out of the ground. Astaroth's hand flew from it to Robert's sleeve and for a moment they both hung in the air like gulls. 'And so we die!' And they were the last words I heard before I watched two faces, milky white in the moonlight, plummet like stones through the rain into the black waves.

I heard nothing above the breaking surf. I saw nothing of their forms in the water. They were no more than the ghosts of the churchyard, wisps that had dissolved into the night.

I staggered backwards, away from the cliff, not knowing what to do. Then I dropped down on my hands and knees like a dog and furtively crawled to the edge to peep over, to make sure they were not water demons flying up at me in some cruel trick to double my terror. But all I saw were waves breaking against the cliff face and the spectral church tower with a bell that now tolled for two more dead.

I turned onto my back, my mouth open, sucking in air and falling water. Was I free? Was I still in danger? Were there others ready to leap out of the shadows to capture me again? I had little idea where I was, and no thought as to what I should do to save my life.

But an instinct for self-preservation is part of our being. And, without an idea, I leapt up, suddenly gripped by the need to run – to sprint as fast as I could as far away as I could make it.

I charged into the dark, through the remnants of

the village – all abandoned and decayed – finding my way by chance to the overgrown road that led to the settlement.

I tramped it for a mile in the dark until the light came on and it met another, greater highway.

I walked that road until I dropped, sobbing, by the roadside, curled into a ball and slipped into sleep.

It took me two days of footsore walking, begging rides, sleeping in ditches and stealing vegetables from cottages to find my way home. I staggered into the Peldon Rose, to the shock of Walter and my friends who were there, and fainted. They revived me with nips of brandy. After gobbling milk and bread, I discovered that the village had been in a minor turmoil since my disappearance. There had been parties sent out to search for me under the watch of Mr Jenkins, the magistrate, but since I had disappeared very far from Mersea itself, the parties had wandered aimlessly and returned empty-handed, without any better thought for what to do. The beadle had been dispatched to neighbouring parishes with a description of my person, but his excursions had been just as fruitless, except in gaining him a few jars of beer to slake his thirst when he came back to the Rose, courtesy of Walter.

'Your schoolmates have been up in arms!' Walter told me. Even in my weakened state, I was sceptical of that claim. They would more likely have been intrigued, excited and, in the case of Fred, perfectly delighted. All in all, it was pressed upon me that I was a child of the village and all the villagers had felt my disappearance as that of their own son or brother.

As soon as Mr Tolson was sent for, and arrived puffed out of breath, I told my tale. Eyes opened wide and jaws fell far. And I had no need to embellish a single fact, for my experience was so astonishing that they were agog at the simplest telling of it.

I was burning to tell my protector of what I had read in the penny blood too, but held back, not wishing to speak of it in company. It seemed too private and dangerous for the open air.

Mr Jenkins was about to raise a hue and cry throughout the kingdom to look for any conspirators in the crime other than those that had fallen from the cliff, but Mr Tolson stayed his hand. Since we still did not understand who was coming for me or why, it might be better to keep quiet, at least for a while.

A hurried conference took place among my friends. Some voices announced that for my protection I should be sent to a safe haven far away in London, or Bristol or even – God help me! – the Australian colonies. Others said I would be safest on Ray, where the sea rose as a moat to keep out intruders. But the presiding voice was always to be my teacher's. After intense consideration, he declared that I should stay at Turnglass House, rather than flit for some ill-defined asylum, because the most dangerous man who was after me was dead, and even if there were more waiting in the wings, my friends could best protect me where they could surround and watch over me. There was assent, though not without some dissent.

For my part, I felt rather lost and at the mercy and whim of others throughout this episode. It was an unmanning and debilitating sensation, like the effects of the drug that had rendered me incapable to defence the day before. I watched the proceedings with the sense that my own preferences would not be so much as heard, let alone entertained. A child of the village? Aye, but a young child at that.

And finally, Mr Tolson took me by the hand and led me once more along the Strood. As soon as we were in Turnglass House, I ran to the schoolroom to show my tutor the item upon so much turned.

'You see?' I demanded.

'See?'

I held in my hand the pocket watch that my mother had carried when she had brought me to the Peldon Rose. My only old possession. A silver German pocket watch, exactly like the one that the narrator of the chapbook owned. 'Maybe he knows who my father is. *Maybe he is my father.*' I whispered the latter sentence, as if speaking it out loud would poison it and it would die.

My teacher's only reply was to silently lead me down to the parlour, ply me with food and water and place me on the settle, where I immediately fell asleep, despite my protests for urgency.

I woke in the morning light to find myself back upstairs in my bed. Mr Tolson and dear Iphigenia were sitting in chairs beside me – my roommates having been banished, to give me a better chance at rest. Even before they had opened their mouths I was babbling of my prized watch and, above all, *The Murderous Deeds in the Village of Lorne in France and How They Brought About the Bloody Revolution.*

'Hush, Lysander,' my benefactor said gently. 'You have been through an ordeal.'

'But . . . but this is . . . this is . . .'

'It is probably nothing. A story that you read. Now, I grant you, there have been events and threats—'

'To me, they were to me!' I did not like the way he

was speaking, as if there had been threats to someone we knew but slightly. 'The story. It is something to do with the story. Roberto said . . .'

'Who is Roberto?'

'The older one. The one who did magic.' He raised his eyebrows. 'I mean the one who did it at the summer fair. He said I should read the chapbook to learn my history.'

'You were very frightened. And understandably so. You could have heard anything.'

'But . . . I did hear that.' I felt the wind going out of my sails. I began, even, to wonder if they were right. Had I, in my terrified, hungry, drugged state, imagined something? I slumped back on the sofa, staring at the timepiece. 'Am I to stay here?'

'You will be safer here. We still do not understand what is behind all this.'

'We will look after you,' Iphigenia added.

I gazed at her.

You might escape me, you cannot escape the Circle.

Astaroth's words rushed back into my head and echoed there like a shout in an empty church. What was the Circle, and what was I to it? To my fourteen-year-old mind, it could have been anything from a body of men to a country, to a grim magical force. But whatever it was, it was a threat to me that I could not see and would not see coming, and I trusted my patron.

I have never regretted doing so. For the first months we – myself, he and our friends in the village – remained vigilant to the point of sleeplessness. Discreetly, Mr Tolson made enquiries too about the penny blood, asking his acquaintances if they knew where we might find a copy, but none had heard of it.

Some days I would stare at the map of Europe on the wall of the schoolroom and try to guess where three days' sail would have taken me if Astaroth had succeeded in his kidnap. Much of the coast of Europe would have been within reach, though, and it proved nothing but empty speculation.

And little by little, our nerves loosened, so that within a year I was back to my usual self.

That usual self was a thoughtful child, a little envious of the other boys who had other homes to go to; at times happy, at times sad. And always, at the rear of my mind, there was a painful absence of self-knowledge.

But I got on with it – what else was there to do? – and grew older and a little wiser as the years rolled past. As my limbs lengthened and my nerves loosened, I put up with less teasing from my schoolmates – who, after a while, drifted away from Turnglass House and joined their parents or went to London or Cambridge. I became quite self-sufficient, in fact, while retaining my loyalty to my first benefactor. And I gained a deepening affection for his daughter that I was sure, in my young man's naivety, I kept as well hidden as Zeus had kept the child Hercules hidden from Hera. I dreamed less, though I spent many hours staring across the dark waters of the sea, and along the road to London, wondering where my future lay.

I began to teach the young pupils who joined the school from time to time, instructing them in grammar, Latin and French, as Iphigenia had instructed me. Over the course of three years, I became something akin to a junior schoolmaster. My hours working thus, however, were not sufficient for my keep and I worked too at the Rose, graduating from wiping the tables to, by the time I was seventeen, serving the beer. I still entertained of a Saturday night, with my renditions of 'The Lincolnshire Poacher' and 'Down Among the Dead Men', and enjoyed the camaraderie of that place, where all were welcome and none were turned away. Good people, forever good people.

The turning time, a day I shall recall always as the recommencement of my adventures, was a Saturday. A man with wide and thick whiskers had entered the inn and taken his drinks to the table. I recognized him as a seller of knives and forks who came to the village every few months. From his speech, I had gained the impression that he had once been of a higher station in life but had been brought a little low by circumstance. That he could read was attested by his voracious consumption of newspapers and social tracts – from my observation, there was rarely a moment when his nose wasn't stuck in one or other of them.

It was on such an occasion in the early summer of eighteen hundred and eight, when I was approaching my eighteenth birthday, that he stumbled in, tripping over the step due to his gaze being glued to a periodical in his hands. I was accustomed to his attention being thus captured and chuckled to myself as he took a cup of beer and went to sit by the chimney that had been my black refuge four years earlier. For a while he supped his drink and turned the pages. I served and cleaned as per my norm, until the work took me over to the inglenook where he stayed. I was wiping down the bench when my eyes caught sight of the front cover of the publication he was reading. And in that instant, my jaw fell quite open. For the cover of that periodical blazed words that had been long-seared into my heart.

The Murderous Deeds in the Village of Lorne in France and How They Brought About the Bloody Revolution. The Second Part.

I stretched out my hand, nervy as a kitten, as if the pages were poison or elixir and I did not yet know which. The hawker peered up at me, curious and confused.

'Do you wish to read it, lad?'

'Yes, sir.' But I was not sure that I did. Four years had passed since I had last traced those letters on a page. Four years for my blood to slow and the memories to fade. Four years for me almost to doubt what I remembered – had it happened? Had it happened the way I recalled? Or had I been a boy whose loneliness had left space for daydreaming and exaggerated impression?

Four years. And now here it was again in my life.

'Are you certain?' There was doubt in his voice.

But his doubt itself hardened my thoughts. *You are seventeen now, you are a man. No longer a child at the mercy of others. Take up your fate in your hands,* I said to myself.

'I am certain.' And I held out my hand. He placed the penny blood in it. I flicked past the words that I had already read when Roberto had shown them to me, and onto the fresh lines I had not yet seen.

Francois had ridden to the monastery to sit in vigil beside the earthly remains of our old tutor. I thought of riding out to see him, but I had not the time - there was an appointment that I was going to keep on behalf of another. I would have to speak to Francois later.

So I took Jackdaw from his stall and brushed down his flanks. 'You will have a good run today, boy,' I told him. He snorted in derision.

Despite his scepticism, he seemed to enjoy himself when we got out of the village onto the road to Versailles. It was faster on horseback than by coach, since we could jump over the chasms in the road surface and canter along nicely until the outer houses of Versailles town hove into view. I have never been enamoured with the town that grew up around the palace - it seems to me a fawning conurbation, living off the King's scraps even more than those of us who literally ate what he discarded.

The palace had been built as a refuge from Paris. A place of safety. The Sun King had been taken there as a child by his mother as they fled the Fronde revolt, when the people of Paris had risen up over taxation and legal privileges. Six hours' walk from the city would discourage any violent mobs from following - especially since they would have to cross through the Bois de Boulogne forest, which was full of brigands and cutpurses even more dangerous than themselves. And yet, six hours is a hurdle, not a complete bar. So I wondered now, now that Paris was in foment once more, how safe the palace would ultimately prove.

I left Jackdaw with a surly ostler at an inn nestling against the Jewish cemetery that Louis had approved just the year before, and set off for the palace. My mission was to find the man who had invited Father Dollet to a secret meeting, in one of the letters I had found in the priest's desk. A harder task would be getting that correspondent to talk to me.

I was also wary of entering the royal estate. Since I had flitted from my bargain with de Rotanne to keep watch on the radical elements in the Third Estate, I suspected the comte's men would be on the lookout for me and they wouldn't be polite about taking me to see him.

I had therefore made two resolutions. First, whoever I was meeting had probably never met Father Dollet, so I would - initially, at least - claim to be my old tutor, who was wearing civilian clothes for the sake of anonymity during our clandestine assignation. And second, I would enter not through the main gates, but by hopping like a little bird through the woods to the rear of the palace.

Helpfully, the appointment had been made to meet in the Queen's theatre. It was a small building half a league behind the palace, where Marie and her ladies-in-waiting would dress as milkmaids and perform pastoral plays - or, if you believed the notorious *Sunrise* pamphlet that I had also found in Father Dollet's desk - where they would strip naked in the dawn light and cavort with the servants in every libertine fashion possible. You made your choice. I preferred the latter as more intriguing.

Anyone in the land had the right to enter the front gate, so long as they bore a sword and hat - and those could be rented from the gatesman - which meant there was little point in making it difficult to enter the rear grounds. A short - rather pleasant, in fact - stroll through the woods and a brief scramble across a ditch and I was then within the estate of the Palace of Versailles. It felt strange to be returning to my supposed home in this shoe-mudding fashion, but time serves oddities for breakfast.

I walked as I had done a thousand times in the direction of the theatre. Discretion was still the watchword, however, and instead of sauntering across the beautifully kept lawns, I chose to wind my way through the maze of monumental hedges, statues and benches in little glades that you couldn't help but stumble across even if you had threaded through many times before.

There was noise everywhere - the palace was absolutely teeming with people of all sorts and social stations now that the Estates-General was meeting. Nobles rich and nobles poor, thin curates and overfed bishops; even, here and there, a lost-looking commoner, his mouth agape at all that he saw, heard and smelled around him. If all this energy could have been harnessed and focused, we French could have been destined for great things. But I knew in my heart of hearts that there were too many voices, too many competing caprices and the outcome was more likely to be havoc than industry and creation.

There was some excitement on the Grand Canal, that long body of water upon which Louis would be rowed aimlessly back and forth. Today, however, it sounded as if one of his great spectacles was in full flow: people were cheering and shouting and as I emerged at the end of the hedge garden, I caught a glimpse of the King and Queen sitting on a gilded dais, avidly watching a number of miniature galleons firing equally miniaturized cannons at each other, in an attempt to sink their rivals. Men stripped as slaves and chained in their seats rowed under the crack of whips, trying to reach positions of strength to blast their rival boats.

As I watched, one of those vessels was indeed holed in the side, an iron ball around the size of a man's fist splintering the wood. The vessel quickly began to list as it took on water and the slave driver jumped out to the laughter of the assembled nobles. Louis himself clapped as the mock-slaves desperately tried to untangle their chains and tear themselves from the wood to which they were attached, before the boat took them to the bottom of the canal. It was a useful distraction for the court as I stole on, towards the Queen's theatre.

Ten minutes later I reached the little cream-coloured building and, after checking that there was no one to witness my entry, I pushed at the door and found it unlocked.

I had never been inside, given that it was used for private performances to the friends of the Royal couple, so was intrigued. I crossed through a small marble lobby to find an auditorium where high windows allowed spears of dusty sunlight to streak in. They half illuminated a glorious horseshoe theatre with seats for perhaps a couple of hundred spectators on benches, and a box reserved for the royal family. Blue and gold coloured the room and I could just make out the three Muses flying across the painted ceiling.

'Who is there?' The words shattered the silence. I heard them but could not see who had spoken. Unless the man was planning to descend from the ceiling on the stage machinery, he had to be in the wings. And then a sound I knew well: the flintlock on a pistol being cocked. As I pulled quickly behind a pillar, the gun showed around the blue curtain to the left of the stage. Yet its bearer remained in shadow. The voice was educated but without the affectations of the nobility. 'Tell me who you are or I will end your life here and now.'

I calculated. At thirty-odd paces he would be damned lucky to hit me. So long as I kept that distance between us, I was safe.

'I am Father Pierre Dollet,' I called.

'Can you prove it?'

'I am at a loss as to how I would do that. But I have read your letter to me, and if I were an enemy, would I not have come armed and with others?'

'That is . . . true,' he admitted. After a moment's pause the man stepped out of the shadow. He was of average height and build, aged in his upper twenties or lower thirties and dressed in clothes that marked him as perhaps a down-on-his-luck writer or actor. He lowered the gun and tucked it into the rear waistband of his culottes - hardly the safest place for a loaded pistol, but his buttocks were his to risk. 'All right. I do not want to dally here, so, to business. You wrote that–' He stopped as a thudding noise behind me resounded through the auditorium. 'What is that?' he demanded. At the same moment as him I realized it was a number of men charging in. 'Who have you brought?!' He slipped into an alcove.

'He has brought no one.' I baulked when I recognized the voice. The Comte de Rotanne emerged into the room, flanked by six or seven of his men armed with swords and led by one with sallow, yellow skin. The comte glanced at me. 'So, it is you, Sévine.' He eyed me with anger. He really was not used to anyone defying his orders for a second time. 'I shall deal with you soon.' He turned his attention to my hidden interlocutor. 'Stop cowering, Marat. I know it is you. My men followed you here. Come out.'

Marat. So that was who he was. The radical journalist who had been writing pamphlets - indeed I had found one of them in Father Dollet's locked drawer alongside the letter he had written to the priest. The man who had positioned himself as a defender of the poor and a thorn in the side of the more moderate members of the Third Estate. He stalked towards us.

'Sévine?' he growled as he came. 'Who are you in truth?'

'You are not to be trusted by anyone, are you?' the comte interposed in my direction, comprehending that I had played

Marat false. 'I was informed you were staying with that dolt Francois d'Agnes.'

I could not tell how he knew that, given that we had told no one at court. It implied the possibility of his network of informants even polluting the ground of Lorne. But that was a question for later.

'My name is David Sévine,' I told Marat. 'Father Dollet was a friend of mine. He was murdered a few days ago. I am attempting to discover by whom.'

Marat made no comment but glared at de Rotanne. 'What do you want, Comte?' he demanded defiantly. I was glad he was no coward ready to roll over at the first bark of a dog, but I could also detect that he was not quite as self-assured as he was trying to appear.

De Rotanne looked between us. 'First, I want to know what you were both doing here.'

'This gentleman and I share an interest in the stage,' I informed him. 'We were rehearsing for an amateur performance of–' The man with sallow skin took rough grip of my shirt and lifted a pistol into my chest. I could have attempted to wrest it from him but there were six more armed men behind.

'We have committed no crime,' Marat said. 'Except perhaps lying.' He cast the words in my direction.

'I will turn to you in due course,' de Rotanne replied dismissively. 'For now, Sévine,' he began, 'I set you to watch dogs like Marat, not take tea and cake with them.'

'I must be a great disappointment to you.'

'You are. But then it is not the first time for that. And I will not be the one to suffer for it. You really should have done what I ordered you to do.' He motioned to his men to take me. 'Now you will–'

I broke away from his heavyset attendant, grabbed the

pistol Marat had tucked into the rear of his culottes, and levelled it at de Rotanne.

'You have seen me use one on the battlefield, Comte,' I spat. 'Your men would grab me afterwards, but you would still have the lead in your gut.'

I am neither a hero nor a fool, but then neither was the Comte de Rotanne. He seemed almost unperturbed. He walked, indeed, to the nearest velvet seat and lowered himself into it. 'As you wish. Leave. I will find you soon enough.'

I saw a huge grin break on Marat's face. I suspected his victories against the representatives of the King were few and far between. And here the risk was borne by another. We may not have been friends, but we shared an enemy, and that is good enough when your back is to the wall. I relieved the sallow man of his gun too. It was an unusual weapon, with a very wide barrel, more like a musket.

'This way,' Marat cried, tugging me towards the door. We backed away towards it, covering the comte and his men with the guns.

'I will collect,' de Rotanne's voice drawled. 'Expect it, Sévine.'

I stopped and looked at him. He was quite unperturbed by the situation. He could have been sitting with the King, watching a comedy on the stage.

'We shall see. And put a leash on your dog.' I spun the pistol around to point at the furthest of the comte's men, whose hand was creeping inside his tunic.

De Rotanne shook his head at the man and his hand fell away. And at that, we ran.

We dashed for the boundary of the estate, checking over our shoulders. But it appeared that the comte did not want to start a gun fight in the palace grounds, with the King himself perhaps within range of a bullet. I cast the firearm belonging to the comte's man aside and we ran through the woods and out into the lanes around the palace.

When we reached the town proper - the poorer part, to be precise - we slowed to a brisk walking pace. We were now in narrow alleys piled with human waste, the crumbling, stuffed houses nearly butting foreheads above us so that only thin streams of light penetrated to the ground. The smell was atrocious. Not just the effluvia, but the stink of human suffering that can be identified by anyone, even though it is forever changing. A clutch of small children played in a heap of dung as women sat smoking in doorways.

On the corner, a man dressed as a butcher was reading out a political tract. His audience - ten or twelve-strong - were listening avidly to the words that promised an end to the salt tax. All they had to do was stand together as brothers and soon they would be breaking the locks on the warehouses and helping themselves to all the salt they wanted. I watched one of them, a white-whiskered grandfather, wring his bonnet in his hands and cry tears of hope at the promise. These were the people Marat had promised to stand behind. By God, they needed all the help they could get.

And yet, my sympathy was tempered by the knowledge that at least one of them would likely be a member of de Rotanne's army of informants, working to keep conditions as they were. Every day he or she would send word to the comte to document who was raising the rabble, who was enquiring about gunpowder, and which of them could be bribed or threatened into joining the ranks of the comte's network. It could be the down-faced youth avidly shouting in the crowd, the old man on the corner tapping out his Meerschaum pipe and paying no attention to the proceedings, or the wife I spied leaning out of her upper-storey window. And to my chagrin I realized that I was playing de Rotanne's game: suspecting each other, we could never truly unite to knock down the walls he had built. It was a clever, layered game.

Marat stopped in front of a house. 'In here.' For a journalist, he was a man of few words.

'Five sous for an upright!' It was called from a doorway opposite.

'No, Elaine,' Marat replied without looking to the source and instead leading me through a leaning doorway. I glanced back. The streetwalker had already moved on to a swarthy fellow who seemed more interested in her wares. But as I followed Marat into the building, I noted at the edge of my vision the old man was still tapping out his pipe. His gaze flitted to mine and back to what was in his hands.

There was no light inside the house other than what was coming through the door. It took me a few seconds, therefore, to adjust to the gloom and see a room utterly bare, nothing more than rotting floorboards. Stepping in, I felt something through my shoes: a thrum through the wood. It was undoubtedly connected to the rumbling and crashing sound rising from a trapdoor in the corner that gave access to some kind of cellar.

Marat, without standing on ceremony, lifted the trap to reveal a blaze of light below. He scrambled down a ladder and I followed him. There we found a thundering iron printing press as the source of the noise and shaking. A man with wild red hair was turning the wheels. He viewed me warily.

'I will take over,' Marat told him. 'You can go for your meal.' The man wiped ink from his hands, scaled the ladder and left without a word.

'A hundred an hour, she can turn out,' Marat informed me, slapping the press. His voice sounded determined rather than triumphant, as if this was a grave duty he had to fulfil. 'We sell them all over Paris, Versailles, Montpellier - everywhere. They read them in the coffee houses, in the streets, in the damn churches.' I picked one up. It was *The Sunrise,* the anonymous scandal-sheet that described Marie Antoinette's notorious break-of-dawn party. 'It sells very well,' Marat laughed. 'No doubt Louis has read it in–'

I cut his revelry short.

'The old man opposite. Smoking a pipe. Bald. Who is he?' I asked.

'That is Nicolas. He was a cobbler but his shop closed.'

'See if he has a new source of income.' Marat nodded, he understood my meaning. 'Tell me what Father Dollet wrote to you,' I said. Now we were alone and away from prying ears, I resumed the interrogation that had brought me to Versailles in the first place.

Marat seemed to recall that I was no idle surveyor of his calling. 'He said he was writing something and wanted it printed quickly and secretly. A broadside.'

Father Dollet had written some sort of pamphlet? And he wanted it printed by Marat, purveyor of furious tracts that had him under the constant watch of de Rotanne? Strange.

'Was it political?'

In answer, he went to the corner of the room where a large armoire stood. The doors had been taken off it and it was stuffed with blank paper, ink, tools, oily parts for the press and the like. Marat ignored the contents and pulled the armoire to one side, exposing a boarded-up hole in the wall. With a claw hammer he drew out a few nails to prise away the cover. Within, I could make out a wooden box in a dank cavity. Instead of lifting the box out, however, he very gingerly reached to its side, out of sight, and apparently manipulated something I could not see. I took a small step backwards. When a man is working something hidden from my sight, I look for anything that could deflect a blow.

I heard a very subtle click. I steeled myself. 'What are you doing?' I demanded in a low voice.

'Believe me, you want me to do this,' he replied with his back to me. Then he held something out to his side, a wire that he had apparently unhooked from something behind the box. 'Now we can do this without being killed.' He hefted the box out and placed it on the floor. Behind him, in the dark cavity, I saw a crossbow with its bolt pointing out towards us.

'That would have been a painful surprise,' I muttered.

He took the lid from the box and looked through a few papers, finding the one he was looking for and handing it to me. I recognized the writing: Father Dollet's.

The contents contained a plea for a clandestine meeting, a brief description of who he was and his hopes for a more equitable nation to come out of the current political machinations in Versailles. And then the explanation of what he had to offer:

> I would dearly love to detail the information that has come to me in the course of my ministry. Yet you, I am certain, are more aware than any of the importance of discretion when communicating other than in person. I feel, therefore, that it is prudent for now to

say only this: what I have learned has the power to change the course of our nation.

Reading these lines you probably either think me a madman or a deluded soul clutching at slogans and half-formed ideas. But I assure you I am no moonchild. Had I wished to live out my days as an obscure country curate drinking wine and growing fat from the plates of my starving flock, I could have kept this invisible weapon to myself. I must confess I have seesawed over the decision, for the knowledge that I keep in my bosom holds power that even I can only guess at. I intend to set this knowledge out in a pamphlet to be published by you and distributed throughout the nation. Sir, I do not exaggerate when I tell you that the pamphlet's contents hold the power of life or death over at least one man to be named therein - and could bear something akin to that potency for a whole generation of our countrymen.

When you read the pages, you may think they describe wicked acts, acts practised only by those abandoned by God to Lucifer. Maybe so, maybe not. But we have a duty, too, I believe, to use any and all knowledge for the greater good of all God's children.

In doing so, there will be a particular guilt on my part, for I will be breaking a sacred oath of my calling: to respect the silence of the confessional. I sent my informant away with a harsh, old penance and yet my own penance - countless years in purgatory, if not hell itself - will be far harsher.

I do not take this decision lightly, Monsieur Marat. And neither must you. Because I must also inform you that possession of this knowledge, I am convinced, puts my - and your - mortal life in jeopardy. And once

> the information is unleashed, the danger to us will be open. But beware: before then, it will come hidden, muffled and masked. I beg you to reply before it reaches me.

And there it ended. Too late those words had been read. Had they been sent a week, a day, an hour earlier then perhaps my old mentor's hand would have now been on the wheel of the press, or his printed words read in every tea house, radical club and tavern from Paris to Strasbourg. Who could say, but God himself? Or the Devil.

Father Dollet's fear was clear to read. Buried far deeper was the matter behind it all. In the times I had spent with him, he had sometimes been poetic in his words, but had never spoken in riddles. 'Have you any idea what he was talking about?' I asked Marat. It was frustrating to hold the letter that had seemingly set my confessor on the path to perdition or death, and not know the dark, poisonous, secret that lay behind it.

'None. Though I considered destroying it after I had read it,' Marat said. 'He seemed mad.'

'I am glad you kept it, although its aid is limited.' I stared at the ink, but it gave nothing more away. 'I should leave now.'

'You should. I think there will be trouble today. After the Oath.'

'What Oath?'

'You do not know?' He spoke with a haughty air, as if only a bumpkin would have not known. 'The idiot King tried to shut down the National Assembly yesterday. He barred them from their meeting salon. But they refused to quietly disappear. Guillotin led them to the tennis court, where they swore an oath not to disband until we have a written constitution! Just think: like America, we will elect the men who set our laws, our rights. Don't you see? They thought - the King, the aristos - that we would be happy with a few changes to the salt tax. Oh no, we have had a taste of what we can demand, and now we will not stop until the Second Estate is smashed and the King is in the Bastille!' Words such as these, ill thought out, reckless, made me tense. He looked deep into my face. 'You think there will be bloodshed?' Now his tone was mocking. 'Of course there will be bloodshed! What revolution has there been without it? There are some treacherous members even of the Third who disputed the Oath. They will be dealt with. The poor clogmakers of Paris will soon swamp the perfidious lawyers of Versailles; and those fat fawning men will pay the price alongside their aristo masters.'

'Primacy of the Third is just a stepping stone for you, is it not?'

He burst into laughter. 'Do you know what they almost called themselves?' He recited from memory. '"The Legitimate Assembly of Representatives of the Majority of the Nation, Acting in the Absence of the Minor Parties". Can you imagine what woollen mind comes up with that?' he scoffed. 'And do you know the oath they took? "We swear to God, to the King and to the Country to fulfil with zeal the functions we have been given." These people will serve their purpose for as long as they serve their purpose.'

A month ago men had demanded an end to the most egregious seigneurial rights. A week ago they had demanded a written constitution. Days ago they had called for elected representation for all. Now some, like Marat, wanted bloody revolt.

'Do not rush into war,' I said. 'You might find it dirtier

than you imagine.' But I was worried by the light of relish in his eyes.

'Pah, you bourgeoisie think that way,' he said dismissively. 'It is a cleanser.'

When men who have never seen cannon-shot and smelled gangrene tell me of the glories of war, then my veins run hot. Men like Marat relish not liberty, but the destruction and fire that precedes it.

'You fool,' I spat. 'Your printed battles would do better floating in the Seine than in men's hands.' He glared at me as I departed. Well, I would have no more aid from him.

There was, at least, one valuable grain of information in the letter that Father Dollet had written: the information that seemed so vital and dangerous had come to him in the confession box. *I will be breaking a sacred oath of my calling: to respect the silence of the confessional. I sent my informant away with a harsh, old penance and yet my own penance - countless years in purgatory, if not hell itself - will be far harsher.* Presuming that it had been a recent occurrence, the man or woman who had spoken to him through the grille was likely a current resident of Lorne who habituated the confessional.

That person might have been the priest's killer - a realization might have come to the penitent in question that Father Dollet was not as silent a cave as he had presumed. Or the murderer could be a third party desperate to keep the information hidden - but if so, why had they not also killed whoever passed Father Dollet the dangerous information? Well, it could be that the one who blabbed was somehow precious to the assassin, despite his or her inability to keep quiet.

Given that the entire village would have regularly entered Father Dollet's confessional, the only individuals ruled out as the source of the information would be the Carmelite brothers and the madman Cotillard. I supposed that was a start.

It was late night when I led Jackdaw into his stable and I wearily made my way into the house, saddle-sore.

I still needed to ask Francois about the village girls who had talked of witches, but I would have to wait until the following day.

22 June 1789

The horses were impatient as the morning sun shone harsh and bright, stamping their shoes into the ground. They snorted their complaint of being cooped up when there were fields to traverse and gates to leap at speed. Louder than them were the dogs. The wave-tailed hounds with tight sinews massed together in a huddle, waiting for one to declare himself the pack leader and set off in pursuit of the stag. The human followers, the servants and the beaters, all looked like the dogs: barely able to hold themselves back from the sprint.

As I walked out of the chateau in musty riding gear that Peugere had found in a storeroom, it felt as if I and the house in which I had been sleeping had been lifted and dropped into another nation - one where the hunt was all and every animal in the world was either pack or quarry. A number of the villagers had turned out too. Francois was chatting to a few of his tenants. I took him aside and filled him in on what I had discovered in Versailles. His eyebrows nearly lifted from his head and I left him to absorb the information.

A groom was holding Jackdaw, who shook his reins as he recognized me. I checked the straps and put my foot in the stirrup, but as I put my weight on it, he took it upon himself to begin the hunt early and started off. I could not hold him and the groom had to chase after him.

'Can you not even control a gelding, Maître Sévine?' I heard from the steps of the house, in a voice strong enough to turn ice into water. 'Surely you have not lost what he has?' Juliana strode down the stone stairway. It took effort on my part not to allow my face to register the surprise at her appearance in full hunting gear.

'You will be joining us, Madame?' I asked.

'I would not miss it for all the gold in Versailles.' Her foreign tones made the royal court sound even more majestic, as if behind the facades and brocades there were centuries of noblemen fighting each other for an empire.

Beside her, Gregory Archer smirked. I could not help but remember his warning - 'advice', he had insisted - regarding his wife. *She will not do you any good at all.* At his side was a young woman I had not seen before, dressed in English fashion, but with an Indian scarf over her shoulders, her arm through Archer's. She was very beautiful, with red hair knotted and thrown forward over her shoulder. She held my gaze as they approached. And behind them all, Catherine trod lightly. The sun was blushing her powderless pink cheek.

Juliana stopped in front of me and introduced the woman who had joined us. 'This is an old friend of mine from London. Annalise Carran. The most talented artist you will find on this side of the Alps.'

I kissed her proffered hand. She gazed at me without reaction. I had the disconcerting impression that she was committing to memory how my chin curved, the hue of my hair, how my muscles made the cloth of my shirt crease. Perhaps every artist does the same, but it was immediately something about her I did not like.

'Should I guess that the portrait that hangs at the top of the stairs is from your hand?' I asked.

Her attention slowly moved up from my waist. 'Yes. It is mine.'

'It is a work of brilliance.'

'It is what it is.'

'Do you take commissions?'

'It depends on the sitter.' She cocked her head to one side. 'You I will do for free. You look different to most men.'

'How so, madame?'

She placed her hands on my cheek and turned my head from side to side. She had emerald-green eyes that bore right in. No woman had ever acted so freely with me. 'I cannot tell yet. I will know when I have a brush in my hand.'

Juliana seemed more than pleased. 'I had hoped Annalise would offer to paint you. It is quite an honour, Maître Sévine. Do you think you will justify it?'

'I am sure that I will not.'

'That is probably true,' confirmed Annalise.

'Yes, that is probably true. So we will have to do what we can to spice him,' said Juliana, thoughtfully. 'Like a *cassoulet*. I think perhaps the costume of a Turkish pasha. Gold thread on a black velvet will draw out your complexion.' She took my arm and swept her hand across the horizon. 'Pictured here, perhaps, on the steps, surveying your lands. And we will put you on one of these fine chargers as if you have just come back from battle, bloodied. With the heads of your enemies on pikestaffs.

Yes, I think that should do it, do you not, Annalise?' The other woman remained still, with her head tilted to her shoulder. 'Oh now, Annalise, do not come the silent mysterious type now. It does not suit those of us who know you have a tongue in your head that is fit to wag when the hour is right. Tell us what you think of our hero? Will he serve for an Eastern king?'

'He will serve.'

'Good. Oh, Maître Sévine. You must excuse us. We have been in the country for too long. We have gone mad in the heat. We need someone to cool us down. I think I will try a cup of that wine that Peugere is spilling everywhere.' She stepped away, somehow graceful still in her man's clothing. Annalise went with her, observing delicately and deliberately all the sights around her.

I was left with Gregory Archer. 'How long will you be with us?' he asked. I saw his son, Charles, saunter out of the house, playing with a riding crop.

'I cannot tell. The baron has asked me to investigate the death of Father Dollet. When that is complete, who knows?'

'I see. You do recall what I said to you last time, do you not?'

'Was it the thing about Cotillard?'

'No, no, it was something quite different, something about my wife. Do bear it in mind. Things became ugly once.'

I looked him down from his head to his feet. He might have once been powerful in both ways - he was well built and had once had the ear of the King. But now he was living as a guest in the house of a minor baron, warning me off Juliana would take more than that. 'How ugly?'

'Maître Sévine, once again you are taking as a threat what I only mean as advice. Learn, perhaps, from my own mistake.'

His own mistake? What could that be, I wondered.

'And what are you two boys talking about?' asked Juliana as she tripped back. 'No, do not tell me. It will be women, will it not? I know what happens in your minds.'

'We were talking about the death of Father Dollet,' I said.

'So sad,' she replied, as if it had been precisely what she had been expecting. Francois shouted over to tell us that we were about to set off. At this, Juliana strode forcefully to her horse, a placid-looking chestnut creature. 'Now, Maître Sévine, if you cannot handle your gelding I will take him and you can have this mare. Maybe it would be more appropriate anyway.'

I walked to Jackdaw, who had been returned by the groom. This time he stayed still while I tested the straps and settled into the saddle. The hounds were leaping in excitement, aware that the hunt was about to begin. Archer went to his horse as the others turned to the direction of the forest they would be searching, and at the signal, the houndkeepers loosed the dogs. They knew the way to the woods where the musk of the brown creature could be found, where they would chase across open fields and through streams until they caught it and brought it down.

At a trot we left, hounds, horses and riders. I watched Juliana. I had never seen a woman ride to hounds and it was an exhilarating sight. She rode like a man. Perhaps the lack of balls actually helped - there had been many occasions I had spent a day in the saddle only to collapse on my bed and look down to see them reddened by the constant thudding onto hard leather. We cantered through fields, and bounded over brooks. And then something changed. I realized the horizon was slipping to one side. Or I was. Instinctively, I pulled my feet from the stirrups and threw myself clear, to see the earth coming up to meet me.

When I woke, it was to a pain like a hot poker in my shoulder and the impression that my ribs had been staved in with a plough. My vision initially failed to register what was going on.

'Come on.' Archer put his arm under my damaged shoulder and lifted me from the ground. Everything hurt like all hell.

As my vision turned from a grey mist to colour, I saw Jackdaw happily grazing by the edge of the field. 'I am glad to see one of us came out of it all right.'

'Your saddle came loose. I imagine you did not check the straps, Maître Sévine.'

'Well, thank you for warning me now,' I said, rubbing my cheek. I had checked the straps. Someone, I was certain, had loosened them. And as feeling and sense returned, I very much wanted to know who that was.

For now, I felt cracked ribs beneath my fingers. We were about a mile from the house, so there seemed nothing for me to do but to return painfully on foot as the others bid me good health and charged away. At least I could use the solitude for a little thought, having had little chance for that in the past couple of days.

I shuffled my way slowly and painfully back, choosing to hole up in the chateau orangery, where I thought I might spend a while thinking over the information I had gleaned.

It was a pleasant time, despite the bruises, in the hot house. The fruit trees bore little bounty, but there was a comfortable wicker seat, and I had a chance to ponder.

I had scratched at the surface of Lorne and found people and places to be so very different to what I remembered. Father Dollet was still the kind man I recalled, but his entanglement with Marat, and subversion of the secrecy of the Confession, was a change. Could Jacob's political excursions somehow be connected? And then there was the downright unholy: witchcraft had always been whispered of, but I could not recall the villagers worrying that among their number were genuine acolytes of Satan.

After a light doze, I prised myself out of my chair and emerged into the day.

At the edge of a small lawn laid out in the neat English style was a copse of thick trees and I could just make out, between them, a young woman sitting on the grass with her back to me.

'Oh, Maître Sévine.'

'Good afternoon, Catherine.'

'Yes, it is. It is a lovely afternoon.'

She glanced about, as if she was trying to discern the propriety of our meeting like this with the rest of the household still on the hunt. 'Shall we take a turn among the roses?' I asked. And I kicked myself for sounding like a novel of the type now being devoured by the worst court ladies.

'Yes, why not?' She beamed.

There was a stone balustraded wall and I sat on it while she examined the flowers and commented on how lovely they were. 'Were you born in Paris, Maître Sévine?'

'I was born here.'

'Here?' She seemed astonished, as if no one who had been born in Lorne could possibly have ever left it.

I thought I might as well tell her the truth. Or some of it. 'I was not especially happy here.'

She paused and considered. 'Oh. Well, let us talk about other things. It is such a nice day; let us not waste it.'

'I have already fallen off a horse and knocked myself

unconscious. I do not think it has been an unremarkable day.'

She blinked and bit her lip to stop herself laughing. 'Did you? Really?'

'Yes. Really.'

'Did you hurt yourself?'

'You mean apart from the point where I knocked myself unconscious?'

'Yes. Apart from that.'

'I am glad my injuries amuse you. If you like I can tell you about many others.'

'I would like that.' She began to walk between the flower beds. 'I heard you fought in the war for American freedom.' I said nothing. 'Will you tell me about it?'

My mood eased downward a little. 'There are stories it is hard to tell.'

Shouts from the other side of the house took our attention away from our own scene then and I guessed that the hunt had returned. We walked around to see the riders dismounting and a large stag being carried to the back of the house to be butchered.

'Will you help me down, Maître Sévine?' asked Juliana. She held out her hand and I took it to aid her out of the saddle. She touched lightly to the ground. 'The hunt went well,' she said.

'Not for the stag.'

'I hope you have enjoyed yourself too?'

'I have.'

She glanced over at Catherine. 'Oh yes, I am sure you have. There are so many flowers in the garden here. What do you plan to do with them all, Maître Sévine?'

'I will start by drying them out. After that I will put them between the pages of a book and sit on it.'

Archer, who had been overseeing the transport of the deer, came over. 'A fine beast, is he not?'

'He is. Venison tonight,' I said.

'The hunt inspired me. I have an aria in my mind on the subject. I will set it down before it disappears.'

'I hope it goes well,' I told him. Juliana took my arm and guided me towards the house. Archer followed behind. As we passed, Catherine gazed at her mistress.

'Have you been inspired by the hunt too, Maître Sévine?' asked Juliana.

'Not exactly.'

'Then we must bring things to a head.' She ran up the steps in front of the chateau and stood on the dais, like, I remarked to myself, a triumphant Roman emperor receiving tribute from the citizens. 'Next week night we shall have a masquerade. A ball!' she announced.

'Here?' asked Francois, who was arriving on his mount.

'Why, where else, your lordship? It shall be here. My husband is completing his greatest work, is that not right, my love?'

'Well, it is turning out quite well, though I would not make such a claim,' replied Archer. 'But a public performance would be a joy.'

'And I will perform its premiere myself. For those who have no suitable costumes I can provide a range of masks from the comical to the grotesque. Come, Maître Sévine, there is a time for work and a time for play. On the night of the ball, we will set the men from the boys.' She spun around and disappeared into the chateau. I was left watching the empty space where she had been.

Francois and I had, of course, other things on our mind. We took a stroll in the grounds.

'All that people would speak of is the death of Father

Dollet,' he said. 'Though that is hardly surprising.' Indeed, it struck me that Juliana's masked ball was in questionable taste at that time, but I was not the one to inform her of that. 'Can you tell me anything? This village. I know it is not much to look at. But it is our home. And it feels like someone has entered our home and smashed it all to pieces.'

'I feel the same. Now, tell me - when you invited me down, you said something about the village girls talking about witches. What of that?'

'Good Lord, I had quite forgotten about that, in all that has–' And he broke off and stared at me. 'Father Dollet.'

'Quite,' I said, seeing that he had put two and two together and come up with the correct sum.

'Upside down. The inverted crucifixion.' I waited. He almost had to slap himself to come back to his senses. 'It was Father Dollet who told me. The girls who work in the bakery claimed to have spoken to them in the forest. One of the girls is Peugere's granddaughter, Odette, as it happens.'

His information contained two points of interest: first, was another connection between Father Dollet and the supposed sorceresses of Lorne. The other was that Peugere had told me of the village's deadly belief in witches but had kept to himself the fact that his own flesh and blood had reported conversing with one of them. 'She said they had actually spoken to the witch?'

'That is what Father Dollet told me. I could make neither head nor tail of it, but you have seen more of the strange world than I, and I thought that perhaps you might comprehend.'

'I want to speak to her.'

'She will be at work now.'

She was probably one of the girls I had seen when I called in there. Aged about ten or twelve, I thought. An age when young minds can be turned to anything. Even the spilling of innocent blood. I mulled it for a while.

'I want to speak to Peugere.' I was not wholly happy with the servant having kept this knowledge to himself.

Francois waved at a groom, who was dispatched to find the butler. My old friend looked at me with discomfort. 'Do you . . . Could it really be that there are witches here?'

I stopped and stared at him. 'Francois, do you really believe there are people in league with Lucifer? Given magical powers?' I was somewhat disappointed in him.

'N-No. But if not, then what are we talking about?'

'We are talking about people who *believe* themselves to be in league with Lucifer, and all too willing to do evil for the sake of evil, in order to please him. Mad or simply stupid.' Or young and impressionable, but I kept that to myself for now. No need to bring terrible suspicion onto childish heads without any proof. 'Peugere took me somewhere - a pool where they drowned an old woman for witchcraft.'

Francois looked astonished as I told him the details.

'But, by the sound of it, she got what she deserved,' he said, uncertainly.

I had to admonish him, even though it was more his affair than mine. Lawlessness cannot be the law. Anarchy only means the powerful thrive and the weak are trampled. 'I prefer the law to be administered by judges,' I said. Though the hole in my argument was that those judges tended to be very little help for poor country folk. And morally Francois was right: whether she had killed her neighbour's cows and made his whole family destitute by witchcraft or simply by poisoning their feed, a sentence of death was not far above what she deserved. 'When was the last time there was a trial for black magic in these parts?' I asked.

He shook his head. 'Good God, I do not know.' He thought for a moment. 'I remember my grandfather telling me he had a sorcerer in the seigneurial court once.'

'Go on.'

'Oh, quite a story. As I recall, the man claimed he had the ability to grow female parts as well as male, and copulate with himself. He had bought that ability from Lucifer, in return for performing a dance every Sunday during which he would leap ten feet in the air while passing water on a statue of the Holy Virgin.'

My eyebrows lifted. 'Quite a trick when you think about it.'

At that, Peugere appeared.

'Your granddaughter told Father Dollet she had seen witches.' He hung his head, which confirmed that he had known and kept it from me. 'Why did you not inform me this afternoon?'

'I am sorry, maître. I am very sorry. Odette is a good girl. She works hard to earn money for us. She goes to Mass twice each day!'

I could not help but feel my heart strings plucked at the sight of the grandfather's instinct to protect. I softened, whether I wanted to or not. 'I understand, but why did you keep it to yourself?'

He glanced at Francois. 'I did not want her to be in trouble. It was a fantasy, nothing more. She is just a girl.'

'What did she see?'

He opened his hands. 'I do not even know. I know that she confessed something to the father priest but I do not know what.'

'Where do I find her?'

'She will be at the bakery now.'

I dismissed him.

Francois was still unhappy with the thought that the villagers' belief in black magic might be at the heart of the mystery. 'But what about Cotillard? After all, he is mad,' he insisted.

'Cotillard might just be the sanest man for thirty leagues.'

'You include yourself in that suggestion.'

'I make a point of it.'

'Well, if not him, the Jacobins? They say they are peaceful but perhaps this is their assault on the First Estate, before they attack the Second.' He was flailing about and he knew it.

'And an obscure country curate would, of course, be top of their list.'

He sighed. 'Yes, yes. You are right.' He did not sound gracious with the compliment.

I took the key to the church so that I could later enter and examine again the scene of my mentor's death, and walked to the bakery. Hubert was, thankfully, out, so I was able to speak to Odette without his doltish presence.

'Odette, you understand that the baron has instructed everyone to tell me whatever they know, without telling any falsehoods, yes?' She pursed her lips - somewhat petulantly, but that was what came with the age of the girl - and nodded. 'Your grandfather has also instructed you to be open and honest.' She glanced in the direction of the chateau. 'What did you say to Father Dollet about witches? What have you seen?'

Her eyes brightened. She wanted to tell. 'I saw them flying at night! Across the moon.'

'The moon.'

'Yes. And I saw one had a cat with her. And a crow.'

'How were they flying? Were they on a carpet?'

'In . . .' she paused for a second while she made up the answer. 'A boat.'

'A boat.'

'With golden sails. And it was full of animals going two by two. And it was raining.'

I had to take a moment to think where to go with this. It was nonsense, but there was always the possibility that something more real had occurred. 'I see. Have you ever spoken to the witches? Has anyone ever spoken to you and said they are a witch?'

'No.' Her irises gleamed. 'Are *you* a witch, sir?'

I sighed. A few more questions and it became clear that the girl had nothing but a vivid imagination and a poor memory for Old Testament stories. And rumours were flying around the village like crows.

Stepping into the daylight, I caught sight of Catherine a little way up the road. She was surrounded by a truer depiction of rural poverty than any artist could paint: three children, a girl and two older boys, the oldest not past ten years of age, dressed in tatters that had once been rags, begging alms. Their hair and skin were more matted with dirt than a river rat's and probably alive with lice. If they had ever known their parents they were alone now and accustomed to calling the nearest roadside verge a bed for the night.

Most of the world - peasant or noble - would have ignored them or kicked them away. But Catherine handed them a few coins and pointed back to the building whence I was emerging. They would be able to buy a little bread, at least.

My eyes met hers and I found myself utterly unable to

move. I simply could not think of the last time I had witnessed an act of sheer kindness. It was in such short supply in our country, it was rarer than rubies.

'If I do not, who will?' she posed, reading my thoughts. Then she read them again, with a hinted note of anger: 'That is right, no one. So I do it.'

We stayed there for what seemed an age, while the children ran into the shop behind me. We exchanged no more words, but we both understood something before she turned and went on her way.

Charity *means something*. It has to in this grim world. A charitable breast carries more beauty than any other. The gilded angels of Versailles had fascinated me when I first attended that place, but on the occasions when I had managed to disrobe them, I had found balls of snow where their hearts were meant to be, and soon lost interest in the game. I painted a mental picture of the scene I had just watched - the girl, the children, *charity* - and guarded it jealously. I might need to remember it some day when cynicism threatened to smother all. I watched Catherine walk away and wondered if her path would cross mine again that day. I hoped it would.

I went on to the church. This time I was there only to look and think. To look for any physical symptom of the murder, that we had hitherto overlooked. My expectations were low, but I was at a loss.

'*Ad poenitentiam te adducit?*' I heard cried from behind me as I walked the nave. 'Do you repent?'

'It is the second time you have done that,' I muttered. 'Do you not get bored of the same role?' I moved to the pew where I had sat before. The door closed and Cotillard the insane lawyer came to sit beside me. Somehow it felt as if we knew each other.

'Poor Pierre,' he said, after a moment. '*Media vita in morte sumus.*'

'I have never had much truck with that thought. I have been in the midst of life and in the midst of death, and the two looked very different from where I stood.'

'A clever lawyer's argument.'

'Should I thank you? You know there are many in the village who think you guilty.'

'But I am not. And since I am not, there is no evidence that I am. And you are of the sort who consider evidence to be more holy than the font water. Have you seen Dom Mathieu?' I inclined my head. 'Ah. How is the madman?'

I thought that description was a bit rich coming from Cotillard, even though he appeared to be drifting through one of his most lucid periods.

'He is sad for the death of Father Dollet.'

'Ha!' He sprang up onto the pew and balanced with one foot on the armrest, one on the back. I readied my hands to catch him should he fall in the right direction. 'May his arse be forever plagued by two-headed vipers!'

'Am I to take it that you and the Dom are not the firmest of friends?'

'And his ears be covered in honey to attract angry wasps.'

'You would have done well during the Inquisition.'

'Oh, the Inquisition was the work of the Devil. I am merely a lunatic. No, what I pray for is not the rooting out of heresy, it is *vindicta*. Revenge. To smite! Smite! Smite!' He pummelled his right fist into his left palm and bared his teeth. Then he stepped slowly down onto the stone floor and knelt on the patch where the curate's blood had collected. 'What did he tell you about Pierre?'

'He told me that Father Dollet was expelled from their

order for theft.' Cotillard scoffed. 'But I do not believe that. So, it had to be something which the Dom was ashamed to admit. And then I recalled how you quoted the Gospel in the church yesterday. Jesus's words to Pierre. "Tonight, before the cock crows, you will disown me three times." But Pierre said, "Even if I must die with you, I will never disown you." But Pierre did disown you, did he not?' Cotillard remained silent. 'Was it a long time ago?'

'Oh, there have been summers and winters. Then summers and winters again. I was not mad then.' He looked sadly at me. 'No, I am not the one who hurt him. I have not touched Pierre for a tenyear. Neither in adoration nor anger.'

I believed him. I cannot say why. No strong, logical reason, but one of those inexplicable senses that were creeping upon me as I returned in body and spirit to Lorne. 'Someone stole some books from Father Dollet's cottage. Was it you?' I asked.

He seemed surprised. 'Have they? It was not me. No, you will have to look elsewhere for that magpie.'

I thought over what I had found in Cotillard's nest in the hay barn, containing many stolen items. And something echoed. 'You took a hairshirt from someone.'

'Yes.' He said it as if it were the most natural thing in the world to steal an implement of self-punishment for sin.

'Who did you take it from?'

'Why do you care?' he asked, casually.

Because Dollet's letter had described how he had come by the dangerous and powerful information that he wanted printed in pamphlets to be distributed across the land, the information that had perhaps got him killed: *I sent my informant away with a harsh, old penance.*

A harsh, old penance. The hairshirt Cotillard had stolen had been that man or woman's penance, spending the days with the rough hair scratching his or her skin.

'I am interested in old punishments,' I said.

His eyes met mine and gazed into them. 'Is that the truth?' he said.

'Some of it.'

'A lawyer first,' he said. 'Always a lawyer first.'

'Will you tell me?'

He pondered for a moment. 'A question for a question. You answer mine and I will answer yours.'

'Agreed,' I said, although I was rather wary. I suspected his question would not be entirely straightforward.

'The question is an old one that all us poor changelings can answer. Thus: *What is greater than God, more wicked than Lucifer, the poor have it, the rich need it, and if a man should eat it, he would surely die?*'

I set my brain coursing like a hare. Taking it all as one universal question bore no fruit. So, I moved to the end, thinking of poisons and bad meat. But they could have no relation to God. Then I reversed to the beginning. The Devil and God swapped places to be greater than the other but that meant nothing. A rich man needs redemption? A confessor? No. I was groping in the dark. I could think of nothing.

And then I realized.

'Nothing,' I replied. 'For nothing is greater than God or more evil than the Devil. Rich men want nothing and every child knows that if you eat nothing you will certainly die.'

'That is correct.' He paused. 'I took the shirt from the chateau. In the middle of the day, I walked in and walked out and no one caught a glimpse of me.'

A felt a sinking feeling in my stomach. If Francois himself was the one implicated, I had no idea what I would do. 'Was it the Baron d'Agnes?' I asked, ready for the answer.

'The baron? Oh no. No, it was his guest. It was Gregory Archer.'

Archer was Father Dollet's penitent. His informant.

Dinner that evening was more crowded than before. At the table, which sported a huge pewter candelabra - I guessed there had once been a silver one, but it had been sold off - were myself, Francois, Archer and Juliana, their son Charles, Catherine and Annalise. I had decided that rather than confront Archer immediately, I would watch for a while. And Catherine's presence set me off-balance. Her dress that evening was more splendid than any I had seen her wear before. I suspected that she had borrowed it from her mistress. It was brilliant white with silver embroidery, tight in at the waist and bolstering her gently tremorous bosom so that I could not drag my eyes away for more than thirty seconds at a time. I did my best but each time I shook some sense into myself and pulled my attention away I glimpsed her stifling a laugh at my expense. I forced myself to turn to the matter at hand.

'And what brings you to Lorne?' I asked of the latest arrival, the English painter Annalise.

'I am to paint Charles,' she replied.

The boy looked haughtily towards me, his green eyes bright in the candlelight. 'Dressed as a soldier,' he said. 'I shall be one soon.'

'You will need your father's permission,' I remarked, pouring myself a little cognac.

'I need no one's permission. I am a free subject of the King.'

There was something of the arrogance of youth about

the lad. But still, I meant him no harm in correcting him. 'No,' I said. 'You are a boy. I am afraid that until you reach the age of majority, you are legally a chattel of your father. He possesses you.'

Fury filled his features, surprising me with its vehemence. 'A chattel? You call me a chattel!'

I saw Catherine roll her eyes and felt a pleasing bond of empathy. We both thought the boy was an idiot.

'I call you nothing. The law calls you a chattel. The law is the power in this land.' I was trying to indulge him, but was reaching my limit.

'Hardly,' he growled like a wolf cub. Young beasts are often the most dangerous because they are spoiling to try out their claws.

'And what do you mean by that?'

'I mean that there are powers hidden to people like you. That's what I mean, Monsieur Sévine.'

'It is Maître Sévine,' I said. 'And do tell me about these powers of which I am not aware.'

'Charles,' Catherine began, attempting to calm him. I wished her luck, but her sensuous appearance distracted my eye again and my attention drifted from Charles. That might have incensed him more.

'Well, know this!' he snapped, pointing his fork at me as if it were a true weapon, rather than an implement for eating fish. I returned my gaze to him. I did not want to, I wanted to keep it where it had been. A thought glinted at the back of my mind that this - this what? Attraction? Fascination? Draw? - could spell trouble. 'There are many of us who see . . .' But he halted. He had caught a black look flashed by his father. 'What?' he demanded.

'You will go to your room and stay there the whole night,' Archer ordered him.

'I will do no such thing!' Charles insisted. 'This man has—'

'Charles, go up and we can play a game later.' It was Juliana.

'I do not want to play a game. No more games.'

'Charles.'

The surprise of its appearance over, I was beginning to take joy in his annoyance. 'Why not enjoy your childhood without adult worries and responsibilities?' I said.

In reply, he stood, threw his napkin to the floor and stomped out the room.

'You will forgive us, Maître Sévine,' Archer said after he had gone. 'He has his mother's spirit. We will punish him later.'

I thought it time to probe very gently. 'I am sure there is no need for a hairshirt.'

'Oh Lord! Do not remind me!' Juliana burst out. 'Gregory has been wearing one of those terrible things of late.'

'Have you?' I asked. 'May I ask why? So few of us follow such practices these days.'

'Do you think so?' Archer replied, recovering his sang-froid. 'Oh, I am sure there are many. I was considering creating a character for an opera I have been working on, the character would be a monk who wore such an item.'

'Ah, and you wanted to know the feeling, in order to more truly represent it on the stage.'

'Precisely.'

'And what was your appraisal?' I asked.

'Unpleasant.'

'It is a poor hairshirt that is comfortable to the wearer,' Juliana added. I wondered if - presuming my supposition regarding the identity of Dollet's penitent was correct - she was aware of her husband's connection to the crime.

'Yes, of course. But not all monks wear them. The idea

must have come to you from elsewhere. Where might that be?' I was coming dangerously close to revealing my knowledge of the situation between him and the priest. As it was, he was probably suspecting it.

And anger visited him too. I was making a habit of inspiring it. 'I thought only of a devout monk who wishes to remind himself of the mortification of the flesh of Jesus of Nazareth,' he snapped. 'And so: a hairshirt.'

I had, indeed, struck home. I surreptitiously glanced at Catherine - yes, yes, I admit it was in the hope that I had made an impression upon her. She was giving her employer a look of curiosity, as if she could not quite work out what he was doing, then her gaze met mine and held it for a moment. Something flitted between us: something akin to a sense of conspiracy, as if she and I were confidantes and all others were outwith our circle of trust. Passion can come on in seconds, but that intimacy, the complicity, grows from knowing someone and realizing that they are like you.

'You are in a passion, my love,' Juliana told Archer, not seeing what had passed between me and her maid. 'Perhaps it will inspire you.'

'Perhaps.'

'Will you work this night?'

'Yes. I want to see all the black land.' I recalled that Archer had told me he sometimes went to the roof to compose his music. 'Now, where is the dessert wine?' He stood and strode irritably towards the kitchen.

At the same moment, Catherine and I lifted our glasses to our lips; then, at the same time, saw our actions mirrored in the other and placed the drinks back down, for fear of appearing ridiculous. After that we each waited for the other to go first and spent fifteen seconds staring, like idiots, until

Juliana laughingly placed the glass in her maid's palm and ordered her to drink it before we all died of old age.

After we had eaten, Francois and I retired to the library. It was a large yet cosy room, well lit, a set of double doors out onto the lawn and a billiard table at one end. The chairs were covered in soft velvet and I could tell that this was where Francois spent the winter evenings, with cognac and a good fire, his feet on one of the thick rugs.

As a boy I had spent many hours between these shelves. Although it was mostly stocked with dry volumes on French history and animal husbandry, here and there I found old copies of Ovid and even Seneca. They were heavy going for a twelve-year-old with only the Greek and Latin schooling of a country curate to lean on, but I became lost in their tales of change and inverted fate.

'What in heaven's name has happened between you and Archer?' Francois enquired as soon as we were shut away.

I lowered myself into a green chair with a rock-hard seat, the stuffing having been compacted by generations of Barons d'Agnes buttocks and never replaced. I contemplated how much I should tell Francois, but decided to tell all. 'When I read the letter Father Dollet sent to Marat it implied that the information he wanted published had been revealed to him in the confessional.'

'And?'

'There was no indication of whom the penitent was, apart from one thing: Father Dollet said he had prescribed an old, harsh penitence for whatever the sin was.' I waited a moment for Francois to recall the conversation over dinner and what had been said when it took a tense turn. I saw the realization steal across his face.

'Archer wore a hairshirt!'

'He did.'

'So you think that was a penance? That Archer was the one who told Father Dollet of some secret sin?'

'It does point to that conclusion.'

He poured himself a generous glass of cognac and drank contemplatively. 'Are you going to confront him?' he asked. 'I mean, I suppose we have to.' He rubbed his cheek. 'I do not want to get it wrong, though. He is a guest in my house, after all.'

'I understand. You saw that I tried probing him a little earlier.'

'Yes, yes, I wondered why you were going on about it. It makes sense now. So . . .'

'We should leave him tonight - his mind is to deny everything.'

'But what if he is the killer?' he said.

'What do you propose to do about it? Lock him up without a shred of proof? Torture him for a confession?'

'Hardly.'

'So let us keep watch on him and search his room tomorrow when he is out. Then I will confront him directly. It is the best hope we have of actually getting somewhere.'

He placed his glass down hard on a side table laid out for chequers. 'So we let him roam the house until then?' he posed. 'What if, from what you said tonight, he knows you are on his scent?'

'I will lock my door tonight and leave a weapon within reach.'

There were no dreams as I slept. I was too deep for dreams, which only come when your mind is still active. I slept unclothed, a habit I had had most of my life, finding nightshirts uncomfortably restrictive. And then, for the second and last time during my stay in the village of Lorne, I was wrenched from my sleep. No light in my face this time, no candle or lamp. No friend exhorting me to throw on clothes as quickly as I could. Nothing from the familiar world but the harsh sound of someone crying out.

'You are guilty, not me!' a voice somewhere outside my room was screaming. 'Dollet! Not me.'

I pushed myself up on my elbows and a sharp stab in my ribs reminded me of my riding injury. The moon outside was high; I guessed we were in the early hours of the morning. And suddenly another cry came through my window, this one a wordless scream that spoke of a visceral fear, something animal.

Then something dark fell past my window. I caught but a glimpse - a sense of it more than sight - before I heard it hit the ground. I jumped out of bed and rushed to look. At the bottom of the wall, spread on the ground someone lay broken - man or woman I could not tell. I took a lamp, pulled on a pair of breeches and ran out of my room, down the stairs, threw open the front door and sprinted to the wall below my window as if I were running for my own life, not someone else's. There on the grass they lay, one arm covering their head to obscure their identity in the night. I dropped to my knees to see who it was and if there was any spark of life left in the body, a glimmer of God-given creation from within. I lifted the arm.

The face of Gregory Archer had sunk into the ground, such had been the force of his fall. His cheekbones and eye socket were beneath the soil. Dirt was spilling obscenely from his mouth, and his neck was twisted and broken. When a man dies there is no look of terror, no image of his murderer burned into his irises as the ancients believed. The only expression I have ever seen on the dead is nothing more than sadness; as if all that inhabits death is regret.

There was little point in checking for breath or pulse. I peered up through the night. Above my own bedroom, there was the upper floor, which was abandoned and all the windows boarded up, and then the roof, with a rough walkway around it. There was a balustrade that a man could easily trip or step over, but nothing else to see - no sign of anyone else. Not then, anyhow. A few moments earlier? Who could say. The same went for the house grounds.

I waited to see if anyone else had heard the disturbance and would come rushing out, but none did. I kneeled again to the body to check for marks indicating violence. There was nothing and Archer was wearing perfectly normal daywear. There was, however, a smell of strong drink to him.

It was inconceivable that his death was unconnected to my belief that he had passed some dangerous intelligence to Father Dollet so I cursed the fact that I had only begun the first tentative steps towards confronting him. Now I would never have the chance to probe properly.

On the assumption that he had been deliberately killed - although I could not yet rule out suicide or an accident - the guilty party must have been motivated by the same belief as I: that Archer had revealed the secret. But that spawned a myriad of more detailed explanations. Archer's killer could have killed Dollet too and wanted to prevent Archer leading me or the authorities to him. Or he could have been a friend of Father Dollet out for revenge. Or he could have been party to the secret and wanted to seal Archer's lips before he blabbed again. Or a handful of other perfectly plausible explanations.

I went back into the chequer-floored hall of the chateau. It seemed to me that there was someone who should be informed before all the others, but first I would check to see if anyone was abroad in the house without good reason. I picked a heavy candlestick from a table. It was unlit but I was not interested in its light - I wanted something I could use if it came to a struggle.

I reached the landing of the main staircase, and then up another flight to the disused floor. The rooms were unlocked and showed ghostly furniture covered in white sheets like unwelcome reminders of richer times. Each was covered in a thick layer of dust that showed no footprints - no one had been in these rooms for years, if not decades. The access to the roof was nowhere to be seen and it was far more likely to be via the servants' wing. That was reached through doors on this floor and the ground floor. I went through to find my steps tapping on stone instead of wood. There were no paintings on these narrower walls, no gay flowers in vases.

I made my way up a spiral staircase to a little wooden door onto the roof, and cautiously stepped out. It was quite deserted, that was clear. Flat and open, I was able to walk around the low wall on its four edges and see the countryside laid out in midnight blue. Up on the hill, I could make out the outline of the church. The wind ripped about me and my skin felt taut and sharp against it. Had there not been more on my mind, I would have found the view and position exhilarating.

At the point where I guessed Archer must have last stood I looked down. I could not see the body, but I was sure it was there on the lightless ground. I pitied the man. He would have had time enough in that long fall to realize he was going to die.

Returning to the house, I hunted through the servants' wing, then the ground floor but there was no one and nothing out of place. For a more thorough search I would have to rouse the household. But first I had to tell Juliana.

Outside the room she shared with Catherine I was about to knock when I hesitated for a moment. And I moved, instead, to the room further down the corridor, which I knew to be Archer's. It was open and I found bedclothes on the floor and a chair turned over. There were papers scattered and falling from a desk including a musical score part-finished. A near-empty bottle of pastis was on its side. Nowhere in the room could I find anything else out of place: his clothes were neatly arranged in the garderobe; a small strong box sat under the desk with the key in it and I opened it to find an amount of money but nothing out of the ordinary for a man with a wife and child to look after.

Frustrated by the signs of some sort of violence, but nothing to indicate its cause, I left the room. Then I steeled myself for what was to come.

Three times I rapped with my knuckles on the thick door to Juliana's room. Nothing. I tried again, louder. I stood back and waited. The air was warm and stuffy, indolent. Then I heard whispers. They stopped, waited, and started again. And the handle twisted down. For some reason it reminded me of the twisted neck on the ground outside.

A crack of light appeared in the jamb. Barely wider than a playing card. It opened enough to see a brown eye, a streak of cheek and the curve of a chin. She caught her breath.

'Catherine, I must speak to your mistress.' For a few seconds she stood there unmoving, then closed the door.

The whispers began again and there was the sound of sheets pulled away and clothes hastily thrown on. It opened a second time and the eye that I saw now was pale blue set in paler skin, though without the powder it had borne before. I could see the mouth beginning a curious smile.

'Maître Sévine?'

'Juliana.'

'No "madame" tonight?'

'I have some terrible news.'

The door opened to show the woman wrapped in a heavy cloak. It was red and gold, surely something she had once worn on the stages of London and Venice as a queen of antiquity. A Cleopatra or Bathsheba. Under the present circumstances, I thought there was something insane about it. 'Then you had better tell me.' I saw Catherine behind, standing in a nightgown with a sheet pulled about her. 'I have had bad news in my time.'

'Your husband has died.' Despite her words, she sank at the knees and opened her mouth, gasping for air as if she had felt a blow in her stomach. Catherine dropped the sheet, exposing her legs from the thighs down, and rushed to her mistress, pulling her in. 'I think he fell from the roof onto the ground.'

'Fetch a doctor. Now!' she screamed.

'I am sorry, so sorry, but he is dead.'

'Fetch a doctor or I will ride to the next town and fetch one myself.' She swiped the back of her hand at me. I allowed it to strike.

'I am sorry. Gregory is dead. I know he is.'

She sobbed on the floor, tears bursting on a plush rug. Her body shook without sound for nearly a minute before she spoke again, this time in a whisper. 'Show me.'

Catherine looked up at me.

'Of course.'

I led the way. Either my movements or Juliana's cries had indeed woken at least one person and brought him quickly from his own quarters. Peugere was on the staircase in an old dressing gown, looking shocked. He seemed to have heard what was said because he did not ask. Instead he followed the three of us down and out the door. Above, I could hear more movement on one of the floors. The flood of sadness that came from deep inside Juliana must have woken more of the residents. They could wait.

Outside, snow-coloured birds dived in a white silhouette across the tarry black sky. I led the two women and the footman around the house. Catherine had her arm around Juliana, who was still wrapped in her cape. They walked barefoot like mediaeval penitents until they rounded the corner and saw the dashed and broken remains of Gregory Archer. Juliana made no cry now, but turned to the wall and beat it once with her fist. Then she walked to the body, turned him on his back and laid his arms and legs out along his body. She brushed the dirt from his lips, and lifted them lingeringly to her own. I could not tell if there was any warmth left in his mouth. I hoped there was and it was more than marble for her. I have seen such tender gestures in the strongest soldiers as well as widows. It is at the deepest part of our common humanity: we do not want our friends or loved ones to leave without a farewell.

She laid her cheek on his chest, above his heart and closed her eyes. Whispered words of a prayer floated to myself and to Catherine, who had tears streaming down her face, her own lips quivering.

Juliana finished her prayer. 'What happened?' she asked.

'I do not know. I was awake and I heard someone fall.'

'An accident?' Catherine said.

'Perhaps.'

I waited. The shock, then the anger, and now there would be sadness. Juliana looked down at the broken man and her face contorted in pain, then she walked away towards the river, her bare feet padding on the dry ground. I took a pace or two in her wake. She stopped about a dozen yards away. I struggled to make her out now, she could have been a ghost with its back to the living.

'She will be strong,' Catherine told me.

'I do not doubt it.' I looked east. 'We have to wake the house. I think whoever did this is gone or lying low. But you should come back in with us anyway.'

'I am not leaving him here alone,' Juliana said, defiantly striding back towards us.

There was little point in arguing, so I left her there with Catherine and Peugere while I returned to rouse the household.

As I left, my mind was in turmoil. The death of Father Dollet had seemed an aberration - something discrete, isolated, that would not touch the living. Now I knew that was wrong. There was far more death in the soil of Lorne than I had seen. And I feared what more might come.

An hour later the household was assembled in the ballroom. Some stood, some leaned on walls, some sat on chairs. None spoke. Francois, with a face like ashes from the grate, stood bewildered in front of them. Only two people were not in the room: Juliana was keeping vigil by the side of her husband, his body laid out on her bed, and Catherine was on a chair outside that room, having refused to leave her mistress.

Eventually, Francois spoke. 'Tragedies. They happen in–' He broke off. I watched the Archers' child, Charles. He stood silent, his arms crossed. I would have given anything to know what was surging through his mind then. 'The acts of God are not understood by men. We will understand this one day. Not tonight. I cannot promise you that. One day. But now, let us pray to God for the soul of Gregory Archer. He was a friend to all of us. A father. A husband. A devout man.' All bowed their heads and closed their eyes. I kept mine open. 'Most merciful father. You have seen fit to take our friend and father to you. We beg you to keep him with you in your house so that one day we will be reunited. Amen.'

For the rest of the night, we waited for morning. Peugere ministered to our needs as best he could but apart from a little water no one wanted anything. He appeared lost. I saw Francois speak to him, telling him to take a seat.

The butler looked scandalized. 'No, monsieur. So long as you need me, I shall stand.'

Francois nodded and took me to the kitchen to talk. 'What can this mean?' he asked.

'If I knew then I would say. But we can be certain now that Archer was the man who confessed some hidden sin to Father Dollet. And we can suppose that his death was connected to Father Dollet's, but whether it was because he killed Father Dollet, or because he knew who did, or because the killer wanted to stop him telling anyone else what he told Father Dollet, it is impossible to say.'

'Tell me what you know, I beg of you. I cannot sit there for another hour berating myself for my empty head.'

'Of course. Regarding Dollet, the most interesting aspect is that he was expelled from the Carmelite order.'

'Expelled? He did not leave of his own will?'

'Expelled.'

'For what offence?'

'It depends upon whom you will believe. Dom Mathieu will have it that a minor scandal erupted when he was found with some pots in his possession that did not belong to him.'

Francois's lip pursed. 'That is strange. But you suggest there is another possibility.'

'I do. If you believe Cotillard . . .'

'Cotillard?'

'Yes. He suggests that he and Father Dollet were engaged in an unnatural relationship.'

Francois's jaw dropped. He blustered. 'Absurd!' I shot him a warning look and he lowered his voice. 'Quite absurd. He would never contravene God's law like that.'

'Plenty of Popes have contravened God's law like that.' Francois looked positively pale. 'And knights. Let us not forget Richard the Lionheart.'

'He was not!' he said, incredulous.

'He was.'

He pursed his lips and thought, briefly. 'Strange people, the Normans. I imagine he picked up the practice while crusading in the infidel lands.'

'It may not be all he picked up,' I mused.

'What is the sentence for that crime?'

'It is a capital offence.'

'By what method?'

'Fire. It is more common than you think. The Marquis de Sade is still in the Bastille under sentence of it.'

His eyebrows lifted. 'Will it be carried out? Not that I care a sous for de Sade.'

'Sooner or later.' He was quiet as he pictured the flames. 'And if the Lionheart tried it now, he would find the law unbending even for his royal person.'

'You think so?' he replied.

'The law is administered by lawyers. Whom do you think are the most regicidal men around? Who make up most deputies to the Third Estate? They would relish the opportunity.'

'Incredible times we are in.' He shook his head. 'Anyway, what of Cotillard?'

'He denies having hurt Father Dollet,' I said.

'He might well, of course. You witnessed how he acted when he burst into Mass on Sunday. Not only did he harangue Father Dollet but he also assumed the position of Christ on the cross, just as we found the priest. That can be no coincidence.'

'Have you ever known Cotillard to be violent?' I asked.

'I have not. But there will always be a first act.'

'But murder as a first act? And in such a fashion?'

He paused. He took my point. 'True. But the man is so mad he might have butchered Father Dollet and forgotten all about it the next day.'

'That is possible,' I admitted. 'Diseases of the mind can hardly be predicted or quantified. And yet, there is something in him that makes me lean to the impression that he tells the truth. Still, there is no good reason for my impression, so we will leave it to one side.'

'And what about the Gypsy boy?'

I sighed in irritation. 'I can see no reason for laying the charge at his door. Had Jacob killed the priest, even for a reason that we cannot fathom, he would have probably run and never been caught. He has friends in Paris.' I did not reveal how I knew that.

'Then among the other villagers? Or . . .' He indicated the residents of our house.

'I have found no link. And there is always the point that Father Dollet was not merely killed, he was crucified like Saint Pierre. It was ritual, not merely functional. It is, from the view of a man who sees through an inverting lens, religious.'

'And that is why Cotillard is the man!' insisted Francois. He would not let go. 'Insane. A man needs be insane for such an act. Who is insane? Cotillard.' He looked at the door to the drawing room, distant and out of earshot. 'And what of Archer? Could Cotillard have killed him too?'

I suppressed my irritation. 'My friend, I do not believe it was Cotillard.'

He shook his head as if he were shaking off a swarm of flies. 'Archer knew of Cotillard's guilt. Cotillard smells the air and knows the hound is after him. The quarry becomes the hunter and he confronts Archer. So he throws poor Archer from the roof.'

I huffed in annoyance. Mostly because I could find no holes to pick in that explanation other than an earthy trust of Cotillard's word that he was not guilty of Father Dollet's death.

23 June 1789

At midday the abbot arrived in the same cart that had taken Father Dollet. If asked, I would have said Dom Mathieu was thinner than on that previous occasion, as if the fear of whatever had entered Lorne was itself sweating the fat off him.

Juliana walked behind the cart. Catherine and Annalise were beside her, and Charles behind. I had no words that would be of use to any of them.

The abbot, for the second time in three days, committed the earthly remains of a Christian to the soil. He said a prayer for the dead man whom he probably hardly knew, if at all. Charles then read from the Bible of how Christians would all rise from their graves on the greatest day and fly to Heaven. He seemed to believe it with the utmost fervour.

Between two houses that we passed I saw another young figure, although his head was that of a far older man. We think of our cities and universities as the places where young men can train and expand their brains. But somehow Jacob had managed it in a country hovel surrounded by failed barley. He was standing upright in the shadow of the sunward cottage. I drifted from the procession and took him a few paces further away so we could talk.

'You did not want to join the procession?' I asked.

'You think they would allow me in? And, Maître Sévine, you too seem out of place among these people.' He lowered his voice. 'I think you think the same as us. You want equality.'

A strange vista. Ahead of me my old friend, the seigneur, was walking from a village that, if he so chose, he could burn to the ground, towards a chateau that had been passed through his line for two centuries. And then on the other side was this young Gypsy inviting me into his cult of revolution, whose congregation would burn down the chateau but leave the village standing.

'Equality is an illusion. You will never achieve it this side of death.'

'Of course we will not.' I was surprised by his answer.

'But we will achieve a part of it. We will not walk the streets arm in arm with strangers. We will not raise cows the size of houses so that there is enough cream for everyone. But we will have a speck of each of these and a speck is more than none. Come tomorrow night. You know the place.'

It did stir something within me, that invitation. He was right that I wanted change - wide change - to the lives of people throughout the land. But fighting the desire to join him were the responsibility I felt to bring my old tutor justice, and the knowledge that the forces ranged against Jacob and anyone who joined him were ten times stronger than he could ever muster. 'I have my own task right now,' I said.

'I know. But we will be visiting someone soon. He is the one organizing our enemies against us and he is no friend of yours, from what I hear. He might not enjoy our visit.' I guessed who he meant but de Rotanne would be no easy target. The boy had fire in him and nothing is more likely to leave a man dead. 'Well, you know the place where we meet.'

'I do,' I said. 'Tell me, do you know anything of the death of Gregory Archer?'

'Nothing.'

'But you watch the house sometimes. The pretty scullery maid, Alice, is it?'

He looked at his feet and blushed, I think. Then he looked up and me and burst into laughter. I joined him. 'But did you see anything the night Archer died?'

'No, I was not there then.'

'Indeed. What about the night of Father Dollet's death?'

'Oh, I stopped by that night. I was on my way to one of

our meetings but when I passed the church to get to the meeting and saw the church open, I looked in. You know what I saw then. And I knew that there would be a lot of noise very soon, so I returned home to make sure my parents were protected.'

'What time were you at the house?'

'I would have left my house at eleven to get to our meeting and been at the chateau five minutes later,' he said. 'I give myself half an hour there.' He smiled.

'Did you see Archer?'

'Yes. He is at his desk most nights - composing his music, I presume. I think I saw him that night. Just sitting there, working.'

Juliana and Catherine had been with Archer until they had gone to bed that night. So, unless they were both lying, it would have been near impossible for him to have gone out, savagely attacked Father Dollet, and returned to be seen by Jacob, quietly composing music.

I bade Jacob farewell and followed Francois back to that chateau, which I now saw in a different light. Could this bastion fall? Of course, all bastions had fallen eventually. The pillars of imperial Rome lay broken and tipped over in that city. The Goths had known not what they did.

We trod the path down to the house. Juliana was bearing it well. Somehow - God forgive me the thought - it suited her. The beautiful tragic heroine was the part she was born to play. The two other women with her were her handmaidens, helping her to the cliff where she would wave farewell to her lover, knowing that he would never return.

The house opened for us as we arrived, revealing the staff lined up in the hall to show their respects. Then, having been awake for a great deal of the night, most of the household went to bed. And yet I heard the pianoforte in the music room begin to play. Painful as the moment was, I needed to speak to her, the sooner to discover the truth of what had happened to her husband. I went to fetch the sheets of Archer's final music.

When I reached the music room, Juliana was looking out the window. 'You want to ask me questions. Do so,' she said. 'I know that time matters.'

'I have come to believe your husband recently made a confession to Father Dollet, and that confession set off this terrible chain of events.' The muscles of her mouth moved beneath the skin, but she said nothing. 'It is possible that whatever he confessed seemed of little importance then but took on greater importance later, or it could have been something obviously severe from the beginning. Have you any idea what it could be?'

She went to the piano, stroked her finger across the length of the keyboard, and lifted her chin to me. 'My husband could tell me anything. I can think of absolutely nothing that could bring someone to murder. Nothing.'

'It might not be something of which he was himself guilty, but some deed committed by another that he had witnessed or heard of.'

'Again, nothing.'

'You will forgive me if I ask the same of others, such as Catherine. It is possible that he revealed it to another.'

'If this great secret exists, I wish you luck in finding it.'

'Will the masked ball now be cancelled?' I expected her to say it would be. I was wrong.

'I have been thinking about that.' She touched a key, ringing a delicate note in the air. 'The best tribute I can make to Gregory is to play his music. His final composition will have its premiere even though the genius that put it to paper is no longer with us. The ball will go ahead.'

Well, it did seem fitting: a headstone is no memorial for a composer of music. A performance of his work is how he would, surely, wish his departure from this world to be marked. I wished her well.

Francois was staring out of the library window with an almanac open on his lap. 'Why do we not take a walk in the grounds?' he said. I agreed and we went down to the river, which was meandering lazily in the afternoon heat. 'I have had an offer for my seigneurie and estate,' he said. There was something in his tone that was, I think, ashamed. I wondered why.

'Well, that is good, is it not?' I insisted.

'Not when you hear who has made the offer.'

I steeled myself. I had a premonition that needed no witch to reveal it.

'It is de Rotanne.'

Of course it was. It was no coincidence. No coincidence at all. 'He knows I am here,' I said. 'This is his way to get to me.'

'Maybe. David . . .' I could guess what he was about to say. I did not blame him - he did not know that I had levelled a pistol at de Rotanne, and the comte would have me cut to ribbons if he could. 'I have to sell to him. If I do not I am utterly bankrupt.'

I thought quickly. While Francois was seigneur, the comte could not touch me in Lorne. But when he was himself seigneur . . .

'What exactly is he offering?'

'Ten thousand livres.' De Rotanne was wealthy enough to pay that without batting an eyelid. Then he could arrest me and take me back to Versailles for whatever unpleasant fate he wished to inflict upon my person. I feared that fate was drawing close.

'That is a pittance,' I told Francois.

'No doubt. But I need it to pay off the bankers. Otherwise . . .'

I knew what the otherwise would be. Francois bankrupt. Everything would go to his creditors and I would be out on my arse anyway. I might as well do my best for him while I still could. And then I would take to my heels once more.

'I will be your lawyer.'

He raised his eyebrows. 'I thought you would want to stay away from the comte.'

'He knows I am here, so there is nothing to lose by presenting myself.'

'Are you certain? What if he tries to arrest you?'

I suspected an arrest would be low on his plan. 'No doubt he will, as soon as the rights are transferred to him. At that point - well, a few days before, let us say - I will saddle Jackdaw in the night and get as far from here and the comte as I can.'

'Where to?'

'England. Italy, perhaps. I do not know.'

A life in France forever running as de Rotanne's pack got my scent would be no life at all. So I would go where the comte had no friends and many enemies. I was thankful then for his prodigious ability to make foes.

'Well, yes, then. I will gladly accept your offer.'

But the development raised again the question: how exactly the comte knew I was in Lorne. Someone must have informed him, but who? Could his army of informants have spread to Lorne? A snake hiding in the grass was not a pleasant addition to the garden. I would have to be on my guard for them.

'What will you do for an income when all your rents have gone?' I asked.

'Join a band of travelling minstrels and play at the houses of the rich.'

'It sounds one of your better ideas.'

'Do you think de Rotanne would have me?' he asked. 'I could dance like a Moor.'

'He might.'

'I will be a whole new creature. Rise like a phoenix from the ashes.' He laughed.

'Or a butterfly from its cocoon,' I mused.

'What? A butterfly?'

'Yes, oh, just something I had forgotten about. On Father Dollet's desk there was a note. It said, "A man dreamed he was a butterfly. When he awoke he could not tell if he was a man who had dreamed he was a butterfly, or a butterfly dreaming that he was a man. But what did HE dream before he changed?" I can't make head nor tail of it.'

'It is probably nothing,' Francois said after a moment.

'Yes, probably.' He was correct: we all scribble notes sometimes, and most of them are nought but the chaff of our daily thoughts.

He sobered a little. 'He will allow me to rent the house from him and live as his tenant.' He paused. 'Have I shown you the hamlet?'

'No.' I dimly recalled him once writing to me to describe his father constructing a strange miniature village on the estate shortly before he croaked.

'Ah!' he chuckled. 'It is part of the reason I am a pauper. This way.' I followed him along the river to the mid-point where it widened out and a tree-covered island rose up from the water. On our bank there was a little boat, big enough to hold three or four men. Attached to each end was a rope. At the near end, the rope was tied around a tree on the riverbank; the other was attached to an iron ring pegged into the ground on the island. We stepped in and Francois hauled us across the river. 'You know this is the same boat we used to play in as a child? Most of the wood has been replaced, but it is the same one.'

'Like Theseus's ship,' I said.

'What?'

'It is an ancient question. The ship that the Greek hero Theseus sailed in was preserved after he died. But every so often the planks would rot and be replaced. Eventually every one had been changed. So, was it still his ship?'

'Of course.'

'Why?'

'I have no idea.'

'No, nor has anyone else. It is a question of identity. What is it about us that makes us us? Are you Francois simply because I say you are, or are you Francois because there is something in you, in your skin and your bones, that is Francois-ish? Or is there a third option: that you are Francois because you think and move and live as Francois does?' I enjoyed the chance to talk of something else for a change, something purely of intellect. And those old paradoxes provided infinite road for meandering discussion.

'It must be in my bones,' he replied without hesitation.

'Why?'

'Because I said so.'

'Good answer.'

I stepped out onto the island. But as my shoe touched the soil, Francois let go of the rope so my rear foot, still in the boat, drifted backwards and I found my legs splitting apart. I had no choice but to stumble knee-deep into the water. Francois found this hilarious. For a minute I could see him as a small boy again. In order to maximize the recollection, I pushed him into the water, full-body, creating a splash that flew up into the air. He did not stop laughing and I hauled him out. 'Ah, father will clip our ears for this,' he said happily. 'Now, it is this way.' He led us through a curtain of trees, which parted to reveal a pair of thatched cottages, one with a miniature waterwheel turning in a thin stream alongside it. 'Yes, my father spent what was left of the family riches on this. It is modelled on the garden of Chantilly.'

'Francois, you obviously confuse me with someone who has the slightest interest in gardening.'

'Yes, I thought I might. Prince Louis-Joseph had a hamlet built at the Chateau de Chantilly about fifteen years ago. All these fake rustic cottages.'

'Oh, the ones that the Queen liked so much.' I knew that her own pretend village at Versailles had been modelled on another she had seen somewhere.

'Those ones indeed. But before she had the idea, my own papa had spent thousands of livres employing the prince's architect to build these. Come on in.'

He opened the door to the first. Inside it was a peasant dwelling, but one where nothing was broken and no one was starving as they did in the real homes of those under-trodden wraiths who harvested our grain and turned it into brioche. I found it a little distasteful. Francois opened a cupboard, found a candle and tinderbox and placed them inside his frock coat. We walked around these strange monuments to folly and then hauled the boat back to the riverbank. 'And over there is the only useful thing my father built,' said Francois. 'Follow me.'

He led me along a roughly beaten path to a small clump of trees on the bank. Within it was a little brick structure, like a short round tower but not much wider than the wooden door that was set into one side. Lichen had turned the outside yellow and ivy had mottled that colour so that it appeared to be a living thing growing up from the moss. Francois pointed to the door and put on an old man's croak. 'Will you enter? Do you dare enter . . .'

'The ice house?' I interjected.

'Oh. So you know what it is.'

'I presume the door leads down to the chamber where the ice is kept.'

'Yes.'

'And it is built near the river because the water keeps the ground cool, so the ice blocks last longer after they are placed in there during winter?'

'They last right into the summer,' he harrumphed, disappointed that I had guessed the structure was nothing more daunting than a method for the cooks to prepare frozen puddings and cold drinks during the hot months.

'I believe the Persians first invented ice houses,' I said.

'Bully for them.'

I was sorry for spoiling his surprise. 'I am sure it is a very fine ice house.'

'The finest,' he replied with a grin. You could not keep Francois d'Agnes down. But as we approached the door, he seemed confused by something.

'What is it?' I asked.

'The door should not be open.'

But it was. It was heavy, insulated with iron on the inside, but clearly ajar. A step inside and our breath was mist in the chilled air. Stone steps led down from the doorway and Francois presented the candle and tinderbox that he had taken from the cottage, but as he was about to strike the flint, I stayed his hand.

'Do you smell that?' I asked, sniffing the air.

'Smell what?'

'Like something burning. Does it always smell like that down here?'

'No.' He looked bemused and proceeded to light the candle. The stairs down were illuminated and we descended into a plain vault the size of a large bed chamber.

A mist of thin smoke hung above the scene. There were seven or eight barrels around the walls, in which the ice was packed, but between two of them there was something alien: a circle chalked on the floor and a small fire, nearly burned out. There were a few glowing twigs but the heart of the blaze was a couple of charred masses that were not natural wood.

I kicked them apart. They smoked and smouldered on the floor but I could tell what they were - or had been: the remains of books. And as they cooled enough for me to pluck them up, I could just make out the title of one: the *Petit Albert* that taught simple people black magic to reign over their neighbours. I presumed the other was the other stolen book - *The Discoverie of Witchcraft* - that had been taken from the locked drawer in Father Dollet's desk. Most of the pages were gone, consigned to the flames like the witches they had once talked of. But I recognized a few that remained: the instructions for making a Hand of Glory, the magical weapon derived from the severed hand of a murderer.

I threw the remaining pages into the fire, where they turned yellow-brown and shrivelled away like the withered flesh they described.

I wanted to know who had been there minutes earlier.

Who had been using this as his secret den. They had much to confess.

Here ends the second part of The Murderous Deeds in the Village of Lorne in France and How They Brought About the Bloody Revolution.

Chapter Six

I wiped my sleeve across my face. I had not even seen that the candles in the Peldon Rose had been lit and the tinker from whom I had taken the penny blood had, in the time that I had been galloping through the lines, taken a meal, finished that meal and lit a bulbous short-stemmed clay pipe with an image of the Devil etched into it. He was gently puffing tobacco smoke.

'Did you find in it what you desired to find?' he asked curiously. Briefly, I even wondered if he had known beforehand of my desperate interest in the publication and had deliberately flashed it in front of me, but then I put the idea from my mind. No, he was an itinerant tinker and lover of printed words. So I asked him where he had acquired it.

He squinted to the ceiling, trying to bring the detail to mind. 'It was within a bundle I picked up in Norwich from a news seller.'

That was not much aid. It could have come from anywhere. I picked it up and gazed again at the back page. And then I noticed: a line of tiny text along the bottom of the sheet, followed by a small cartoon of a fort or castle on a huge rock, with a town below it. 'What's that?' I said to myself.

The hawker, taking my words as a question to him, held a candle close to the page. 'Printer's mark,' he said, tapping the tiny picture.

'What is one of those?'

'What do you suppose it to be? A mark to say who printed the publication.'

I felt a thrill. 'Do you know it? Can you tell me who they are?' I asked, hoping against hope that this man would know the printing house, and be able to send me their way.

He shook his head. 'No, no. There are hundreds across our nation.' I felt the thrill ebb into disappointment. But he was still staring at the page. 'What does that say?' he said, pointing to the fine text. 'Your young eyes are better than mine.'

I held the page an inch from my nose. The orange candlelight enabled me to – barely – decipher the words. 'Printed upon the University Press,' I said. 'University.' There were but two universities in England, so the possibilities were narrow. 'Oxford or Cambridge!' I had two cities to choose from, and I could reach either by coach in a day or two.

'Could be, could be,' said the hawker. 'Something, though. I have been to those cities many a time. And each has a castle. But not like in this picture.'

'How so?'

'Those castles were knocked to pieces hundreds of years ago. And neither sits on a cliff.'

So that militated against Oxford or Cambridge. A thought struck me. 'Are there universities in other countries?'

'Of course. But any publishing house is hardly likely to print a pamphlet in English. Except for . . .'

'Yes?' I burst out heartily.

'The Scottish universities,' he said thoughtfully. 'Aha, my lad. I think we have it. There are four universities in Scotland: in the cities of Glasgow, Edinburgh, St Andrews and Aberdeen.'

'Do any of them have a castle like this?' I could barely contain myself.

'One, and one only. I have seen it twice and will never forget it.'

'Please tell!'

'A majestic castle on a rock that towers over the town.'

'Where?'

'The home of the Scottish kings,' he said. 'Edinburgh.'

Edinburgh. And as I drew from my mind the map of Britain that I had imprinted there over the years, I calculated how long it might take to sail there.

Three days. The length of time one-eyed Astaroth had told me it would take to sail to 'the Circle'.

I was for Edinburgh.

Mr Tolson was taken aback. 'Edinburgh? Whyever there?'

'I have read it is a town with opportunities for young men,' I replied. Had I said that the reason was that my past – and most likely those that made it their business to capture me as a result of that past – might well be found there, my protector would have ruled the town to be the very last on the face of the earth whither he would send me. For he would have taken far more heed of the danger to my being than I did.

A part of me, you understand, was naive enough to see the forthcoming chapter of my life as a Sunday fireside tale, told to wide-eyed youths. The lone heroes of those stories were always bloodied but alive and triumphant at the close of the novel. And not a single one ever took their schoolmasters with them on the errand. Yes, I was younger than my tutor.

So young that I did not know the adventures of life as often as not left the good as the victims, their life leaching from them into the cold earth.

So now I blush a little at my recklessness; and yet, on the other side of my face, am I not simultaneously proud of the young man who rushed headlong into the cyclone? Well, yes, I am, reader. For I will not be him again. And perhaps that is a little tragedy of age: our brains overtake our passions. Of course, it must be so in order that we can protect our reckless young, but who does not also miss the adventurism of youth? Show me that man or woman and I will show you one without the flower of romance in their soul.

In the end, I am far from certain that Mr Tolson believed my feigned reason for going, yet he was thoughtful for a while before stating: 'Well, I could make some enquiries. Perhaps we could find a gentleman in need of an assistant. He might train you in a profession. You are of the age now to begin such an education.'

An assistant? Why not? So long as it was in Edinburgh, and a step on the path to knowing who I was, I would take any such offer.

'I should like to go soon.'

Through the doorway I could see Iphigenia, carrying a basket of clothes to the schoolroom. I had known from the moment of fixing on Edinburgh that it would be harder to inform her of my departure than her father.

So, after the interview with my benefactor concluded,

I sought her out. She was placing the younger boys' clothing within the shared press. The lads themselves were outside, playing with sticks and wooden shields.

'Iphigenia,' I said, my heart in my mouth.

Her back was to me as she folded a nightshirt. 'I overheard what you said to my father.'

'I must go.'

'Why? I could tell what you told father was untrue. I am sure he knew that too.' She turned to face me and I sat upon the bed I had occupied from my very earliest memories. I knew every lump in the mattress and knot in the frame.

It seemed to me familiar, but something I had outgrown. Something bigger than I, or Iphigenia, or Mr Tolson or Mersea was reaching out a hand to draw me away.

'I think I can learn something of myself there.'

'You mean, of where you came from?' I felt a breeze on my cheek from the open window, and nodded. 'Be careful,' she said, softly and wisely. 'It might not be what you wish it to be. Sometimes we are better off not knowing.'

She was right, of course. Why is it that we always believe the truth will set us free? The truth can be a prison. Gaoled men can dream of being released, but one can never un-know the truth. A painful knowledge will always be at your side, whispering in your ear, driving you mad.

'You are right. But I will take the chance.'

Had I been an older man then, my mind would surely have weighed the consequences. But a young man with a burning curiosity glides over any evil in his future and plunges fast into the maelstrom.

'Take care. I wish you to return one day, Lysander.'

I felt the two-year gap in our ages keenly then. She was the voice of maturity and reason. I was not. I was anything but. We both missed mothers we had lost in infancy. It gave us a bond of the saddest kind. And I think it made her fear further loss.

'I will take care,' I told her. But I may as well have had my fingers crossed, for that was a falsehood.

Chapter Seven

The time of my leaving proved to be two months later – a span of time that saw me turn eighteen years old – after letters were exchanged with one Angus Baird of the Castlehill, Edinburgh, a surgeon who had advertised for a junior. Cutting into bodies sounded gruesome to me, but I was fixed on the location, not the trade.

And so it was that one drizzling morning in September I found myself deposited as dawn broke, in a puddle of human waste on a steep hill, before the gates of a fearsome-looking ancient castle. I blinked. While the address might have given me a suggestion as to what to expect, I had not predicted that an actual stone fort, complete with towers, turrets and unshaven musket-carrying guards was to be my destination. I absent-mindedly stared through the gates, and as I shuffled I moved my feet and felt foul liquid seep in through the leather.

'Naw, naw, naw,' chuckled a voice at my back. 'Ye'll no be gaun in yon place.'

'I . . . I do not . . . what did you say?' I replied, turning to meet the speech and finding a rosy-cheeked and well-fed lad my own age, dressed in scuffed breeches and coat, his hands in his pockets.

'Och, it's tae be English, is't?'

'I . . . I'm sorry. I do not . . .'

'Naw, ye'll no, will ye? Och well,' and his tone changed to an exaggerated form of my own speech. 'I shall be hospitable to the new gentleman and discourse in his own pretty tongue.' And he swept a low bow.

I was as discombobulated by this excess of courtesy as by the near impenetrability of his former language.

Wracks of laughter lifted his shoulder once more. 'James McPhail, at your service. Ye mus' . . . I mean you must be Lysander Rose.' And he thrust out his hand.

'I am, yes.' And the warmth of his grip placated me.

His speech settled into the English that I knew, but with a distinct Edinburgh burr.

'Mr Baird has sent me to find ye and make sure ye find the path to his house without bein' murd'ert.'

'"Murder't"?'

'Aye. Ye know, bashed on the head, dirk between the ribs, that sort of thing.' He mimed thrusting a knife into my chest and I flinched. He smirked. 'Featherish one, are ye not?'

I huffed at that. After what I had encountered as a boy – two tough men bent on abducting or killing me – I felt myself no poltroon. I should have liked to have seen this James McPhail fight them off and escape without crying. He looked at me quizzically. 'No, wait, there's something there I can spot.' And he came close to examine me from little more than an inch away. 'Yes, ye don't look like much from the outside. But I can see a lot deeper than most. Ye have some lead in yer veins.' I had never heard such an expression before. But I could grasp its meaning. 'All right, Sergeant Rose, follow me.'

The street ran down hard and steep from the castle,

with its granite-faced guards, to what looked like a more regal palace at the bottom of the mount. 'Ye see before ye the Palace o' Holyrood. That's where our kings and your usurpers live when they're up in Auld Reekie.'

'In where?'

'Auld Reekie – why look about ye. This town. Edinburgh, man. Och, yes. I forgot. *English*. It means "Old Smokey" or some such to ye.'

I could well comprehend the name then. It wasn't just the smoke from houses that was mingling with a light mist, it was that every building seemed utterly coated with thick soot, as if they were wearing clothes of wet black wool.

We passed a middling-sized squarish cathedral. St Giles, I was told by my guide. Edinburgh seemed to me to be a city both fearsome and fearing. It feared God, and its enemies must have been afeared of its military might. There was something in the tall, spiring buildings – a jumble of homes, shops and coffee houses – lining the street shoulder to shoulder that warned against crimes against this state. But as we walked, out of the corner of my eye, I saw something flitting, tripping through the shadows. I halted sharp and stared through the gloom but could make nothing out.

'Aye, that's why Mr Baird wanted me to come for ye. They'll not hurt you while I'm here. They ken me.'

'But if you weren't here?'

'Why, then I would not give tuppence for yer life.'

I was more sceptical at this melodrama than I think he had intended. 'Oh yes?'

'Yes.' He turned and stared me down. 'These are the folk of the tenements and the wynds. Some o' the tunnels underneath.' He pointed to the ground under our feet.

'Do not think yer safe just because ye wear breeches.'

'I do not think that.' No, I knew what lurking danger truly meant.

It was little more than thirty paces to an imposing five-storey house made of soot-clad sandstone. Unlike its neighbours, no lights shone out, so that it had the air of a coiled black cat hiding in the undergrowth and ready to spring on some hapless rodent.

James lifted a giant claw-shaped knocker and slammed it home onto a brass plate, releasing a din like a cannon firing. He did it again and within seconds we heard a whining from behind the threshold of 'All right, all right, I hear you, I hear you.' And the door wheezed open to reveal a prodigiously tall but stooped-over man with yellowish skin, like the bulb of a dim lamp. 'Oh, Rose, is it?'

'Yes, sir,' I said, bowing as formally as ever I had done so.

He looked unhappy with the answer. 'Well, you had better come in.' And at that, my guide left me, with a smirk and wink.

The only similarity between my old teacher and my new master – for so I must call him – began and ended with the number of eyes and limbs. Where one was affable and loved music, the other was intense and dour. He informed me, leading me into a freezing front parlour, that his household consisted entirely of him, with functional morning visits from a housekeeper to provide breakfast and an evening meal of pickled oysters and ale that was left to be taken cold.

'You are shivering,' he observed.

'Yes, sir,' I replied, brightening at the prospect of a fire being lit to ward off the chill.

'You will become accustomed to it.'

I learned that my duties as his apprentice would revolve around student tutorials in anatomy that he gave in the rear parlour of his house, preferring, for some reason, to dissect his subjects there than in the university. 'This way. You shall see it.'

He led me through and I found that part of the building had, indeed, been converted into a small dissection room complete with raised benches to accommodate those observing. In the centre stood a granite-topped table with carved rivulets that ran down to a hole. But it was not the design of the room that made me catch my breath – it was the fact that the dissection table was not then unused. For upon it lay an immensely fat man, his flesh tinted grey, his bulging eyes open and staring upwards, but seeing nothing.

'He will be the first for you,' Mr Baird said solemnly.

And for a moment, the unbidden thought that inhabited my mind was nothing of the prospect of cutting open a human being and peeling away the bloated flesh. It was instead a sort of self-doubt, self-questioning – it was simply: 'Why does death follow you? Are you part of it? Is it a part of you? Will it always be thus?'

'Fetch the pails.' He indicated a row of metal buckets. 'That one is for the fluids.' He pointed to the hole in the table and I gingerly placed it below the hole in the table. 'That one is for the organs. That one for the stomach contents. Do not spill them on your shoes. They are a devil to remove and I do not wish them trampled into the rugs.'

I was afforded no simple time to come to terms with my new position in life. For that very night, his students assembled with their notebooks and I assisted in carving up a human being. I wish I could say I stood bravely through it. But the truth is that it wasn't just that man's stomach contents that ended up in the pail; my own mingled with them to the hilarity of the students and the utter uninterest of my employer.

I went to bed in a bare bedroom above the back door, shaking not from the cold but from a degree of natural shock.

Chapter Eight

What to say of those first weeks? Well, the shock waned as they passed, with dissections every Wednesday morning. Indeed, I came to find my job interesting, as the human form and its soluble mysteries is fascinating when one comes to be elbow-deep in it.

The corpses would be delivered before dawn, ready to be cut apart that day. Any longer and they would begin to make the house smell. 'Who are they?' I asked early on. 'The . . . the people.'

'Murderers. Thieves. The dregs of humanity,' Mr Baird informed me. 'The law civil says I am only to use the corpuses of hanged convicts. All other bodies are to be respected in their integrity before God.'

They arrived courtesy of a freakish-looking pair. One, a wiry tall man with teeth that projected before his lips like a monkey, looked me up and down the first time as if gauging what price he would get for my young form. His companion gave the impression of a cud-chewing fat bovine. If he said a word it would be at least a week before another emerged. Sometimes their wares came fresh, with the mark of a rope around their necks. Others came without such mark – perhaps, instead, with a wound to the side, or broken skull, or no mark at all but a damp smell that suggested a few days under the earth before unexpected and unwanted resurrection.

And Edinburgh was an astonishing city to a lad reared in rural climes. There were majestic streets and vistas down to the sea, raucous students running riot in the streets and music in the inns. When the richest of the city travelled, they were carried in sedan chairs by four footmen – a sight I had never before beheld.

I gained a few acquaintances, such as the mercurial James McPhail, although they could hardly be called friends. James delighted in taking me to the underworld of Edinburgh: the whisky dens in the New Town and boxing matches on the Grassmarket. I enjoyed even learning the customs of the city: that night soil was thrown from the upper windows of the houses with the warning 'gardyloo!' and if you were walking below and did not want to be covered in it, a quick yell of 'hold your hand!' was essential. I learned, too, the local dialect, and even began to mimic it a little as I spoke.

My money was very tight. Mr Baird, grumbling about the cost of the cadavers, kept a tight grasp on outgoings. For instance, when the students were in attendance, the lamps burned sweet spermaceti whale oil. When they were gone, we used fish oil that made our clothes stink. And my own allowance was scarcely above that of a market-stall boy.

Still, I managed entertainment. For a penny, once a week, I took myself to the theatres where one could gawp at the Scottish aristocrats who took the gilded boxes by the stage, clad in their finest rubies and furs. Then an apple or perhaps a cup of small beer on the way home rounded off an enjoyable night.

Sometimes, out for messages or walking by myself

on the High Street, I would observe the swinging corpse of a criminal who had been sent to the gallows beside the cathedral of St Giles, and know that twelve hours later, his – or occasionally her – body would be on our dissecting table. You may find this ghoulish, but to us it was merely the way of medicine and learning.

Neither did I neglect my true calling. For during this period, I pursued my secret task like a demon. Hidden from my master and all the world, I sought two things: one physical and hard to the hand, and one spectral and mist-like. The first was the penny blood. I had to find a copy of the third instalment of the chapbook that detailed my own history. The other question was to discover the nature of the Circle, which the fallen angel, when he had abducted me, had assured me would never let me go. Was it a gang? A philosophy? Was it even some sort of disease that would never leave me? That I had to pursue these quarries hugger-mugger made success all the more elusive.

I tried the first with the booksellers of Edinburgh around Parliament Close, where the society ladies would order improving religious books and secretly slip *Tom Jones, a Foundling* into their bundle of purchases.

The initial time I called into one I was immediately greeted with a sceptical – bordering on the contemptuous – eye from the owner. 'We do not sell such *material*,' he told me with an audible sniff when I explained my quest. The others declined in similar fashions. Over time, I tried the booths between the taverns of the Cowgate, where the disreputable side of Edinburgh's populace drank themselves into the gutter, blanketed by the urine fumes from the surrounding tanneries. But I met with no more success.

My enquiries with friends, acquaintances and even casual strangers for intelligence on the Circle brought only a similar void of knowledge. So that after a while, I felt my energy to pursue the subject falter, and I decided to leave off my enquiries and to enjoy the city – the first city in which I had ever lived.

Something of a breakthrough occurred one day quite by accident. I had often watched with envy while the wealthier inhabitants of the city attended chocolate stalls. The steaming drink seemed to give them warmth and pleasure like a ten-hour sleep on a feather mattress. It was a Saturday, I had a penny in my pocket and strode to one of these stalls close to the palace of Holyrood. The seller – he was, I think, an Irishman – took my coin with as much politeness as he afforded those who wore wigs, and handed me my cup. It was like drinking heavenly manna! I had never before tasted anything so sweet and fulfilling. If I had had enough money for ten cups, I would have bought ten and begged for five more. But still, the natural economy stayed my hand and I had to make do with licking the last remnants from the cup before handing it back.

'Good one, aye?' said the seller happily.

'Aye.'

He leaned in conspiratorially. 'I charge you less than I charge *them*, you know.'

I was bemused. 'Less than who?' I asked.

And he shot his eyes towards a procession of carriages that were then turning into the mews attached to the palace. '*Them*. The Frenchies.' My expression must have been utterly blank, for my mind was. 'The French court. Their King Lewis. All them over here to escape having their heads chopped off.'

'The French court?' I gasped. Thoughts tumbled through my head. The chapbook. My father. The French royals. I had known they were in Britain, but had thought them in London. The French émigrés were often depicted in the newspapers as paupers pretending to riches, living on the munificence of their Anglo-Saxon brethren. Even their putative exiled king, Louis XVIII, was known to be more close with his money in private than in public. It was, doubtless, less than the life to which he had been accustomed, but at least his head and his neck had not been parted by 'Madame Guillotine' like his elder brother's had been.

'You did not know? They live at Holyrood. Our King had enough of them in London and sent them up here where they can't cost him any more. They were all away for a while somewhere, but they are back now. Always so loud in the streets. Still, I can charge them twice what I charge you.' He served another customer while I stared. This had to be the reason that I had been bound for Edinburgh: a population of émigrés. Among them, I must be able to learn of my history and the fate of my family.

I could approach members of that group, but I knew not how they would take my presence – it could as well be a boon or a threat to them. No, instead I resolved first to redouble my efforts to learn more of the chapbook that narrated my beginnings.

I went back to all the book shops I had attended before, and asked anew. I met with only raised eyebrows and huffs of irritation. 'I told ye before, no!' was the common reply. The final straw was the canine laughter I received from a dog-like delivery boy with wild ginger hair in the last shop that I tried. I gave up once more and sauntered away.

I had not gone far when I felt a tug on my sleeve. I spun around to find the dog-like boy.

'You will not find what you seek,' he rasped at me in a guttural voice (that I here translate).

'Oh, will I not?' I replied off-hand, for the impression he gave was of one mocking me.

'Not unless you can furnish me.'

'Unless I what?' I demanded, turning more attention upon him.

He did not answer the question, not directly anyhow. 'That penny blood. Funny thing about it.'

'What do you mean, "funny thing"?' I was becoming annoyed with this strange meandering.

'None left of it. I know it. I read it. Good one, it is.'

'You read it?' I demanded, actually seizing him by the shoulders. 'Tell me how it ends! Tell me now!' He shook me off as roughly as I had snatched at him. But he seemed not angry, he seemed pleased. And I realized why. For he understood that he had a fish in his net.

'It was so long ago that I forget the story.'

'Then sell me a copy! I will pay well for it.'

'Ah, that is the problem.'

'How?' I yelled, my temper escaping me at his deliberate avoidance of answering my needs.

'It was a year or so ago. One of the sellers here had it. Hamish Blythe.' He pointed to one of the booths that was shut up. 'He was drinking in Mother McTavish's when he sees his hut being knocked over by two men, one big, one not so big. He runs over and screams at them – he had been at the whisky or he would never have had the courage, Hamish. "There is no money there, leave it alone!" But the big one comes up to him, draws a knife and puts it to his chest. "We seek a chapbook," he says.' The dog-boy smirked his widest them. 'And you ken well which one.' I did. '"Give us every copy. And tell all your pals." He waved his dirk around. "No more selling of it. If you do, we return with fire-raisers." Now the clever thing would have been for Hamish to say, "Yes, sir. Whatever you say, sir." But instead, he demands to know on whose word these orders are given. "The Circle," says the small man. But at that, the big one turns and swipes his fist across his pal's jaw and tells him to hush.'

I caught my breath. There was no mistaking that name. The boy looked at me queerly and instantly I regretted letting my face speak for me. 'Oh, does that mean something to you?'

'Never you mind if it does or does not.'

'Oh, I will mind all right.' He bared his teeth.

'What happened next?' I demanded.

'Next? Why, they took the two or three copies of the tale that Hamish had, and dumped them by a pile of trash. Then they poured a wee bit of oil on the pile and put a flame to it. Whoosh! Up it all goes in smoke. "Remember, no more selling of it!" the big man warns Hamish. And then they go their way, up Candlemaker Row.'

'What about Hamish?'

'What do you think? He went back into Mother McTavish's and drank enough drams to fall off his stool and sleep it off in the street.'

I felt like having a drop of the hard stuff myself. It was frustrating all the way to my bones that there had been copies aplenty of this chapbook, and now there were none. 'Could there be any in other towns?' I asked hopefully.

He scratched his fluffy chin. 'Those two looked fair determined to make sure not. And penny bloods like that one, well, they only print a few copies at a time.'

'So it is lost!' I moaned.

'Well,' said the boy slyly. 'Perhaps I could find a copy. Just perhaps.'

I could see that he knew where one was to be found. I reached into my pocket book to offer the third-guinea and few shillings that I had saved from the meagre allowance that Mr Baird gave me for entertainment. He took them. 'That is not the price.'

I felt stupid and angry, and snatched his hand back, prising the money from his fist. 'Then what is?' I snarled at him.

He remained smug and cool. 'I know you. I have seen you at the house of the doctor. The one who cuts up the killers.'

'Mr Baird instructs in anatomy.'

'Whatever you call it. He cuts up the hanged men.'

'So?'

'The penny blood. Have you read any of it?'

'I have read some.'

'Have you read of the Hand of Glory within it?'

I was knocked back. Yes, I had read of that. It was detailed within the narrative as witchcraft pure and simple. The hand of a hanged man when preserved in some concoction could be used as a magical weapon to paralyze one's enemies or open locked doors and boxes. The belief in the power of witchcraft was almost as strong in Scots city folk as in French peasantry and it dawned upon me what this boy wanted.

'If you want me to bring you the hand of a dead felon, that is something I cannot do. Here,' I said, offering the money back to him. 'I can get you more.'

'I do not want your money. I want a Hand of Glory!' he snapped, coming so close I could smell the stink of bad meat on his breath. 'There is one I would use it on.'

Even though I should not have been, I was astonished by this: the boy not only believed in black magic, he also had a foe that he intended to petrify like Medusa. Well, he probably had a dozen such enemies. With a Hand of Glory, he could quite rampage through the city until his lust for revenge was sated.

I analysed the question as quickly as I could. I would feel no guilt over giving him an impotent tool. The hard part would be acquiring one. He was quite correct that my apprenticeship placed me in the company of dead felons, but that hardly meant that I could go about hacking off their limbs willy-nilly to bestow on idiots. And yet, it seemed the only way I was going to gain the prize that I so desperately needed. And the fact that this boy referred to its presence within the chapbook tale demonstrated that he had, at least, held and read that text.

'I will get it to you.'

He grunted in joy.

Five days later, wondering if I was in my right mind, for the task I was about seemed the errand of a lunatic, I crept towards a hut at the north end of the Nor'loch, that foul body of fetid water at the foot of the Castle Rock. In the night, it was a black mirror that reflected the castle above it, like Hell looking up to Heaven.

My lungs filled up with the rotten vapour from the

Loch as I approached. It was the reek of decaying wood and dead animals. Thrice I fancied I heard feet slapping in the mud behind me. Thrice I whirled around at the sound but saw only mist and the dim outline of the stone Castle high above.

It was no easy task to discern the broken-down hovel where I was to meet the boy. When I found it, I observed that it had no roof and the doorway was empty, as if the building itself were crying out in distress. Closing on it, my nerves tightened like viola strings as night creatures glared at me before scampering out of my lamp beam and into the surrounding, suffocating blackness.

When I reached the tumbledown structure, I shone my beam in, to find the dog-boy there, perching like a bird on a pile of stones and wood.

'Do you have it?' he demanded breathlessly and urgently, skidding down the mound.

'I have.' I lifted the linen sack that held a hand that I had stolen from a dissected cadaver.

'Show!' And he plunged his own hand inside the bag, plucking it out and lifting it to the light of the moon. Thrilled, he knelt on the sodden ground and lit a candelabra that I had not seen. He examined the grisly ware more closely. 'Yes! It is right.' Unable to contain his excitement, he hurried to a niche in the wall, wherein there was a mass of metal that might have once been a bread oven. He placed the hand on a grill, covered it in plant cuttings that he took from a bag, and lit a little pile of wood below. I could not remember the instructions within the chapbook for creating a Hand of Glory, but it was obvious that this was the process. The boy stood back. 'It will take until dawn,' he said.

'I have supplied what you wanted. Now, give me my return.'

From his jerkin he drew the object I had coveted. It was my turn to snatch, nearly tearing the pages apart as I took from him *The Murderous Deeds in the Village of Lorne in France and How They Brought About the Bloody Revolution. The Third Part.*

By a Gentleman of the Law.

It was dirty and stained, but still the words were as legible as the day they had been cheaply printed. I could not bear even the time it would take to tramp back to my lodging. I sat among the rats on the boy's cathedra of corruption and read.

As I tramped back to the house, I saw Catherine alone in one of the little gardens. I was somewhat surprised to see her without Juliana, who must have still been in need of friendship and comfort; but then I thought Catherine, like anyone else, had her limits. She only had so much sympathy to give without tending to her own grief. She was sitting on a lichen-covered stone bench, her elbows on her knees and her chin in her hands and did not move when I sat beside her.

'Days like these are hard,' I said. Her lips twitched, as if preparing to speak, then halted again as whatever thought she was about to voice lost its appeal. 'But we need them. We need to say goodbye to people we cared for.'

'Is there anyone you care for?' she demanded, a little too harshly. I was not offended but she immediately relented. 'I apologize. That was not fair. You have been . . . kind to me.'

'I have tried.' I had. Kindness was not a great part of my everyday job, and it was far removed from the enquiries I was then pursuing into two murders. But I had tried.

I wanted to speak more deeply to her. The occasion made me want to feel a connexion with her, but also made any conversation too far removed from the sorrow of the morning seem frivolous and selfish. I think she felt the same. We were caught in that impossible tide pulling us in two directions at once. Then I gave in and spoke for an hour. My childhood in Lorne. My manhood in the Americas. My isolation in Versailles. It felt natural. 'I must go,' I told her. For I had sharper, colder work to do and it could not wait forever.

'Can we talk another time?' she asked, turning her face to me, so that the sunlight picked out shimmering tracks of tears that she had wiped away.

'Yes, we can.' I wanted to.

'Thank you.'

I placed my hand on hers - another gesture that was only half what I wished it to be - rose and left.

A little-used room at the rear of the chateau had been given to Annalise the English painter to use as a studio. It suited her task well: large windows facing east, sparse furniture. Dust sheets lay on the floor and the settle. Two easels took pride of place in the centre and boxes of paints, pencils, sharpening knives and the like were scattered throughout. I went to the smaller easel. A square wooden block on it was covered by another sheet. I began to lift it.

'You are curious, Maître Sévine.'

'I am, madame,' I replied, without looking behind me. I could not say Annalise was the sort of woman whose company I relished. There was something of the bitter winter about her.

'You are very curious about other people, and there is something curious about you. I wonder if I will be able to record it.' She paused, as if deciding the answer. 'Lift the cover if you like.' I did so. It was a family portrait of the Archers. 'Juliana is an enslaving subject. Of course, this work is pale compared to my other portrait of her. That one reveals her true beauty. This is a cheap family bauble.'

I looked at the three faces on the canvas; all were staring at the viewer as they played wind instruments. The flutes and recorders seemed to be emerging from their lips like snakes' tongues and I felt an aversion to the part-finished painting.

'I am sure that you are right. I am a lawyer and we are not known for our artistic understanding. Now, tell me: why are you in this house?'

'I told you yesterday.'

I turned the painting so that the sun hit it directly through the huge windows. The pale, unpainted surface seemed to glow with heat. Annalise turned her unblinking green eyes from it to me. 'Of course. I apologize,' I said. 'You did inform me that you are here to paint a portrait of young Charles.'

'He is a handsome young man.'

We both looked at his youthful, unblemished image. And

I saw something I had not noticed before. 'Yes indeed.' I paused. 'Why are you here?' I said again, this time more darkly.

'For the portrait.' Her lips pursed in irritation.

I grabbed her and dragged her to the painting. She fought with her fingers against mine but it meant nothing. 'Have you no wits?' I demanded. 'Do you not see how you expose yourself with this? The eyes, you fool. The eyes.' She stared at the blue eyes of Gregory and Juliana Archer, then the emerald green eyes of Charles. The same emerald green as Annalise's. I let go of her and she stumbled to the side of the room, hanging on to the back of a chair and panting like a dog. 'You were in love with him. You bore Charles for him.'

Her jaw dropped. 'You know?' she stammered.

'Of course I know.'

Amazement turned to anger. She flung the chair aside. 'Yes, I loved him with all that I was. He was the only man I had loved and I have loved no other since.'

'So, you are Charles's mother.'

'They came to me. They could have no children. I agreed to carry the child. Gregory's seed in me. I was their brood mare. But it meant a part of me would always be with the man I love.' She hesitated. Then her expression changed, narrowing into suspicion. And something new - triumph - flitted across her face. She lifted her head and I could see her lips turning to a grim, taunting smile. 'But no. No, I see you do not understand.'

'I understand better than you think.'

'Oh no. Not at all.' Her rictus grin widened horribly. 'Do as you will, I will not say another word to you.'

I looked at the painting. It seemed to me as though she was in there too. No longer just drawing the brush over the surface, but visible in between Archer and Juliana. She had no instrument to play, but she had a talent that could whisper things to you. It could at once tell you truths and hide them. All was doubled. Double truths, double loves, double people. They were all to be seen on this canvas.

Frustrated that there was something I was missing, I went outside and wandered through the gardens, trying to discover my own ignorance, and eventually finding myself at the spot where I had found Archer's body. There was still nothing there to tell me if he had fallen, jumped, or been cast down. I kicked my toes into the ground, turning up the soil like a pig sniffing for truffles; but there was nothing under that hard-baked surface.

I returned through the house to my chamber. As I entered, dust and dirt shaking from my shoes onto the polished floor, a sight made me stop still. There was something strange and alien there - something that had been placed under my bed sheet. It was a small mound a couple of handspans in diameter; and stranger than that, in places it was moving. Tiny patches of the sheet were rising to become taut, then sinking back into rippling pits. Warily, I took the corner of the sheet and threw it back to reveal, to my astonishment, the sight of a black cockerel, pathetically attempting to flap its wings away from the nails that bound it to a wooden cross. The poor creature's neck had been tied to the crossbeam and it was trying to twist its head away from the bond. The tight string had robbed the animal of its famous voice and it was attempting to cry, raising its head and opening its beak, but each time brought forth nothing but a faint scratching noise.

My presence seemed to frighten it into renewed efforts and its wings made useless short flaps against the nails while its legs jerked back and forth without ground to push against. It must have been in terrible pain. I slowly passed my hand towards it and it struggled harder to pull away from me. The string around its neck was cutting into its flesh, pinhead droplets of blood appearing on the feathers. And I found then that it was not the only dark gift in my bed - for lifting the sheet further, I saw a small pile of stones, grouped into a rough pyramid. This was surely what Peugere had said was a familiar's cairn, where witches' demon servants - bloody-clawed birds of prey, or spitting cats - lay in wait for their quarry.

I did not like thinking that I had an enemy who could steal unseen into my quarters. Only an arrogant fool thinks he can ward off a knife in the guts while he sleeps. Yes, Lorne, it seemed, was more dangerous to my person than I had given it credit for.

I took a clasp-knife from my trunk and probed the blade through the feathers of the bird's neck until I found the twine. With its head freed, the bird threw itself back and forth against the nails that held it. The wood was soft so I pulled them out with some ease, and opened the window, setting the bird on the sill in the hope that it would stalk out and flutter to the ground. But the nails and the string seemed to have done too much damage and it could not stand on its own, instead crumpling onto its side and impotently waving its wings. It was dying. I broke its neck, as the kindest thing.

After that I set to examining the debris. The cross was made of unremarkable wood and the string no more distinctive. I would have no help there in identifying my secret visitor. But it had clearly been meant as a mocking echo of the execution of Father Dollet.

I left, walked to the library and rang the bell. Peugere arrived quickly. 'Have there been any visitors in the house in the last hour?' I asked.

'No, maître.'

'Have you seen anyone enter my bedchamber in the same time period? A member of the household or staff?'

'I have not.'

'Thank you. Now, I would like you to enquire quietly among the other servants if any of them noticed someone going into my bedroom.'

He took this instruction without comment, but I knew it must have worried him. 'Will there be anything else, maître?'

I shook my head. He bowed and withdrew.

For twenty minutes I browsed Francois's bookshelves, until Peugere reappeared, more silent than any grave and every bit as confidential. 'No one was seen entering your bed chamber, maître.'

'I understand. Peugere, could you watch for anyone doing that?'

'Yes, maître.' He said it as if it was the most natural request in the world, rather than one that boded ill for the household.

'And tell the groom to have my horse saddled.' He bowed and was about to leave when I decided to throw mores aside in the pursuit of the truth. I needed to know what was secret in this house, this village, and what was known. 'Peugere, this is a delicate task.' His expression changed. He was an old servant and, like all old servants, he knew sometimes delicate tasks were required of him but they had to be carried out. 'Do the servants gossip?'

'I am sure that in all houses, the staff talk.'

'Of course. Now again I will have to broach a delicate subject. Have you ever heard anything to suggest that Madame Juliana could not have brought forth her son?'

He blinked. On a second attempt, he was able to speak. 'I have not heard such a thing said.'

'I understand. That will be all.' I lowered myself into what I knew to be Francois's favourite chair.

He hesitated and swallowed. 'But there was something, maître, that might be connected,' he added.

'What?'

'The laundry girl. I once overheard her say something strange to the cook.'

'Which was . . .?'

'The girl remarked that Madame Juliana's sheets were always clean, maître. If you understand my meaning. When one would expect, from time to time, a lady's linen . . .' He left off delicately.

'Yes. Yes, quite so. Thank you, Peugere.' I felt sorry for having pressed him to be indiscreet, against his instincts.

24 June 1789

I lay on my bed as the morning light filled my chamber. My brain was jumping here and leaping there and it was the strains of a distant song that brought me from my strange reverie. With a cloth I scrubbed my night sweat away and then pulled a shirt from my trunk. The door to the music room was closed today. I knocked on it.

'Come in, Maître Sévine.'

I entered the room. Juliana, dressed in black, was playing the harpsichord. Although I know little of music, I knew that this was a lament. Notes that seemed somehow unnatural to the ear were left hanging in the air. There was a knock on the door. Peugere brought in a note on a silver salver. 'For you, madame,' he informed her with a slight bow. She unfolded and read it. 'Has she gone already?' she asked.

'She took the coach to Avignon this morning.'

'It seems Annalise has left,' Juliana muttered. 'She was contracted to go to Avignon next week to paint the Papal legate. She has made the journey a week early. Do you know why?' She showed me the note which contained the briefest of farewells.

'I think that it is so that I cannot touch her,' I answered. In the Papal enclave of Avignon even the king of France could not touch her. I kicked myself. I should have seen that she had secrets about her still. 'She told me something about you.'

'Did she?'

'It was something that I discovered and she expanded upon.'

'I am all ears, Maître Sévine.'

I walked to the window. 'I saw from her portrait that your son's eyes are green. So are Annalise's. Yours are blue. So were your husband's.' I left it hanging in the air. 'You cannot have children?' I asked.

She sat and thought for a while. 'No, I cannot.'

'Has it always been that way?'

'Maître Sévine, I cannot imagine how this has any bearing on the matter of my husband's death.'

'Has it always been that way?'

'Yes, it has.'

'I understand. Thank you for answering my question. Why did you choose Annalise as the mother of your child?'

'I believed she would be discreet.' She said it with bitterness. I was sorry to disabuse her of the illusion that her friend could be trusted to keep her secrets.

'Yes. We are often mistaken in others. I asked you before if you could think of anything that your husband could have confessed to Father Dollet that would have put both their lives in danger. Has anything come to you?'

'Absolutely nothing.' She began to play, then slammed down the lid. 'Maître Sévine, I want you to know that if the person who killed my husband is identified, it would be better for him that you find him before I do.' She lifted the lid and resumed playing.

'If you will excuse me, I shall take my leave of you.' I left the room, followed by the sound of the harpsichord.

Reaching the hallway, I sent Peugere to fetch my riding boots, because I thought a ride would clear my head. But as I drew the first on, I felt something prick the sole of my foot. I tipped it out and out came a small mound of stones and broken animal bones. Disconcerted, the memory of how my sleeping chamber had been violated in order to threaten me still very fresh, I stared up at Peugere, who looked as if he was ready to break in two at the sight.

Recovering himself, he took the boots and disappeared, returning with a pair of Francois's that were tight but would do. I did not ask what he had done with the others, but I was certain I would not see them again. Whoever my quiet stalker was, they were coming closer.

Well, I said to myself. *Let them come.*

We had barely an hour before the Comte de Rotanne arrived in a splendid carriage. His bewigged footmen riding on the rear must have felt quite out of place in Lorne and their livery was spattered with dirt by the time they came to a stop in front of the house. I was standing nonchalantly by the steps up to the door because Francois had decided to be discovered in his drawing room, as if he had forgotten that the comte was coming to buy his seigneurie - the comte's first step to laying his hands on me.

As de Rotanne stepped out of his vehicle, his eye fell on me. 'Captain Sévine,' he said with mock surprise.

'Comte.' I bowed.

'If only you had done as I instructed.'

'I fear I am no natural spy.' I quickly sized up the men who had come with him - old or fat, and while that was no guarantee they could not handle a firearm, it put me somewhat at ease. I would still be on my guard, however. 'I believe I shall be engaged in the business that brings you here. I am lawyer to the Baron d'Agnes.'

'Since when?'

'Since yesterday, Comte.'

He steadily held my gaze, carefully choosing his words. 'Perhaps you will prove a better lawyer than soldier.'

'I think we both pray that is the case.'

Then he came closer to me. His breath pricked my skin. 'It will not be long, Sévine,' he said quietly. He stepped back and raised his voice to a normal level. 'My own lawyer, Matrick.' He indicated a hawk-faced thin fellow clambering out of the carriage, his greasy hair lank to his neck. He was clad in a black velvet coat with fur cuffs. 'He has the purchase contract. Now, I would like to conclude this business.'

De Rotanne's lawyer and I wrangled for four long hours over the contract. I struck out many potential snares the man had set for Francois. Matrick grimaced and bared his teeth, but eventually we inked the quills, and with a few strokes it was all signed. Two weeks from then, the Comte de Rotanne would be seigneur of Lorne. That gave me two weeks to slip away to foreign lands. 'Congratulations, gentlemen,' Matrick said. His accent was Alsatian.

'Thank you,' Francois replied, mustering a sad smile. 'Shall we go in to dinner?'

The comte agreed and I started for the door. But de Rotanne's lawyer held a hand in my path.

'I believe order of precedence would be for the new seigneur to lead out,' he said.

I held myself back from knocking him to the ground. It was a struggle as hard as any I have had in the past.

'Yes indeed,' said the comte as he passed me.

As we ate, we made small talk. 'We are to host a ball,' Francois said. 'We would be honoured if you would come.'

'A ball? Well, my dancing days are perhaps behind me.' The comte smiled. 'But as new seigneur I shall indeed come.' He drank a draught of wine. 'I will bring my son. It will all be his in time, so he might as well see what he will have to deal with.'

'Do you have any plans for improvement of the village, Comte? I have long had the ideas but lacked the capital,' Francois enquired.

'Better irrigation of the lower pastures,' de Rotanne said through mouthfuls of fish. 'The church tower needs raising.' Francois inclined his head in a manner that said he agreed and would look forward to seeing the work completed. 'And your quit-rents are absurd. The standard throughout this region is one chicken in three, not in four.'

Francois tried to smooth over the situation. 'Comte, you are quite correct. Many of the other seigneurs in the area deduct just that proportion. Yet they have richer lands. If I believed my peasants could hand over that fee, I would certainly demand it. Yet, if I were to do so, I am certain it would last one year and then there would be no chickens at all for the peasants would have all starved to death.'

Matrick piped up. 'If it is possible a few leagues from here, then surely the comte is correct in thinking that it is possible here.'

Francois ate no more of his fish. 'But there is a more pressing issue in this land,' de Rotanne declared, finishing his last morsel. 'Your sodomite priest.' He turned a cold eye on us. I caught Francois's expression of muted alarm. 'You did not think that I would be ignorant of this?'

'No, indeed, I did not,' Francois replied quietly.

'And your lawyer, if you call him that. Did he think that such deeds would pass me by?'

I remained silent. I wanted to know exactly what he had been told.

'I am informed that the priest was buggered before or after he was cut up.'

I nodded in confirmation, although I would rather have knocked his face to the side.

'No doubt it was part of his behaviour. He liked to open himself to men's pricks. Well, animals tear each other apart. It is in their nature. And do not think I do not know about his sympathies with the seditionaries. No surprise that a man who goes against nature also goes against France.' De Rotanne's spy in our midst certainly knew his business.

There was something especially foul about having a man I held dear slandered and abused in that off-hand manner. Francois had provided a meal to de Rotanne and the comte was relishing his defamation of our old tutor as he ate it. I could well have taken him by the neck and dashed his face to the table. One word from Francois to say that it would do him no harm, and I would have accomplished it in a heartbeat.

'Sedition, Comte?' Francois asked, perturbed.

'My men located an illegal printing press this morning. Thankfully, one of the men there was loyal to me.'

So, someone had discovered that Father Dollet had wanted something printed on Marat's press.

'Neither the machinery nor its operators are now in any state to produce any further libels.'

Had he done for Marat? Perhaps. Either way, I felt the implied threat of de Rotanne's ever-present informants. 'But to the matter in hand: locating the man who killed your priest. Well, sexual inverts can never hide long. They stink of the filth of it - where they have been. My seigneurial court will find such an animal.'

'What if he denies the murder? You cannot execute him without a shred of evidence,' I insisted. Even two decades of seeing justice bought and sold hadn't entirely extinguished a flame within me that held hope for its equity, that innocent men should - more often than not - be set free.

'It hardly matters, does it?' de Rotanne said, drinking more. 'We will have him for buggery instead - the sentence is the same: death by burning. Burn a man for homicide or burn him for sodomy. Either way his flesh becomes no more than meat.'

The fire stake. I pitied any wretches under such a sentence. Early in my legal career I had been told that if the workmen building the bonfire felt charitable towards their victim, they would use damp wood, for the smoke would suffocate him before the flames burned through his flesh and his eyes popped. But for a sodomite they would use the driest sticks they could find.

'The priest is lucky he is dead,' de Rotanne continued. Francois's jaw dropped at the pronouncement. 'If it were proved he consented to such deeds, I would have him in the same flames.'

It did not surprise me. De Rotanne was not a man for mercy.

'Comte–' Francois began angrily.

De Rotanne raised his palm and spoke loudly over Francois. 'It is what the law and the Holy Church mandate. Pauper, priest or king, the sentence is death by burning. No question.'

I would have liked to have disputed, but he was correct; legally, there was no question: 'pauper, priest or king', the sentence was indeed death by burning.

'Tell me, Comte,' I asked, 'how did you come to hear that the baron was offering his seigneurie for sale?'

'Oh,' he said dismissively. 'Someone mentioned it.'

'Mentioned it? Oh, well I suppose they must have done. Who?'

He merely smiled thinly at me.

Before I did something else I would regret - I had done enough in the past few weeks - I excused myself to visit the water closet.

The privies within the house were poorly aired so I preferred to use those in a block to the rear. As I left the dining room and approached a narrow corridor that led to them, I heard very soft footsteps behind me. Peugere was serving and I doubted one of the other servants would keep quiet pace with me like that.

More alert, but not wishing to let the man stalking me know that I was aware of his presence, I continued a little more slowly, to give myself time to decide. It had to be one of the comte's men. Would de Rotanne risk an assault on me in Francois's home? I had not thought so, but perhaps he had his reasons. And whatever my pursuer's intention was, it wasn't to invite me for a friendly cup of beer.

We passed one of the ancient suits of armour that Francois's ancestors had probably never worn. And then the glass in a picture frame allowed me to catch sight of the man behind me. It was the comte's sallow-skinned lackey with whom I had tussled in Versailles. He must have been concealed in the comte's coach and stolen into the house.

The armour, unfortunately, carried no weapon. A mace or broadsword would have been welcome at that point, if a little mediaeval for the task. I slowed, allowing the man behind me to close the distance by a pace without realizing. I felt his feet on the floorboards. Then I snatched the helmet from its place, wheeled around and windmilled the metal at the mangled face of my foe. Startled, he stumbled to his side and reached inside his tunic, drawing out a pistol. But I still had the helmet and smashed it down upon his wrist. The gun fell to the floor and clattered away. I had taken him by surprise, but he quickly recovered himself. I guessed that like me, he was a veteran of war and not shocked by violence from unknown directions.

He launched himself upon me in order to prevent me swinging at him again with the steel in my hand. His weight crashed us both against the wall and I had to drop the helmet to grapple with his considerable strength. His knee lifted into my gut, but I put the piercing pain from my mind and cracked my elbow hard into the ridge of his eye socket, knocking him away.

We both jumped back to gain better stances for the fight. There was nothing more I could use as a weapon, but his gun was no more than a stride behind him. I saw that it was an air pistol, a rare weapon that uses compressed air in a bulb to shoot a small lead bullet. The range is low but the gun is silent, making it a good weapon for a cowardly assassin, and just as deadly if shot into the soft flesh of the face or neck. He spun around and reached for the pistol. I threw myself forward and kicked out his knee, dropping him to the floor, but in the flick of an eye the gun was turning to me. With one hand I grabbed his wrist, twisting it upwards, and with the other hand pulled the trigger. There was the sound of a dry stick breaking. No more than that. Then blood spurted from his face, droplets hitting my tunic.

His mouth fell agape and he slumped to the floor. I stared at a bloody pit of ragged flesh and broken bone that had been his left eye socket. Air pistols shoot a light bullet, but it had been heavy enough to break that ring of bone to pieces and lodge in the eyeball itself. He was lucky the strength of the weapon was low, or the lead would have gone right through into his brain. He cried in pain but could form no words and I stopped the sound with my heel driven into his mouth before I wrenched his face to mine.

'When they come, you will say that you accidentally discharged your weapon,' I told him as his hands grasped at the air. 'Better to look a fool than a coward creeping on a man to shoot him in the back.' And I threw him back down. Perhaps I was not entirely above such a surreptitious approach myself, but I would not have funked it like this idiot.

He made no answer, possibly because I had dislodged a few teeth, and seconds later Francois and de Rotanne were indeed with us. 'What the Devil . . .' Francois began.

'A terrible accident, Baron,' I said. 'The danger of carrying a primed pistol in one's jacket. For your lordship's protection on the road, I presume, Comte?'

To his credit, de Rotanne did not bother lying. He looked no more than annoyed at a plan gone awry. The man at our feet looked up, bloody-mouthed and torn-faced. It was, I supposed, the end of his employment.

I could see from Francois's expression, darkening by the moment, that he was working out what had really taken place. I counted myself lucky it was not me on the floor, my flesh blasted. And from thereon I would be a damn sight more careful with my guard. 'Comte,' Francois began angrily.

I stopped him. There was no point. De Rotanne would do what he would do. Francois needed the sale, or bankruptcy would be his new companion. We would deal with the aftermath when the time came. 'Let us leave this for the day,' I said. I looked down. 'It looks like a minor wound to me. I am sure you do not need a doctor, do you?'

De Rotanne looked at me with a face as blank as a sheet of virgin paper. Then he stepped to his man and kneeled, examining the blasted eye like a surgeon.

'Dear me,' he said to himself. 'It does look bad.' He gripped the wound in his hand and squeezed this way and that, spurting blood and gore over his own fingers, without concern. The man fought to suppress any cry of pain. 'Does it hurt? Oh, yes it must. And we cannot leave the bullet within, any surgeon will tell you. No, it needs to come out. Do not worry, I will perform the action.' And, to my surprise, he plunged his right forefinger into the exploded flesh. The pain to his lackey must have been astonishing, and his fist beat down on the floorboard. 'Yes, this will not do,' the comte said, quite without concern. He was pushing around the lead ball, which had become misshapen by the impact, causing as much damage and suffering as he could without effort. 'You must remain still or it will hurt you more,' he told his man as a red stain seeped up his wrist. 'You see?' and he tore at the edge of the gash with his fingers, ripping the flesh, all the while with a disconcerting air of slight curiosity. 'Do you see how it hurts?' The man could hold his tongue no longer and cried out.

'Monsieur! I . . .' I noted that he had an English accent. A rough soldier hired from that country, no doubt.

'When you speak, you distract me.' And de Rotanne employed his other hand now, both tearing the ragged lips of the wound apart, spraying a thin line of blood up his fine sleeve, before gripping the bullet between his finger and thumb. His underling's face twisted in such pain I thought he would have welcomed death to end it. And then de Rotanne plucked his digits away with the dripping lead between them, leaving the exploded eyeball dropping out of the gory wound. 'There, you see? I have it now!' And at that he abandoned his demeanour of the uninterested surgeon and flung the bullet angrily across the hallway before striding towards the door. 'Throw him in the coach,' he spat at Matrick. 'If he is weak now, let him get weaker.'

But the lawyer had no need to exert himself, for the torn man half walked, half hauled himself in the comte's wake. I almost felt sorry for him.

I did not quite reach that point.

'Was that meant to scare you, or more than that?' Francois asked darkly when they were both gone.

'Your guess is as good as mine.' Although it had turned out in our favour, weakening de Rotanne in arm and spirit, as the dust settled I felt sobered. His man had come close - very close, now I had a moment to replay the episode in my mind - to putting a denier's worth of lead right through my neck. I did not attempt to fool myself that my life had never been in danger. And no matter who you are, that realization leaves an after-tremor of fear and fury.

'Then you had better watch out,' he added. 'The Comte de Rotanne has more men to call upon.'

And as I thought of the comte and what he had intended

for me, it was then that I resolved to join Jacob in his conspiracy to bring equality to this land and to make de Rotanne understand that pain could be visited upon him too.

Reckless, oh yes it was reckless. And how I learned my lesson.

Chapter Nine

I halted reading. There was so much to take in. For first, I had met a man with a missing eye before. Could the one who had attacked the narrator of this tale be the man with a brass eyepatch that I knew as Astaroth? I could not know for certain, but a belief grew. My only lifelong possession, the silver watch, was surely the one that David Sévine had mentioned early in his narrative. It was not too much of a leap, I hoped, that this meant he was my parent. In that case, Astaroth had come for my father, then my mother, and then for me. And now he was at the bottom of the sea. I thanked God for His vengeance. And went on.

25 June 1789

Riding out to take some air late the next morning, Francois glanced in my direction. 'You seem well rested,' he commented.

'I slept well,' I replied as we passed a paddock with two horses. It was a pleasant day, and I was a little put out when Jackdaw began inexplicably to throw his head around, and would not run straight. He stamped and struggled towards the paddock fence.

Before I could stop him, he had jumped it and we were trotting towards a dappled grey, which I saw turn and present its rump to him. He leaped straight on. I thought it best to dismount and watch with both my feet on the ground. Francois was in hysterics. I saw him wiping tears from his eyes as he struggled to stay in the saddle with the shaking from his laughter. 'Oh, my dear fellow!' he shouted over. 'You must learn to control your horse when there's a pretty mare in season nearby. He may be castrated but no balls is no barrier to what he is doing now.'

'And now what do I do?'

He trotted over to the fence. 'I would say watch and learn. It would be rude to interrupt him.'

We stood there, conversing, while my gelding horse pumped his sterile seed into a mare. I wondered if she knew that she would have no foal to show for it and she was just doing it for pleasure. Well, after a while he withdrew like the rake that he was and ambled over to where I stood against the fence. 'Have you finished?' I asked him with my arms crossed. His tarse was now spilling some seed on the ground like Onan but he seemed uninterested. 'Will you not even thank her for her time?' He snorted, which set Francois off into fits of giggles once more. 'Well, Don Juan in the shape of a horse,' I said, 'it is time we left. If you are a good boy I might let you come and play with the trollop again tomorrow.' I was actually rather pleased to see him enjoying himself. He was a good horse and deserved to play from time to time.

'Oh dear,' Francois chuckled. 'Anyway, now that we are on the subject, David, what precisely is between you and the sweet Catherine?'

Jackdaw's quality as a steed notwithstanding, I was rather put out by the comparison - in part for myself but the greater for Catherine. 'Your guess is as good as mine,' I told him. It wasn't, of course, but I felt a little sensitive when it came to that burgeoning connection. I was far from certain myself where it was leading.

'Do you think you can prise her away from Juliana?'

I considered his point. Sure it was that what Juliana and I offered was very different, but he was right: Catherine was utterly devoted to her mistress, perhaps in a way that she could never be devoted to me.

'I cannot say.'

'No, I suppose not.'

A pleasant ride, then I bade farewell to him, for I had a longer journey to make.

Upon arriving in Paris, I trotted into the Faubourg Saint-Germain, where the greatest nobles had their *hôtels particuliers* - elegant, imposing country chateaux transported to the middle of the city. De Rotanne's was an especially fine example. The gravel-laid *grand cour* that I rode up must have been forty *toises* long - the length of forty tall men lying end to end. The frontage was that sum in width. As I rode, I had to skirt a fine fountain decked with a spouting whale, dolphins and other denizens of the sea.

Nearing the house, a liveried footman opened the door and stared at me, clearly not expecting visitors. I rode past him, around the right-hand wing of the building and up the side, towards the rear gardens.

They were as fine as Versailles itself, I found. *Cabinets de verdure* salons had been cut into the greenery and a short gallery connected the house to a wooden pavilion. It was quite charming, containing ornate furniture arranged for the taking of tea while viewing the English lawns. On the other side was a magnificent orangery full of ripe fruit. I returned to the front of the building, where the footman looked bemused.

'Sir?' he asked, uncertain whether to address me with respect or shout for the watchman.

'I wish to see his lordship the Comte de Rotanne,' I said casually.

'His lordship is not at home.'

'Ah, that is a pity. I wished to invite him to a meal. We shall be dining outside.'

'I will make the comte aware,' he replied warily. 'May I ask your name?'

'Ask away.' I turned Jackdaw around and cantered off.

De Rotanne had demonstrated that he was quite prepared to have an assassin shoot me in the back. Now that I had little to lose, I would soon show him that ordinary men were not defenceless. We could touch him where he lived too.

26 June 1789

Late the next morning Juliana sent word to me that she and Catherine would be visiting Paris in order to withdraw some money from her husband's bank. The city was tense and anyone carrying a bag of gold from a bank would be watched by regiments of thieves. She therefore begged my presence as an escort.

The prospect of a day's excursion with Catherine excited me far more than I even wanted to admit to myself. We had shared little more than glances and hours, but I could feel a golden chain stretching and linking between us.

We rode out in the baron's carriage with its fading green paint just as the clocks sounded the hour of one in the afternoon. Peugere had, with an embarrassed cough, provided us with horsehair cushions to place under our rumps to make up for the lack of springs in the old coach. They did little to reduce the rattling of our bones and prevent any bruising, though, as we shuddered over ruts and scars in the bad road.

Juliana was as striking as ever, in a silk dress with detailing in a part-Chinese style that suited its part-Chinese wearer. Catherine looked even prettier than she usually did - her dress was cut low at the front, a fact to which her mistress made frequent allusion. 'Much more of this bouncing around, my dear, and what you have there will soon be roaming free,' Juliana mentioned casually, to our general laughter, soon after we began the journey. I appreciated the commented because from then on, I had no need to pretend I wasn't as captivated by the motion as any man would have been.

We thudded and ricocheted onwards, by turns complaining about the journey, then suffering like the Stoics, and finally bursting into laughter about it all. 'As soon as the Jacobins take over, I will be writing to Monsieur Robespierre to request he personally take charge of this road. He can roll up his sleeves and toil like an honest peasant,' Juliana announced.

'You believe a change is in the air?' I suggested.

'I do. There is nothing so good for a nation as an occasional upheaval. A good war or the deposition of a ruler.' Catherine laughed and clapped. 'Come on, let us get on with it. Louis out, that absurd prig of a wife of his shoved into the deepest trench below Versailles. Have someone with a bit more panache on the throne. A Habsburg. I think we need one of them. Or a Borgia - if you want a ruler with some fire in them, you must look to Italy, Maître Sévine.'

'I am sure Italy is the orchard where to pluck the fruit.'

'Quite right,' agreed Catherine.

'And the Italian men, Catherine,' her mistress said. 'We must find one of those handsome brutes for you.'

The girl blushed. 'I would not say no.'

'Ha! Maître Sévine, you are witness. I will write to everyone I know in Italy, asking if they know one who can show Catherine what my countrymen are made of.' We laughed together even as the left-hand side of the vehicle lifted into the air, then crashed down with the sound of splintering wood and the whole coach came to a halt leaning to one side. Catherine was thrown quite into my lap. Even then she did not stop laughing. Of course, her mistress was laughing the hardest.

'You seem to have won a prize, Maître Sévine,' Juliana said, bracing herself against the roof of the carriage so that she would not topple out the door. 'And a very pretty one at that.'

Catherine pushed herself off me as the coach rocked and the footman jumped down. Truth be told, I would gladly have had her remain where she was - we men are simple creatures at times, and have simple mechanisms that work in simple ways.

The coachman came to the window and nervily asked if there had been any injuries. 'Only to our pride,' Juliana informed him through the window. 'Now be a good fellow and help a lady down.'

He pulled the door open and gave her his hand. All the while Catherine and I could do nothing but gaze at each other with a series of emotions including amusement, faint discomfort and, in my case, mild pain occasioned by smacking my head on the roof.

We emerged into the mid-morning sun. The coachman told us the wheel was broken and the coach would be going nowhere until it was replaced. 'A nice day to walk to town, then,' I suggested.

'Maître Sévine, you can walk, I am going to ride,' replied Juliana. 'It is the wheel that is broken, not the animals.'

'Bareback?' I returned. 'In your fine dress?'

She gritted her teeth. 'Blast it all. You are right, of course. Well, walk it is.'

'I am sure Maître Sévine would not be so ungallant as to expect two ladies to walk through this dust,' interjected Catherine with a smile edging from her mouth. 'I say we wave him off and wait until he returns with a coach and four.'

'You might find Maître Sévine goes home and does not come back,' I told her.

'How ungallant.'

'You should get used to it.'

And so the servant returned on foot to Lorne to have the coach repaired, and we went on foot to Paris.

An hour later we passed through the city gate and gladly found our way to Archer's bank, whence Juliana retrieved a moderate sum of money. We strolled along the Champs-Élysées, where the glittering shops selling the finest perfumes and silks in the world were near deserted. Juliana and Catherine were the only ladies walking. A few gentlemen strolled with sticks in their hands and loyal footmen with years' experience in the Household Guard behind them to show they were not afraid of the ragged scores milling in the Jardin des Tuileries at the end of the road. These two worlds were divided by the octagon of the Place de la Concorde.

Juliana insisted on strolling even more nonchalantly than

these men, and put her nose into many an otherwise empty shop. I walked with Catherine while Juliana smelled scents she could not afford. 'There is no one like her,' said Catherine.

'No.'

'Men look at her.' I could not deny that. 'You look at her the same way.'

I gazed at Juliana's back as she walked.

'Men look at you too,' I said. And it was true. Juliana had majesty. But Catherine had something else. She had - how to put this without sounding like a simpleton? - a good heart. A heart that beat with fine feelings. I had seen so much suffering and anger on the field of battle, in the courts, on the streets of France, that simple goodness threw its arms around me and held me.

I noticed Catherine's fingers, no more than a hand's width from my own. I do not know if she noticed. But I felt it all the time that we walked and all the time that we stood still and took in the vistas of Paris. I could tell you when it lengthened and when it shortened. At one point I kicked myself: any more and I would be sighing like a victim of Cupid in an Italian comedy.

'What do you want, Maître Sévine?' she asked, as Juliana strode ten paces in front of us. Catherine waved her hand over the horizon. I understood her meaning. I just did not know the answer.

'Allow me a lawyer's trick. Let me turn that around. What do *you* want?'

'To find my place,' she said.

'Then there are two of us.'

'Perhaps many more.' Juliana eventually tired of shopping without buying and we stole onto the île de la Cité. With our backs to the great cathedral dedicated to Notre Dame, we sat on the riverside, dangling our feet above the water.

I bought us cups of spiced red wine from a street hawker and we threw sticks into the Seine to watch them drift away with the tide. Children make friends easily, it is not so simple when you are grown. But there are times when you meet others and you feel a bond form.

'Wake up,' Catherine instructed me. I did wake up. I had been idly lobbing stones into the water. One had gone too close to a ferry and the pilot was waving his fist at me. 'You are a danger to yourself.'

'If only I was the sole danger,' I replied.

'And who else is?' she said, smiling too sweetly. I was used to suggestive petulance from her mistress, but now Catherine was showing that she could exhibit it too. I did not answer. 'How old are you?' she asked, perfectly naturally.

'I am thirty-four years old. You?' I could not help asking.

'I thought a gentleman never asked a lady that question,' she admonished me.

'Perhaps I am no gentleman.'

'But you are,' she replied quite seriously and ingenuously. 'I am twenty-four.' She broke a blade of grass in two. 'Very old.'

'Just you wait for thirty. It will hit you like a tonne of bricks.'

At that, Juliana laughed and threatened to push us both into the river if we didn't stand up because she had had enough of making her rump numb on the grass.

We needed to find somewhere to put up for the night, until the repaired coach could be sent for us. I thought it best to plump for one of the hostelries close to the Sorbonne on the Left Bank.

After a while we turned down a street where buildings were lit and men were lying drunk in the gutter. The houses were double-storeyed with enough smoke billowing from them to engulf the nearby great twin towers of Notre Dame and make any man think the city itself was alight. There should have been city guards dashing down the alley, carrying troughs of water to throw through the doors. Instead, single-toothed crones and men broken in the middle like a sprig of wheat after reaping stumbled in and out with no more discernible purpose than the cats sitting quietly at the end of the street.

I walked to the entrance. An enormous man - wider than he was tall - blocked my path. I had no idea how one could get so fat when there was a famine throughout the land. Perhaps he had eaten the other starvelings. Or perhaps there had been no famine until he came along. His face was burned to a deep plum colour and I guessed he was a blacksmith who forged horseshoes all day long in front of flames. He put his arm across the doorway, barring my entry.

'Who are you?' he demanded.

'My name is David Sévine. I and the two ladies require rooms for the night.' He saw Juliana and Catherine waiting a few yards away and squinted.

'Are you for the Third Estate?'

'We are.'

He leaned in. I could smell the soot of his daily toil on his skin. 'And what makes you think there are rooms here?'

I leaned in too, so that our noses were almost touching. 'It is an inn,' I replied.

He burst into laughter and threw a beefy arm around my shoulder. 'Ha! Indeed, indeed it is! Come in, monsieur.' He dragged me in, leaving the women outside, and I saw the taproom stuffed with humanity - if you could call half of them that - all laughing at me. It seemed this was some ritual joke to welcome strangers. No blacksmith he, but the innkeeper whose face had been burned red by rough wine, and his skin sooty from the pipe smoke he bathed in all day long. The clientele sat on benches or sprawled on tables, all of which were covered in dirty bowls and tipped-over pewter tankards. Some tables sported small dogs and one had a brown bird on it, pecking at a bread crust.

'Now, monsieur, you will be wanting a room. One big bed is it?' asked the man who had dragged me inside. He winked three or four times as if he was afflicted by the dropsy. I looked back at Juliana and Catherine peeping in. I discovered that he had, when pressed, two rooms for rent.

'And something to eat,' I added.

'To eat? Ha! What part of the country are you from, friend? We have no food in Paris for anyone less than a duke.' Paris's bread stores had run dry, he said, and the only meat to be had was the flesh of the rodents running between houses. 'If you want fresh bread, go to Versailles and present yourself as a noble. Then you may drown under the loaves they have.' He minced across the room. 'I am Marie Antoinette and I wish to eat my own weight in brioche!' His friends all cried in laughter. 'Here we have this to put in our bellies.' He pulled from under the counter a lump of black stuff that looked like bread soaked in tar. He banged it on the wood to show how solid it was. 'They call this bread. So rough that it scrapes the throat on the way down. So heavy that you cannot pass it through you. Fancy it, my friend?' He laughed again and tossed it across the room.

So we drank a little, then headed for our beds, rather hungry.

That night I lay in my bed, shifting my body every few seconds as I tried to slot my bones and muscles around the solid lumps that felt like the mattress had been stuffed with horses' hooves. The wall had a thousand holes through which the wind was whistling on an unusually breezy night. Outside I could hear the cats fighting for territory. And then something new: a tap-tap on my door. I listened, and there it was again. I moved not, but the latch lifted and the door crept open. Through the gap I could see an arm in a white nightgown - where she had got it, I do not know - and Catherine's face was slowly revealed in the faint glow of a distant lamp.

'Can I come in?' she asked.

This instant was one of the instants in my life when I was presented with a choice that had already been made for me by God, fate, or the stars, depending on your view of who pulls our puppet-strings. I knew what I would say, I had no real power over the word. At best, I could speak it uncertainly, as if deciding then and there. We can rail against such controlling powers, insisting that we are free men with our own muscles and movements, but deep within us we know that there is nothing we can do. Sometimes there is a higher power and we cannot fight it.

I sat up. 'Yes.'

I felt warm and heavy blood swamping my brain. For all I had once congratulated myself on controlling my passions, I had to admit that all it took for that wall to collapse was a chink of light between the bricks. Well, it is better to discover where our limits lie and where we are vulnerable.

She stepped through. Neither of us said a word but I could hear the floorboards creak as she moved to me. Then a faint rustling sound as her nightgown fell to the floor. I slid to the side of the bed, giving her space to enter. Her warmth came to me, even though we were not touching. The bed dipped slightly towards the middle and my body rolled towards hers.

There was still space between us, warm air, but I could

hear her breath in and out. She was on her back. The bed had a thin, hard pillow and as I moved closer, I felt her hair spread out on it, the wisps touching my cheek. I waited, even though she was waiting for me too. Then, lying on my side, I reached to her and placed my hand on her stomach. I felt the muscles tighten and her breath quicken, light panting now replacing easy breaths. I let it lie there for what felt like more than an hour before I moved it up to her neck, then her cheek and turned her to me.

An hour later she slipped out of my bed and pulled on her nightgown once more. I could hear her bare feet on the boards as she walked away, to the door. She lifted the latch and walked through, turning at the last moment so that I could see her smiling at me. I felt, more than anything, grateful for her presence that night.

27 June 1789

It took the whole of the following day to repair the coach and send it to collect us, so we ate, strolled around the safer parts of the city - Catherine's arm through mine, as Juliana walked ahead of us - and returned to Lorne at night.

I found Francois in his study, reading a pamphlet. 'Have you heard what is happening at court?' he asked. 'The King has attended a combined meeting of the Estates-General. It seems he berated them for not having come up with a plan. But he will agree to tax reform.'

'Tax reform?' I shook my head incredulously. 'He thinks that will stem the tide of what is happening? He is stupider than I imagined.'

'David,' Francois berated me. 'He is our king.'

'For now,' I replied. 'I cannot see this turning out well for poor Louis.'

'You think he will be forced to cut down on spending?'

'No, I do not think the King will be forced to cut down on spending, Francois. I think the change will be rather more fundamental than that.' I was a little frustrated with my friend's lack of foresight.

He was quiet for a moment. 'I heard the bishops were attacked afterwards.'

'In the street?' I perked up at the news. The corrupt bishops were an excellent target for street violence, in my estimation.

'In their lodgings. Stones through their windows.' That was, indeed, a step. We French are not averse to throwing stones at one another, but to cast them at the princes of the church, that was a strong step across the chalk line. 'What do you think they want?' He looked at me almost plaintively. Francois was a good man, a man who cared for his villagers. But he was still a noble, and I think he knew that it was but a sideways step from throwing stones at wealthy bishops to throwing them at poor barons. And I could not answer him, because there was no answer to give.

'The problem is, there are twenty million of "them" and five times as many demands. Not a chance to satisfy them all.'

'You are probably right,' he admitted, with more than a hint of worry.

We moved on, talking about books we had read, places we would like to visit (I had a hankering for the sights of Egypt during the winter, when the air would be warmer than that of northern France). We drank deeply of some Madeira wine he had brought up from the cellar.

'Catherine is a sweet girl,' he said lightly, peering into his glass.

'She is. Yes, she is.' He looked at me, then we both burst into laughter. 'Yes, she is.' I felt a little wall crumbling. Francois had seen that my feelings for Catherine had gone far beyond the young man's passing lust for a pretty girl. Her presence made me feel lighter.

'You are too young to be an old bachelor, David. Make her your mistress. Do not live alone, man is not made for it.'

'You are so very romantic, Francois.' It was true that a bachelor's life was a limited one - limited in its horizons and possibilities, and I felt them keenly sometimes. Solitude often suited me, but the longer it went on, the more oppressive the quiet became. Still, there were limits about how much I wanted to talk about Catherine in that way. And, in particular, I did not want to make her just a mistress, visited thrice weekly to dine and bed. I redirected the subject matter. 'Why do you think the King has not taken a Chief Mistress?' I pondered.

'Oh God knows. The same reason it took him and Marie Antoinette years to consummate their marriage, I would guess. Not much ink in his pen.' He looked a little sheepish for talking of the King in this way. He rummaged about in a chest by the wall and took out a box of dominoes and set them on the table.

'And what about you?' I replied. 'You have not so much as made a stab at marriage. Double six.'

'There is less choice here, I am afraid, old man. The third and best-fed daughter of the Duc de Reims made eyes at me and feigned to blush when I was forced to attend a ball in Marseilles last year. That was the closest I have been to the marriage altar. Anyway, come on, old chap. Let us have something with a bit more spirit than the Madeira.' He took a bottle of cognac from his drinks cabinet and poured out two measures of the stuff. 'To love!'

'To love, you old romantic,' I said, thrusting my glass to the ceiling with him. We both drank the draught down and threw our glasses into the fireplace. It was like being aged ten again, but with hard drink.

'What is that?' I asked, pointing towards the window.

'What?' Francois followed my index finger. 'Some sort of light in the church.'

'No,' I said. 'It is outside. In the graveyard.'

'What on earth is it?'

'Let us find out,' I replied. Concern was beating in my veins - the glimmer might have an innocent explanation, but the last time there had been a light in the church after dark, the very ground of Lorne had ruptured. We hurried, on foot, so as not to alert whoever was there to our presence.

As we closed in some minutes later, I shuttered my own lamp, to remain unseen. A hundred yards away we slowed and padded carefully, to muffle our footsteps. And now we could make out a figure among the gravestones. Closer and we could hear sounds of work - metal against wood or stone. I indicated to Francois that we were to creep in on this scene before us. We slipped to the side of the church and viewed what we could. In the boneyard, a figure was kneeling, hunched over something on the ground. Between the headstones we could make out the sight of a spade and some other tool obscured by shadow. This man, or woman, had been digging down into the graves.

'Who is–' Francois said, too struck by the sight to keep quiet. I silenced him with a grip of his arm and pressed behind a buttress in the church wall, but it was too late. The figure twenty yards from us had stopped whatever he was doing. He looked this way and that. And then he shot a glance straight at us. I unshuttered my lamp and the beam fell on his face: Charles. And below him I could see what work he was accomplishing. For at his feet, surrounded by the shards of his coffin, lay the body of Father Dollet, rendered horrible by time in the ground. My body started at the horrific picture. I had seen men torn to pieces by grapeshot, but what remained of them had been treated with respect, buried with honours. This was foul work.

And then I saw more. An added offence against the good priest that threw an even fouler tint on the scene. With his right hand, Charles had hold of the priest's wrist, in his left was a small saw, ready to cut through skin and bone and take that piece of a man. My mind raced to the detailed preparations for making a Hand of Glory, the magical weapon derived from the hand of a dead criminal, as set out in the *Petit Albert* that had been stolen from Father Dollet's desk.

Charles's mouth opened but he had not time to speak before I sprang out, as full of fury as I had ever been. He turned on his heels and fled.

I charged between the graves, stumbling in the murk. Charles vaulted into the street and ran into the shadows.

As I reached the point where he had been kneeling, I stumbled over the moonlit face of my old tutor, his cheek hard against the dewy ground. There was no blood in that flesh, only the white of the beams shining on it.

Through the looming black shapes of the village, I cast my lantern aside and sprinted after the boy. He was younger than me but his limbs had not yet grown to their full strength and I saw the distance between us shrink, pace by pace. Behind me, I heard Francois afoot too. He flitted between puddles of utter dark, as if he had fallen down a deep well, never to be seen again by human eyes. Those from the city will never know the true, true darkness of the countryside, where there is no light for leagues around. Charles fell into such a void and as I reached the spot and whirled around I could find no trace of him. Francois arrived a few seconds later.

'Where is he?' he managed to puff out, his lungs heaving.

'Slipped past us. I do not know how!' I snarled. Francois set off on the road again, in the direction we had just come from. 'No, wait,' I said, realizing that the wall beside us was not sheer. Right by our backs were the shutters of a window that began at waist height. I tried them. They were bolted but the bolt was ill-fitting and with a heft they opened. There was no window glass behind. 'He must have come through here,' I told Francois under my breath. 'Try the door.'

He went to the door but it was evidently locked. And so, I swung a leg over the windowsill. I doubted Charles was the type to attack - he was the sort to run and hide - but still I was ready in case a blow fell. My other leg went over and I silently eased myself to the floor. I tried to work out which house this was; my best guess was that it was the bakery. I moved inside, feeling a heavy table in front of me, making way for Francois to follow. He did, kicking something wooden that skidded on the floorboards.

I pushed him slightly to indicate that he should move around the room in the opposite direction to me and so we parted and began feeling our way about. I was sure, when I came across a large porcelain bowl, that this was indeed the bakery. It is strange learning where you are by touch alone. No doubt the blind think it is strange that we can learn of the world any other way, but for those of us with the gift of sight, it is disconcerting to the point of fright.

I heard something. A scratching sound from the floor underneath the shop table. A rat, perhaps.

Or perhaps not.

I bent down to examine.

And then a ball of bright fire seemed to engulf my vision

and a body knocked me to my side. Charles must have had his lamp shuttered and smothered in his cloak to hide all glimmer, and then uncovered it all to shine in my face, disorienting me. He was up and running through the shop. 'Stop!' Francois shouted at him, although it would have done about as much good as writing the boy a letter.

I righted myself. The burning in my irises dissipated and I could just see Francois bowling out the room's rear door in pursuit of the boy. I pulled my wits together and set off at speed. We were in a narrow rear room with a sleeping room above. Thudding feet above us said the baker was up. 'Who is there?' he shouted down the ladder. I had no inclination to wait and explain, so followed Francois out a back door of the building. We were now on the edge of the woodland that touched the village. Charles, ahead of us, shuttered his lamp again.

Our feet found soft turf and suddenly we were dodging around trees, feeling our way through the wood. 'There!' I had seen a flash of light some way off. He must have been checking his way. We moved towards it, but picking between clawing branches and over treacherous tree roots made the going slow. We blundered on, in truth hoping against hope that we would stumble across him. When another flicker appeared ahead, we thought we were on the right track and we would take him despite his best efforts, but it shut off and we were back to feeling our way. Francois tripped and turned his ankle and our going became even slower. For fifteen minutes more we felt around, before it was obvious he was gone. 'Let us go,' I said wearily.

'Leave him?' Francois asked, surprised.

'What choice do we have? Besides, we can guess where he is going to go.'

'My home?'

'That is possible, but I doubt it. He would know we would easily catch up with him there. He cannot run from the village in the dark - where would he go? No food or money, and with enough oil in his lamp for an hour. No, he needs somewhere else he can hide until he can get away properly.'

'So, let us go there.'

I was conflicted. It was galling to let him run but I could not shake away the image of my old tutor, splayed on the ground like a hunted and torn animal. 'Give him time. I do not want to leave Father Dollet as he is. We need to go back and bury him. Then we can lay hands on the boy.'

'Yes, all right.' For human decency will sometimes trump the application of justice.

Back at the churchyard, the priest lay as we had left him. His neck was twisted horribly, but the rest of his body was rigid in the position in which it had lain under that earth. The rigour of death had, at least, given him some semblance of dignity and the boy had not had time to begin his incisions into the wrist.

I picked up my discarded lamp and managed to light it. The yellow glow almost seemed to bring some vitality back into him. He was so small, laid out in the dewy grass. I had spent many years looking up to him - metaphor, literal truth - and hanging on his words. Now he was cold and still, never again to explain or admonish.

I looked him over for marks of abuse by Charles: new cuts on his flesh or in the alb in which he had been buried. Thankfully, I could see none and we placed him back in the remnants of his coffin.

Before we reburied him, I placed my hand on his. It was hard as wood. I thought over what he would have wanted - I had thought little about the man during these past few days, only about what he had done and what had been done to him. But he was a man, no more, no less; and he should be mourned as such. If I had believed it would have gone anywhere except the air, I would have said a prayer for him.

So I squeezed his hand by way of a goodbye. And it was then that I noticed something missing. The signet ring that I had seen so many times in my youth was no longer on the little finger of his left hand. It had glittered at me as a youth. I recalled the device on it: Father Dollet's initials set within a scroll that he said exaggerated his scholarship. My father, being illiterate, had no need for such a ring to press into sealing wax and thus testify that a letter was genuine, and I had wanted to own one when I was older, although I never got around to it.

I felt a bolt of lightning strike me in the head to cure me of my utter idiocy.

'Oh, good God!' I exclaimed. 'Now I understand!' All this time in my childhood village, I had been looking entirely in the wrong direction. I had been a child indeed! Convinced by foolish old folklore when the modern era contained far more insidious dangers. Dangers to men, women and entire nations. 'Witches indeed! I am a numbskull,' I berated myself. 'Francois, I am a veritable dolt!'

He was becoming concerned by my explosive mood. 'What do you mean?'

I shook my head, I wanted to recover my self-image by at least apprehending Charles before revealing how I had overlooked the simple truth. 'The boy. He thinks he is safe now. Let us prove him wrong.'

'I will be glad of it.'

We placed the coffin as gently as we could back in the ground. It was a shallow grave so we could do it without great indignity to the dead. Then we piled the soil back on him.

'Let us not tell anyone about this unless we have to,' I said. 'We could do without having the villagers up in arms again.'

'Yes, agreed,' Francois sighed as he shovelled more earth down into the plot. We were both dirty on our clothes and palms. 'I feel like I should say a eulogy.'

'What would you say?'

He thought it over for a moment. 'He was a decent man. Good to us, good to others. You cannot ask for much more than that.'

'No, that is true.' It was a simple claim, but just. I hoped that Father Dollet had been right all those times he described heaven. A place of both wonder and serenity. It would suit him well.

'What now?' Francois asked.

'Charles.'

'Where do you think he is?'

'In his den. The ice house.'

We strode down the hill to Francois's estate and the low round tower that was the entrance to that cold subterranean cell. A thought was resounding in my head. For days, someone had been playing with me like the cat plays with the mouse.

Thick undergrowth muffled our approach as we crept up to the ice house. I pulled the door open and it swung on hinges that had been oiled since we were last here. A waft of freezing air made my lips tighten and my nose sting. Looking down the stone steps, a light glinted from below. A shuffling sound told me that there was movement. 'I am with you,' Francois said under his breath. The movement stopped. I steeled myself for what I guessed was to come.

Foot by foot, step by step. It is strange how solidity

can melt away under examination. I could feel the damp stone beneath each foot and yet it seemed to be giving way.

The glow beneath brightened and as my head ducked under the low ceiling, I saw that it came from a fire blazing on the floor.

On the other side of the flames, a figure sat on a stool, his elbows on his knees. 'Hello Charles,' I said.

The boy slowly grinned at me, then his forehead furrowed as he heard more feet on the steps. He lifted his chin and craned his head to see who was with me. 'Oh, your friend. Our benefactor,' he muttered.

'You desecrated the grave of a man I respected,' I said. 'You stole his books, then his dignity in death.'

'What books? The ones about black magic?' Francois asked, staring at Charles. I nodded. 'Is he . . . does he believe himself a witch?'

'Oh, hardly,' I said. 'He took those books, yes, but they were not what he was looking for, were they, Charles?'

A sly smile spread across Charles's face.

'What was?' Francois asked, still barely able to form coherent sentences.

'The letters in Father Dollet's desk. But when I interrupted him, he grabbed everything and ran.'

Charles looked quite satisfied. 'Oh, I see that you understand,' he said.

'Understand what?' interjected Francois.

'You placed that dumb strangled cockerel in my bed too,' I said.

'What cockerel?' Francois asked. It was all too much for him.

Charles slapped his palms onto his thighs. 'Ha ha. Such a good friend of yours that you have not told him. Tell him now. Go on. Tell him now.' He seemed more and more like a ten-year-old child enjoying the limelight.

'Charles crucified an animal and left it in my bed.'

'So it is witchcraft!' Francois insisted. 'To mock the crucifixion of Jesus.'

'In a sense.'

'And he does think himself a witch!'

'No, you fools,' Charles laughed. 'I am–'

'A wretched little spy,' I said.

'A spy?' Francois burst out. 'For whom?' He was quite dumbfounded.

'De Rotanne. Is that not right?' I said. Charles laughed haughtily again. 'Perhaps you heard of my run-in with the comte and you thought you could inform him of my whereabouts?'

'I am a spy, if you will, but not for de Rotanne. Not in fullness,' he insisted, pulling himself up to his full height and puffing out his chest. 'I am loyal to our King, as we all should be!' His voice rose in triumph and anger. 'That priest was a seditious old man. A traitor to France!'

Yes, I had fixated on the books Charles had stolen, whereas it was the letters from Father Dollet to Marat and other radical minds that he had wanted.

'What did Dollet want? Peasants ruling us all? They cannot even spell their own names. Go on, look at them. See them in Versailles instead of the King and Queen.' He thumped his right fist into the other palm. 'We owe him our allegiance. Our lives! The King is set on his throne by God and he who rebels against the King rebels against God himself!' At that, he seemed to burn himself out. I imagined he had been rehearsing this speech in his mind for months.

'So, he was the one who killed Father Dollet?' Francois

sounded suspicious but wary, aware that he was treading behind others who knew the way better than him.

I snorted in derision. 'No, not at all. He is a child and nothing more. But when we were chasing imaginary witches, he thought he would add to the confusion by placing that poor bird in my bed, and sprinkling mounds of stones around me. We were looking for witches and he supplied them.'

'So why did he desecrate Father Dollet's grave? If anything was devilish, that was it.'

'He was not desecrating it, he was robbing it. He took Father Dollet's signet ring so that he could impersonate the priest in correspondence. Then he could expose all those with whom Father Dollet had discussed such matters - priests in particular.'

'Traitors to God and their king. They do not deserve holy title!' Charles insisted, lifting up his hands as if in supplication to the Almighty.

'Oh, hold your tongue, you half-witted child.' My anger was too close to the surface to wink at what he had done.

'The sodomite priest is burning with the rest of them,' he spat.

That was too much. My anger boiled over and I was about to do him violence, but Francois stopped me. 'I think it is time for us to leave,' he said.

I was torn for a second between doing as he suggested and shoving the boy against the wall and giving him something to think about, but it had been a long night, and retiring to my bed was a more sensible action.

We climbed the steps to the door. I closed it behind us and shot the bolt on the outside of the door, locking it quite fast. 'Let us return tomorrow,' I said. 'Or perhaps the day after.'

'Will there be enough air for him in there?' asked Francois as we walked away in a warm wind.

'How would I know?' I replied.

Here ends the third part of The Murderous Deeds in the Village of Lorne in France and How They Brought About the Bloody Revolution.

Chapter Ten

And the narrative stopped. I knew so much and understood so little. 'Where is the last part?' I asked the dog-boy.

'What do you mean?'

'There is another part to it. A continuation. This leaves much unsaid.'

'I never saw another part.'

'Was it published?'

He shrugged.

'I want to speak to the publisher.'

'Dead. Killed last year. Found in one of the closes.'

'Who killed him?' I asked darkly.

'None can say.'

None could say. That was ominous. I was sure that David Sévine was my father. I presumed Catherine was my mother. But I had no idea what had happened to tear us three asunder. It occurred to me that they were not the only personages in whom I should take an interest.

'Do you know anything of the French court at Holyrood?' I asked the boy.

'Something.'

'Is there a Comte de Rotanne among them? Or his son?'

He sneered and held out his hand. I sighed and dropped a crown into it. 'Count Rotten is one of the French King's best men. His son is a fat arse.'

'Where would I find the son?'

'Hinney's coffee house on the High Street. He gambles.'

They had been right under my nose! Well, I would have to spin the tables and inveigle myself into their lives without them knowing who I truly was.

In my bed that night I tossed and turned as ideas rushed around me like so many soldiers in the midst of battle. I knew the shape of my plans – to gain the trust of the people whom I thought were mine enemies or the friends of mine enemies. But there was a barrier to action: I was barely more than a boy. Yes, I was eighteen years old but my sensibilities were still those of the child at Mr Tolson's school: lies stuck in my mouth; the shame of dissembling or twisting another to my will blushed my cheeks; wrath was a sin.

I had to unlearn all that, for my path of vindication would not be a straight one. It would not be grassy underfoot. It would require wicked deeds – or, at the very least, a mind prepared to execute them if the time called for them. I had to baptize myself with fire.

It is strange and taxing to tell oneself that one has to change in *this* way. To become *this*. When *this* is not within our nature. I thought on it as silvery clouds sped across the black sky and night birds screeched to one another. An image formed in my mind: a picture of my father that I had taken from his narrative. He was a lawyer, a soldier. A man of persuasion, a man of action.

I noticed my window had become unlatched and was banging in the wind. I got out of my bed, starting a little at the frosty air, and peeked out into the night. Somewhere out there my parents lay – alive or dead. I would take all my enemies' sins as my school lessons, and I would better my teachers in their art. I made a plan.

'Sir, are you not the esteemed Vicomte de Rotanne?' I said, sweeping my lowest bow.

Gaston peered up from his game of faro. I recognized his person from the penny blood, despite the passage of time.

'I am, sir. And who might you be?'

Hinney's coffee house was the den of the wealthy and idle. I had often been attracted to the sweet smells wafting from the establishment, but my apprentice's clothing would have had me sneered at before I had crossed the threshold – even though the French court with their outmoded *culottes* and hair pomade raised titters in all they passed on the streets.

I could hardly afford to have such clothing as would be at home in that place, so I had helped myself to my employer's possessions. His finest silk apparel and his best wig were mine for the afternoon while he was at the university, and fitted me well enough.

I powdered my face and stained my teeth yellow in order to make my skin seem even paler, as the French aristocrats did. The effect was to make it seem that one had never seen the outside, but had spent one's whole life in the salons and gaming parlours of the great palaces.

'Oh, sir. I am the most unfortunate you have set eyes upon since the poor deceased King Louis himself. De Tarre is my name,' I explained. 'And I spent seven long years in the foul prisons of the seditious dogs before I could bribe my gaolers to allow my escape.'

'Really?' He looked much intrigued.

'Yes. I managed to come here almost penniless. But your name has spread as a leader of us exiled loyal Frenchmen.'

I was laying it on a bit thick, I knew, but I credited Gaston with more vanity than sense. And there truly had been such stories of oppression and escape.

Gaston was attended by a small gang of pals. Like him, they were blatantly overfed and probably unencumbered by brains. They were in their fifth decade of life and yet seemed as juvenile as those who had not reached the third. It was their straining waistbands that gave the game away. There was, however, one among them who clearly ate less, laughed less and watched more. He was older than the others and had greasy grey-blond hair. His black velvet coat was less ostentatious than those of his companions.

'De Tarre,' Gaston said ruminatively, his jowls gently wobbling. 'I do not know your name.'

'We are of Corsica.'

It was a source of amusement in England that there were thousands upon thousands of French nobles, as anyone born to a noble thus became one, and that had been the rule for five hundred or more years – the result being that every village contained a man with an aristocratic title, even though they may be no richer than the local miller. I was therefore confident that my assumed name and rank would not be detected.

He nodded in acceptance of my explanation. The one in black spoke. 'Your accent is strange, too.'

'And I apologize for my poor French. I was in the prison from a young age with my English mother and none other to whom I would wish to speak. Monsieur . . . ?'

'Matrick.'

It was like a bolt from the blue. I knew that name well. Perhaps it should not have been such a surprise. The man was the hawk-faced lawyer to Gaston's father, the Comte de Rotanne, against whom my father had butted heads.

But Gaston was not so guarded as his father's lawyer. 'Sit down, de Tarre. It is nice to know more people from France.' The others agreed.

We chatted for a while about local entertainments and the coarseness of the local manners, the beastly Scottish weather and the barely edible food. I wanted to ask why, if they disliked it so much, they did not decamp elsewhere. But the answer, of course, was that no one really wanted them. The British court and those of Europe, too, found them to be a deal of 'work' to administer, and costly far beyond their worth. And so they were stuck in Edinburgh, where they spent their days reading the *Evening Courant* for news of Bonaparte and railing about the drizzle.

'Do you think we will defeat him?' he enquired, looking at me keenly as if my – supposed – more recent experience of France qualified me to pronounce on the subject.

'Without doubt. It is God against the peasants and atheists.' He looked pleased, and there were universal murmurs of assent. I thought it prudent to invent a rumour that Bonaparte was sick with the pox, which he had caught from his wife. The information was gladly received.

After that, we settled down to empty a bottle of pastis

and talk of hunting stags, during which I made up various opinions about the best ways to trap such a beast, despite having never seen one. Some of my suggestions were revelatory, members of the party declared.

Eventually, Gaston scratched his flabby buttocks, checked an ornate clock upon the mantelpiece, and announced: 'It is time for the opera.'

'Oh, the opera?' I replied. I had not expected music lasting hours at a time to be Gaston's bent.

'Yes, it is boring but we have to be seen there. A work by Gluck, the story of Orpheus and Euridice.' He beamed. 'Come with us.'

'I should be delighted.' I only hoped it would not be excessively expensive, for I had only the two guineas I had been able to save from my allowance.

'Then let us be off!' announced Gaston. And his servant helped him to his feet.

We processed through the evening stink to the New Town's great thoroughfare, Princes Street, led by link boys holding their torches aloft so we could see where we stepped. Then, for ha'pennies, the crossing sweepers cleared a path through the horse dung to the grand Theatre Royal.

I knew the story of Orpheus, the Greek bard with the beguiling voice, and his wife, Euridice, whom he led out of the Underworld after death had taken her, only for her to be snatched back again by Hades. It had been among those we had learned at school and I had enjoyed its story of redemption, spoiled by ill-luck.

Arriving at the theatre, I viewed a throng of carriages outside the large but plain-looking edifice. I had rarely seen so many tailcoats and bonnets together and the alcohol in my veins made me forget my dark mission such that I was quite happy and giddy at the gay sight. Gaston's man flourished our metal tickets and we were duly ushered under the great chandeliers to the prince's box, beside the stage. It was one of the pricier ones and was replete with a feast of cured meats and fruit that Gaston had thought to have catered in advance. The fizz from the limelights at the foot of the stage lent a constant crackle to the air.

I had been to plays here, usually in the standing pit – where I was, at first, a little surprised to see men relieve themselves in the corners and jades touting for business – and once in the more genteel stalls when I had felt especially flush. But I had never attended the opera and knew not what to expect.

I was about to discreetly enquire when the whole theatre rose to their feet and bowed or curtseyed. I followed, not comprehending, until I saw a bored-looking man in the very finest pink silk coat and brilliant-white cravat saunter into the royal box. The box was between us and the stage, and level with the performers, so that its occupants might have been part of the action. There he was: Louis XVIII of France, a king without a country. A man revered only by émigrés and doomed to live and die on foreign soil. Yes, he, his wife and his courtiers were very much part of the entertainment rather than the audience. Fortunately, he looked quite theatrical with his long dark moustache and longer chestnut-coloured tresses. He was only three yards from us, so I could have smelled his perfume – had the room not already reeked of a hundred other expensive scents.

He sat, and at that signal we took our seats again. I was at the front of the box with Gaston, while Matrick's breath moistened the back of my neck. I must say I enjoyed the sweeping overture that summoned the pastoral joys and then the hellish terrors to come. And when Orpheus, played by a divinely statuesque woman aged, I supposed, in her fifties, strode onto the stage and enchanted us all with her voice, I was quite captured. 'She is something, is she not?' Gaston said slyly.

'She certainly is.'

'I could introduce you.'

Albeit I had only heard her sing, the prospect was bewitching. 'Could you?'

'I could. Juliana is part of our court.' I jerked up from my seat involuntarily, attracting the stares of those around me, even the King. Gaston pulled me back down and scowled.

Matrick leaned his face between mine and Gaston's. 'Is something a-matter?' he asked.

'N-nothing. Juliana. I believe I have heard of her.' I had read so much of this woman, but never thought to have seen her in the flesh. And to think: all my time in Edinburgh, she must have been here too.

'Is that all?' Matrick knew there was more.

'Yes, quite all.' I stared at her, this enticing woman. Her age had not withered the beauty that my father's narrative had set down. If anything, the years had rendered her more bewitching. As she sang of her lost love, I could have plucked out my heart and offered to it her.

'She plays a man's part well,' Matrick said. 'But then, Juliana has had a lot of practice playing with a man's parts, has she not?' There were meaningful sniggers all around from Gaston's coterie. 'And Gluck wrote it for one who has lost what she has lost.' This time there were no more laughs, yet, glancing back, I saw Matrick smiling to himself as if he had made a very satisfying private joke. But then her voice hit a note that could have soared above the very clouds and the entire theatre held its breath, waiting for the note to fall back down to earth. I felt my hands grip the edge of the box tighter, as if the music itself was controlling me, turning me into its puppet.

'Calm yourself, de Tarre,' Gaston whispered, amused. 'We shall meet her after the performance for wine.'

'We shall?' The whirlpool of sensations churned within me. Would she have news of my father? My mother? I grabbed a glass of chilled wine and threw it down my throat, hoping that it would settle my nerves. 'Will you tell me about her?'

'Oh, if you like,' Gaston sighed. 'She is His Majesty's mistress. She came over in, oh, '92, '93? She performed at the grand courts of Europe until the peasants took our nation.'

'Has she . . . family?'

'Family? I believe there is a son somewhere. I know not.'

A son somewhere. Yes, I was certain that was the case. I fell silent, enslaved by the music. There was an interval, during which we drank more, but I cannot recall what else occurred. My whole body itched until the second part of the performance. And then I sat, rapt, watching every step the woman took, every twitch of a delicate finger, and entranced by every note that she lifted to the rafters.

I understood how the French King had chosen her as his entertainment and his life beyond his family and court. I saw her painted in portrait by her friend Annalise; riding to hounds; crying for her husband, Gregory Archer.

And then, as she lifted that heavenly voice in the passion of loss, portraying Orpheus in the moment that he realizes that his beloved wife will never return to him, her eyes swept to the royal box, and bowed down to her kingly patron. Then they lifted again and travelled on to our party. And they met mine and widened in an ecstasy of shock. The notes cut out. Her voice faltered and ceased. The orchestra fell into a disarrayed halt. And still Juliana Archer's eyes were locked on mine. Without a word, her hand lifted up as if to touch my face. It reached into the void between us. Boos and jeering erupted from the pit as those who had paid a penny for entertainment found themselves robbed of it. At that, she seemed to come to herself, shaking her head and dropping her hand. She smiled apologetically at the conductor and bade him strike up again. When the music rose once more, her face was a theatrical mask of sorrow for her Euridice. And only once after that did I catch her glance at me, quickly and surreptitiously, before returning to her performance. But I knew that she recognized me – as my father's son.

'Who are you?'

It was whispered in my ear. I knew the cold breath. Matrick.

'De Tarre,' I replied mechanically.

'Are you? Are you really?' And I could feel him sit back in his seat.

I was still for the rest of the performance as if my limbs were bound up, unable to move. I was unable to do anything but say to myself: *What does she know? What will she do for you? Will she embrace you? Deny you? Expose you to your enemies?* I was in a dark forest of danger and promise.

Eventually the show ended, and the King rose and swept out. 'Let us see Juliana,' Gaston burbled, the amount of drink he had swallowed now taking its toll.

'Would you like that, de Tarre?' posed the voice behind me. 'I am sure that you would.'

I said nothing. But even in his inebriated state, Gaston could tell by his chaperon's tone that something was afoot. 'What? What'sat?' he mumbled.

'I believe our new friend is an admirer of Juliana.'

'Oho, is he, by God? Well, she's gettin' on a bit. But yes, let us see her in th'flesh.' And he stumbled out of the box and down the stairs. We followed in his bullying wake to the back corridors of the theatre, where he made a point of leering at some ballerinas in a state of semi-dress and bursting through a door putatively guarded by an ancient porter.

'Juliana!'

She was seated before a mirror, removing her make-up and wig. She did not seem surprised to see him or me. They exchanged pleasantries, he slobbered on her hand. Matrick congratulated her, while watching what I did. I was close enough to see the blue eyes that my father had described. They had seemed pale to that author, but to me, by the candlelight in her dressing room, they were a rich, velvet hue.

Juliana served us wine. But as she placed the cup in my hand, I felt something else come with it. A note that she must have had ready. When the others were distracted, I took a moment to read. I should have waited, of course, but I could not contain myself.

You look just like him. Come to me later.

It sent a jolt of fire through me. So, there was no doubt now. David Sévine was my father. I glanced at Juliana. She was back to playing hostess but she gave me a meaningful look.

For half an hour we played at polite companionship until it was time we all went to our beds. Outside, in the smoky air, I bade them farewell and promised to see them again at the coffee house soon. Instead, I doubled back to Juliana.

To the truth of who I was. And the truth of who wanted me dead.

'I never thought I would see you.'

The voice, unmistakably hers, drifted through the empty theatre corridor even before I reached her open doorway.

And yet, here I am, I thought to myself. I could barely believe it had come to this either.

And then there she was in the centre of the room. The candelabra in her hand sent shadows flickering all around us like devils.

I said nothing, waiting for her to continue. She looked magisterial, like Shakespeare's Cleopatra before her death. And yet . . . yet there was something else flitting in her eyes. It was not fear, no. Neither was it pity. It was . . . could it be dread? Yes. Dread. She was dreading something: an event to come, or a memory of things past.

'My father?' I blurted out, not even a sentence, a question, just a plea.

'Your father was a brave man. A good man.'

'*Was*?' I said, quoting her, wondering at the tense. 'Is he dead?'

She steadied herself on the table before her. It was strewn with the paint with which actors and singers bedeck themselves to turn into other beings from other times. A pot of rouge had tipped over and spilled its contents.

'Dead?' And my heart turned to stone. But she caught my blanched looks and came to me quickly, placing her warm palms on my cheeks. Even with the life drained from me, her touch seemed to pulse on my skin and for a moment I could understand how she had entranced kings and commoners across Europe. 'No, he is not dead. At least, I do not think that he is. I have not seen him for more than a year, but I begged them to keep him alive.' The elation I felt was indescribable. It felt like being drunk on words alone.

My father alive! For a full ten seconds, I was no longer in that room, but soaring through the clouds above Scotland and France and everywhere in between. Then I brought myself back to find her searching my face, and I could tell, somehow, that it was for some spark of forgiveness. Forgiveness for what? What had been her part in the capture or downfall of my parents?

'Where is he? Tell me,' I demanded, my blood rushing back to my limbs and my tongue.

She lifted her hands away and stepped back from me, as if I were now a danger to her, as if my pores seeped poison.

'I know not.' She lifted her face to mine. 'I wish to

God that I did. They do not tell me these things. They distrust me. They have good reason.' Her voice fell ruefully.

'They? Who are *they*?' I growled, losing what temper I had exhibited until then. 'Tell me who they are so I can kill them.' And the vehemence, the black hatred that poured through the final words struck even me dumb. I had not known until that moment how much I wanted to plunge my dagger into their chests and twist it, to see the distillation of pain in their faces that I had suffered for my whole life, my life robbed of parents' love.

The violence of my hate made her catch her breath. For a moment she was unable to pronounce a sound. She might have even feared for her own life and being. Then she nodded, for I had a right to know. 'The Circle. They are the Circle.'

'What is the Circle?'

She did not answer.

'I have only heard of them. Who are they?' She began to move away from me but I caught her wrist. It was delicate as a painting.

'De Rotanne,' she whispered.

'The count?'

'Him.'

'Then I shall find him.' She shook her head. 'Is my mother alive?'

'She is—'

She was cut off by a heavy rap on the door, which opened instantly to present to us a sight royal: Louis XVIII of France flanked by two equerries dressed by someone who had not been informed that the finest hours of the Bourbons were behind them. The King scratched his cheek while his men entered the room, shoved me aside and made a tunnel for their monarch to enter.

Juliana dropped into a low curtsey and a swift glance in my direction told me it was time to bow. I did so, but surreptitiously watched as one equerry displayed to all a tortoiseshell snuff box with a flourish, which he then handed to Louis. The King, obligingly, tapped the lid three times to settle the powder and demonstrate the quality of the box, before flicking the lid open with his thumb to demonstrate his dexterity and taking a small pinch that was placed within his nostril. I could detect the aroma of lavender, which seemed to be his preferred variety. With a practised and decisive sniff, the snuff went straight up his nostril, we all waited and then he sneezed well, but not excessively, into a linen handkerchief proffered by the equerry.

'*Qui est-il*?' asked Louis, without much interest.

'*Personne, mon seigneur*,' Juliana replied, negating my presence in just three words.

The King held out his hand, and Juliana kissed a giant emerald on a ring that surrounded his left index finger. He lifted her to her feet and the two of them departed.

I was left watching her skirts trail in the dust of the floor on the corridor. She turned and silently mouthed. *Do not come again. I am watched.*

Chapter Eleven

For a month I inveigled myself into Gaston's party. I laughed at thin jokes, I frequented bawdy houses, I quaffed wine and pastis until my vision blurred. Most of all, I lost money at cards. By good fortune, my master was spending a term teaching at the university in Glasgow. He had no need of me there, so I was left to keep watch on the house. With no other idea for how to maintain my place in the pleasant company to which I had been admitted, I took to pawning some of the silver plate that was locked away in the scullery. I had a vague intention to recover it in time, before Mr Baird noticed its absence – although how I was going to do so was a mystery to me. Even the coffee in Hinney's was extortionate, because one had to pay with the little brass tokens that the house used instead of common money, which disguised the price of each cup. And that was without the fashionable taste for turtle soup and blancmanges that my new companions sported.

But on one score, my stratagem was a success. I became a cemented part of Gaston's coterie. Once, when I returned from visiting the lavatory, I happened upon Gaston and Matrick whispering with animation between them. Matrick appeared annoyed.

'Your father will hear of this.'

'He is in London to get loans. So I run the Circle. He will—' He hushed at Matrick's insistence, but as I sat before them, Gaston's face was the picture of satisfaction, while Matrick's was like thunder.

It was two nights later that I arrived at Hinney's after nightfall to find Gaston and three others silently waiting for me. Matrick sat apart, scowling. I began to order a drink but Gaston stayed me with his hand.

'My friend de Tarre,' he began. 'Things will be different tonight.' And he leant in close enough for me to smell garlic on his breath. 'Tonight and for ever.' I asked his meaning. He put a hand up to stop my speech. Then he led the way, followed by the others, outside. We wended through the dirty air, across the soot-covered Old Town, and down the great hill into the damp valley below, where the air in the park around the ruined Holyrood Abbey was sweeter and cooler. All the while as we walked, though, I felt Matrick behind me like a vengeful spectre.

The abbey, which had been the origin of Holyrood Palace that lay beside it, had long ago been destroyed by the Protestant forces and poor engineering, so that it now seemed a threatening ribcage of stones rising from the earth.

As I came closer, I heard the murmur of men's voices. The walls of the abbey church had long ago split apart, as if a giant fist had punched through, and we processed in.

And there, and then, is when my fate first appeared to me. Six men, each wearing courtly dress, with a blue silk sash from the right shoulder to the left hip. One stood watching our entry, a couple sat on lichen-encrusted stone blocks, one perched in a niche in the wall. A subtle smile played on Gaston's lips as he walked me in. Then he glanced to the ruined sacristy, where a stone altar still stood, ready to bear the blood of Christ, the body of Christ. On the stone a dozen candles had been placed in a ring around a silver crown.

Gaston grinned more widely, beckoning me with enthusiasm.

'Do you see this? Do you see it?' Such excitement! *Of course*, I thought. *This is not his place. He is standing for his father. He is forty-five years old and yet like a child left alone at home for the first time, going through his parents' wine cellar.*

'I see it.'

'De Tarre. You are a loyal Frenchman, yes? Loyal to God and his servant, King Louis?'

'I am.'

'Then you will prove it now.'

Instead of opening the secret to me, he motioned to one of his fellows, a huge man, powerfully built, barely encased in his extensive clothes. His tree-like beard accentuated his monolithic image. This man reached for my hand. By beast-instinct, I drew it away. But he grabbed it by the wrist and slammed it down on the damp altar stone, facing upwards. Two other men, less powerful than he but with a combined strength that beat my own, thrust my left hand onto the silver crown.

'Hold it hard,' one ordered me. I did so.

A man appeared from behind me with a flaming torch. He held it to the silver. Soot appeared on the glistening metal but it was clear that was not the point. The point was the heat that began to surge through into my skin, warming, then burning it. I knew that this was an ordeal I had to go through to be admitted into the Circle and its secrets. I could smell my own flesh burn.

'We have all been through this. To an extent,' Gaston told me, his little eyes glittering with amusement. The pain sliced through my nerves. I would have wagered all the wealth I owned that Gaston had not endured half so much as I had already. I gritted and gnashed my teeth so as not to cry out. I thought of my mother, my father. Of Mr Tolson and Astaroth. All that I had endured on this path. 'Does it hurt so much?'

'Yes,' I growled, uncertain if I was supposed to brave through it and deny any pain.

'It is a test, you see.'

Of course it was a test, you fool. And your idiocy was just the spur I needed to endure it. I crushed my teeth into each other and hissed like a snake. I pictured myself wringing his neck.

And then, just as the pain grew so great that I thought my very hand on fire, and I was about to drop the crown and dash all my hopes, Gaston cried: 'He has endured!' and my hand was plucked away and thrust into a bucket of icy water, numbing the pain to a dull ache. 'You are now of the Circle.' He seemed delighted with what he had seen.

I said a prayer of thanks to God that the trial had ended before I had driven my fist into his puckered lips.

'It is an honour, but I know not what it is.'

And then, for probably the only time in his dull life, Gaston said something intelligent. 'But you have guessed, have you not?'

I smiled conspiratorially. 'I have, yes. I think you mean to place the King back upon the throne.'

Gaston opened his arms. 'And then we are going to

put Robespierre on a spit.' It did not seem to matter to him that Citizen Robespierre had been dead since 1794, and if he was to be put on a spit, it would be his dry bones they would be cooking.

Gaston nodded to the big man. His size made one think of him as an oaf, but his brain was clear and quick. 'There is more, de Tarre,' the man said.

'Tell me.'

'We have much to accomplish so we have two great aims: the first is to build alliances. Russia still stands hard with us in the fight against Bonaparte the usurper. But we need more friends for soldiers and funds. What was the Holy Roman Empire is now an anarchy of cowards under Bonaparte's boot and that was a blow; but we have established a secret mission to the Turk and one to the new rulers of Sweden, in the hope they will soon commit troops to the great war of restoration.'

I was struck. Inviting the Mohammedans to send soldiers into Christian lands was an astonishing, risk-filled move for a Catholic dynasty. It was therefore no surprise that the Circle had to keep the mission *sub rosa*. No doubt, if the British government had caught wind of the pact, they might well have kicked their royal guests out of the country.

'Who else will help?' I asked. I knew that Boney's French empire had gobbled up most of Europe. 'America?'

'Ingrates. They offer us nothing. Fifty years ago, we emptied our coffers to fund their war against England, and now they turn their backs on us. They sell cotton and tobacco to the Atheist usurpers and buy the wine that comes from our stolen vineyards.' If he had been an uncouth man, he would have spat the name of

America upon the ground, I could tell. Others around us looked similarly angry.

These men of the Circle were playing chess, but against five opponents on one board. They were hosted by England. All well and good. But they wanted the support of America, and America and England were fighting each other at sea over trade, so there was no fruit from that tree; and if Christian Europe were to learn that the Turk, who had been defeated at the gates of Vienna a century ago, was to have those very gates opened by Louis XVIII of France, it would most likely mean Louis exiled to lands where men shared their caves with bears.

'I wish to be of use,' I said. If I am to be frank, I said this in part to endear me to them, and in part because, in my boyishness, I rather relished the idea of life as an intelligencer. How romantic to fly at night, to sail to America, to smuggle myself to Constantinople! That these missions had, to date, been failures – and to say nothing of the fact that they were in aid of mine enemies! – registered little in my adventure-seeking mind.

'In time, perhaps,' the big man answered me, thoughtfully. 'For now, you will aid us in our second course. Seeking out the spies of the usurpers.'

'Spies . . . here? In Scotland?'

'The little snakes are everywhere. Some are street punks, spreading lies through pamphlets about our old regime. Some are cleverer than that. They are agents of influence and try to turn Britain's parliamentarians against us by saying that we waste their money, and England could safely trade with Bonaparte. We uncovered one plot to kill his Highness King Louis.'

'Did you? What happened?'

'The girl was dealt with.'

I hesitated. 'How?'

'The Nor'loch.' I felt those cold waters, that I had passed many times, swirl around me. He continued, with scant concern for his prior words. 'You, with your English accent, will be of use to us in this area.'

'What should I do?' I asked falteringly. An image of a woman floating through the blue-black water of the Nor'loch, her hair entangled in weeds, drifted before me and I felt sick.

'Different things. Ask about if anyone knows of publications libelling the King or praising the usurpers. The inns around Dover and Folkestone can be sources of information.'

My head spun a little. I was to be a traitor twice over. The French court would set me to spy upon the English, unknowing that my heart was set upon peeling away the layers of secrets to find what that self-same court had done in the shadows to my father and mother.

The Nor'loch. I winced to blow it away.

'You will be a loyal servant to the crown,' Gaston said. And they all cheered for the life of Louis and thanks to God.

Out of the corner of my eye, I saw Matrick standing as motionless as a statue, observing me.

Despite my entry into their league, over the next week I found myself no closer to discovering what I needed and I was mulling the problem for the hundredth time as we sat in our box at the Theatre Royal, waiting to hear Juliana sing Orpheus once more. I was frustrated and a little bored while I peeled an orange and cast the skin on the floor.

Lifting my opera glasses, I gazed at the stage, looking for Juliana. Her divine presence would, at least, pull me out of my funk. Two discs of the stage appeared through the glasses, one side sporting a grassy hillock constructed of wood, the other a vision of hell made from the same. Chitter-chatter about Juliana rose among my companions once again about how Orpheus was her part to play, when a shout arose from the stalls below us.

'There he is! Thief!' Startled, I turned my glasses to the seats below us. To my shock, the lenses found my employer, Mr Baird. He had returned early from Glasgow and was pointing at me, his face like red brimstone. 'Thief! He stole from my strongbox,' he was yelling. 'My servant. He is my servant and I take him in the name of the law. Call a constable. Clap him in irons! He is a thief! He took my best silver plate! Thief!' Amazed, I dropped the glasses. My companions had stopped talking and were staring as hard as I was from him to me.

'De Tarre?'

I do not even recall whom it was who spoke. Gaston? Matrick? Did it matter? Not one jot. I jerked to my feet. It was the wrong thing to do now, I know, an admission of some sort of guilt, but Baird was marching towards the staircase that would bring him to me, and had enlisted the aid of two or three other just men on his path, shouting that they would be helping him apprehend a common criminal in the hue and cry. 'A common criminal! I took the boy in. A criminal!'

I had envisaged having to run from Gaston or his friends, had even made a point of looking for the safest exit upon entering certain abodes with them. But the need to flee my employer had not crossed my thoughts. That is, perhaps, why I panicked and attempted to dash like a hunted fox.

'Come with us,' yelled one of my companions. 'We shall get you safe.' In that moment, with my mind on fire, I was overjoyed with gratitude for the help, and three of them, with Gaston on our heels, drove me at speed towards an exit.

'Stop him! Thief!'

I looked around. They were no more than ten yards away, striding towards us. One of my companions ran to hold them back while I was bundled away, out the side of the building. We sped through streets, hearing the shouts grow more distant, until we stopped, our lungs heaving, in the doorway of a milliner. Gulping air, my heart ready to burst, I spoke. 'My friends, I th—'

And then the heavy blow to the back of my skull cut off all thought.

Chapter Twelve

Waking in the blackest dark, unable to think, not knowing your name or where you are, unable to conceive of anything but that you are alive, is a sickening sensation. It reduces you to the life of a beast. You might as well be a dog living among the trash and gutters of mankind.

I woke with nothing. My mind was an empty expanse of ocean. All I had were the sensations of cold, pain, restraint.

Restraint, for I could not move my hands. When I tried, something bit into my wrists. A rope, rough and tight. I could not see it, though my eyes were open. I could see nothing at all.

'If you move, your life will be over.'

It was hissed in my ear. It could have been the voice of an angel or devil. I twisted towards the sound, and then realized why I saw nothing, even with my eyes wide open. The movement of rough hessian upon my face and neck told me that my head was encased in a thick hood.

'I . . . I . . .' I stammered, but I could think of no words. Words themselves seemed beyond my reach.

'You seem less sure of yourself than the last time we met. Do you remember that? Do you?' And then a little throaty chuckle. 'I remember it. I'll remember it 'til they put me under the ground.'

'Who are you?' I croaked. 'Where am I?'

'Where are you, or *who* are you?' And another little chuckle. And those words resounded in my head, echoing from a time years ago when I had pronounced them. 'You have been a little fool, have you not? Meddling when you should have stayed away. When you should have kept to your toys and poppets.' I groped for a memory. It was there, but I could not reach it. 'Take care, lad. Or there is worse to come.'

'Who are you? Show yourself. Or are you coward?' I yelled.

And there was silence. Silence but for the heavy breath of the man who held me.

'Enough of this.' It was another voice, spoken out loud. Richer and more refined. 'I have affairs to attend to.'

'So have I,' muttered the first man. He was so close that I could feel the heat of the blood in his veins.

'Come, remove the hood. I wish to see him.'

'As you will,' grunted the first man.

The hood was ripped from me and flares burned into my eyes, through the iris, along the optic nerves. I saw nothing but a ring of suns until, bit by bit, my vision became human again to show a circle of torches burning. I was back in the abbey church. My hands were tied to the stone altar. And as my swimming vision became natural, I saw a face – a face I had been sure would never appear before me again. A man I had named myself.

Astaroth, the fallen angel and keeper of the Devil's secrets. A man with a shield of brass where his eye had been blasted out by my father.

'You are surprised.' And he broke a grin. 'You thought my bones were on the sea bed.'

'But you . . .'

'A hundred men have tried to kill me. Your father too. None yet did it.'

'Then I will do it!' I know not what depths of defiance originated it, but the thought burst from me.

But his only reaction was laughter. It shook his body. 'Spirit.' I became aware that sheets of rain were washing across us, driven by gusts of hard wind that the crumbled walls of the abbey church could barely slow.

He appraised me, looking me up and down with his one eye. I took the time to stare to my sides. There were five or six other men in that bust church. Matrick was one, standing some way off.

'So this is the child that you failed to take, Vinerre,' said a man aged around sixty, wearing a fine wig and clothes – though they had been well spattered by the mud and standing water of the abbey grounds. He stood sheltered in the lee of one of the walls, where a tiny patch of roof remained to provide enough dry ground for him and no more. Matrick looked at him and nodded, deferentially. Oh, of course. This was Gaston's eminent father. The Comte de Rotanne, back from persuading the bankers of London to lend upon Louis XVIII's name and distant hope of regaining the French throne from Napoleon.

And I knew the true name of the man who had stalked me for my entire life. Vinerre.

'This is the boy.'

'Well, I want you to proceed as instructed. This wreck is fit only for pigs or those of your estate.' The comte stepped stiffly away, holding his coat above his head to ward off the rain. 'Have it done before I reach the palace,' he said. Matrick followed him. The others remained.

These men. These men who encircled me looked like nothing so much as a squad to murder me. I feared death. I was young and any young man who says he fears not death is a liar or a halfwit. I had searched my life for my parents, for the truth of my birth because I wanted to live, not to die.

'It took much to find your ma. Less to take her away,' Vinerre said, as much to himself as to me, enjoying it. I snarled and twisted at the bonds on my wrists. 'You want to kill me, do you not?' And I saw his fingertips stained brown. So, he had come up enough in the world to afford snuff now. But still it was a cheap blend that left its mark on the skin. I felt a welcome thrill of contempt for this man who wanted to be among his betters but had found his way barred.

I had before me a picture of my mother – blurred and vague. Full of maternal love but enveloped by sadness. I know not whence it came – perhaps in that moment my fingertips had touched the first real memory I had ever had of her. Perhaps it was all of my own fabulation. And yet, there she was. And here was the man who had ripped me from her, and her from me.

'Face me now. Face me like a man!' I yelled, shaking my wrists in their bonds.

'You want to fight, boy?'

'I want to kill you!'

'Ah, yes. Yes, you do.'

I felt electricity surging in my limbs, as I had seen on the demonstration table. I wanted to tear him apart with my hands and teeth. We were all soaked to the skin, as the rain fell like the flood of Noah.

'Fight me!'

I jerked at my bonds and felt the warmth of blood trickling down my wrists. He chuckled. 'I could break you up with both my hands tied back, boy.' I shouted such oaths and threats that I cannot even recall, but they only made him laugh harder. 'One day you will have the chance. I will be waiting. But for now, you are going in the pit.'

Even through the red mist of anger that enveloped me, what he said made me halt. I was to be taken somewhere where the very name was a threat of disappearance.

He and three of the others prised my arms behind my back and bound them. A leather line was thrown around my neck, tight, to choke and drag me. Yet still I hissed threats and demands. 'Where is my mother? Why are you doing this to us?'

But Vinerre was finished with conversation. He led the way towards the nave of the church. I struggled at first, but the noose around my neck tightened and they choked that fight from me as they pushed me towards what seemed no more than an empty niche within the wall. What had once been there – a tiny chapel or statue to a saint – had long since been plundered. Were they going to tie me up there? Kill me there? But I was destined for 'the pit'. My feet kicked up sprays of filthy water.

As we reached the niche, I saw that there was a hole in the ground, and ancient steps, covered in turf, leading down. Vinerre went to their edge.

'Follow him,' ordered one man twisting my upper

arm enough to break it. Now fear's clutch wound around me, to replace the blind fury.

I did as I was told. The steps were running with rainwater and utterly impenetrable to vision once they had descended under the ground. Vinerre smiled a taunting smile as he stepped down towards hell, and then his head was swallowed up by the black. I heard none of his footsteps. It was as if he had been rapt by the Devil himself. 'Where is my mother?' I called down. I was calmer but still jolts of anger shivered through me.

'Your mother.' A little whispering laugh to himself echoed. 'Down here? Up above? Who can tell you?'

'You can,' I hissed.

'Can I?' And his voice changed, become less a playful taunt and more a demonic threat. 'Come down.'

The promise of knowledge, not concern for my life, dragged me down those filthy steps, into the bowels of Edinburgh. And then a shaft of light suddenly erupted and I found his face inches from mine. I would not give him the satisfaction of laughing again at my please to know of my mother's fate. But there was something else I wanted to know.

'When you tried to take me . . . You fell into the sea. I thought you dead. Why did you not come back for me?'

'You think that you are all there is in this world? Ha! After I fished myself out, I went back to the Circle. And they had other plans for me. There was fighting to do. Battles against Bonaparte. They took me away from all this for a time. But now I'm back.'

He turned and moved from the moonlight to the darkness.

I could see nothing in that passage, and had to feel my way with my feet for fear of tripping and tumbling down – all the way to hell, for all that I knew. Vinerre's feet tapped carefully ahead of me, telling me that he, too, was finding his way by touch.

The flight was not as deep as I had thought, though. Soon the ground was flat, albeit an inch deep in chill water. I started to walk forward but was halted hard by a hand on my chest. A spark flew in the darkness and caught on dry char cloth where it burned red and lit a beeswax candle.

I had a head full of questions. 'Why did they send you for her? What do they want with her?'

He made a satisfied little grunt in his throat. 'You have no idea, do you, my boy? Take my word. Know the battle before you fight it.'

At that, he led the way again. The walls were so tight they squeezed my shoulders. I wondered where we were. It was the depths of the ancient abbey, that was for certain, but it was no part that had ever welcomed the prying gaze of outsiders. It reeked, too, of the Nor'Loch's brackish water, which splashed around our feet.

We turned a corner and suddenly the light from his candle burst to walls ten yards away and a barrel-vaulted roof of carved stone.

'Where are we?' I asked in surprise.

'Crypt.' He said it as if he felt comfort here – perhaps he did. It was a place with only the passage we had travelled as entrance or exit. Here and there were a few rotted sticks, which suggested long-gone wooden chests. It might have been the abbey treasury, stuffed with reliquaries and silver plate – all thieved five hundred years before. One of the side walls was crumbling to the waterlogged floor.

I heard a sort of moaning from somewhere, rattling around the room, but could detect no origin for it. Shoved to my knees, I could see my reflection in the dark pool. It was only then, kneeling with my arms bound behind me in an underground cavern, with no friends and only enemies around me, that the thought entered my head: I was to die there. My life was to be torn from me, my body perhaps to rot in the cold water drifting around us. I sighed. I did not cry for mercy or friends. I only sighed. I had searched for my parents but would never behold them.

Vinerre must have seen the look on my face that said I expected death to pounce upon me before the hour was up. 'Oh no, we haven't decided what to do with you.'

I glared at him, somehow resenting even this – for at least if I were to die, I would no longer be under their suzerainty. From somewhere I heard a moan again. It must have been the wind through those bricks.

'Do what you will,' I muttered. It was a passive defiance, but the greatest that I could summon while bound and friendless.

He laughed. 'Oh, we will, boy. Your father owes me this.' And he lifted the brass patch over his left eye. Beneath it was red, uneven flesh and skin, yellow pus seeping here and there. The eye was gone and there was only a dark mass. He took a small flask from his pocket and poured the contents over the blasted ring of bone. It smelt of rough spirits and he grimaced in pain, before grinning at me. 'I will have my reckoning,' he said.

He motioned to the others who shoved me towards a break in the side wall. I could not understand where I was now being taken – into the wall itself? I blinked. They pushed me right at the breech. Yes, somehow I was being thrown into the very wall. But then I saw that the wall was not now, and never had been, solid. Within it was a dark cavity, a little more than the thickness of a man, a sort of tiny monk's cell.

The bricks that had fallen from the wall had exposed this crypt-within-a-crypt. And from the back of my mind I dragged an old memory of the history of the church: how, in the mediaeval times, monks and nuns had sometimes been incarcerated in the walls of their abbeys, either through religious zeal at the thought of holy self-inflicted privation, or as punishment for some offence of the spirit or flesh. For most of those prisoners, they would be bricked in, with a small hole through which food would be passed, to live out their natural lives there. For others, body-wracking death by starvation was the sentence pronounced by their religious order. Immuration, it was called.

But none had been subject to it for centuries.

I was to be the first to break that gap.

'No!' I cried out, struggling with renewed vigour. I was prepared to forfeit my life, but not in such a painful way. 'Kill me and be done with it!'

Vinerre laughed. 'I told you. They haven't decided what to do with you yet.'

I lashed out with my feet, but they were quickly kicked away and I was dragged on my knees to the tumbledown of bricks and stones. The moaning of the wind was louder and closer.

I was thrown in and my cheek struck the damp wall.

I half collapsed as a fist across my temple added to the pain. It stunned me while my captors twisted me around and replaced the ropes on my wrist with chained manacles that were locked to a ring of metal set into the stone slabs underfoot. I was unable to stand, let alone walk or struggle, with my hands thus bound behind me.

'You'll stay there until you are called for,' said the man I still saw as the blackest fallen angel.

Before I could snap back some threat or oath, he was gone. One of his gang – short but solid-looking and armed with a cutlass – was to be my guard. He watched his comrades leave then cast his gaze back. His expression was strangely blank, as if this was a common duty for him.

He disappeared from view to some perch and I peered at my surroundings by the dregs of lamplight that found their way into the cell.

It was, as I had surmised, little thicker than a man, and extended at least a few yards in each direction. The impenetrable darkness at the ends might have contained the bones of long-dead rebellious or self-flagellating monks. I kicked at the wall but the broken edge was solid – and even if I had been able to smash it to pieces, I could not have escaped the metal set into the hard floor with mortar. Water from the storm above us was running in sheets down the walls and pooling on the stone floor.

At one end of the thin cell, I made out something utterly ominous: a rotten box that contained the broken and fragmented skeleton of a man. The bones had, perhaps, once been those of a monk who had long since been drawn into the arms of his maker.

I was about to shout out something: I knew not what, probably an offer of a bribe combined with a threat to my captor's life. He would know that neither was serious, of course. I halted when I heard the moaning again and my heart skipped another beat when I realized that the sound was not a draught between the stones, but the sighing of a human, immured, as I was.

The sound was coming from the darkest corner. And there was something else this time.

At first it looked like the shadows themselves were animated with life. They moved and warped, rolling over one another. And then, slowly, they resolved into a form.

A face, as black as the darkest recess, loomed out of the gloom, glaring at me.

He was tall and well-built, lank hair of a colour I could not discern in the murk that engulfed us. The shadows played still on his face, so that I could hardly make it out. It was like the livid pit in which we were both encased: mutating and unknowable.

For a full ten seconds, he scowled at my bonds and at the break in the wall.

And then his first sounds: a mumbling that I could not understand. It was not quite human. He took a step closer and I stiffened. Trussed as I was, I was quite defenceless if he turned out to be a lunatic intent on snapping the neck of anyone sufficiently reckless to enter his madman's cell.

I opened my mouth to yell for the guard, but the man's head slowly turned from side to side, telling me not to cry out.

I stopped myself and he came closer so that I saw why he was making only animal moans: he was gagged, with a rag between his teeth, tied around his jawbone. He twisted himself around in the narrow space to show me his back. His wrists were bound in metal like mine, only with a longer chain to the ring in the floor that allowed him a couple of yards of movement through the two inches of water around our feet.

Somehow, the sight of this offered me some relief. When we are in the direst circumstances, it is a selfish desire, but we want company more than anything else. We need another human to go with us to face whatever fate we are destined to face. Dying alone is perhaps the cruellest fate of all.

My fellow inmate carefully lowered himself to the floor, his back to mine. I offered him my bonds and his fingers tugged at the fetters on my wrists, trying this way and that. I hoped to be first to be freed because I was still very wary of him. He tried and tried but they were impossible to remove, of course. With a sinking heart, I tried his but was just as impotent to open the metal as he had been. He gave up and seemed to jerk his body in frustration.

All this took perhaps ten minutes, during which the water was still trickling in, so that I wondered if the nearby Calton Burn had burst its banks and was flooding Holyrood Park.

My cellmate took hold of the ring to which we were both bound and attempted to wrench it from the stone into which it was cemented. He must have tried before and failed, but it was worth trying with my strength added to his. The two of us dragged it up with all that we had, all the lust to remain living that was in us; for this was probably our last chance for life, we both knew. But it moved not the breadth of a hair. I dropped back onto my haunches and he did the same. All the while neither of us had uttered a word or a sound.

Hopeless and helpless, he twisted about so that his head was close to my hands. I realized what he wanted and found the gag in his mouth. With much probing I found the ends of the rag and managed to untie them, freeing him from his dumbness. I heard him take in a deep breath, as if the fetid air in that crypt were the sweetest country air he had ever tasted.

'Thank you.' He whispered, so that we should not be overheard by the gaoler. His words had a French sound to them. 'Who are you? Why are you here?'

My despondency almost kept me as d[illegible]b as he had been. Then I summoned what rema[illegible] and dignity I had. 'Lysander Rose is my [illegible] I am here through misfortune.'

There was silence. 'Yes. Misfortune. We are both misfortunates.'

At that, my mind played over all that I had suffered, that night and a thousand days before it. The memories seemed almost distant, now that my life was almost at its close. They drifted away. I realized I had not asked who he was in return. 'What is your name?'

He was silent for an instant, as if trying to remember. Then he answered.

'David Sévine.'

Chapter Thirteen

It felt like I had been lifted up from the earth and dashed back down upon it. The man I had been searching for, the man upon whom I had settled all my hopes of family and history and place in the world. Here he was and here we were both fated to die. I could have laughed the bitterest laugh.

I caught my breath. It was to be the deepest question of my life. 'Did you have a son?'

He replied, guarded. 'I did.'

'How old would he be now?'

'Eighteen years.'

You look just like him, Juliana had told me.

'Did you give him a silver watch?'

I felt the the air wrap me in a chill blanket. He hesitated. 'Yes.'

And at that, everything around us seemed to crumble away, to leave us on an open plain. 'My father. You are my father.' I twisted my body to look at him. He was kneeling in the pool of water around us.

His eyes widened and then shrank again. That was as deep as his reaction went. For an instant, I was happy for that. It meant he was a strong man, as I had always imagined him to be.

'I thought I would never see you again.' And a silence

the like of which I had never known. It was pregnant with the spirits of lost years. Of sadness untold and unwritten. Of a man who lost his son, and a boy who lost his father. What could the wind do to give us those days of humanity and love that we had never known? Nothing. It could do nothing but bear witness to a gossamer chain of feeling that was reaching through the air from one to the other of us. 'Lysander.' He looked up with keenness and sorrow, blown into curiosity and abated protectiveness. 'Who gave you that name?'

'Mr Tolson. He was my schoolmaster. He took me in.'

'He was kind?' I heard the hope in his voice.

'Very.'

He nodded thoughtfully. 'I am very glad of it. The only good news I have had in a long time.'

Who am I? So many times I had thought those words, fewer times I had spoken them. Never before had I expected them to be answered. Now I could see, with mine own eyes, where I had come from. Whom I might one day be.

'There is a chapbook. It has been published in parts. It tells your story.' And it occurred to me that it was my story too.

'It has been published!' he declared triumphantly, banging his hands against the wet bricks. 'I thought it never would be.' His joy sparked into me.

'It led me to you.'

At that, he sighed. 'This was not the outcome I wanted,' he said grimly. 'I wanted to make you safe.'

'I wanted you to be my father.' In the narrative he was brave and clever. All that I wanted my father to have been. I felt his hands on mine. It was the first time in my whole memory that my father had touched me. But I pitied not the bereft child, I was only thankful for a moment of knowing my parent and knowing that he had cared for me. 'Who is my mother? Is she Catherine?'

'Yes, she is your mother. And she loved you.' His hands remained on mine. It was a comfort.

'What happened to us?'

'They came for her and we had to run,' he told me, stoic, but with an undercurrent of anger.

'Why were they after her?'

'For what she knew. That is why they wanted you: if they had you, Catherine would have done whatever they willed.'

'But the man who came for me. With him, it was a vendetta. His name was . . .'

'Vinerre.'

'Yes,' I said.

'I am sorry. He came for you because he was not allowed to kill me. Someone begged for our lives. Someone with influence over Louis.'

With all my heart and all the hopes I had ever had, I asked a question. 'Is my mother alive?'

His eyes locked on mine own. 'I believe she is.'

And those hopes turned to flesh and blood. I took a second to feel my blood turn warm in my veins and fingers. I turned my face to the heavens and thanked them. Then, before me, I saw the dark heart of the mystery of my birth and life. The secret that had dragged me from my mother's arms. The water was running fast down the walls and had nowhere to drain, so it was now up to our ankles. I began to wonder how high it would rise. 'What was it she knew? Who protected you?'

'Juliana.'

'Juliana?'

His chains clanked on the floor. 'You have read my story?'

'Not all of it. I have never seen the final part.'

He paused briefly considering. 'The murders that took place in Lorne all those years ago. They were . . .' And he halted short. I glanced at him. He was staring at the ceiling above us. A stream of water had punctured through and a large block of plaster was dropping out of place. As we watched, it seemed to hang on, and then crashed to the ground. I winced but my father – how strange it felt, to call him that, and no longer 'Sévine'! – remained unmoved, turning his gaze from it to the break in the wall of our prison cell.

Immediately, the guard appeared, looking amazed. He ogled the hole in the ceiling, through which muddy water was now pouring. 'What did you . . .' he began stupidly. But then another, larger section of plaster followed the first, and then a lump of wood with it, falling from the hole and bouncing off the slabs. He could see the future. We all could. Without another sound, he turned tail and fled.

'He is a coward. How lucky for us,' my father said sardonically as he rose to his feet. He was tall and had to stoop under the low ceiling. The fallen plaster had revealed a roof of ancient and rotten timber joists. I watched while he stared at them. 'Yes, here.' And then I thought he must have gone mad because quite without warning he began to smack the top of his head against the bottom of one of the beams.

'What are you doing?' I said, astounded. Was his plan

for suicide to rob our enemies of their triumph in killing us outright?

He ignored me and kept hitting his skull on the wood. And then he instead placed his head on the underside of one joist and pushed up with all his might. I was as amazed as before. I was about to beg him to stop when I caught his eye. There was something in it that made me hold, something in it that I trusted.

And at that, the beam he was pressing against broke apart, and a chunk fell to the flooded floor. Immediately, he dropped to his haunches and felt for it with his hands bound behind his back. That was when I saw what he was after: not the beam itself but the long, rusty iron nails embedded in it.

'I have it!' I declared, shoving it to him with my foot.

He broke apart the wood on the metal ring that held us both. And then he had an iron tool, like ancient man. He bashed it on the ring to bend it. 'Yours first,' he ordered. 'You will drown first.' He fitted this form of key into the lock on my shackles and twisted it. 'An old skill I never thought to need again,' he muttered.

And in mere seconds, the lock was free! The manacles fell away. He handed me the pick and I tried to liberate him too but I twisted and turned it and nothing came. I handed the pick to him. 'Damn it. The lock is too rusted. I cannot pick it,' he growled, attempting it. I felt the hope drain from me. He was to die there after all. 'Wait. There. That old box of bones.' He was staring at the small coffin in the corner that held the bones of a long-dead monk. 'You see that . . . yes, that powder!' he exclaimed. 'Pull the box here. But for God's sake, be careful about it.'

Without comprehension, I dragged it across the wet

floor with my feet, then watched as my father took a part of what I recognized as a tibia bone from the box – that it had once been part of a living, breathing man did not cause him any concern – and used it to gingerly scoop up a small grey nugget of what looked to me no more than compacted grime. What he could possibly want it for was beyond my ken. 'You do not know what this is, do you?'

'No.'

'Well, these old bones did not dissolve themselves. This is quicklime. And it has turned the flesh and skeleton of Brother Deadman to salt.' With the utmost care, and without touching it, he pressed it into the lock. Then he bent down and put his lips to the floor. I was as amazed as ever when I saw him sucking up some of the foul water. He jerked his head to tell me to get back, then spat it into the lock and pulled back as far as he could. For two seconds, there was nothing but the sound of the water around us. And then a bang like a firework and grey smoke from the lock. Praise the heavens, it came apart as easily as a child's bootlace!

We said nothing – we had no time for back-slapping – but started for the door through which we had come, kicking through the dank knee-high water. Then we stopped dead. There were voices outside: at least two, maybe three, and coming this way.

'What now?' I whispered.

He was not looking at me, he was looking all around to the corners of the chamber.

'This was the crypt. They would have washed the bodies here before burial.' I did not understand. He pulled me as he searched in the submerged corners of the chamber with his hands. 'There will be a culvert somewhere to pour away the burial-wash water. It could . . . There!' He pointed to a dark corner where I saw movement. Horribly, the movement was not the waves of the water, but of black rodents swimming from our chamber and disappearing, causing a new shiver to shake my bones. 'We will follow them.'

'Through there?' I gasped. But at that moment, the door to the chamber opened, and three men with swords entered. They stopped and stared at us, then began to charge.

Where the stream led we could not say, but the rats seemed to know, and without another word we plunged into the freezing tide.

As the dirty water engulfed me, I opened my eyes then immediately closed them again. The filth was blinding me, and sightless, I had to feel my way through what was now an underwater pipe, hoping and praying to God that there would be a way out that was not open only to rats. It felt like an age, swimming through dank, icy water, as if we were a hundred miles from the world of man.

And yet, we were lucky! Although it seemed like a mile, the pipe was no more than two or three yards long and my heart soared as I stumbled out, shivering and disoriented – straight into a brick-lined pit full of filth and animal bones, knee-high in water. My father was right behind me and we both sucked in air, cold as it was, like they were the first breaths of our lives. But we had no time to waste. Our pursuers might come through the pipe, or around the broken church. So we ran.

'I wish you had raised me,' I blurted out as we flitted and hid between walls and tree stumps, watching for pursuit.

He fixed me with his eye, paused, then spoke gently. 'I was your father. I am he. We missed so many years, so many name days and holidays. But nothing will ever change that I am your father.'

I confess now to unmanly feelings. My heart all but burst at these words and I turned from a young man into a young boy before my dad. I threw my arms around him and sobbed twice before he pushed me gently away and held my head up. 'We will have time for this.' And he pointed to the distance, where flaming torches were moving in the wrong direction, away from where we were, confused by the pipe and the storm.

'What is my name?' I asked. I had so long wanted to know the name my parents had given me. It was the part of my being that was missing. 'What name did you give me?'

He put his hand on my shoulder. It was warm. 'Olivier. That is your name.'

I tried it on my tongue. It felt foreign, although it was older than the one I had borne as long as I had been able to speak. 'I will keep "Lysander", I think.'

He laughed. 'As you wish. Now, we must run. But I have no friends in this city. Do you know where we can hide?'

'I have one friend here,' I said, thinking of McPhail.

'Is he trustworthy?'

'Not one bit.'

'Then he is just the man we need.'

We took a path north. We were skirting the Abbey Hill so as to approach the Old Town from the north.

'The chapbook, why did you write it?' I asked.

'For leverage over them.' I stumbled. He caught me.

'Did you think we had abandoned you? Olivier, when we knew they were coming for us, we fled France. Our countries were at war so I had to bribe fishermen to take us to Dover. You and Catherine were in another boat and the pilot was afraid of the British navy, so he took you by a smuggler's route. I had no idea where you had landed. But Vinerre followed you and found you. I spent years searching for you both. And that was how they caught me.'

All that time I had thought myself uncared for, yet the truth was that my parents had risked everything to save me. Knowing that softened some of the old pain at their absence.

'How did you have the book printed?'

'I gave it to a printer. I told him to publish it in parts, but only when I told him to do so, because it was meant as a threat to the Circle: if I found you and they let Catherine go, there would be no more chapters. But then they caught me and because the printer did not hear from me, he must have stopped.'

I told him how the Circle had destroyed the copies of his story. Then I related how I had spent years searching for him and the complete narrative. He was pleased at my fortitude and perseverance.

'Juliana could protect you like that.'

'Yes, but also I think de Rotanne enjoyed too much seeing me filthy and in chains to kill me. And a dead man is of no use. A wily spymaster always keeps men who might one day prove useful. I had too much potential to throw into a grave.'

And then, in the night air, with all the white-hot passion of vindication we spoke of how we would break open the chests of those who had harrowed our lives, and tear out their hearts. Only the wronged man knows the joy of vengeance.

I thumped on the door of McPhail's tenement. He eased it open, peering curiously at my father – his rags were no cause for attention where McPhail lived, but he had a nose for things that carried danger. He gave us admittance, carefully checking that none had marked our arrival. Then he was all hospitality by the side of a fire that was more smoke than flame.

I told him much of our story. His eyebrows shot up here and there but he enjoyed it while drinking tea, sat in a chair that he must have purloined from some fancy house.

'And you will be needing James McPhail's help for what?'

'Somewhere to hide. Then we need an introduction to one who prints chapbooks. And will do it quietly.'

'Chapbooks, you say? Maybe I know a man. Maybe.'

'And we want guns,' said my father.

McPhail smiled. 'Oh, that I can do.'

Chapter Fourteen

We spent the night and the following two days at McPhail's. Then he found us a conveyance to Glasgow after nightfall. It was a hair-raising journey concealed under a cargo of hemp, and we were undecided as to whether we were more likely to be stabbed by an agent of the Circle or shot by highwaymen.

Over the course of a night, as the tallow burned, my father set down the missing and final part of his tale and a poverty-stricken printer from Dublin set his type. I lay on a straw rug, exhausted by our recent travails and spent that night in awe. Awe that my life could turn like a child's top. A month earlier I had been respectable. Now I was an outlaw revenger with a wronged father by my side, and a man with one eye casting a shadow before me.

After two days of laying low, McPhail appeared in the print shop with a box under his arm.

'Good ones, these. From a cavalry officer. Been fighting Boney.' He placed the case on a press that was still warm from churning out my father's story.

My father opened it and lifted a pistol to the lamplight. 'New Land Pattern,' he said. 'Good gun.' He said it with respect and confidence and I knew he was adept with such things. He handed it to me. I had never held a firearm, let alone shot one. He could see that. 'Frizzen. Stock. Trigger,' he said, pointing out the parts of the gun. 'I will show you how to load and shoot it.' I looked into his eyes. He spoke like he was speaking to a man whose life hung in the balance. He was, of course.

'Are you ready?' My father asked it in a low, determined breath, that frosted in the air. We were watching from a side street, as braying members of Scotland's aristocracy barged through the Romanesque entrance of the Theatre Royal on Princes Street. Juliana was to perform Gluck's *Orfeo and Euridice* again that evening, but it was not her that we were waiting to see, with our pistols concealed under our cloaks.

Something inside me despised the people before me. Their loud laughter was hollow, like a man throwing his voice to entertain children. Their gilded clothes seemed far worse than an honest beggar's rags.

Our escape, we witnessed, had put the Circle on edge so that where the King went, there were now guards everywhere. A squad of six stood before the main entrance and another patrolled the rear. There was no chance of entering armed – a fact that my father had realized an hour earlier when we had first spied them. 'We must divert their attention,' he had said ruminatively.

'A fight in the street? A theft?'

'That they would but watch and laugh. No, I have something in mind.'

We had then, cloaked by the early evening night, run through the town and scrambled over the wall into the royal mews. While the grooms drank bad beer in one of the lofts, we had quietly hitched two horses to the King's gorgeous coach, opened the gate and walked the beasts out. The hapless grooms were no doubt by this time cursing and searching high and low for the fugitive vehicle.

It now stood behind us on the lane.

'It is time,' my father said in his familiar resolute tone. And at that, he leaped up onto the seat and hied the horses. They jumped to it, and I watched as he rounded the corner away from the theatre, rattling over the stones. There was half a minute's wait until I heard the beasts' hooves again, and this time they were coming at a gallop on the icy road, the iron-rimmed wheels of the coach clattering like Doomsday and raising sparks on the cobbles. Horses and men ran from their path as my father drove like the Devil. Nearing the theatre, he stood and wrenched the reins to the left, spinning the coach and sending the horses tripping and slipping and then falling, with the vehicle itself overturning onto two wheels and then no wheels at all as it twisted and crashed into the road. At the last second, my father jumped for his life, away from the conveyance, landing heavily but upright.

At the crying of the animals and the crashing of the wood onto the frozen ground, men and women ran to help whoever they thought was inside. The King's guards – who had recognized their liege's coach the instant it had burst into view – were the first, abandoning their post; and giving us a way to slip unseen through the great entrance.

Inside, two servants paid us no attention as they stared at the wreckage and we found the pass door that took us down into the depths of the theatre.

'I can hear you are nervy,' my father said.

'What?'

He halted. His short yet thick beard made him seem like a Viking to me. 'The way you are walking.' I glanced down, feeling like a child or a coward. He took me by both shoulders. 'This shall be your first fight, I know. I have been in more than I want to remember. Listen to me: do not think. Do what you are here to do. And do it quickly.'

I comprehended. Thought was then the enemy of action. I had to be keen as a knife and no more thinking than one. I made my step easy, or as easy as it could be while each of my hands gripped a loaded pistol beneath my cloak. 'You lead now. You know the way.'

Yes, I knew the way. The last time I had walked through this building I had little imagined how I would return: a revenger, with guns in my belt and a dagger in my boot. I could have come from one of the plays that performed on the stage above us. Fate will treat men as playthings to be thrown from game to game.

'This one,' I muttered, tapping a door.

'This is her?'

I nodded. We looked around us. A slovenly woman stumbled past, reeking of strong drink and belching. My father opened the door. It took us seconds to see that Juliana was not within. A magnificent costume of red satin lay across a chair and a bottle of wine stood uncorked, but Juliana's intoxicating presence hung only in the air.

We left and headed for the auditorium. I stopped and caught my father's arm, telling him to wait. I was listening. A sound floated all around us and I knew what it was. I had heard it twice before but if I had only heard it once in my life it would have stayed with me.

It was Juliana's singing. It was her aria, '*Che farò senza Euridice?*' The song that had made her famous in the opera houses of Europe. It soared and it plundered our hearts, tugging them from our bodies as she became Orpheus crying in anguish for his lost wife, taken down to the Underworld.

Che farò senza Euridice? Dove andrò senza il mio ben? Che farò, Dove andrò? What will I do without Euridice? Where will I go without my beloved? What will I do, where will I go?

I could have lost myself in her song. My father too. But I knew he understood it differently to me. To me it was music, to him it was a song that told his own pain: a wife taken from him, a future lost.

'This is the song that told me everything,' he said grimly, with his back to me. 'And condemned us all to hell.' He turned to face me. 'I am changing the plan. Go. You can achieve on your own.'

I knew his meaning. It was not what we had intended, but I understood. Plans change in the face of changing facts, changing threats, changing opportunities for repayment exacted at the point of a knife. Justice does not fall from heaven, I had learned in the past few weeks. It must be roughly taken.

'Good luck,' I bade him, and ran quickly up an unlit flight of bare stairs, trusting that they would take me to the gallery of boxes. Well, this time, fortune smiled and I stepped out onto the lush carpet of the gallery, where the aristocrats gaily tripped. I untied my cloak and it shook to the floor with a rumpling textile whisper.

A girl with a tray of oranges stood back politely then dropped her tray when she saw me pull the guns from my belt and kick open the door to the royal box, beside the stage.

There they were, lined up like mute chessmen ready for a game: all the fools of my play: Matrick. Vinerre. Gaston. De Rotanne. King Louis XVIII of France. All – bar Vinerre – powdered and wigged. They turned their heads to see who had entered, perfectly ready for me to put a ball of lead through their skulls if they moved a muscle. I cocked both weapons.

'Do not move,' I growled. On stage, devils in costumes of black feathers and red velvet masks were spinning madly around Juliana as her voice soared to the rafters.

'What are—' hissed de Rotanne. But even before he completed his sentence, Gaston, in a fit of bravery that I would never have credited to him, and could only have been the bravado that comes from a bottle, had jumped up from his seat and grabbed for one of the pistols that I had trained on him and his fellows.

His hands snatched the barrel of the gun in my right hand. Just what he thought to do, I could not tell. But I remembered my father's command: do not think, act. And I turned and fired the gun in my left hand.

All then seemed to happen at half the speed of life. The sear released the cock. The mainspring snapped it down. The flint struck the frizzle and sent sparks into the pan to ignite the priming powder. There was a moment of silence and calm. And then the main charge blew. I felt an explosion in my hand as the bullet left the barrel and blasted through Gaston's left kneecap.

Blood and bone sprayed across the fine chairs upon which the King of France and his loyal attendants rested their thighs. Gaston screamed and fell. The audience before us screamed and stood. But as he collapsed, Gaston's hands gripped even tighter on my pistol, pulling me down and I felt a blow to the side of my head as Vinerre punched me hard, making me drop both guns.

At that, the lawyer Matrick summoned up what courage he had and wound his arms around me, throwing me back, so that we two splayed over the side of the box onto the ledge of the next one, known as the duke's. Its denizens recoiled from us as if we carried the Plague, cowering at the back. I felt a pang of terror then, that all might turn against us and it would be my death, not my triumph, that the night would see. All the while, the orchestra, in their own world of deafening drums and bursting trumpets, played on, oblivious to the royal struggle above them.

But I fought back and struck Matrick's temple with my elbow, trying in vain to reach the knife in my boot. I saw, behind him, Vinerre pounce on the loaded pistol that I had dropped. Guessing the next, I rolled to the side and managed to get my fingers to the hilt of the knife. I thrust it into the shoulder of Matrick, who roared in pain and let go. I sat up but at that moment I saw Vinerre take aim. Matrick saw it too, and the two of us twisted as one, off the sides of the boxes that held us in the air, falling into the stalls below us. Still Juliana sang like a siren tempting sailors onto sharp rocks, for the dazzling lights before her must have kept her blind to what was happening in the auditorium.

A searing pain in my hip told me I was still conscious, and I fought myself free of hands grabbing at me, scrambling into the aisle. It was fortunate that the royal box was less than a yard above the stalls, so the fall was not severe and I still had hold of the knife. Its point glinted like a spark, reflecting the limelight as the patrons who had attempted to seize me – two well-made men – stepped forward. Then they stopped and looked up. Vinerre was standing with the pistol, cocked, in his hand. He was no more than three yards from me and could not miss. I saw his finger twitch on the trigger. Juliana's magisterial voice rose in sublime crescendo with the music and then turned shrill, shifting into a terrified scream.

'Hold your hand!' My eyes flicked to the stage, to see my father pointing two guns, one at Vinerre and the other at Juliana's neck.

The devils around her ran for the wings of the stage like the petals falling from a dying flower. For her part, dressed in white and lit like a flame, she stood, shaking. I knew my father would not hurt her and she probably knew it too, but she had a pistol pointing at her and fear was wrapping its knuckles around her throat. Slowly, my father moved the barrel of the gun so it no longer pointed at her.

Now it pointed at Louis, King of France. And the stakes of the fight were higher than they had ever been.

'If you pull that trigger, I will pull both of mine,' my father said to Vinerre. His voice resounded with a calm fury. The King began to rise but de Rotanne put his hand on the royal shoulder and pressed him back into his seat, murmuring something. Around us, there were whispers and frightened mutterings. 'And I am a better shot than you.'

'Lower it,' de Rotanne calmly instructed the man with a brass patch for an eye. He kept his seat. Vinerre, the dark angel who had haunted my life, lowered his gun but I feared still that he would suddenly lift and fire at me or my father. Perhaps my father was indeed a better shot, but at this distance, the chances were that I would feel half an ounce of lead rip through me.

Well, I resolved I would be no man's sport, so I jumped up and climbed into the duke's box. Its denizens – three fat women dripping jewels, and a skinny man with bowed legs – cowered still at the rear. They had not even the wits to flee.

'Place it on the ledge,' I said, holding my blade out towards Vinerre. His eyes moved slowly from the gun to my chest. He hesitated. I could see him calculating the time it would take to lift the gun and fire against the time it would take for me to thrust the blade into his neck.

'Do as he says.' De Rotanne's blood was cooler than his lackey's.

He did as he was told. His fingers slid the pistol onto the edge of the box and I slowly breathed out. And then like a bullet from a barrel, they flashed it back up towards me and wrenched back the trigger. I had less than a second and spun myself on my foot. The first explosion cut across my inner arm, drawing a line of blood and tattering my shirt. The second shattered Vinerre's jaw, knocking him to the ground, draining the blood from his face, stopping his heart, and sending a wisp of smoke from the barrel of my father's pistol.

The women behind me screamed loud enough to shake the building to pieces, but I could not hear them, as the sight of Vinerre dead on the floor of the royal box wrapped me in a blanket of comfort and ease. I laughed at the sight, righted myself, and pointed my dagger at de Rotanne.

The comte made no sound but I saw a bead of sweat slide down his neck. The King was outright shivering in his seat. 'What is it that you want?' de Rotanne said.

'What do we want?' snarled my father. 'Your head and our lives.' The comte stiffened a little at the threat. 'But we will settle for our lives.' Out of the corner of my eye, I saw members of the audience creeping out the exits, no doubt calling for the city watch. 'Catherine is alive, I know. Have her brought here. Then we three shall leave.'

De Rotanne, recovering his calm, drummed his fingers on his liege's seat, as if mulling what he wanted to eat that evening. I stepped up onto the ledge of the box. My knife now levelled towards the King.

De Rotanne beckoned a terrified footman and muttered to him. The man sprinted away, delirious at his chance to escape. None of us said a word, but within seconds there was a sea of movement below as all those left in the auditorium dashed for the exit, some shouting, most silent.

From then, the vast room echoed only to the breaths of those of us left in the two boxes, my father and Juliana.

For an hour we waited, an hour without speech, only hopes and fears. My father and I reloaded our discharged pistols, while keeping our other weapons trained on our targets. An hour can seem like the blink of an eye or a hundred years. For a young man longing to see the woman who gave birth to him and nurtured him and loved him, it seems longer. All the while, all those ticked seconds and unmarked minutes, I kept my hand steady.

Before I saw my mother slowly and quietly enter the auditorium, I saw Juliana start, and I followed her gaze to the rear of the room.

My mother, Catherine, had been washed by the years of suffering. Her hair was grey, her skin without the lustre that my father had once seen. She walked favouring her left side, as if the right caused her some pain.

But then her eyes met mine and she put her hands to her head. I knew not whether she had been told by the flunkey who brought her that I was there, or whether, like Juliana, she saw my father's face in mine and knew me as her son. Something in me hoped it was the latter, that there was a golden thread between us that had never been severed nor ever could be. Then she ran, with the vitality of a younger woman. I abandoned my post and climbed down to embrace her, feeling the warmth of twenty years of love put aside.

'Olivier,' I heard her say. And she stared at my father on the stage. 'David.'

'Catherine.' But he kept his guns trained on the King and de Rotanne.

And the comte spoke, his voice haughty and arrogant. 'And tell me. After I let you leave, what will stop me having you all hunted down and slaughtered like dogs a month from now?'

It was my time. 'Read this,' I said. I drew a white,

cheaply printed chapbook from the breast of my jacket and tossed it to him. Our greatest weapon was not the pistols in our hands, it was the words on the pages that we had had printed in a little shop in Glasgow.

He quickly glanced at them, raising an eyebrow in recognition. I knew every word.

The Murderous Deeds in the Village of Lorne in France and How They Brought About the Bloody Revolution. The Final Part.
By a Gentleman of the Law.

28 June 1789

The moon had risen by the time I was at the inn stable where I had previously witnessed the gathering of Jacob's fraternity. The room was full of smoke from long-stemmed peasant pipes. It was rough as acid and burned the throat and nose. I could not understand why those who had stuffed the tobacco into clay bowls wanted to scratch away all the softer parts of their entrails but it was not my position to discover for them their own system of pain.

The inn was a safe place for all sorts of radical groups to meet - the innkeeper, although he kept a low profile, being sympathetic. While those of the urban poor met during the day, Jacob brought those from the countryside around Paris together at night - the peasant having a well-founded fear of retribution from his seigneur that the town dweller did not have to contend with.

Tonight, after a day when crowds had formed across the city to spread rumours that the old guard aristos were plotting a coup, the number in the hut had swelled like the belly on a farmhand's new wife.

'My brothers,' Jacob began. 'It is five days since we last met.' He waited. 'In those five days our friends in this city have talked, and walked, but done little.' There were murmurs of agreement and he took those mumblings of assent and built upon them like the best courtroom barrackers I had seen. 'But change is coming. Who here lies in his bed when the land is black but does not know that the sky will soon be blue, the trees green and the barley a golden yellow? None? No, for we all know that life will get better. God has decreed it. He put us in Eden so that we would know sweet life. Hunger and pain, they are to be banished by food and ease. God's bounty is to be taken. We have only to pluck it from the trees.'

A recalcitrant older member of their union interrupted him. 'And where is this bounty? In my fields there is nothing but broken stalks.'

'The bounty, my brother - for every man is my brother whether he be French or Spanish, legal or a bastard - the bounty is France itself in all its glory. The fields are dying, aye, we have all set foot in them. But there is so much more that we can pick and pluck and reap if we just have the minds and the hands to do it. There are grapes on trees, there are fields of corn, there are sheep groaning under their own wool. This is our Eden! It belongs to us. We need only take it!'

'Us?' asked one.'

'Us, my brother!'

A few of the men murmured their agreement. One clapped his hands. Another, named Jean, looked perturbed. 'Jacob,' he began. 'We all want to eat our fill, but steps. We have to take steps, not strides.'

'Christophe,' Jacob said, ignoring Jean. 'What rights does the fat Comte de Rotanne have over you?'

Christophe's words sped from his mouth. 'His quit-rent is one fifth of all my sheep.'

'And you, Emmanuel?'

'His rights? He has the right to enter my home at any time and require myself, my wife and my children to work for him without payment.'

Jacob called out to the whole room raising his hands to the ceiling. 'Who here has worse?'

A man between Jacob's age and my own shouted out in anger. 'Me! On my farm he has *droit de ravage*!' There was a moan from one or two men there. 'If he wants, he can destroy all the fields, burn all the crops, kill all the animals as far as he can command.'

'And what would that mean?'

'We would starve. Not just hungry. But dead!' There were well-founded cries of outrage at the picture.

'Well, tonight,' Jacob declared, matching his volume, 'our brother David here will send him a message. A message that the wind is changing.'

Jean spoke. 'What do you mean?'

I stepped forward. 'I have a battle with the comte,' I told him. 'It is a private struggle, but I intend to prosecute it tonight.'

'We want to come with you,' Jacob said. 'We want to stand shoulder to shoulder.'

That had not been part of the deal. Much as I could have done with friends, I was not prepared to risk drawing others into my private war with de Rotanne. His response could not be predicted. 'You are brave men. But I cannot take you. Afterwards I will gladly tell you blow by blow how it went, but it is not a venture for men who have anything to lose.'

Jacob did not reply directly to me, but instead addressed a member of his group. 'Roger. My dear brother, Roger. The Comte de Rotanne is your seigneur. Why should he have the right to take your granddaughter for whatever purpose he wants?'

'No reason,' replied an old man.

Jacob turned to me. 'He has nothing to lose.' Three or four others concurred and begged to join the expedition. I was torn. Was there such a difference between them and the Frenchmen who had joined the war in America against Britain? The only real difference was that these men were fighting for their own freedom, not for others' liberty.

'Only those without a family to support,' I relented. 'Men without ties.' Six stepped forward.

Jacob was elated. 'We will not take de Rotanne's life as he is able to take ours,' he said. 'But with you, this night we will just exercise our own *droit de ravage*!' They cheered. 'It is the twenty-eighth day of June in 1789. One year from now, France will be a land of free men. Brothers, free and equal. One year from now!' They cheered louder and more jubilantly.

The candle he was holding flickered in the gust from their throats. It strained against the movement of the air, but could not hold. And then it was gone, leaving only a glowing amber wick.

We tumbled urgently through the dark streets, carrying

with us a bag full of torches swathed in oily rags. Here and there we saw groups of five or six men, more often than not with bottles in their hands. Many wore red bonnets like Jacob's and their lamps lit them from below, turning their features grotesque. They had their own missions that night.

We ran along the banks of the Seine, picking out white wave-crests. As we passed the Bourbon Palace, home to Louis-Joseph, the prince of the Conde who preferred dressing as a girl when enjoying whores, two of our number stopped, awed by the Roman imperial lines. I guessed that they had spent their entire lives less than three leagues from the centre of Paris and yet had never set foot in it.

'There,' I said, when we were in view of de Rotanne's house.

Its rear gardens were surrounded by a high wall but the iron gate was secured by a simple warded lock. I had borrowed a few hair pins from a bemused Catherine that afternoon and bent them into picks. They opened it in less than a minute and I saw in the moonlight the wooden pavilion and orangery I had witnessed by daylight a few hours earlier.

'Our masters eat oranges while we have no bread,' Jacob declared.

'Their food is raw now, but we shall cook it for them,' I replied. I opened the bag and handed out the torches. 'Once we are alight we will have no more than a minute before his men are upon us. Five more minutes and the whole house will go up. It will be enough time for the servants to get out. But go. Go quickly.'

I lit my torch and the others touched theirs to it, two per man. Suddenly a pyramid of flames, a bonfire of sixteen torches, burned.

The pavilion was my target - an edifice bigger than three peasant houses laid end to end. I peered through the dark glass to see furniture within that was as ornate as any I had seen at Versailles. Above the chaise longues, a delicate clock bedecked with a hunting scene chimed the midnight hour. Around it were a number of pistols arranged on the wall as if ready for a duel and one was the spitten image of the air pistol with which de Rotanne's lackey had attempted to put a bullet in my neck. I smashed a glass pane with my elbow and threw my torches in. The satisfaction of an act of burning vengeance flooded me.

A few yards away, Jacob touched his torch to the wood of the orangery. Its trees would soon be fuel for a fire. Alain, a farmhand, was next, running to the corner of the building and touching his to a break in the planks. I felt the heat on my face and in my heart that night. It had been a long time since I was part of a corps of men, united in purpose, and it was good to know that solidarity once more.

A dry breeze blew sparks from building to bush to pavilion, blazing in the dark faster than I had imagined. Lights began to glow within the house. The servants were awake. There were shouts from within. Somewhere close a dog barked and snarled, no doubt eager to tear after us.

It was time to leave the way we had come. As we did so, we circled around to the front wall that stood before the great house and I took from my pocket a sheet of paper with writing upon it in large, bold strokes. 'What does it say?' one man asked.

'It says we have just cancelled the comte's seigneurial rights,' I told him as I nailed it to a post.

We did not have time to enjoy the sight of the note, the heat from the fire, the drug of having begun something that could not be stopped. We ran.

Our lamps were spluttering but already on the horizon we could see the first rays of the sun, making all grey where it had been black.

Jacob whispered in my ear. 'The land awakes. Now we will see what the chickens make of their coop.'

It was well done. We had plunged a scalpel into the wen; but any surgeon will tell you that when the bad flesh is cut from the bone, the whole body shakes. Over the days to come we would feel the force of that bloodletting.

As we ran, I wondered if this was what Father Dollet had wanted. Archer had entrusted to him a dark, powerful secret. Was it powerful enough to lead to scenes like this throughout France? Perhaps that was precisely the power it held.

29 June 1789

Shouts and sounds of bustle woke me. Catherine was by my side. In bright dawn light, I opened the window and leaned out to see a number of servants I did not recognize walking across the lawn with bundles in their arms. I stumbled out of my room to find Francois watching more of them carrying furniture about.

'Who are they?' I asked him.

'Gaston's staff.'

'Gaston de Rotanne?' I had little interest in seeing the comte's oafish son.

'For the ball. It is tonight. He has taken over the hamlet on the island in the river.'

I had forgotten about the ball Juliana had decided upon.

'Sévine.'

The face of the Comte de Rotanne rose up the stairs. A

less welcome figure at that moment I could barely imagine. And yet, I had to quell a smirk, for the memory of what we had done secretly warmed my heart.

'Comte.'

He came closer and closer until his nose was no more than a hair's breadth from mine. 'Last night, criminals burned my house.'

'That sounds terrible, Comte. I trust the damage was light.'

'It was not.'

'Do you know who did it?'

'No. But happily, information has come to light regarding another severe crime. Your dead priest.' My eyes narrowed. What game was he playing? 'I have been informed that a local Gypsy boy did it, out of hatred for the Mother church.'

I took this accusation with less humour. 'There is no evidence for that.'

'That will be easily obtained when I turn every one of your village vermin out of their homes until I gain the information I need. I will begin the minute this absurd ball is over. And your Gypsy will be hanged by this time tomorrow.'

He stalked down the staircase and I stumbled back to my chamber, followed by Francois who glanced at Catherine without comment. My mind sped like a horse, throwing images around. Dollet's eyes flicking open; the seed left upon him; Archer's broken corpse. I thought of the riddle that Cotillard had set me. Of the one Father Dollet had written down: 'A man dreamed he was a butterfly. When he awoke he could not tell if he was a man who had dreamed he was a butterfly, or a butterfly dreaming that he was a man. But what did HE dream before he changed?'

I knew that locked within my mind was the truth. All it needed was a key, a single fact that would turn all. Think. *Think*! Who knew a fragment of it? How could I save Jacob and my own soul? All the knowledge that I had absorbed from books; all those days with a weapon in my grip and dirt on my face; all was for dust now. *Think*! In which forest could I hunt for the truth?

'Cotillard. Is there something else we can ask him?' I burst out desperately. 'Can he know something without knowing it?'

'The madman?' asked Catherine. She knew little of our struggles so far to find the truth. If I had had more time I would have explained to her but there was no chance. 'You want to speak to the madman?'

'Sane or mad, if he knows just one fact, one thought that can . . .' I broke off as Peugere brought us some fruit and buttermilk. I drank it down and felt the fat warming me. I would start my quest afresh. 'We go one more time to the church,' I told him.

'I will have the horses saddled immediately.'

He left to call for the groom. I walked to the window and for a few minutes I looked out at the chateau's grounds, where the birds were wheeling and the trees shimmered in the wind. In the distance farmhands walked through their fields, waiting to crop the barley for the second harvest of the year, going about their business as their fathers had and their children would. The clear river rippled with movement.

When Francois and I entered the church a thin layer of dust lay everywhere - the few days without use had already begun reclaiming the building for the elements of the earth. 'It is here. The knowledge begins here,' I said. 'His head to the ground, like Saint Pierre. A man inverted like the apostle.' I walked to the spot where we had found the priest. Some of his blood still lay dry and rust-brown in the cracks. I knelt to it, turning in my mind every sign that we had met to show us the way to a knowledge that would save. 'It has to mean something.'

'You want it to mean something.'

'I want it to. If not . . . If not then I cannot help him.'

'Could there have been a gang of them?'

'It is possible.'

'And you think this man also killed Archer.'

'He might have done. It might have been someone else entirely, but it is connected, there is no doubt.'

'And you will not countenance the possibility that it was Jacob, who we know knew of Archer's nocturnal work habit?'

I sighed. 'I will countenance it.' I went to the confession box and sat where the priest had sat. He was the keeper of the village's secrets. The man best placed to tell me where the guilt lay. But all his knowledge had been drained from him. It was now in the nooks of the floor.

'You know, to the boy, we are old men,' Francois mused. 'Have you thought of that?'

'That is true. Where did the summer go, Francois?'

'Oh, my old friend, I still feel like a young colt let loose in the mares' field.'

'You would,' I replied.

We roved the village and the fields. We spoke a hundred ideas and accusations, but none had any more substance to them than the seeds of a dandelion, blown away in the summer wind.

It was early evening when got back to the house. We found it alive with servants and guests milling hither and thither, all searching for the beauty they had been promised. I saw de Rotanne some way distant on the lawn, apparently in discussion with his lawyer, but I walked past quickly, having no time for a confrontation. We passed the portrait of Juliana as we climbed towards the music room, the one that Annalise said showed 'her true beauty', and just as on the first day, I saw her face turned away from the viewer, a musical score spilling from the table to the floor. The painting was silent but through the warm air we were surrounded by her voice as it burst from the music room so strongly that you would think the door had been broken down. 'What is that song?' I asked.

'I do not know,' replied Francois, misunderstanding and peering at the score in the portrait. 'The sheet says it is Gluck. I will find out.'

The door opened and for the last time I saw her in that music room, with the harpsichord and the piano. 'Tonight, messieurs, I will be singing my husband's last composition,' she announced. 'Because that is love, is it not?'

'It is,' Francois told her.

'And when you love someone you will do anything for them.'

'You will.'

'What will you do, Maître Sévine?'

I glanced over her shoulder to Catherine, who was behind her, looking out the window. I had no time for this. Soon the comte would commence harrowing the village, demanding false information that would point the finger of accusation at Jacob.

In any case I could make no answer because a footman arrived, summoning Francois to de Rotanne's presence. Grateful for the interruption, I went to my room to think in peace, but before I could shut myself away, Peugere appeared with a note on a silver salver. It was from Gaston and was cryptic and promising without detail. *Come to the hamlet. I have something that you want*, it read. *Just you.*

What did he have? And why would he help me? Perhaps his father had told him something regarding Jacob. I could not tell if Gaston had forgotten our argument over his cheating at cards at the palace, or if he was the type to scream and bawl at a man one day and be bosom friends with him the next. Both types were unpleasant.

I hurried away, then stopped and considered taking a weapon - but that was foolish, if Gaston wanted to do me harm he would be surrounded by his men and nothing less than a cannon would protect me. So, while my mind ran this way and that, desperation seeping in at the edges, I resumed my journey out to the river, running to the tethered boat and pulling myself across to the island.

It was while I was hauling across that I spied the King's coach rolling up the driveway. Francois and his few servants hurried out to line up in honour of their guest, who promptly jumped out, followed by Marie Antoinette. I noted the royal couple were simply dressed for now, their costumes and retinue no doubt ensconced in the six other coaches arriving in their wake. I had no time for them, for ritual, for artifice.

Yet, as I breached the curtain of trees, I saw lamps swaying on poles, decorated with silken streamers wafting in the wind. Servants carried food and musical instruments. And there in the middle was Gaston himself. By his side was a friend of his - judging by their intimate laughter - a man as thin as a stick and tall as a tree. His feet were like roots planted into the soil.

'Good evening, Sévine,' Gaston said. 'Glad you could come here for all the joy.' He snorted and wiped his mouth with his hand. I could not tell what he was wiping off it, grease or spittle. He really did seem to have forgotten all about our previous contretemps.

'Hello, Gaston.'

His brow furrowed and he checked to see if any of his servants had seen someone address him in public by his Christian name.

'"Vicomte",' corrected his friend, bowing slightly. Gaston gurgled in appreciation.

'Yes, Vicomte,' I said, bowing too. 'You said you had something to show me?'

'Not yet, not yet. Let us take a drink first.' He waved to a passing servant and mimed drinking from a bottle. The servant scampered away. Gaston was stalling me. I did not know why, but I had to go with it. 'Now, I understand from father that you have a little revolutionary Gypsy?' Resisting the urge to punch him in the mouth, I agreed that I had. 'Dear dear. A revolutionary and a Gypsy.' His face cracked in two again. His thin friend guffawed so that his body shook and his head at the top of that stick of a neck wobbled back and forth like a child's toy. He looked over to where the servant was hurrying towards us with a bottle and three glasses on a gilt tray. 'Ah. The wine, yes.' He wiped more spittle from his chin, then grabbed it eagerly as it arrived.

'Vicomte,' I began.

'Wait, wait.' He screwed up his face as he attempted to draw the cork from the bottle. The additional distraction of answering whatever question I was about to pose would have tasked him too much at this moment. With the servant holding the bottle, he managed to pull the cork with a pop and wine fizzed over his hands. He licked his hands and the neck of the bottle. 'It is a good one, is it not?' he asked the servant.

'Yes, Vicomte, the best.'

'The best,' echoed the thin friend. I was reminded of the lawyer Matrick. It was a family trait of the de Rotannes to surround themselves with thin men who answered 'yes' to any question.

He poured and drank a glass. 'Now, it is becoming cold out . . .' It was not and his whale blubber should have protected him from an arctic winter. 'Let us go indoors.' We stepped through the door to a cottage that I had entered a few days before to see a neat and sanitized model of a peasant cottage, as imagined by a man who had never set foot outside the Palace of Versailles. That image had been utterly transformed now, with silk drapes, cushions and furniture all in the Turkish style, giving the impression of a pasha's boudoir. More servants, indeed, were dressed in Oriental style as if they had been shipped in from Constantinople, stopping only to scrub away their tawny complexion. Between men around my own age, lying louche on the furniture, they carried trays of coffee and wine. Gaston grinned wider than a cat as he took in the vista. 'Good men. Good men all. Now sit, Sévine, sit.' He indicated an empty chaise longue, covered in purple velvet brocade. I did as he asked, although I was increasingly frustrated by his time-wasting. I needed to know what he had to tell me. 'You will take a drink.'

'I am grateful, but I am not thirsty.'

He clicked his fat fingers to the same servant. 'The bottle that I put aside for Monsieur Sévine. Now.'

I waited what seemed an age while the servant went to an unseen room and returned with a bottle on a salver with one glass. He poured it and offered it to me. I looked inside and recognized the bouquet. It would taste bitter on my tongue and then my vision would blur and I would be in a warm, soft cocoon fearing nothing, caring about nothing. 'Vicomte, I am most grateful, but I must need my legs for dancing this evening,' I forced myself to chuckle.

'Take it,' he insisted. 'The poppy is from Turkey. The best. My friends.' He swept his arm around to indicate that the others had partaken.

'But think of the ladies disappointed by my lack of dancing,' I joked.

'Take it.'

I had no choice. I took the glass. If this was the price to pay, I would pay it. I sipped and the bitterness stung my tongue. Then I knocked the rest of the glass back. It would take a few minutes to take full hold. I had that time to get from Gaston what he knew, what could perhaps save Jacob's neck. 'A very fine grain. I thank you, your lordship. Now, you said you had something that I wanted?'

'You did not want that?' he asked. I felt a clench in my stomach - was that all he had dragged me out here for? Then he smiled. 'No, no. There is something else. Something far more valuable. After all, I know of your exploit with my father and that pile of sticks you burned. Frankly, I am happy for anything that makes the old goat angry. So, here is your reward.' He stood and walked towards the door, beckoning with a sausage finger. I stood too and began to move. The grain in the wine must have been potent because already my vision was beginning to swim. I had to steady myself on the back of the seat. A couple of the men lying down laughed at me.

'He has had too much already,' one chuckled.

Gaston chimed in. 'Come on, you can walk, can you not? Or do we have to carry you?' I made no answer but walked steadily out, having shaken off the waves in my head. We left the cottage and walked to the next one. I wished the night were colder to freeze some sense into me. The door and shutters were closed. Gaston stood in front of it, with his fingers on the handle. 'In here.' He turned the handle and pushed the door away from him. It was dim inside, with a strange spectrum of moving lights made by coloured cloth stretched over lamps. The effect was disorienting but Gaston's hand on my back propelled me forward and through the door. When my eyes adjusted, I saw those covered lamps were suspended from the ceiling and spinning and wafting in some unseen breeze. The cottage was larger than the first and had been divided by screens into a series of four closets. While his thin friend remained by the door, Gaston pushed me forward and directed me to the farthest booth. He pulled back the drape hiding its contents from the casual visitor. 'All for you,' he said. Inside was a bed of oriental design to match the great theme of the day. And upon it sat a girl aged around eighteen years, dressed like an Arab, with huge gold earrings. Her eyes were glassy as a mirror and barely turned to us as we stood. 'She has drunk the same as you.' This was what he had for me. No information, no insight. Just a girl drugged into lifelessness. 'Do you know what gave me the idea?'

'No,' I replied, with nothing but emptiness in my voice.

'The Banquet of Chestnuts.' I dropped my eyes to the floor. 'No? The Banquet of Chestnuts? One of the Borgia Popes. His son, a cardinal and brother of Lucrezia Borgia no less, threw this wonderful banquet in the Vatican where they had all the best whores of Rome. They threw armfuls of chestnuts to the floor and the whores had to crawl around picking them up. Of course, while they were on their hands and knees, they were free for any of the cardinal's friends.

He, the Pope and Lucrezia watched and kept score to see who could tup the most jades. So that will be our game for the evening. You may start with her.'

I had no words left, so pushed past him, out the door, around to the back of the cottage. Among the dark trees I could see a few sparkling animal irises. As I stepped through the thick vegetation, spines clutched at my clothes and something stung my neck. I took a few more paces in, stealing behind a wall of ferns that would veil me from the cottages where I could hear men walking about, although I could not tell if they were looking for me. The land was turning liquid, I felt a blanket of warm wool wrapping itself around me. The qualms melted away and I was lifted from the soil below, floating without care in the summer of all.

And yet, at the back of my mind, there was a thought that would not be stifled. Indistinct, yet stubborn like a thorn in my palm. There was a sadness to it that I could not ignore.

Violently, I shook my head, knocking it against the trunk of an old thick tree. The sharp pain gave me a space in which to push back the wool. I supported myself against the trunk and pushed the fingers of my right hand down my throat. They tasted of salt. The flesh of my mouth was soft as water as I pushed further in and within a few seconds I felt my throat, then my stomach, heave up. Then the poppy I had drunk came back out of me in a brown liquid that poured onto the ground. It is a foul thing to have to do that to one's own body, to hurt oneself in order to have the use of one's brain. I had no choice then.

I collapsed and lay on my back, breathing as deeply as I could, hoping that it would clear my head. For a time, I was caught in a half-life between sleep and waking hours. I saw the people of Lorne, the crimes of Lorne, the jealousies and envies of Lorne all dancing around and into each other and proving their own opposite. Father Dollet had a powerful secret that could change the nation. Francois, counting his few remaining coins. Jacob, living on the boundaries of the village but by night searching for a path to Eden.

After a few minutes - minutes wasted when I had needs for every one of them - I peeled my head up from the scratching leaves and stalks below.

I had no desire to return to the hamlet and instead stumbled through the undergrowth back to where I knew the boat was tethered. Even dozed as I was, I noticed that the river was rising, the waters higher than I had ever seen them, threatening even to burst its banks and flood the land around us. With my head heavy, I pulled myself back across the swell and walked to the house, where the lights were blazing and the blare of music was bursting from the open windows, despite the wind having grown in strength to whip around my head.

I could only have been gone for forty minutes, but during that time a crowd of men and women had arrived. They were laughing and singing, spilling out onto the lawn like water. People milled about in fanciful costumes. Here there was a woman whose face was a green bird's, there a man with a huge coat and hat like a wizard, covered in red stars. On the lawn a band of lithe tumblers wearing only oriental-style silk pantaloons were forming a pyramid and then flipping backwards off it, to the gasps of the audience.

Through them, I caught a glimpse of someone I had not expected to be there: Annalise, who held a white faceless mask in her hand as she threaded her way through the mass of bodies, hot with the wine they had drunk and their proximity to each other. I hurried after her as she went through the doorway but then everyone started moving as one and I realized I had missed some unseen signal. Losing sight of her, I went with the tide of the crowd as they washed into the ballroom.

There, in the centre of the room, Juliana wore a dress that seemed to be spun from pure silver. She stood beside something covered in a sheet that rippled as the candles moved. It was as tall as she was.

But even she was not the only focus of the eye. For at the end of the room closest to me, on a wide dais, sat King Louis XVI, staring at her, his sometime mistress, his mouth open like a lascivious dog. One could tell from his face that he was considering taking her again that night, regardless of her recent widowhood. He was dressed for dancing, with a blue-feathered mask in his hanging hand and there was something animalistic about him that I had not seen before. Something guttural.

'I do not want to be here forever,' I overheard him telling one of his entourage as I passed by. 'Tell her to come at eleven. No, ten. I do not want to be here longer than I need. What is the Queen doing?'

Marie-Antoinette was up and flitting around, decked out as a cloud with stuffed birds in her piled hair, giggling like a child with one of her ladies-in-waiting. The jasmine-scented pink gloves with which she always travelled were ready, arranged alongside her perfumed handkerchief on a gilt table to her side. The King glanced at her, then returned his proprietorial gaze to Juliana and his tongue touched his lips.

The noise in the room was rising as everyone spoke over each other, trying to make themselves heard, until a single repeated note, a tapping on an empty glass with something metal, pierced through it all, cutting into our minds. I could not see where it was coming from and yet I knew to whom I was to give my silence.

'Your Majesties.' Juliana curtsied low, and rose once more. 'My lords, ladies and gentlemen, my friends, my family, you all know that tonight there is a space in this room. You have seen the empty air at my table. I stand beside it and I am cold where I should be warm, I feel nothing where I should feel nothing but love, I can touch no one where I should touch a husband.' There was no murmuring, no shifting of feet. I saw Gaston, that garter-snake, stumble through the doorway. Charles had joined his party and smirked when he saw me. 'Love is the most powerful medicine we have found.' She looked at her son. She must have known nothing of his petty intrigues for de Rotanne. I would deal with him later.

'Gregory Archer was not a husband to me,' Juliana said. 'He was a lover. We were married in law, but that was just one star. We blazed like the night sky. He found me singing friendless in a tavern and without him, I would have been destined for a circus or begging for coins on the streets. He made me a person.' For the first time I could see Juliana's duality. The theatre, the performance was there in her voice and the way she stood as if all the lights were shining on her. But there was humanity too. Honesty, one might say. It was as if her costume were halfway off her, as she sat in a dressing room after the flowers had been thrown at her feet. 'Gregory–'

She stopped. She did not sink to her knees or cast her face up to the royal box. She did not weep. She merely stopped to remember. I had hardly known the man and yet I too remembered. I think that at that moment the room was full of memories of him. Then she took hold of the sheet near to its tip and slipped it from the wooden frame below. The Archer family, blue-eyed parents, green-eyed child, gazed out from Annalise's painting. It seemed more vivid to me now with two of its subjects nearby. The colours were both subtle and lush. The tones of their skin were true. And always those eyes.

I could not help but recall what had occurred the one other time I had seen the picture, when it was in Annalise's studio. The power that it had possessed to reveal what had been hidden. Without it I would never have realized that Annalise had given Juliana and Archer their son. Her son.

You were in love with him. You bore Charles for him, I had said.

You know? she had stammered to me then.

Of course I know, I had replied.

Without that painting I would never have known the love that she bore. *I loved him with all that I was. I met him when I was fourteen. You. You do not understand this,* Annalise had told me.

Out of the corner of my eye I glimpsed her. She was looking not at the portrait but at me. I recalled the triumph in her voice when she told me that I did not understand. And in that moment, I felt an ocean of blood rush to my head. Thoughts thundered, visions swam. Such thoughts.

I dropped my glass. It exploded on the bare wooden floor, breaking the silence. Everyone turned to look at me and I put my hands to my head and stared down at the shards as the realization washed over me like a terrible wave. Juliana started and I could see Annalise's lips stretch out into a triumphant smile, exposing sharp little white teeth. Unable to contain myself I ran forward to the painting and tore it from the stand. Juliana grabbed hold of my arm, and another pair of hands took hold of me as voices shouted. The King was ushered away by a courtier. I felt myself pulled to the side of the room and pushed into a chair. All the while the realization was becoming clearer as I stared at the painting until it was ripped from my fingers and all that was there was the image of the family emblazoned in my eyes.

Now some were glaring at me, others were comforting Juliana. Charles was with her and Annalise was retreating. She went out the door and I did nothing to stop her as the room began to spin around me.

You. You do not understand this.

Understanding. It can be so fleeting or so ill-timed that you wish later in the days, weeks and years to come that you had never had it. You can wish clocks turned forward or back, your memories destroyed or enlarged. And all because of an understanding too late.

Around me the three or four men who had pulled me away and wrested the painting from my grip were standing back and talking amongst themselves. They were discussing me, I could hear.

'Throw him outside, let the man cool,' one said gruffly.

'He is calming down, I do believe he is beginning to see sense,' replied another. He put a glass in my hand but I did not grip it.

Then there was a third, dressed differently and peering at me like a strange and dangerous animal. Peugere was pushing between them as forcefully as he could while retaining some decorum.

'Maître, his lordship said this is urgent.' I blinked, stared at the scene in front of me, then at the folded paper Peugere had thrust into my hand. I opened it. It had Francois's crest at the top. It had been scribbled at such speed that it was confused, barely legible.

> David. I am in the library. Come right now. It cannot wait a second. I now realize something of Juliana that all should know. It was from the painting. I have sent word to Catherine to come too for I believe she is in danger. Come now.

I dropped it to the floor. The painting? He had not seen it. No, not this painting. *The other painting.* Annalise had said the portrait above the stairs was the only picture that revealed Juliana's true beauty. And now Francois had seen it and understood.

I leaped up and the three pairs of hands immediately found my chest, thrusting me back. They thought I had lost my mind. They did not know what I knew, that Francois was standing before an abyss of danger. I fought them away, grabbing their fingers and prising them from my clothes, threatening and pleading. One of them, the one who had been the first to speak, now began to laugh at what they were doing. 'Throw him outside!' he cried again. I could see the others considering the idea. 'Let him cool down.'

'Yes!' I shouted desperately. 'Please, let me cool down. I have had too much wine. You gentlemen know how it is.' The second speaker, tall as a tower, chuckled and slapped my cheek in a friendly way.

'Ah. There is a good fellow. Yes, a bit too much of the Chablis, I declare.'

'Yes. Look, I am much calmer already.' I sat back, away from their stinking hands, and lay my head against the back of the seat. I dropped my voice. 'I just need a little fresh air, and then why do not we all go to visit the girls on the island?' Having to humour these fools felt like blades in my mind.

'Ah! Spoken like a truly sober chap now! I am about ready to give that little Louisiana mulatta a taste of what French men can do.'

They cheered and stood back. One put his hand under my shoulder and lifted me. I thanked them all generously. Forcing myself to walk to the door, without running, was the hardest task I have ever done. I have charged into battle and out of it. I have dived for the blasted ground to avoid being stung by bullet and blood. But knowing that you cannot run to save your life or the life of someone you love is like a fire inside your chest. You pray that it will burn itself out before it spreads and destroys you from within.

As I drew closer to the door that led to the hallway, I felt the muscles in my legs stiffen, my feet tripping over as my pace quickened. I just had to make it far enough that when I began to run the others could not react so quickly as to bar my path. Ten yards from the door my heart beat, then five, my hands became fists; three yards and my back was drenched with sweat; a yard away and I thrust my head down and pushed myself off my feet. My stride was like a horse's at that moment and a shocked servant threw himself from my path. I sprinted through the hall and out the door. I could hear the shouts behind me, furious. *Let them come*, I thought. *Let them come, but let us not be too late.*

On the horizon I saw the top of the amber sun dipping behind the church, leaving that edifice black on the raised horizon. Faster than I had run around the walls of Yorktown I ran for the outcrop of the house that was the library. But something was making the going harder. The ground was soft, like mush. Each footstep was sending up a spray of dank water. The ground was sodden to the point where the water was shimmering across it. The river. The river had burst its banks as it had been threatening to do, and was creeping across the land, reclaiming it from men. I heard the shouts behind me die away as my pursuers gave up, not caring what I did.

I skidded, my hand sloshing into the soaked earth, but the glass-panelled doors that opened from the library onto the front of the house were blazing with light. I reached them, but they were bolted shut.

Through the glass I saw Francois before his green leather winged chair, his arms wide, and Catherine backed into the corner of the room with a stiletto knife in her hand, pointing it desperately at Francois and thrusting to keep him back, as if her life depended on it. It did.

I shouted her name.

Francois, startled, turned his head towards me. Catherine took the chance to run for the doorway and I threw myself body and soul through the glass, blasting shards of wood across the room. It hurt like hell but I cared not, and, righting myself, I grabbed her wrist so that the weapon fell to the ground, and she stumbled to her knees.

She could do nothing but stare at me as tears coursed down her cheeks. They dropped into a pool at her feet, the unleashed river having found its way through the little gaps and mouseholes in the wall to seep through the carpet too.

'Christ!' Francois whispered, his eyes wide, glaring at her then me.

I think I said Catherine's name but cannot remember. She was shaking, sprayed with dank water, her face oiled with tears.

Francois, lost for words, stooped and picked her blade from the floor. He looked down at Catherine. She did not seem to notice, her eyes locked on mine. Tears coursed and her body shook.

Francois stared at me.

'It was her?' he asked, his words little more than breath.

I kneeled to Catherine until my lips were almost touching hers. I held her wrist still. It was cold to my touch. 'You did not strike the blows,' I told her. 'They were by Juliana, were they not?'

She struggled to speak and I could barely make out the words, whispered and mumbled. They came from deep inside her. 'I had to protect her,' she said. 'You understand why, do you not?'

I did.

'The painting,' I said to Francois. 'Juliana's portrait above the stairs. What did you see?'

He blinked. 'The aria you see on Juliana's sheet music. It is *"Che farò senza Euridice"*. By Gluck. It is only sung by castratos.'

I turned to Catherine. 'Annalise wanted people to know,' I said. I knew I was right.

'Annalise was so foolish, so arrogant.' She spoke slowly, a dangerous secret she had kept for so long, now escaping from her into the world. 'Juliana sang it in the inns before Gregory discovered her and turned her into someone new. She was always meant to be a woman, he could see that. Annalise was taunting those who did not know.'

Gregory Archer had loved Juliana as a woman. Annalise had loved him as a man. Catherine had borne a different kind of love for Juliana, but one just as fierce and protective. So many kinds of love there are.

Time too has more than one face. There is what was and what could have been. I think of what would have happened if Archer had never confessed all - Juliana and the King - to

Father Dollet. And if the all-too-human curate had not allowed his baser senses to lead him to propose a bargain with Juliana. Her for her secret.

'Tell us,' I said.

'The priest said it would only be once,' Catherine said quietly. 'A penance for what she had done. But if she did not, he had written a pamphlet, an exposure of her and the King together and he would have it sent all around the country.' Death was what the law decreed for those acts between them, king or pauper. And she knew it. 'That would have been like a death for me too. But we knew the priest would go back on his word. He wanted to use her for himself, then against the King.'

Yes, Father Dollet would have denounced the King and Juliana to diminish him. To make the people mock and pillory him. And by so doing, to foster a land no longer ravaged by hunger. New lives would have sprung through their fallen bodies. But for Juliana it would have been the end of hers.

And so death visited neither Louis nor Juliana, but Father Dollet.

'Juliana used the knife?' Catherine nodded, saltwater droplets falling from her eyes. 'What did you do?'

'I tied him to the cross after and turned him upside down, so people would talk about witches and look away from us. I grew up on a farm. We butchered our animals. I was used to it.'

Father Dollet had written of a man who dreamed he was a butterfly. I had seen the surface: a man who dreams. I had not seen what lay below: a man who transforms into something more beautiful.

Knowledge too late is no knowledge at all. If I had listened to Francois telling me about gelding horses and their barren seed instead of dismissing it as the folk learning of the peasant. If I had stayed in Lorne instead of running through Paris to take personal vengeance on de Rotanne. If I had never left the court at all. We would not have been there.

'And Archer?'

'I went to him. Over dinner you said things about his hairshirt and I knew you understood some of what had happened. I wanted to warn him. But he was furious and drunk. He thought I was doing it to hurt Juliana. I tried to get away from him. He kept coming and I pushed him away. He fell.'

Francois stood above us, unable to speak. He was a trusting man. I was sorry for all that had happened to him, all that we had brought down on him.

With a chaos of voices warning us that the house was flooding, some of the ball revellers wandered into the room. They stared at us with confusion on their faces. They could not begin to guess. They should have left us to our purgatory.

Through the broken doors, I saw people in masks and costumes spilling out onto the lawn, trying to escape the cold water surging through the house, the river that had burst from its course and claimed the land for itself. Some were yelling, some running, although they knew not where would offer them asylum.

Gaston waddled out, shouting for his carriage, his thin friend hurrying in his wake, stripped bare of his arrogance and dumbfounded by what he saw. The balletic tumblers from before now looked like famished beggars as they huddled together ankle deep in marsh-soil. I saw a man dressed as a wild beast fighting with another in a cape. They tripped, still struggling, to the sinking earth. The one in the animal costume tore away the other's mask and threw it aside while others stumbled over them.

Then the King emerged, hurrying for his coach, surrounded by courtiers with their rapiers drawn and shoving men and women from their path. But the wave of humanity began to rebound and started pushing back, advancing upon their monarch. Seeing their approach, he scrabbled hard for his carriage even while it still moved, letting his velvet shoes sink into the muddy water and crying to the driver to go. De Rotanne was a stride behind him, attempting to gain the carriage too, but the King kicked him away. Marie Antoinette was nowhere to be seen. I witnessed, in that scene, a time when such lives would be forfeit, although ten thousand others would be offered up in their place. All knew that the chateau was lost.

And then I saw Juliana, standing still in her silver silk dress while everyone around her spun like a whirlwind.

'How did you do it?' I asked Catherine softly.

'I watched her go into the church. I wore my hood up so no one would recognize me and waited for what seemed like an hour. Then when she had done it, I went in and we arranged his body.'

Francois seemed to recover his wits. 'We can lock them in the cellar until–'

'Please let them go,' I said.

'What?' He stared at me, dumbstruck. 'In God's name–'

'It is all done now. What can be served?' I let go of her wrist. I cannot tell how much I was trying to convince him, and how much I was trying to convince myself.

'They killed Father Dollet.'

I needed no reminder. But she had been right. I knew that after he had used Juliana, he would have broken his promise to her. 'He was not the man we remember,' I said.

Francois's brow turned to thunder but he took a step away, clearing the way to the door.

Catherine stood unsteadily. 'I had to protect her,' she said. 'No one else would.' Then she walked away from me.

Before us I could see the rippling ground crowded by people pretending to be things that they were not.

Here ends the final part of The Murderous Deeds in the Village of Lorne in France and How They Brought About the Bloody Revolution.

'Olivier. Tell me who you are, what you have been.' My mother's tears wetted my cheek. I knew not where to begin. Memories and thoughts tumbled from my tongue like drunken sailors. She laughed and cried at them.

After some minutes, de Rotanne folded the papers, the deadly final chapter of my father's story, and neatly slipped them inside his frock coat. 'I presume you have scores of these ready to be released around the country?'

'Oh no, my lord,' my father replied. 'We have two thousands of them ready to be released around the country. They have been deposited with a variety of men. Some we do not know ourselves.'

'Well, well.' He said it dismissively, as if to deride was his only reaction; but I could see a plum-red anger rising up his neck. 'Then . . .' But he could think of no more words, no more sneers. Before him, the King looked blanched, abandoned like a lame hound.

'Juliana,' my father said. 'You have not finished your song. Sing for the King, will you not? It is time for us to leave.'

And, at that, he left her on the stage, with the lights upon her. Juliana. It had all been about her. My suffering, my father's privations, my mother's solitude. One person can be the centre of a whirlwind that destroys all around. One can bring destruction without meaning to.

There was no orchestra now, no strings or drums. But she sang and my father came to us. We left the theatre treading lightly, looking back, with pistols in our hands; but no man or woman followed us. Only her voice followed. Only her voice.

Epilogue

My parents and I live now in a city. I will not tell its name, but it has tall stone walls, built to defend against armies and raiders. We are, I think, happy. We have settled into our ways. I teach a few pupils the rudiments of Latin, my mother teaches them music, my father teaches French. We talk occasionally of what happened before and after my birth, but not often. On one of those rare junctures, I asked if they knew what had become of Jacob. 'I heard he became an officer in Bonaparte's army,' my father informed me to my surprise. But then, was it so astonishing? A young man with fire in his belly and javelins in his eye? Surely not. And what of Francois?

'Oh,' chuckled my father. 'Francois landed on his feet. A Portuguese duchess took an unexpected liking to him. That she is just about old enough to be his mother does not appear to cause either of them any distress.'

I had often struggled with the idea of my mother, who gave me life, taking the life of another. My father had done so on the battlefield, but that was as directed by the law of men. Was not murder against the law of nature? I had, in the end, decided that moral absolutes could not hold. They just could not. It had to depend on the right and wrong of the other. Morality is not a hill, but a city of streets, passages and undercrofts.

'How guilty was Father Dollet?' I asked my father.

He was thoughtful for a while. 'Legally? Entirely, both for his acts and for his demand dressed up as a bargain. Morally?' I waited. 'It is a question I cannot truly answer. I have lost perspective. But he was many leagues from innocence.'

My mother and Juliana may have been right to do it, and yet I still cannot knit the sight of the gentle and caring woman before me with the bronze willpower of one who had done what she had done. I shake my head at it, and then catch her eye. I think she knows what is running through my mind. Maybe, for her part, she wants to answer: 'Love, not hate, is the greatest fire for determination.'

I write each week to Iphigenia. She writes back the next day. It is the sunlit land of my week.

I wonder sometimes, while the three of us sit reading or sewing beside the hearth, what is between my mother and father. Their friendship was first constructed upon the mudflats of untruth and deception. But it became, I know, something far more solid. Their love is real. We are, I hope, allowed to repair our mistakes. If not . . . well, then much of the human race is doomed. But no, I choose to believe there is always the chance of a redemption into the bright grace of love.

If you enjoyed *The Riptide*, discover more mind-bending mysteries from Gareth Rubin, the master of ingenious crime fiction.

The TURNGLASS

'Vivid, resonant, melancholy and beautiful'
Janice Hallett

1880s England.
Idealistic young doctor Simeon Lee arrives on the bleak island of Ray, off the Essex coast, to treat his cousin, Parson Oliver Hawes, who is dying. Parson Hawes, who lives on the only house on the island – Turnglass House – believes he is being poisoned and he points the finger at his sister-in-law, Florence. Florence was declared insane after killing Oliver's brother in a jealous rage and is now kept in a glass-walled apartment in Oliver's library. And the secret to how she came to be there can be found in Oliver's tête-bêche journal, where one side tells a very different story from the other.

1930s California.
Celebrated author Oliver Tooke, the son of the state governor, is found dead in his writing hut behind the family residence, Turnglass House. His friend Ken Kourian doesn't believe that Oliver would take his own life. His investigations lead him to the mysterious kidnapping of Oliver's brother when they were children, and the subsequent secret incarceration of his mother, Florence, in an asylum. But to discover the truth, Ken must decipher clues hidden in Oliver's final book, a tête-bêche novel – which is about a young doctor called Simeon Lee . . .

'A stunning, ingenious, truly immersive mystery. *The Turnglass* is a thrilling delight'
Chris Whitaker